PRAISE FOR RHYS BOWEN

"Rhys Bowen is a gift to all who love great writing, rich and complex characters and a plot that grabs from first words."
—Louise Penny, #1 *New York Ti*   *lling* author of the Chief
                                              or Gamache novels

"Thoroughly entertaining."

—*Publishers Weekly*

"A truly delightful read."

—*Kirkus Reviews*

"Keep[s] readers deeply involved   .l the end."
—*Portland Book Review*

"Entertainment mixed with intellectual intrigue and realistic setting[s] for which Bowen has earned awards and loyal fans."
—*New York Journal of Books*

"[A] master of her genre."

—*Library Journal*

"An author with a distinctive flair for originality and an entertaining narrative storytelling style that will hold the reader's rapt attention from beginning to end."
—*Midwest Book Review*

"Bowen's vivid storytelling style holds readers enrapt. [She] perfectly develops both narratives with absorbing details about several characters and different geographical environments."
—Historical Novel Society

THE
ROSE
ARBOR

ALSO BY RHYS BOWEN

CONSTABLE EVANS MYSTERIES

MOLLY MURPHY MYSTERIES

Murphy's Law

Death of Riley

For the Love of Mike

In Like Flynn

Oh Danny Boy

In Dublin's Fair City

Tell Me, Pretty Maiden

In a Gilded Cage

The Last Illusion

Bless the Bride

Hush Now, Don't You Cry

The Family Way

City of Darkness and Light

The Edge of Dreams

Away in a Manger

Time of Fog and Fire

The Ghost of Christmas Past

With Clare Broyles

Wild Irish Rose

All That Is Hidden

ROYAL SPYNESS MYSTERIES

THE
ROSE
ARBOR

A NOVEL

RHYS
BOWEN

LAKE UNION
PUBLISHING

Text copyright © 2024 by Janet Quin-Harkin, writing as Rhys Bowen
All rights reserved.

Published by Lake Union Publishing, Seattle

www.apub.com

Amazon, the Amazon logo, and Lake Union Publishing are trademarks of Amazon.com, Inc., or its affiliates.

ISBN-13: 9781662504211 (hardcover)
ISBN-13: 9781662504228 (paperback)
ISBN-13: 9781662504204 (digital)

Cover design by Shasti O'Leary Soudant
Cover image: ©Peter Greenway / ArcAngel; ©Cyrille Redor, ©posmguys, ©christinemg, ©Lanova Daria, ©Zoran Pajic / Shutterstock

Printed in the United States of America

First edition

This book is dedicated to Lisa Brackman, who keeps me in order and keeps me sane.

And also dedicated to the real Marisa Young, who was the high bidder in a charity auction and lent her name to one of my characters.

PROLOGUE

Tydeham, Dorset, England, September 1943

There had been no advance warning, apart from an army vehicle that had appeared one blustery afternoon three weeks earlier. This in itself was strange, as there was no proper road to the village, only a lane that became rather muddy after rain. And it didn't go anywhere, apart from down to the tiny harbour, where there were currently no fishing boats, the war having made fishing too dangerous in these waters. The open-topped Tilly army vehicle had driven down the one street, past the church, the schoolhouse, the pub and the row of cottages, to where the village ended in the overgrown track with steps down to the harbour. An officer, wearing a smart peaked army cap, had climbed out, looked around, and was heard by Mary Norton, who was getting in her washing before it rained, to say, "It will have to do. Luckily there's nothing of historic value here."

She never bothered to pass along this statement, or the inhabitants might have been better prepared when the post office van came sloshing through puddles to deposit the mail at the village post office cum village shop. Mrs Jenkins, the postmistress/shop owner, had looked at the pile of letters bearing no stamps.

"More rubbish from the government," she had said to Fred Hammond, the driver. "I wonder what it will be this time?"

"Probably cutting our sugar ration again," he said. "Or the meat ration. But I bet that don't affect you so much out here with your chickens and pigs."

"We do all right, I suppose," she said. "Although the rats keep getting at our eggs, bloody nuisances."

"He don't have to worry too much, do he?" The post office driver nodded up the street. "Him at the big house. Don't he still have cows?"

"No, they're long gone," she said. "Government took them. Now he don't have that much more than we do. A couple of pigs and chickens. But a fine lot of fruit and veggies, and I must say he's good enough to share with us."

"Well, he should, seeing as you're his tenants, right? You pay him every month to live here, don't you?"

"We do, I suppose." Mrs Jenkins smoothed down her apron. "Now I better get that lazybones Ned to take these around."

~~

It turned out that the letters were not about the sugar ration. Instead they said:

To the inhabitants of Tydeham. This is to inform you that His Majesty's armed forces have need of your village to further the war effort. It has been requisitioned for invasion drills, commencing October 8th, 1943. You have two weeks to remove your belongings and vacate the village.

Every adult occupant of Tydeham is required to attend a meeting at the village hall on September 24th, at eight p.m., where there will be further explanation and questions will be answered.

"Bloody 'ell," Ed Jenkins muttered when his wife showed him the letter. "They've got some nerve, haven't they? Turning folks out of their homes? Homes they've lived in for generations?"

"I suppose it is for the war effort, Ed," Mrs Jenkins said, trying to be brave but not really any happier with the news than her husband had been. "They'll have to rehouse us, won't they? They can't just turn us out into the street?"

Ed shrugged. "I hear that's what they've been doing in the cities that were bombed. Oh, your house just got flattened. Too bad. Don't you have a relative to live with?"

"We could go to my sister in Dorchester," Mrs Jenkins said. "They have that spare bedroom now that young Jack . . ." She did not complete the sentence. Young Jack had gone down with his ship.

"They'll have to rehouse us," Ed said firmly. "What about my vegetable patch, eh? I haven't harvested half the stuff yet, and there's the taters and onions I've put in." He stood up resolutely. "I'm going to have a word with Mr Bennington. If anyone can set these army blokes straight, he can."

He grabbed his jacket and shoved his cap on to his head, then stomped off up the street, past the church and along the narrow path that led to what locals called "the big house." Its real name was Tydeham Grange. It was an elegant stone manor house, set in grounds that had been manicured before the war. Now the croquet lawn had become a veggie patch. There were sheep grazing on the parkland behind the house, and a pigsty had been built beyond the stables. Ed met Mr Bennington himself coming out of one of the barns, carrying a pitchfork.

"You've read the letter, have you?" Ed called to him.

"I'm afraid I have. And I've already been on the telephone to London. It seems there's not much we can do, Ed. They have to practice invasion tactics somewhere, and we seem to fit the bill. Come inside and have a cup of tea."

Ed followed him into the flagstone hallway of the manor house. The kitchen at the back of the house was warm, with the wood stove now taking the place of gas. At least there were still plenty of fallen trees on the estate. Mr Bennington put the kettle on.

"Take a seat," he said.

Ed sat at the round kitchen table. "It didn't say anything about compensation, did it?"

"Not so far." Mr Bennington took down the tea caddy in the shape of an Indian temple. His family had had connections to India for generations, and he himself had served in the Bengal Lancers as a young man.

"They'll have to give you something, won't they? You own all this land. You own the bloody village, for Pete's sake. Do they expect you to move to a council house?"

Mr Bennington shrugged. "I expect we'll be able to return after the war if they haven't damaged the place too badly. They'll give us money to rebuild and spruce the place up."

"That is, if we win," Ed said drily. He accepted the mug that Mr Bennington handed him.

"Oh, I think the tide has definitely turned. They wouldn't be practicing invasion tactics if they weren't hopeful of going across the Channel. And look at the success we've had in North Africa. Egypt, Malta, Sicily and now Italy. And how about those Dambusters? Marvellous stuff. Oh, we've got Hitler rattled all right."

"What does your wife say about this?" Ed asked.

Mr Bennington looked worried. "She doesn't know yet. She's taken young James to Sherborne to look at the school. It's about time we put his name down for a school somewhere, although I went to Marlborough, so he'd get in there easily enough. But Amelia doesn't want him too far from home, in fact she doesn't want him to go to boarding school at all. She's become so anxious since the war started. Especially after Simon . . ." He paused, gave a sort of cough in his throat to hide emotion, then went on. "She never was the strongest of women to start with. I'm afraid this will really unsettle her. She does love her home."

"It will unsettle us all," Ed said. "I reckon almost all the families have been here for hundreds of years, haven't they? Working your land or fishing. It's only the schoolmistress and the vicar who are outsiders, and they don't live here, do they?"

Mr Bennington sighed. "I suppose all we can say is that it's a damned sight better than what those poor blighters are going through in Burma or on the Italian beaches."

Ed nodded. "You've got something there. I can't tell you how happy I was when they said I was too old to join up."

"They didn't want me," Mr Bennington said. "I had rheumatic fever when I was in India. It's affected my heart. I'm supposed to be taking it easy, although mucking out pigsties, digging up vegetables and picking apples because the young lads are off at war can hardly be described as a quiet life, can it?"

Ed drained his mug, savouring the taste of sugar at the bottom. Sugar was a luxury these days, and Betty only allowed him one small spoonful in his tea. He stood up. "Well, I'll be getting along then, sir. I'm right sorry that you'll be losing this lovely place, too. But I can tell you I'll be giving those army fellows a piece of my mind at the meeting. We're not going to give up without a fight."

Charles Bennington watched him go, shaking his head. "They can fight all they want," he muttered, "but they are not going to win."

～

The fighting sentiment was echoed at the Golden Hinde pub that evening.

"First it's no bloody whisky, then it's bloody beer that's watered down, and now it's no bloody house to live in," Bert Thatcher said, banging his pint mug on the counter for emphasis. "When we get to that meeting, we'll just tell them we're not going to take it. They can practice their invading somewhere else. I'm not leaving my cottage, and that's that."

"You tell 'em, Bert!" said Tom Pierce, the landlord of the village pub, but he was smiling and shaking his head. "If the army listens to any of us, they'll listen to you."

Bert was a strapping chap, over six feet tall and quite broad. He'd tried to join up but at forty-eight was considered too old. And, as a land worker, too valuable.

～～

The tiny village hall stood behind the church on the south side of the village street. To access it, you had to walk through the churchyard, past the graves of generations of ancestors, which the villagers had never paid attention to until now. On the evening of September 24, Ed Jenkins paused on his way to the hall.

"Come on, Ed. We don't want to have to sit at the back." Betty tugged his arm.

"I'm just wondering if they plan to move my poor old mum and dad," he said, gazing down at the tombstone. "And my grandparents, too. I don't like the thought of them being disturbed in their graves."

"It can't do them too much harm now, can it?" Betty was always pragmatic. "It's us I'm worried about."

The hall was packed. Not just the adults of the village were in attendance, but parents had brought young children, and men had brought their dogs. The air was thick with cigarette smoke, and an angry muttering echoed. The Benningtons had seated themselves on the front row. Mr Bennington was in a blazer and slacks; Mrs Bennington was wearing a smart hat and kid gloves, as befitted the occasion. Six-year-old James beside her looked at all the angry and anguished faces and wondered what it was all about. His mummy had been upset all the time, ever since his brother had been killed in the RAF. And now everyone else in that hall looked the same.

The vicar came in through a side door and stood off to one side. He was still a youngish man, and he surveyed his congregation helplessly.

"So you reckon a few prayers would do any good, Vicar?" Tom Pierce asked, having spotted him. As a well-known atheist, he was only goading, but the vicar shook his head.

"I don't think prayers seem to be very effective in this war, Tom. I'm afraid we'll all have to make the best of it and presume that God has a long-term plan."

"It's all right for you," Bert Thatcher said. "You don't even bloody live here."

The vicar nodded in acknowledgement of this. He was in charge of two small churches, ten miles apart, and lived at the rectory of the further one. "But I've grown very fond of this place, and its inhabitants, you know. I'll be sorry to lose you all."

"As if it's not bad enough having our men off and fighting," Joan Lee said from the row behind the Benningtons. She was a tiny woman in her forties who had produced two very large sons. "And they'll be wanting my boys before you can say Jack Robinson. Of course they're raring to go, silly sods. Aren't you?" She nudged one of the strapping lads sitting beside her. The boy gave an embarrassed grin. She turned to Amy Pierce, whose own son, a gangly boy who seemed all arms and legs, was engrossed in a small glass puzzle box. "You're lucky your Freddie will be out of it."

Amy grunted. "That's right. Lucky old us," she said. She was about to say more but broke off as two army officers came in. A hush fell as the men walked up to the front dais and stood, surveying the crowd.

"Right," one of them said, not looking as if he was going to enjoy the next few minutes. "It's good of you all to come."

"The bloody notice said we had to," muttered a voice from the back.

"I'm sure this has come as a big shock to you all. You are, after all, being asked to leave your homes. And we would not be doing this if it were not absolutely essential to the war effort. We have to practice for the eventuality of an invasion, you see. And the terrain here is ideal for what we need. Tricky cliffs beyond the village. Buildings that we can pretend are occupied by the German army. We looked at several sites and felt that yours presented the least disruption. Only eight families displaced, and fishing is temporarily banned, so not enough work here."

"So what do you plan to do with us?" a voice growled from the back.

The officer cleared his throat before answering. "We'd like those of you who can go to relatives to do so. For the others, we'll find you council houses in the area for the time being."

"What about Mr Bennington up at the Grange?" The voice was Bert Thatcher's. "You don't expect him to live in no bloody council house, do you?"

"I'm sure arrangements will be made for Mr Bennington's family," the officer said. "And of course there will be compensation for the lost crops, for all of you."

"You mean you'll pay us for what we're growing in our gardens?"

"Exactly."

"And what about compensation for leaving our homes?" One of the women stood up. She was young and fresh-faced with red cheeks and neatly permed hair. "I'm Sally Purvis. I were born here, lived here all my life. And my William is off on a merchant marine ship, risking his life every day. Me and my William have worked hard to make our cottage nice. William's put up lovely shelves in the kitchen and a cupboard in our daughter's room. What about all the effort that's gone into those?"

"I'm afraid there will be no compensation for the actual dwellings. They do, after all, belong to Mr Bennington. You are just tenants. But naturally you'll be able to take your furniture. In fact, the army will even supply the lorries for the move—at no charge to you."

"That's big of you," someone growled.

Bert Thatcher stood up. "So you're telling us we have no say in this? There's nobody we can appeal to? We're out of here whether we like it or not?"

"I'm afraid that is the case."

"And what if we won't go?" Bert folded his muscular arms. "What if we all refuse to budge?"

"Then I'm afraid you'd be forcibly removed and you wouldn't have a chance to take your possessions. That's not what you'd want, is it?" He paused, glancing at the other officer for reassurance. "You have to understand, I'm afraid, that in times of war His Majesty's army has complete jurisdiction over civilian property. We have requisitioned many fine houses across the country. It has been a wrench for all those people who've had to move out."

"So what about after the war?" Betty Jenkins stood up. "When it's all over? We can move back in?"

"That will have to be decided later," the officer said. "Let's hope we win this war soon and everybody can return to their old lives."

He didn't say what he already knew, which was that the invasion exercises were going to entail using live ammunition. There would not be much of the village left.

CHAPTER 1

London, October 1968

The first word that Liz Houghton uttered as she stepped out of the revolving door at the *Daily Express* building into bright afternoon sunlight was a four-lettered one and began with *f.* She glanced around, glad that nobody had heard her. She had been raised not to swear, and her mother would have been horrified that she even knew that word. But she felt the moment merited the use of strong language. Her heart was still racing. Colour flooded to her cheeks again as the scene she had just experienced replayed itself in her head. Miss Knight's smug smile, her innocent, cow-like face looking directly at Liz as she blocked off her retreat, coming out of the ladies' bathroom.

"I just wanted to have a word, Miss Houghton. About Mr Green."

"Mr Green? What about him?" Liz had tried to sound disinterested.

"I've noticed you two have become quite . . . friendly lately."

She had felt herself blushing. "We've been for a drink a couple of times."

"A drink." The smile broadened. Miss Knight was head of the typing pool and made it her business to notice everything. "Anyway, I thought I should say something, for your own good, you know. Before you get in too deep."

"What do you mean?" Liz heard the sharpness in her voice.

"You do know he's married, don't you?"

Liz tossed back her long hair, eyeing Miss Knight defiantly. It felt as if she were confronting one of her teachers back at school. "Of course. But I don't see what that has to do with anything. I'm sure a married man is allowed to have drinks with a colleague, in a professional capacity."

"A professional capacity." Again that condescending smile that made Liz want to smack her face.

"What your colleagues do in their spare time is none of your business, Miss Knight."

"I'm on your side, dear," Miss Knight said. "I just wanted to warn you. You wouldn't be the first young girl he's led astray. And just so you know, he always goes back to his wife in the end. You girls are just a bit of fun for him."

Liz fought to keep her features composed. "Thank you for your concern, Miss Knight, but I'm quite capable of looking after myself," she said. "Now if you will excuse me, I have to be getting home. I'm going to the theatre tonight."

She pushed past the older woman, stalked down the hallway and went down the stairs and out into the street. The setting sun shone directly into her face. She worked her way down Fleet Street to the Strand.

WHERE'S LITTLE LUCY? news billboards read while the vendors shouted out, "Has Little Lucy been spotted? Read all about it! Get your *Evening Standard* here."

Liz did not notice, pushing blindly through rush hour crowds to the Tube station, then forcing her way on to the District line to Victoria. It was a long walk from the Tube station to her flat in Fulham. Normally she relished it, that chance to wind down, looking for that first glimpse of the Thames, but today she couldn't wait to get home, to shut the door between herself and the world.

"How dare he," she said out loud. "How bloody dare he!"

Liz reached her destination in the middle of a row of Victorian terraced houses. Her flat was one flight up with a nice bay window overlooking the quiet street. If you leaned out of the bathroom window, you could actually spot the Thames between buildings. She had been there for a year now, sharing the place with a former school friend. She had felt hopeful when she moved in—finally out of her parents' clutches. She had a new and exciting job, and she was going to make the most of her life, not ever think about Edmond Harrington again.

Liz turned the key to the flat, came in, threw down her bag and kicked off her shoes.

"You here, Marisa?" she called.

"In the bedroom. Putting on my make-up. I've got a hot date."

Liz went through to the bedroom. Marisa was sitting at their dressing table, deftly applying fake eyelashes. She was a stunning young woman. Her father, a London cockney policeman, had met her mother on the island of Malta when he was stationed there during the war. Marisa had inherited her mother's olive skin, luxuriant dark hair and big, dark eyes. Those eyes sparkled when she laughed, which she did often. Understandably she had no shortage of boyfriends and showed no intention of settling down any time soon. She was a complete contrast to Liz, who was quiet and reserved, tall and slim with ash-blonde hair and blue eyes.

They had been friends since the age of thirteen when they'd both arrived as new girls at a posh London convent school. Marisa had been a scholarship girl, looked down on by some of the other girls because of her cockney accent, because she looked different and because she was smart. Liz had been mostly ignored because she was quiet, shy and bookish, or scorned as a teacher's pet when she excelled in English or history. And so they formed an unlikely friendship—"Us two against the world," Marisa used to say.

They had lost contact after school, only to bump into each other in the Strand, where Marisa was in the process of arresting an intoxicated man. It turned out she had gone into the Metropolitan Police, following in her father's footsteps. They started meeting again, and when they both needed to get away from the stifling and protective atmosphere of home, they had moved into a flat together.

"How do I look?" Marisa flashed that dazzling smile. "Are the eyelashes too much, do you think?"

"You look fine," Liz said. "You always look fine whatever you do."

Marisa caught her friend's tone. "What's up with you?"

Liz flung herself down on her bed. "You know that nice chap I've been seeing? That nice Bob Green who loves to read and go to the theatre and on long walks in the country, and has invited me to his cottage in the Cotswolds?"

"Yes?" Marisa looked at her suspiciously.

"The only thing he failed to tell me was that while I would be at the cottage in the Cotswolds with him, his wife and kids would be at their London flat."

"Bloody hell." Marisa had no problem with swearing. "What a prick. Letting you think you'd found a soulmate, someone you could talk to."

Liz fought back angry tears. She sat up. "What's wrong with me, Marisa? Am I doomed to keep meeting the wrong men? First it was Alistair, who was so suitable but as boring as hell, and then I meet Edmond and I think I've found the love of my life and I'm sure a proposal is coming, then he gets his dream job in Australia and off he goes, and I don't hear another bloody word from him."

"He is a mining engineer," Marisa pointed out. "He could be in the outback, miles from the nearest postbox."

"For a year?" Liz demanded. "Even if he sent a message by camel, it would have reached me by now. Even if he'd crawled through the bloody desert to the nearest post office. No, I have to accept that he was never as serious about me as I was about him. And now I think I've met safe, reliable Bob Green, and it turns out he's bloody married." She picked up the pillow in the shape of a heart and flung it across the room. "I'm doomed, that's what I am. Doomed to be a lonely old spinster working in the obituary department at the *Express*."

Marisa got up and came to sit on the bed beside her. "Things will improve. You'll see. It was just a stroke of bad luck that you stepped on the wrong toes at your newspaper. It could have been the scoop of the year. You could have been famous by now." She patted Liz's knee. "How were you to know that the bloody MP was an old school chum of Lord Whatsit who owns the paper?"

Liz shrugged. "I should have quit then. Being sent to obits is a fate worse than death." She nudged Marisa. "You know what, Marisa? I think I will quit. I can't face Bob Green every day, or that cow Miss Knight. I ought to be able to get a job with another paper, don't you think?"

"Unless Lord Whatsit has put out a bad word about you?"

Liz sighed. "Yes, I suppose he could do that. He's spiteful enough. He did make that veiled threat, didn't he?"

"Threat?"

"That if I took the story to another newspaper, he couldn't vouch for what might happen to me. I took that to mean I'd wind up floating in the Thames."

"Bloody men," Marisa said. "Why do they have all the power? Speaking of which." She stood up and went over to the window. "I've got an assignment. Could be a good one. Better than continual domestic abuse cases."

"What is it?"

"You know the little kid that's missing? Little Lucy?"

"Of course. How could I not? It's on all the billboards."

Marisa continued. "You know that tips have been pouring in? Well, a girl about her age and fitting her description was spotted in the back seat of a car in Dorset. The person who reported it said the girl was peering out of the back window and she looked anxious. So I'm being sent down to the South Coast to see if we can find anything."

"If she's still alive, that's good news, isn't it?" Liz said. "If someone had abducted her and was going to kill her, he'd have done so by now."

"Probably," Marisa said. "Anyway, it will be like looking for a needle in a haystack, I expect, but the Met is under a lot of pressure. People think we're not doing enough. After all, how can a child simply vanish from a garden in a Central London square in broad daylight?"

"I think it's terrific that they've assigned you," Liz said. "They must think a lot of you to give you such an important job."

Marisa shrugged. "I think I was something of an afterthought. Someone said we ought to have a woman PC along, just in case the child is found and needs a woman's touch."

"I see. So you'll be working with male officers?"

"One male officer. And I'm not thrilled. His name is DI Jones. He must be at least fifty. Chubby, unmarried. Doesn't take care of himself— you know the type. And he doesn't like women. He made that very clear when I met him today. I came into the room, and do you know what the first thing he said was? He said, 'Oh good. Help has arrived. Go and get me a cup of tea, love.'"

"Damned cheek." Liz nodded sympathetically. "But then too many of them are like that, aren't they? I've had my share of blokes who talk down to me and think they are superior because they are wearing trousers."

"Now that the fashion is long hair and flowery clothes for men, perhaps that will change," Marisa said, chuckling. "But not for old DI Jones. He really didn't want to work with me until he was flat out told he had to. I have a feeling it's going to be a barrel of laughs."

"So when do you leave?"

"Tomorrow morning. Nine o'clock train to Weymouth." She jumped up. "Which is why I'm going on a date tonight. It may be my last for a while."

"You going out with Des again?"

"Des? No. That's over. Too boring. He talked about racing cars all evening. No, this one is a fellow plainclothes officer. Ronnie. Tall. Good-looking and from East London like me. So we've got something in common."

"Have fun," Liz said. "If we have that bottle of vodka still, you'll find me passed out when you come home."

Marisa's smile faded. "You won't do anything silly, will you?"

"Apart from drinking vodka?" Liz smiled. "No, you won't find me dead in the bathtub. Frankly, no man is worth that."

"I could telephone Ronnie and call it off if you like." Marisa still looked worried.

"Don't be silly. Go on. Go and have a good time. Someone has to." She gave Marisa a playful shove. Then she lay back on the bed. *I've had a lucky escape,* she told herself. She would surely have slept with him when they'd gone down to the cottage. He seemed so nice, so intelligent, sensitive, a little older, calmer. Just what she needed right now after the heartbreak of Edmond. How could she ever face Bob? If she told him what a rat he was, someone would overhear, and then it would be all over the newspaper. That girl who trod on the wrong toes and is now in obits? Well, it turns out she's been seeing Bob Green, and they had a big bust-up.

Liz closed her eyes in an attempt to shut out the pain. She'd hand in her resignation tomorrow morning and look for another job. But what if she couldn't find one right away? She didn't exactly have savings to keep paying the rent. She'd have to leave this place, leave Marisa in the lurch and move back home. Her parents would like that, of course. They'd been quite devastated when she announced that she was going to share a flat with a friend.

"Are you sure that's wise, dear? I mean, London is a big city, and you never know who might be living next door." Her mother had grabbed her hand. "Don't go, Lizzie. Don't leave us. What's wrong with living here? We make it nice for you, don't we? You have everything you want, and we're on the Tube line. It's not as if we're in the middle of nowhere. We even moved to London so that you could go to a good school."

Yes, and then wouldn't let me go on to university, she wanted to say. Even though my teachers told me I was bright enough for a scholarship to Oxford and I should go into a good profession. But her father had shaken his head. "No point in wasting money on university for a girl, Lizzie. All that studying, and what for? You'll only go and get married like all the other girls." And so they'd suggested a secretarial college instead. "Good secretaries will never be out of work, Lizzie." Except that she wasn't a good secretary. Her typing and shorthand were passable at best. She'd suffered through time in a solicitor's office (where she had met the very suitable Alistair, whom her parents had liked) before landing at the *Daily Express*. There she saw opportunity and got herself moved to the newsroom, being given more and more challenging stories to cover. Until the fateful one. The one that sent her to cover obituaries.

The thought of having to move back home was more than she could bear. Mother, who had always been over-emotional and clingy, whose mental state was clearly deteriorating, would start fussing over her, worrying about her, wanting to meet her every need. Dad being jolly and reassuring: "Don't worry, Lizzie. You'll find another job soon. And in the meantime you're safe here, and you know how happy it makes your mother, don't you?"

That was the worst of being an only child. Not only that, the child of older parents. A late miracle in their lives. Naturally they wanted to hold on to her, to cherish her, especially her mother. But their constant overprotective fussing had left its mark. Her father never failed to remind her of the time she'd lost her wallet or got on the wrong train and he'd come to the rescue. Added to this was the shock of losing Edmond, and she found she was less sure of herself, scared of making a mistake.

How she envied Marisa's home life: the crowded backstreet terraced house in the East End with five children younger than Marisa, the exotic cooking smells, Marisa's mum laughing and singing and hugging Liz when she went to visit. It was always full of noise and chaos, and it seemed like heaven to Liz.

And now Marisa would be gone for a while. It might be a few days. It might even be longer. And she had a chance to do something important. If she could find the missing girl, she'd be a heroine. Probably promoted. Her picture in the papers. And the little girl would be safe.

If only, Liz said to herself, wondering what she meant. *If only that were me, and I was on this story and* . . . She sat up, mouth open in anticipation mixed with trepidation. *Could I?* she asked herself. *Dare I?*

Then she answered herself. "What have I got to lose?"

When Marisa came home at eleven, her make-up clearly smudged from a snogging session somewhere, Liz was still awake and dressed.

"Oh, you're still up," Marisa said. "I had such a nice evening. We went to the pictures. Back row. He's a good kisser."

Liz nodded. Then she said, "Listen, I've had a thought. A way to redeem myself with the paper. What if I came with you down to Dorset? And I helped look for this missing girl?"

"What?" Marisa eyed her suspiciously, then laughed. "Liz, I'm on police business. I can't take friends along."

"I understand that. But what if I just happened to bump into you down in Dorset, and you introduced me to your DI Jones as a newspaper reporter who was also hunting for the missing girl . . . and you suggested we could work together, cover twice as much ground?"

Marisa shook her head. "You haven't met DI Jones. Working with one woman is going to be painful enough for him. But two?"

"It's worth a try, isn't it?" Liz said. "I've made up my mind I'm not going back to the paper, at least not to obits. I'm going to telephone and say I'm sick. So you tell me where you are going and where you are staying, and I'll arrange to run into you there. And we'll see what happens next."

Marisa was frowning now. "I don't know, Liz. You might get me into awful trouble. I'm on shaky ground as it is with this DI. Don't do it."

"But don't you see, Marisa, if I got a scoop . . . if I helped find the missing girl, my paper would have to take me seriously again. Look, I promise I'll tread cautiously, and I won't say the wrong thing. I won't get in your way. I won't hamper your investigation. But it's a chance

I've got to take if you don't want me to quit my job and move home to my parents' again."

Marisa was standing half turned away. Liz stood up and put a tentative hand on her shoulder. "Come on, Marisa. Please."

Marisa turned back, shaking her head. "I think you're bloody barmy, love," she said.

"But you'll let me do it, won't you? Who knows, I might even be useful."

Marisa shrugged. "I suppose I can't stop you if you happen to want to take a quick break on the South Coast. But I can't tell you where we're going, because I don't know. All I've been told is nine o'clock train to Weymouth. The local police are supposed to be meeting us at the station. And you absolutely can't interfere in what we're doing. I mean it, Liz. What if you tipped off a kidnapper that we were looking for him, and he killed the little girl before we got to him . . . ?"

"Don't worry," Liz said. "I promise I won't get in your way. And I'm actually quite good at surveillance, remember. I was the one who found out about the MP and the call girl."

"And look where that got you," Marisa said as she unzipped her dress and let it fall to the floor.

CHAPTER 2

No more was said that night. Liz lay awake, too wound up to sleep. What did she really think she could achieve by doing this, and what if she got Marisa into trouble? She almost decided it was a foolhardy idea but heard a small voice whispering that she was giving up too easily. Chickening out. If she wanted to prove herself as a crack reporter, she should take risks. At least it would be far away from Bob Green and the poisonous Miss Knight. It would give her time to think, if nothing else. At last the distant city noises died down, and she drifted off to sleep.

She was up early, shoved some clothes and toiletries into an overnight bag and was gone before Marisa woke up. She made her way to Waterloo Station and bought a coffee and bun at the station café. She found a phone box and called the *Express*, getting Dick Haskell from the night news team still on duty.

"Can you do me a favour, Dick?" she said. "Can you leave a note that I'm calling in sick? I've got stomach flu."

"Why not call in yourself when everyone is in the office?"

"I might not feel up to telephoning later."

There was a pause, then he asked, "What are you up to, Houghton?"

"I told you. Stomach flu. Not pleasant. You don't want details."

"Righty-oh. I'll pass on the news. Obits will fall apart without you." He laughed, then hung up.

Then she waited and watched until she saw Marisa walking beside a portly, balding man. The latter was wearing a fawn mac that seemed to be the trademark of plainclothes policemen. Marisa was dressed in a pleated navy skirt and suede jacket with her new white boots. She looked stylish as always. And not very happy. She was glancing around, trying to spot Liz.

Liz moved on to the platform, still keeping out of sight. This part was fun, rather like a child's game. Playing a part. Liz, the intrepid investigator. She tried not to consider that she might be making a stupid mistake that could get Marisa and herself into a lot of trouble. Instead she pictured herself tracking down the child whose disappearance had dominated the headlines for the past week.

Oh, you're offering me a job with the Sunday Times? *How nice, but I've already told the* Guardian . . .

The train gave an impatient toot, and she hurried to board, getting into the next coach, seeing nothing of Marisa until they disembarked in Weymouth on the South Coast some three hours later. It was only a small group of people who left the train, since it was out of season for seaside holidays. Liz made sure that Marisa and DI Jones were ahead of her. She handed in her ticket, then paused as a policeman approached the two detectives. Words were exchanged that Liz couldn't hear, but they nodded and went with him. Liz hurried to catch up with them. A police car was waiting at the curb. Then she heard Marisa saying, loud and clear, "So where will we be staying, then?"

"We've put you up at the Seaview Lodge, on the front. It's nice enough and empty at this time of year," came the reply.

Liz smiled to herself and asked for directions to the Seaview Lodge. Coming out of the station, she saw the harbour off to one side with fishing boats moored and pastel-coloured houses. A pretty scene on a sunny day, except at that moment the sky was heavy with the promise of rain, and the wind off the Channel was bitter. Liz wrapped her scarf more firmly around her neck and started walking in the direction of the seafront. It was only a short distance up King Street to the esplanade, with the sandy beach curving around the edge of the bay. Seaview Lodge turned out to be part of a row of Georgian houses facing the beach. The houses had clearly seen better days, dating from a time when this would have been a fashionable destination for middle-class Victorians. Several of the houses had been turned into small hotels, each bearing a name like Seaview, Seagulls, The Breakers. The proprietress was surprised and delighted to see Liz.

"Usually we've little business at this time of year," she said. "We close at the end of October. I was saying to the hubby maybe we should just go ahead and close now, and then today we get two sets of customers. There's another party booked in besides you. They haven't arrived yet, but they are booked in. The hubby's going to say, 'I told you we should stay open.'" And she laughed. "I'm Mrs Robinson. And your name?"

Liz was tempted to give her a fake one, but said, "Miss Houghton."

"Pleased to meet you, love. Was it a single room you'd be wanting? And for how long?"

Liz told her she wasn't sure but probably for a week.

"Down from London, are you?"

"Yes," Liz said. "Taking a break for a few days."

"I don't blame you, love," the proprietress said. "You wouldn't catch me living in a big city. All that noise and bustle. It isn't healthy, is it? Do you work there?"

"I do," Liz said. "I'm a newspaper reporter, actually. Stressful job."

"It would be." The woman paused, mulling what Liz had said. "You wouldn't be down here on a story, would you? Scandal in Weymouth? Something dodgy going on under our noses?"

Liz attempted a light laugh. "I couldn't tell you if I was, Mrs Robinson."

The woman laughed, too. "Well, I don't suppose anything too juicy would be happening down here. Usually a lot of old fogeys come down for their holidays—retired colonels who take their constitutional walks along the front. And as you can see, at this time of year it's pretty much deserted. Most of the attractions are closed. Dead as a doornail."

"Just what I need at the moment," Liz said. "Peace and quiet."

Mrs Robinson nodded. "The other party coming today is from London, too. A Mr Jones and a Miss Young. I don't know if there's anything going on there or if it's just business. You never know these days, do you, with all this talk of free love and what have you." She gave a knowing little smile. "But you have to learn to be broad-minded in our line of business. Turn a blind eye, that's what the hubby says. I suppose we'll find out more when they get here."

She took Liz up to a narrow single room that faced the beach. It was spotlessly clean, if spartan, with a washbasin, a small chest of drawers and some hooks for clothes with hangers on them on the wall. But there was pink eiderdown on the bed, a mirror on the back wall and over the bed one of those needlepoint pictures saying, *There's no place like home.* Liz felt that this defeated the purpose of a welcoming hotel and smiled to herself.

"Bathroom down the hall, love. Watch the water from the geyser. It comes out really hot. And will you be taking your breakfast and dinner here?"

"Yes, I think so, thank you."

"Then dinner's at seven. We get nice fresh fish down here. Hope you like fish?"

"Oh, I do." Liz gave her a smile, hoping she'd go away and leave her in peace.

"Then I'd better get cracking, hadn't I?" The woman smoothed down her apron and left Liz alone. Liz unpacked her hastily packed items, noticing that she hadn't brought a spare pair of tights and had forgotten a hairbrush. She'd have to go into town and find a Woolworths. She went over to the window and looked out. It was clearly about to rain. She should have brought a mac. Still, she could buy one of those cheap plastic ones in Woolworths. Looking out of the window, she took in the scene: the row of brightly coloured beach huts, strung along the sandy curve of the bay, and in the other direction the harbour walls, a Victorian clock at the seafront and a war memorial.

Then she paused, pushing back her hair from her face. Had she been here before? It seemed vaguely familiar. She had taken several seaside holidays in England and Wales with her family right after the war, before going abroad became fashionable. Torquay she remembered fondly. And Newquay in Cornwall. Maybe Bournemouth? She'd only have been four or five, when beaches and buckets and spades and ice creams and donkeys were more important than place names. But her parents always stayed at rather more grand hotels than this—the sort with a glass-fronted lounge where they would take their coffee and read the papers before the stroll along the waterfront. Utterly boring to a small child. She noticed several grander-looking buildings further along the bay, but none of them stirred a memory. She wrapped her scarf around her head and set out again.

Having completed her purchases at Woolies, she stopped for a sausage roll and a cup of tea in a small café. The sausage tasted like sawdust, and she wished she had gone to the Indian place she'd spotted from the train station. Still, there was the promise of fresh fish tonight, which cheered her up. The rain had held off so far, and she walked around the town, on the lookout for any small girl. She realized this was a hopeless quest: if a kidnapper had brought Lucy Fareham here, he would hardly be parading her around for all to see. After all, her picture had been in every newspaper and on the telly.

"Let's face it, Houghton," she muttered to herself. "You don't know what you are looking for. You have no idea how to set about this, and you only came down here because you are running away from your life in London."

Having agreed all that was true, she went back to the hotel, where she had a satisfying afternoon nap.

CHAPTER 3

She woke to hear voices outside her door, coming past her room.

"One of you can take the room with the sea view, and the other gets the room upstairs at the back, where it's quieter." That was Mrs Robinson's voice.

"I don't mind being where it's quiet, if Inspector Jones wants the front room." That was Marisa. "He'd probably not want to climb the extra flight of stairs."

"Too bloody right," said a man's voice. "My knees aren't what they used to be."

"Oh, so it's Inspector Jones, is it? I'm sorry. I had you down as Mister."

"That's all right, love. We don't exactly want it broadcast that we're police."

"Oh. Right you are. Mum's the word, then." And the voices moved away. Liz heard doors shutting. She was dying to go up and chat with Marisa, but she stayed in her room, made a cup of tea with the electric kettle provided and then spruced herself up for dinner. She waited until she heard the others going down and gave them a chance to get settled before she headed for the dining room. It was a pleasant room with a bay window looking out over the seafront and now contained five small tables, each with a white lace tablecloth and a vase of artificial flowers in the middle. Marisa and DI Jones were already sitting at the table in the bay window. Liz hesitated, waiting for them to look up and notice her.

DI Jones did so first. "Oh hello," he said. "We've got company. I thought we'd have the place to ourselves at this time of year. Take a seat, miss."

"Thank you." Liz went to sit at a far table, then exclaimed. "Wait a minute. Marisa? Is that you?"

"Oh my God," Marisa exclaimed with authentic surprise. "Liz Houghton! What on earth are you doing here?"

"You two ladies know each other?" Jones asked.

"We certainly do," Liz said. "We were best friends at school."

"You went to the same school, then?" He glanced at Marisa. She's posh and you're definitely from the East End, his look said.

"We did. St Ursula's Convent in Highgate. A very snooty girls' school," Marisa said.

"It was a very snobby school," Liz agreed. "Most of the girls only wanted to snag the right husband when they left. We bonded over being odd girls out. They thought I was strange because I liked to learn and I was a teacher's pet, and they were horrible to Marisa because she was a scholarship girl."

"What were you doing at a school like that?" DI Jones asked Marisa. "I thought you came from the East End?"

"My mum wanted to make sure I got a good Catholic education and didn't meet any boys until I was eighteen." Marisa grinned.

"I bet you've made up for it since," Liz said, and they all laughed.

"Grab a pew. Come and join us," Marisa said. "You don't mind, do you, guv?"

"No, I suppose not," he said grudgingly. He waited until Liz had taken the chair beside him before asking, "So what brings you down here, Miss Houghton?"

"Work," Liz said. "I'm a reporter with the *Daily Express*. I've been put on the story about little Lucy Fareham. The paper has sent out reporters everywhere. The paper would love us to be the ones who find her and get the scoop."

"Really?" DI Jones eyed her with interest now. "And why down here?"

"I understand we've been getting tips from all over the place," Liz said, not wanting to make eye contact with Marisa.

"Oh, and where have you been getting these tips from, may I ask?" Liz could hear the belligerence in his voice.

Oh dear, she thought. "I don't know. I'm not told who logs the tips in, but I do know several have come from the South Coast. But it's like looking for a needle in a haystack, really, isn't it? We know so little. It could have been family or a friend who abducted her. We haven't been told anything, only that she was playing with the au pair in the square outside her house in London and she loved to hide amongst the bushes, and when her au pair called, she wasn't there."

"That's about it," DI Jones said. "We don't know that much more."

"So what is your theory, Inspector?" Liz asked. "You must have handled cases as perplexing as this before."

She was unprepared for the look of distress that crossed his face. "I have," he said. They paused, waiting for him to say more. Then he took a deep breath. "I was put on a similar case when I was a young copper in the war years. Actually, several cases. Three little girls. All from London being evacuated to the country. One was found, murdered, in a wood near the train line. But the other two simply vanished. Gone without a trace. It was wartime. Everything was chaotic, you know. People getting bombed, moving in with relatives, sending their kids to be evacuated. That's what these girls were, you know. Sent off to be evacuated to the country, and that was the last their parents saw of them."

"How terrible," Marisa said. "Wasn't there paperwork to keep track of them?"

DI Jones sighed. "Like I said, it was all a bit chaotic in those days. Parents panicked, came to a station and shoved their kids on to a train with a label around their bloody necks. If they were evacuated with their school, then the teachers were with them, and they all went to the same place, but if they were travelling as individuals, then the train stopped at various stations, kids got off and local people took the ones they liked the look of. Half the time there was no official record if the local volunteers did not keep tabs on who went where. The parents in London had to wait until they got a letter telling them where their child was." He looked up as Mrs Robinson came in with a tray.

"It's vegetable soup tonight," she said and put a plate in front of each of them. DI Jones toyed with his spoon.

"That's what made it so hard," he said as Marisa and Liz started to eat. "Each time it was over a month later when the parents came to the police and said they hadn't heard from their child."

"How awful," Marisa said. "I bet my mum would never have let me go. And if she wanted me evacuated, she'd have taken me herself, and vetted the place I was staying first."

"There was such a feeling of panic in those first years of the war." DI Jones took a spoonful of hot soup, then went on, "When the Blitz started and people were being bombed every night, all they wanted was for their kids to be safe. Anything to get them out of London and to the country. They thought they were doing the right thing."

"You found no clues at all?" Liz asked. "Were all three of the girls you mentioned supposedly sent to the same part of the country?"

"They'd all been sent southwest of London: Hampshire, Dorset, Wiltshire. Inland, of course. You didn't want to put kiddies near the coast, where there was always danger of invasion. The little girl we found—her name was Valerie Hammond. She was supposed to be going with her school to Dorset. Only nobody knew whether she even got on the train. Her mum had to work an early shift and told her to walk to the station to join the others. As I said, it was always very chaotic on the platform what with all the kids, parents and volunteers." He looked up, the distress still on his face.

"That's terrible," Marisa said.

"Not what I'd have done with an eight-year-old kiddie. They did actually live quite close to the station, so I suppose it wasn't too unreasonable. It was different in wartime."

"You say you found her body near the train line?" Marisa asked.

"I didn't find it. A local farmer came across her. I was part of the team sent to investigate." He tore off a piece of roll, then played with it on his plate. "I tell you, I'll never forget that scene as long as I live. The kid was lying as if she was asleep in a little woodland, and there were flowers all around her, and a crown of flowers on her head. Like a ruddy fairy princess."

"Had she been—you know—assaulted?"

"Oh yeah. I can't tell you what I wanted to do to the bloke who did it."

"But you never caught the murderer?"

"A bloke was caught red-handed, so to speak. In the act of putting on the crown of flowers. He was . . . not quite all there, you know. One sandwich short of a picnic." He grinned at this attempt at a joke. "His name was Dan Harkness. He never actually confessed, but he never denied it either. He was sent to a mental institution, deemed not fit to stand trial. We thought that was that. Then another girl was reported missing. Rosie Binks was her name. Same thing. Same time of year the next year. Put on a train to Dorset and never seen again. And then a third girl the year after that. Gloria Kane. All about the same age."

"A serial killer, then?" Marisa asked. "Presumably you had to release the barmy bloke?"

DI Jones toyed with his spoon, not looking at them. "We did, since the other girls vanished when he was already in custody. He was eventually handed over to the care of his sister."

"Were they all on the same train line?" Liz said, looking up sharply from her soup.

"Same general direction but not the same route."

"That makes it more complicated, doesn't it?" Liz said. "If there was a child predator who kept his eye on one train line, you could understand it."

"That's what made it so bloody impossible," DI Jones said. "I can tell you it hit me very hard. I was a young copper. I'd joined the force in '38 and just been promoted to plainclothes when I was assigned to this. I was feeling pretty bad about not joining the army, you know. Doing my bit. But police work was a protected occupation, so I was stuck in London, identifying bodies that had been blown to bits after a bombing. That sort of stuff. I really thought I could make a difference if I found these little girls." He paused, took another noisy slurp of soup, then went on. "It was just the one at first, but when we got the call about the same time the next year, my old guv said we needed to find out if other girls had gone missing and if there was a pattern."

"And then the third the next year," Liz said. "That must have been shocking to you."

He nodded, tearing off a bit of roll and dunking it into the red-brown liquid before popping it into his mouth. A trickle of soup ran down his chin, and he mopped it with his napkin. "I felt so bloody helpless," he said. "I did wonder how long it would go on. Was one girl going to disappear at the same time every year?"

"You don't think Lucy's disappearance could be linked, then, guv?" Marisa asked. "Same time of year? Same pattern?"

"Linked? Not really." He looked startled at this suggestion. "I mean, come on! After twenty-something years? The circumstances are quite different, aren't they? Lucy was taken from the gardens outside her own home, in broad daylight, in the middle of London."

"And nobody saw anything," Marisa said. "That's amazing to me. There is always someone peeping through the curtains in London. Someone housebound, or someone who just happens to be looking out of the window at the exact moment."

"You'd think so, wouldn't you? Or a taxi driver waiting in the square, or someone at a bus stop . . . but no. We've asked the public to come forward, and nobody has. That's why I begged them to put me on this task force and let me help them look. I've had this sense of failure all these years. Sense of guilt, actually, that I couldn't save them. I'd dearly love to do something to solve this one."

"I'll help in any way I can," Liz said.

She saw his expression change. He had been mopping up his soup plate with the last of his roll. He seemed to remember that she was not a member of his team, not a policewoman.

"You can help by leaving us to get on with our work," he said. "It was bad enough being stuck with one woman on my team. But two? This is police business, understand, young lady. No outsiders needed."

"I'm sorry," she said. "I only thought . . ." She paused. "The more boots on the ground the better, you know. I am rather good at interviewing people. It's my job." She gave him an earnest stare. "Look, I'd love to get the scoop, of course, but more than that I'd like to save a child's life."

"If she's still alive," Marisa said. "Prior cases would tell us the chances aren't too good."

"Depending on why she was taken," DI Jones said. "Is this a kidnap for ransom, a child murderer or a deranged woman longing for a child?"

"Let's pray for the latter, shall we?" Marisa said. "So what's the plan, guv?"

"It could be a complete waste of time down here," DI Jones said. "The tip said the kid was spotted looking out of the back window of a car. The person who phoned it in said she had thought it looked a lot like the little girl in the newspaper, and she wanted to follow, but she was taking her own child to a doctor's appointment, and she knew he wouldn't see them if she was late. She tried to note the number plate, but all she got were the first two letters. It was one of those winding lanes with the high hedges, you see, and the other car was moving quite fast."

"What kind of car was it?" Marisa asked.

"A blue Morris Minor. Not very clean."

"That could apply to half the cars in the county," Marisa said.

"Were they heading for Weymouth?" Liz asked. She had finished her soup quickly, having been starving. It was clearly out of a tin, but it was warm and comforting.

"Out of Weymouth," DI Jones said. "On a back road. That's what makes me a little hopeful. It wasn't the sort of road you'd take to get anywhere, apart from the villages along the coast. So that's what we'll be doing. Tracing that route, visiting villages and farms along the way. In country areas like this, people will know if anyone new has come to visit."

He looked up as Mrs Robinson came in to remove the soup plates. "I hope the soup was good," she said.

"Lovely, thanks," they all muttered in that way the English do to avoid being rude or complaining.

"I'll bring in your plaice, then," she said.

They waited until she had put three plates of fish in front of them. A small fillet of plaice was accompanied by mashed potato and cabbage and decorated with a dab of parsley sauce. A first mouthful proved that the fish was indeed fresh and delicious. Silence fell on the room as the three occupants ate with obvious pleasure. DI Jones finished his first. He put down his knife and fork. "You can't beat a bit of freshly caught fish, can you? It's always bloody frozen in London." Then he seemed to remember what he had been talking about. "Look, miss. I know you mean well and you've got a job to do, but if you really want to help the little girl, you stay well out of our way. Look around Weymouth, by all means. See if you can spot the car. You can even ask at the hotels if they've any new guests with small children. But if you find anything, you report it to us first, is that clear?"

"Of course," Liz said. She avoided Marisa's gaze.

CHAPTER 4

"You're wasted in your profession, you know that?" Marisa had come into Liz's room later that night when snores could be heard coming from DI Jones's room down the hall. "You should have been a bloody actress. Your look of surprise when you saw me. Oscar-winning performance."

"Well, he bought it, didn't he?" Liz sat on the end of her bed, brushing out her hair. The cheap Woolies hairbrush caught in the tangles, and she winced. "Look, Risa, I don't want to make any trouble for you, so I'll keep out of your way, but do let me know if you find anything, won't you?"

"If I can," Marisa said. "If we're dealing with a homicide, then . . ."

"Don't." Liz shuddered. "I can't bear to think of those little girls, all those years ago. And their parents never knowing what had happened to them."

Marisa nodded. "If that had been my mum, she'd have gone stark raving mad."

"Can you picture what it would have done to my mother then?" Liz asked. "She'd have gone right over the edge. It's bad enough now . . ."

"She's getting worse, is she?"

Liz shrugged. "Sometimes she seems quite normal, asks me about my week, comments on what she's read in the newspapers. And on other occasions she asks me the same question three times or tells me the same anecdote again and again. And she gets upset really easily if anything unexpected happens or the schedule changes. Clearly in the early stages of some sort of dementia. I can tell Dad's worried, but what can you do?"

"She's not even that old, is she?" Marisa said. "I thought that kind of thing was an old-age disease."

"She is over seventy, and she did live through the deprivations of the war. That upset a lot of people's mental health, didn't it?"

Marisa laughed, shaking her head. "You should have seen what my mum went through in Malta. Bombed incessantly. They had to live down in tunnels night after night. She said they even had a school and a chapel down there."

"That would have finished off my mother. She's claustrophobic as well as everything else," Liz said. "Look, you'd better go, in case your charming DI wakes up and hears us talking."

"What could be wrong with that?" Marisa said. "We're old school friends catching up on years."

"That's true."

"But you're right. I am knackered. It's been a long day, especially putting up with a continual barrage of sexist remarks that I have to pretend I haven't heard. See you in the morning, then."

She went to the door, then turned back. "Liz, I'm glad you're here."

～

Breakfast the next morning was quite satisfactory—a full English with egg, bacon, sausage, fried bread and tomatoes. Used to only yoghurt eaten hurriedly before she went to work, Liz mopped up her plate with relish. So did DI Jones, who added three slices of toast and marmalade. Clearly food was the big love of his life. A police car arrived for them, but no mention was made of where they were heading.

"Remember what I told you yesterday." DI Jones turned back to Liz as they approached the front door. "You stay out of our business. And if you find anything at all, you report to us first, not some bloody news rag."

"All right. I've got it." Liz nodded.

It was raining again, and frankly she wasn't sure what she should do. She put on the plastic raincoat and went out, bending her head against the bitter wind from the sea. She visited hotels along the seafront, asking if they'd had any recent guests with a child of Lucy's age. When they learned she was trying to find the little girl, they were more than helpful, but none of them had seen a child matching Lucy's description.

Liz then walked through the town, looking out for a dirty blue Morris Minor. There were plenty of those cars but not a dirty blue one. She asked at the sweet shop and the toy shop, figuring that if Lucy had been kidnapped, her kidnapper might want to keep her quiet with sweets and toys. Of course the shop owners were most interested. "You from the telly, then?" she was asked.

"No, a newspaper. I can't tell you which one. But I'm staying at the Seaview Lodge if you can think of anything that might be helpful."

She found the big breakfast kept her going well past lunchtime, and instead she treated herself to a cream tea at a local café. Then she came back to her room to dry off and surprised herself by taking another nap. Napping was not something that usually came easily to her. Maybe she had found the last year and its ongoing stresses to be a bit much and she was now letting go.

It was a good thing I came down here, she told herself, although a nagging voice at the back of her head whispered that she could be sacked if they found out what she was doing. She debated calling personnel and making sure they had been given the message, but then they might find this more suspicious. As darkness fell she heard Marisa and DI Jones come in, stomping up the stairs and parting with a "See you at dinner, then."

Liz changed into a frock and went down to the dining room at ten to seven. Sherry and glasses, along with a bowl of Twiglets, had been put out on the sideboard, and she helped herself. She took a table off to one side this time, not wanting to intrude, and was halfway through her glass when the other two came in.

"Nasty old day, wasn't it?" DI Jones said. "We had to have a pub lunch to dry off. Decent meat pie and peas. I wonder what the innkeeper's got for us tonight, then?"

He took his seat at the table in the window. Marisa sat opposite him. "Did you have a good day, Liz?"

"Apart from getting soaked," Liz said. "I did what you suggested, Inspector. I asked around at the hotels, but nobody has a small child staying. Well, they wouldn't, would they? They'd all be back in school. I tried the sweet shop and toy shop, too. Just in case."

"Good thinking," Marisa said.

"And I looked out for the Morris Minor, but no sign of it. How about you?"

"I reckon we visited every village and farm between here and Lulworth and nothing. Not even a dirty Morris Minor. We've now got a nicely dirty police car from driving through all that mud to the farms. I hope we aren't supposed to clean it before we turn it in."

"What do you do next?" Liz asked. "Move on to another town and fan out from there?"

"We'll give it another day or so," DI Jones said. "There's one place we haven't looked at. It shows up as a village on the map, but it's also marked as a restricted area, government property. I've no idea what that's about. When we tried to drive there, the road was blocked. And yet a bloke we spoke to at the pub says he saw some kind of vehicle going down there a couple of days ago."

"That's interesting," Liz said. "I wonder why it's off-limits."

"We're going to find out from the local police in the morning," DI Jones said. "In the meantime, I'm starving, and I could do with a beer."

It almost seemed as if Mrs Robinson had been listening because she came through with a bottle and a glass.

"I thought the gentleman wouldn't want a sherry," she said. "Ready for your dinner, then? Miserable old day, wasn't it?" She put the glass in front of him and poured efficiently. "Weather's supposed to improve tomorrow, according to the telly. Sunny for a few days. Not that I believe a thing they say. I said to the hubby, 'Is there any other job in the world where you can get things wrong every day and they don't sack you?'" She tittered at her own joke. "I'll bring your soup, then."

"Annoying woman," DI Jones said. "I hope we haven't said too much in her hearing. It will have been all around the county by tomorrow morning. That's the problem with women. Too nosy and can't hold their tongues."

"Maybe that's true of some women," Marisa said, giving him a withering frown. "I can hold my tongue perfectly when needed, and I'm sure Liz can, too."

"I've always said it's not natural, women wanting to join the police," he said. "Not that I'm saying you're bad at it, mind you. It's just not natural for women to want to go after criminals."

"Perhaps we want to help make society a better place," Marisa said. "Protect families, you know."

"I suppose there is that." He finished his beer with a swig and asked for a second bottle when the soup was brought in. This time it was cream of tomato, again from a tin, but the main course was shepherd's pie and more cabbage. Quite tasty in its way. And the pudding was jam roly-poly.

"Remind you of school food?" Marisa asked, grinning.

"I thought it was quite satisfying," DI Jones said. "I don't hold with foreign muck. All these Indian places everywhere. It's bad enough they want to move here, but now they're forcing us to eat their bloody food."

"I love Indian food," Marisa said, shooting a glance at Liz and rolling her eyes. "And nobody's forcing you to eat it. At least it has some flavour, which is more than can be said for most English food."

"Give me good old roast beef and Yorkshire pudding any day," DI Jones said.

"Nice, if you can afford it," Marisa said. "A Sunday roast was always a luxury in our house growing up."

Mrs Robinson returned with coffee for the women. DI Jones announced he was going up to bed, but Marisa stayed with Liz to drink their coffee.

"This is a complete waste of time, isn't it?" Marisa said.

"I'm beginning to think that way," Liz agreed. "I'd like to know more than we do. Was the kidnapping quite random, or was it something to do with the family? Are they rich? Was it a revenge act of some sort?"

"All I've heard is that the mother is distraught and can't imagine who could have done it. She also can't think how someone could have taken Lucy in broad daylight. The au pair was there, watching, all the time." Marisa shrugged. "I expect someone higher up at the Met is looking into all connections—family business dealings, et cetera. The husband is quite an influential bloke. Something in the city to do with trading."

"If you stole a child in London, why would you bring her all the way down here, unless you wanted to keep her?" Liz said.

"Or you've got some kind of family connection and a place where you could hide out."

"Right." Liz nodded. "Now I'm even more keen to keep digging. I wonder if my newspaper has turned up anything. Or if they'd tell me if they had." She got up. "I expect it will be back to obits for me, anyway."

CHAPTER 5

The next morning dawned bright and clear, the sun sparkling on a smooth sea. Liz got up early and went for a walk along the beach, admiring the brightly painted beach huts. Apart from a couple of dog walkers, the beach was deserted, and she stopped to pick up shells and white pebbles rounded by the water. Even though the trip had yielded nothing of interest so far, and she might be in trouble with her paper when she returned, she was glad she had come. She could feel the tension of the past months slipping away. She had never really liked city life, she realized. Having been raised at a lonely house in the country until she was twelve, she had hated to move to London, hemmed in by buildings on all sides. The move had been so that she could attend a good and proper girls' day school, since her mother did not want her away at a boarding school, and also her father, a career army man, had accepted a job at the War Office.

She came back in time for breakfast and ate with relish, finishing the whole full English this time. There was no sign of Marisa or her DI, but Marisa came in just as Liz was eating her second slice of toast.

"We've been to the local police station," Marisa said, "and it turns out that the village called Tydeham on the map has been deserted since the war. It was taken over by the military and used for target practice ahead of the D-Day invasion. It's just ruins. Nobody's allowed there now, because of the unexploded ordnance."

"So you won't be visiting, I take it?"

"DI Jones thinks we should take a look, because of the vehicle that was seen going towards it. He's had to call the army for permission. They are sending someone down since we would not be allowed in on our own."

"And in the meantime?"

Marisa smiled. "In the meantime, let's go for a walk and enjoy the sunshine."

The army, in the form of a young corporal in a Land Rover, arrived that afternoon. He seemed quite keen when he learned they were looking for Little Lucy.

"You think someone might have taken her to the deserted village?" he asked. Then he shook his head. "I wonder why they'd do that. It's pretty much all ruins. I was there once. Not the most pleasant place to hide out. But you'd know more than me about how criminal minds work, wouldn't you?" He addressed this to DI Jones. "It has to be some kind of pervert, doesn't it?"

When DI Jones didn't answer, he went on, "Are these ladies your secretaries?"

"I am a detective constable, assigned to this team," Marisa said coldly. "And this lady is a reporter from a London newspaper."

"Blimey." His face flushed with embarrassment. "I didn't realize they had women detectives. I mean, I know they have women coppers these days, but I didn't think . . ." He couldn't finish the sentence.

"I don't blame you, son," DI Jones said. "I feel a bit the same way myself. But this one's all right."

"High praise indeed," Marisa said.

Surprisingly, DI Jones had not made much opposition to Liz's tagging along to the village.

"Frankly I think we're wasting our time here," he said. "And I doubt you're going to get a story out of it."

They set off in the Land Rover with DI Jones up in front beside the corporal, who had revealed that his name was Dave. They drove out of the town and then along the same back road that they had covered the day before, past farms and cultivated fields in rolling countryside. The road was little more than a lane, really narrow with high hedges on either side. At this time of year there was old-man's beard growing in the hedgerows and berries forming on holly bushes. They drove through a couple of good-sized villages, each with its pub and small row of shops, then the corporal consulted his map, and they turned down an even narrower lane that soon became an unpaved track after about a mile. There was plenty of mud after the rain, and the Land Rover bumped and slithered until they came to the gate across the track.

Corporal Dave stopped the jeep and switched off the engine. "It's on foot from here, I'm afraid," he said. "I hope you haven't worn your good shoes."

"You can't open the gate?" DI Jones said.

Dave shook his head. "Not allowed without permission from the top brass, and that would take days. You're lucky they are letting you in at all. It's only because it's so urgent."

"We have to walk from here?" DI Jones asked. "How far is it?"

"About half a mile to the village," Dave said.

"And we have to climb that bloody gate first?"

Dave nodded. "Afraid so."

"Then if you don't mind, I'll leave this to the girls," DI Jones said. "They are younger and fitter than I am. I'll take a little nap in the jeep while you two go exploring. You know what you're looking for, don't you?"

"You're trusting me to confront a psychopath holding a little girl?" Marisa said. "I am flattered."

"Only because I don't expect they'll be here," Jones said. "I mean, would you drag a little girl for half a mile to a ruin? Probably not. But someone has to check it out because we have to cover our rear ends when we get back to London."

"Fine. If that's what you want. I'm ready to go exploring, aren't you, Liz?" Marisa climbed out of the back of the jeep.

"Absolutely." Liz got out of the vehicle. "I hope your new boots survive." She looked down at Marisa's tall white boots.

"They're patent, or probably plastic," she said. "They'd better survive. I paid enough for them on Carnaby Street."

"Right, then." Dave nodded to them, and they headed for the gate. There had been barbed wire on top, but over time it had been pulled aside, and they were now able to climb over. Dave went first, then held out a hand to the women. Liz was glad she had worn trousers.

Marisa was already scouring the ground around them. "There don't seem to be any recent tire tracks," she said. "It doesn't look like anything has come down here for a while apart from us. But we should look for recent footprints, especially a child's footprints. Although it rained so hard yesterday that a lot will have been washed away."

There had been a continuation of the track on the other side of the gate, but it was now horribly overgrown. Wet grass and weeds brushed against their legs, and it was heavy going, avoiding mud and puddles. The track was lined with large trees, oaks and beeches, their leaves already turning gold, and a carpet of yellow leaves was forming beneath them. Dave chatted with them as they walked, telling them that he had joined up because he hoped to be sent abroad and see a bit of action, but so far he hadn't been any further than Salisbury Plain.

"Still, it's not a bad life," he said. "Someone else feeds me, clothes me, and tells me what to do. It's like living with my mum." He laughed. "A bit different from my brother, who's run off to join one of those new hippie communes. He's into love and peace and all that junk. I can't talk to him any more. I mean, it's all very well to spout love and peace, but someone has to defend the country if we get another Hitler or the Russians decide to attack, right?"

"From what I've seen, the talk of love and peace is an excuse to experiment with drugs," Marisa said.

"Quite right," Dave said. "You should see my brother. He's not even the same person any more. Of course, he won't come home now because he knows what Mum and Dad think."

"My mum would personally kill any of my brothers who tried the same thing," Marisa said.

"Strict, is she?"

"Ever so strict. She's from Malta, where you obey your parents or else."

"Good idea," Dave said. "We need more of that here."

"My father was an army man," Liz said. "I was certainly raised to do what I was told or else."

"Career army or just in the war?"

"No. Career army," she said. "A brigadier, actually."

"Blimey, then I'd better watch what I say, hadn't I?"

Liz smiled. "He's retired now. He worked at the War Office for his final years. But he was very active during the war. He was part of the D-Day invasion and went all the way across France and into Germany."

"Good for him. They were tough blokes in those days. I don't think today's army would be up to it. We've got a bunch of sissies."

They came to a place where a tree had fallen across the path and had to work their way around it. On the other side they stepped out into what had been a street. The road surface had been paved but was now cracked with weeds and even saplings sprouting through it. On one side stood a row of what once had been grey stone cottages, although now they were roofless, and all that was left were crumbling walls, open to the sky. Here and there they were covered in ivy and red Virginia creeper, making them look almost part of the natural landscape and the hillside that rose behind them. A tree had grown up through the middle of what had once been rooms. On the other side of the street were the remains of a couple of bigger buildings, one still standing two stories high, although there were gaping holes where windows had been. At the far end of the street, the land rose, forming a V-shaped valley with a glimpse of blue sea beyond. It would have been an inviting location for the people who once lived there, if a little too remote.

Liz stared, taking it all in. The utter silence apart from the soft stirring of dying leaves in the breeze that came up from the sea. Not even the cry of a bird, as if all living things had abandoned this place.

"Oh, how sad," Liz said. "To think that people lived here once. It's like the trips we used to take with the school to old castles, but they were from centuries ago. This was within my lifetime."

"Just the same as the bombing in London," Marisa said. "We used to see whole streets of rubble. I remember seeing a doll lying half buried in a collapsed wall and wanting to go and take it, but my mum wouldn't let me."

"I suppose you're right," Corporal Dave said. "I wasn't born until 1946, but I remember there was still a lot of bomb damage when we went up to London."

"Well into the fifties in our part of the city," Marisa said. "Oh look, there's a church back there. That's still standing."

Liz looked off to her left. There was a wall with a gate in it. A line of giant yew trees led to a little grey stone church with a square tower at one end, still looking completely as it always had done.

Dave nodded. "I think they were told to try and preserve the church. I believe the former inhabitants of Tydeham are allowed back for one service each year."

"We should take a look inside that," Marisa said. "If it's still inhabitable, someone might shelter in it." She pushed open the gate that creaked on rusty hinges.

Amongst the tall grass and dying brown bracken, they could see gravestones. Marisa started to walk forward.

"Stay on the path and let me go first," Corporal Dave said. "You never know where there might still be unexploded shells."

"Oh, right." Marisa looked around her before stepping forward. "But keep a lookout for any sign of recent activity. A sweet wrapper. A footprint. People usually leave some trace of themselves." She turned back to Liz and Dave. "And we probably shouldn't talk any more. In case they are still here and they hear us."

They made their way up the narrow path to the church door. It was a massive thing of old oak and was locked. Dave checked around, then shook his head.

"Well, nobody came in here," Corporal Dave said.

Off to one side there had been another building, but it had been made of wood, not stone, and was now completely flattened. They made their way back to the street. Liz looked at the gravestones, some overtaken with ivy, others now hidden by tall weeds. *People have come here to visit their loved ones in my lifetime,* she thought. *The folks who were buried here expected to be remembered.*

They came out through the gate and now started along the village street. In what had been cottage gardens, weeds now ran rampant, brambles tumbled over walls. There was no sign that people had once lived here, no washing on a clothesline, no toy dropped when a child was called in to a meal. Nothing.

"This is all there was of it?" Marisa looked around. "Hardly much of a village."

"There was a big manor house, too, off to one side up there," Dave said. "I think the village was built by the family who owned it. They had workers living on the spot. There was a harbour, so perhaps some of them were fishermen."

They continued forward, stepping over the great fissures and craters that had formed.

"They certainly gave this place a beating," Marisa said. She looked back at Liz.

Liz was standing, staring down the street, frowning.

"What's the matter, Liz?" Marisa asked. "Have you spotted something?"

"I've been here before," she said in a puzzled voice.

"You can't have," Dave said, chuckling. "It's been off-limits since the war. It was taken over by the army in 1943 to prepare for the invasion. You weren't even born, were you?"

"I was born in 1941," Liz said.

"You'd only have been two when the people were turned out," Dave said. "You don't remember much from when you were two, do you? I know I don't."

"They say some people remember their birth," Marisa said. "That's why they are claustrophobic, coming down that long, dark tunnel." And she laughed.

Liz was still frowning, looking around her. "I'm sure I was here once."

"Maybe another village like it. There's plenty of them on the coast here," Dave said. "But probably not during the war. The coast was mostly off-limits for civilians. They had mines and tank traps on the beaches. And this wouldn't have been the sort of place you'd come on holiday. No hotels or caravan parks nearby in those days."

Liz shook her head. "I can't remember anything else. It just came to me that I'd been here. I've no idea when."

"Like I said, it would have to have been before 1943, and you'd only have been a toddler."

They continued walking. Liz stopped, looking up at the shell of what once had been the two-story building. "There was a pub here called the Big Boat," she said.

"The Big Boat?" Dave looked amused. He examined the building. "I suppose that could have been the pub. It's the only larger building on the street other than the church." He trod gingerly over to where a door had once been and peered inside. "Can't see much in here," he said. "Just rubble where the upstairs floor has caved in."

"But there is a metal hook on the side," Marisa said. "Where a pub sign might have hung once."

She, too, tiptoed forward and peered into tall grass. Then she stopped and looked up, her mouth open. "There's a sign," she said.

Liz and Dave went to look. The painting on it was faded and discoloured, but they could just make out the shape of a ship in full sail and the words "The Golden Hinde."

CHAPTER 6

"The Big Boat," Marisa said in a shaky voice. "That's what a little child who couldn't read would have called it. She would have just seen the picture." She looked at Liz. "You really might have been here."

Liz was staring from the pub to the sign and then back out to the street beyond. "It's so weird," she said. "As you say, I could only have been two. When would we have come here?"

"Like I said, it's not the kind of place you come on holiday, even if there isn't a war on," Dave said. He paused. "Unless you were related to the people at the big house, and you came to visit them?"

"What was their name?" she asked.

"I've no idea. We could look it up."

"I'll telephone my parents and ask them," Liz said. "But it does seem strange, doesn't it?"

"Did you live down here, during the war?" Dave asked.

Liz shook her head. "Nowhere near. We lived in Shropshire, on the Welsh border."

She caught Marisa staring at her. "What else do you remember?"

Liz stared down the street to the triangle of blue sea beyond. "Nothing. It just came to me in a flash that I'd been here. But that's all. I can't remember anything about it."

"Perhaps more will come back to you as we look around," Dave said.

They walked on, past what once had been a shop. Here there was a hint of former human habitation. A red postbox stood beside it, and there was a sign over the door, the paint now almost gone, but it seemed to say "Post Office." There had been a proper shop window on one side, the glass now gone, and as they looked in, they saw what looked like a tin of something—the metal now half corroded away—lying on the shelf inside. But the roof of the shop had caved in, and the rest of the shop beyond was in ruins.

"They had to leave all their stuff behind?" Marisa said. "That's hardly fair. I wonder if they were given compensation?"

Dave shrugged. "Who knows? It was wartime. The army took over what they wanted, didn't they?"

Liz had still been fighting to recapture the fleeting memory. Had she been to this shop? Bought an ice cream, perhaps? But it stirred no recollection. After the shop, the paved street ended, and steps ran down to the sea. Below they could see the broken remains of a harbour wall. Clouds were amassing in the west with the promise of more rain coming in.

"I don't see how anybody could have hidden out here for long," Marisa said. "There's nothing standing, apart from the church, and it's locked. They can't have got in there."

"There is the big house, you said," Liz pointed out.

"Yes, but I think that's a complete ruin, too," Dave answered. "And if you just came in here on the off chance, you wouldn't know about it. It's way off to the left, through those trees." He pointed to a small wood. They started to walk towards it. Through the trees Liz could just make out some sort of building in the distance. There had once been a path, but it was so overgrown in places that it was now indistinguishable from the undergrowth. "I'm not sure about going down there," Dave said. "Who knows what's lying under this bracken? We don't want to get a foot blown off, do we? I was told to keep you safe."

Liz peered through the trees, trying to make out what she saw there. She was fighting with a strange sense of dread. Something told her she didn't want to go that way.

"But if someone brought the little girl in through here?" Marisa asked.

"Taking a big risk," Dave said.

"They'd already taken a big risk in kidnapping a child," Marisa said sharply. "This is only a narrow path. Is there another way in? Wouldn't the residents have had a car? And what about deliveries?"

Dave thought about this. "I suppose there must have been a back entrance, or rather a front entrance, further up the lane. We could look, but I can't let you go this way."

They retraced their steps back to the waiting Land Rover, where DI Jones now sprawled blissfully asleep, his mouth wide open, looking quite unappealing.

"All done, are we?" he asked, stirring and opening his eyes as the women scrambled into the back seat. "Anything at all? No signs of them?"

"No signs," Marisa said. "It's all quite ruined. Depressing, actually. But we are going to try and see if there is another way to get to the big house. The path from the village has been quite grown over."

"All right. But let's get a move on." DI Jones sat up. "Looks like more rain is coming in. I don't fancy getting wet."

"But we should try to check it out, guv," Marisa said.

He sighed. "I suppose so. But to be honest, I've thought this was a wild-goose chase from square one. If you really want to know, I've always thought that they sent me down here to keep me out of the way of the real search. I begged them to put me on the team. I told them how important it was to me. I think they humoured me, but who'd want an old bloke who'd already failed three times?"

Liz heard the bitterness in his voice about the other missing girls and felt a wave of sympathy. She knew how it felt to have been brushed aside only too well. In her case it hadn't been failure, but stepping on the wrong toes, and the result had been the same—shoved off where she couldn't do any damage.

Marisa must have felt the same because she said, "Don't give up now, guv. If the girl is not here, we'll move further down the coast. But let's try and find the big house first."

There was no room to turn around, so Dave reversed the Land Rover until they came to a five-bar gate leading into a field. He managed to turn the vehicle without going into the ditch that ran on either side, and they headed back to the road.

"I say let's give up on this," DI Jones said. "It's almost time for my beer. I'll shout you one when we get back into town."

They had only gone about a hundred yards when Marisa grabbed at the corporal's sleeve. "Wait. Look. There's a driveway."

Off to their left there was a clear track, not too badly overgrown. They turned into it and followed, with a wood on one side and a newly ploughed field on the other.

"This obviously leads to a farm," DI Jones said. "These fields are being cultivated."

"We should try it anyway," Marisa insisted.

"You're keeping your governor from his beer?" he said, but he was joking.

The track plunged into a thick woodland. They had to duck as branches reached out across the road. Dying leaves fluttered down on to them. On the other side they came to giant rhododendron bushes, overgrown topiary hedges and other remains of a formal garden. And beyond they glimpsed the walls of what once had been a large grey stone manor house. It now stood roofless, with the same gaping holes replacing the former windows.

"Bloody hell," DI Jones said. "So this was it. It must have been a pretty impressive place once. Fountain and all over there. All right for some."

Dave stopped the vehicle, and they got out. Marisa was already examining the ground. "There are tire tracks here," she said, looking up excitedly. "Someone has been here quite recently."

DI Jones came over to where she was indicating. "Not a Morris Minor, that's for sure. That's something much bigger. A van, I'd say."

Liz was staring at the ruin of the house. Had she once stayed here? But no memory stirred. She didn't think she had ever seen this place before. Surely she would have remembered a fountain, beautiful gardens? It would have seemed like a fairy palace to a little girl who had spent a lonely childhood in fantasy worlds.

The men had started towards the house. The flight of steps leading to the front door was pockmarked and cracked. Dave went up. Broken glass lay strewn around, along with slate tiles from a roof. A great oak door now swung crazily on a hinge.

"Nothing here," he called back. "The upper floor has fallen in. There are beams lying across, and the floor is piled with debris. What's more, it's all open to the sky, and there's a couple of trees growing in the middle."

"Well, that's that, then." DI Jones turned back to the jeep. "I can't see anyone wanting to keep a little kid hidden here. You wouldn't want to venture in there. It's too bloody dangerous."

"Someone came recently," Marisa said, still staring down at the tracks.

"Probably the same farmer that just ploughed that field," DI Jones said. "Those tracks could be some sort of farm vehicle. Maybe he's helping himself to slate tiles for his own roof, or timber from the beams."

Marisa walked beside Liz to the jeep. "Any memories of this?" she asked. "Do you think you stayed here once?"

"What's that?" DI Jones turned back sharply.

"It was so strange," Marisa said. "We were in the village, and Liz was sure she'd been there before."

"Before the war? You can't be old enough. Or do you look young for your age?"

"No, I was born in '41," she said.

"And this was requisitioned in '43," Dave chimed in. "So she'd only have been two at the most."

"Then you can't have been here," DI Jones said. "It was wartime."

"But she remembered the pub, that was the weird thing." Marisa looked at Liz for confirmation. "She called it 'the Big Boat.' And you know what? We found the pub sign, and it was the Golden Hinde. A picture of a ship in full sail."

"So I suppose you might have visited this house?" DI Jones asked. "Your people are obviously posh. Perhaps you knew the family."

"I don't remember the house at all," Liz said. "I'll have to telephone my parents and ask them. But it's strange, isn't it? We didn't live anywhere near here. I grew up in Shropshire. Miles away."

"And people didn't travel much in wartime," DI Jones said. "There was no petrol for civilians."

"My dad was a brigadier," Liz said. "I'm wondering if perhaps we didn't accompany him when he had to come down here. I know he supervised part of the D-Day operation."

Dave laughed. "You don't bring your family along when you're on army business, especially not during wartime."

They got into the Land Rover and drove away. Liz looked back at the house and frowned. She could remember a big house—just vaguely. She remembered looking through the banisters down at a square foyer below. And someone had said, "What are you doing out of your room, you naughty girl? Come away from those stairs."

She flinched at the sudden memory. A woman's voice saying it. Not her mother's. And then it was gone.

Tydeham, Autumn 1943

The lorries arrived as the church clock finished striking nine. A whole line of army Bedfords, backing cautiously down the village street.

"They're here, Betty," Ed Jenkins shouted to his wife. "Come on. Get cracking."

"I'm finishing my cup of tea first," Betty said. "They'll not make me do without my last cup of tea in my own kitchen. Is there a whole lorry for us? And who's going to help us load all the stuff?"

"It looks like there's only four of them," Ed said. "Not one per family."

"Well, that's no ruddy use, is it? I've got all the stock from the shop to take. I'm not leaving that behind, not when I've paid for it with good money. They're not going to cheat me out of everything I've worked for . . ." Her voice broke with emotion.

Ed came over and put his arm around her. "Steady on, old girl," he said. "I know this is upsetting for you. Ruddy hell, it's upsetting enough for me, who was born here, and my old dad before me. But there's a war on, isn't there? And there's nothing we can do about it, so we just have to make the best of it. Come on. Drink up, or we'll find that the Nortons have got all their stuff loaded before us."

Betty drained her teacup, washed it up, dried it and shoved the tea towel and cup into an open basket. She stood, looking around the kitchen and out to the shop beyond, with its shelves now almost empty, gave a big sigh, took off her apron and went to join Ed.

Across the street, Reg Norton was already tottering out towards the lorry with a chest of drawers. "Here, give me a hand with this, young fella," he shouted to the army private who had just descended from the cab. "I'm not as young as I was." The private obliged, and together they lifted it on to the lorry bed. "You better come inside and help with the rest," Reg said. "And God knows how we're going to get the bedstead out through the front door. But the wife will insist on taking her brass bed."

His wife, Mary, met him as he came towards the cottage. "Here, Reg, what about my clothesline?" she called. "I'm not leaving that. Always been a good clothesline, that has."

"No time for that now, love," Reg replied. "We've got enough to get on to the lorry as it is before my old back gives out."

"Didn't they send soldiers to help us?" Mary demanded. She spotted the private. "Here, you over there. You're supposed to be moving us, not standing there."

"I'm just the driver," the boy said. "They didn't send no one to move you."

"Damned cheek, that's what it is," Mary said. "And how are the Purvises going to manage, eh? She's a slip of a girl, and the old man can hardly walk two steps. You'll have to go down and help them, Reg."

"When we're finished here. You'll have to give me a hand, my love."

"Damned cheek," Mary said again.

Further up the street, Tom Pierce came out of the pub carrying a captain's chair. "Come on, Freddie," he shouted to his son. "You can help with these. Get cracking."

"Those lorries are big, aren't they, Dad?" Freddie just stood there, wide-eyed, staring at them. "Big lorries."

Tom shook his head and went back into the pub to bring out the next chair.

Bert Thatcher, strong as an ox, had clambered up on to the truck and was piling boxes handed up to him by Molly. "Take care with my china, now," she called to him.

"It's all right. Keep your hair on. It's not going far, is it?" he said. "And if it won't all fit on the lorry, I'll come back with the tractor and trailer for the rest."

"I can't believe we're going," Molly said, looking around her. "I never thought this day would come."

"Cheer up, love. At least you're going to get a real bathroom for the first time." Bert did not seem too upset.

"You should go and see if Mrs Purvis needs help. She can't load furniture by herself, and those two little girls to look after."

Bert stared, then shook his head. "Joan Lee's got one of her boys helping them."

"They should have sent army blokes to give us a hand," Molly said as she handed up a kitchen chair. "Leaving us to our own devices like this . . . it's not right."

"None of it's right, is it?" Bert said. "But then it wasn't right of Mr Hitler to invade Poland and start a war, was it? Nothing's bloody well right any more."

And he threw a big sack of potatoes up on to the lorry.

Old Mr Purvis was more concerned with onions. "We can't leave now," he shouted, waving his stick at his daughter-in-law. "My onions aren't ready yet. And taters in the ground."

Sally Purvis pushed a strand of hair back from her face. "I told you, Dad, they're going to compensate you for your crops. You'll get money to start a new garden."

"Money don't feed nobody come winter, do it?" he said. "And that pocket handkerchief of a garden won't feed anybody."

They looked up as they saw the Lee boys approaching. "Ma says we should give you a hand," one of them said.

"Are you already loaded?" Sally Purvis asked.

"That's right. All done. Can't wait to be out of here. Best thing that ever happened to us, I reckon. Now I can join up when I turn eighteen and not have to worry about Mum."

"What about the big house?" Old Mr Purvis asked. "Are they moving out today? Does someone have to go and give them a hand?"

"Ma says they've got their own moving van coming, with men to help."

"Well, they would, wouldn't they?" Old Mr Purvis said. "All that fine stuff they own. You couldn't put that on the back of a lorry."

Amelia Bennington stood on the steps of Tydeham Grange as a van came up the drive. "This van is nowhere near big enough," she said. "Didn't you tell them we wanted a proper pantechnicon?"

"It's all they have, my dear," Charles Bennington said. He came up behind her and put an arm around her shoulder. "And you have to understand that we can only take the bare minimum. There's not going to be much room in the new place. Just enough to keep us going for now."

"But our lovely pictures. Our vases, our decorations. We must have those. I do need some beauty around me."

"The best of the pictures are going into storage. They'll be all right," Mr Bennington said. "But the rest of the stuff, well, we'll just have to leave it in the hands of the gods and trust it will still be here when we come back."

Amelia Bennington walked through the house ahead of him, running a hand over a chair back, a sideboard. Then she froze. "My dining table," she said. "We have to have our dining table, Charles."

"It won't fit, old thing," Charles Bennington said. "It's only a small, ordinary house. You've seen it."

"Horrid, poky little place." She shuddered. "Nasty, dark little rooms. I can't stand it. How am I ever going to cope?" And she burst into tears.

"We'll manage somehow, my dear," Mr Bennington said. "I'll help in any way I can. We'll get a girl in from the village to do the housework, I'm sure. We'll get through this."

"Everything has been taken from me." Her wail rose louder. "First my daughter, then my son and now my house. I've nothing left. Nothing at all."

Six-year-old James had been standing in the doorway watching as men carried out boxes, knowing that his rocking horse would be left behind. He knew he was too old for such toys, but it had been such a splendid rocking horse, still big enough for him and in the family for generations. He had spent hours galloping on it to imaginary battles. Now he was trying to be as brave as his father had urged him to be. A big man, right, James? Doing our part for our country. But it was hard. And seeing his mother going to pieces like this was most unnerving. She had always seemed so poised, remote, elegant—the sort of figure to be admired from afar. He went over to her and slipped his hand into hers. "You've got me, Mummy," he said. "I'll look after you."

She looked down at him as if she'd noticed him for the first time. "You're a good boy, James," she said. "I just wish I could love you better."

CHAPTER 7

Weymouth, 1968

Clouds had swallowed up the sunset by the time they drove into Weymouth and the first drops of rain spattered on to the bonnet of the car.

"Time for that beer, I think," the inspector said as they drew close to the seafront and the hotel. "What time do you have to have the Land Rover back, Corporal?"

"No special time. It's signed out for the day," he said.

"And you'd be allowed a beer on duty?"

"Who's to notice, sir?" Dave grinned.

"That looks like a pub over there," Marisa pointed out.

Dave turned to their left and brought the vehicle to a halt outside the Black Dog. It was a pleasant-looking whitewashed building with the image of a running dog painted on it. It was beginning to rain in earnest as they sprinted for the front door. Inside was warm and cosy with a large stone fireplace on one wall and a dark oak bar. They took their seats at a table near the fire while DI Jones went up to the bar to order. Liz had followed mechanically, but her head was still spinning as she tried to recall those flashes of memory. All she wanted was to get back to the hotel so she could telephone her parents, but the others, it seemed, were in no hurry to leave the pub. DI Jones ordered the first round. Marisa had a half pint of lager. Liz ordered a shandy. Then Dave ordered a round. Even with the smaller amount of alcohol, Liz began to feel detached from reality. *I might have visited that village,* she told herself. *I might have stayed at that big house before the village was abandoned. So what?* But then why, she wondered, did she have this deep feeling of dread?

The rest of the crew were quite merry by the time they were dropped off at the hotel.

"I hope that lad makes it back to camp all right," DI Jones said. "He could certainly knock them back, couldn't he?"

"You didn't do too badly yourself," Marisa said.

"Ah, but I can take it, love. Got hollow legs, you know." He giggled.

Liz noticed that he had called his colleague "love." She would have found this amusing, but she was itching to make that phone call. However, as they entered the hotel, they were met by Mrs Robinson.

"We wondered where you'd got to," she said. "And look at you. You're soaked, poor things. I said to the hubby, 'I hope they haven't had an accident in that army car. That young fellow hardly looks old enough to drive.'"

"We're just fine, Mrs R," Marisa said, presumably preventing DI Jones from revealing how much he had been drinking. "We were out investigating that abandoned village near here."

"Tydeham, you mean? I didn't think anyone was allowed in there."

"We got special permission," DI Jones said.

"Oh. In case the kidnapper had taken the little girl there. I get it." She gave a conspiratorial nod. "And did you find anything?"

Marisa shook her head. "No. The place is a complete ruin. There would be nowhere to hide except the church, and that was firmly locked."

"We all felt so badly for those folks when they were turfed out," Mrs Robinson said. "I was a land girl, working on a farm nearby. I volunteered to do my bit. We all did, didn't we? And actually it was a lark. We girls worked hard, but we had a lot of fun, too. And an army camp nearby." She chuckled at the memory. "But I remember some of the boys from the camp said they'd had to drive the lorries to help those people move out. They said the kiddies were crying. Some of the grown-ups, too. One old man was furious he had to leave his onions behind before they were ready."

"Where did they go?" Marisa asked.

"I couldn't rightly tell you. I do know that the family from the big house were put in some kind of council house nearby, and all their lovely things had to be shoved into storage. This army bloke said it wasn't right. They should have been treated better than that. He said the wife was proper upset about it."

"What was the family called, do you remember?" Liz asked.

"Let me see. I did hear the name, but my old head, it's like a sieve now. Boddington, was it? Something like that. It will come back to me."

"Do you have any idea where they are now?"

"No idea at all, love." Mrs Robinson shook her head. "I was a farmworker's daughter. We didn't mix with the likes of them." She smoothed down her apron. "I shouldn't keep you here chatting. Go and get those wet things off, and the dinner will be waiting for you on the table."

They came down to find no soup tonight but a plate of Russian salad with some tinned tuna. This was followed by smoked haddock, potatoes and peas. The DI accompanied this with another beer, and Marisa had a white wine. Liz stuck to water. There was tinned fruit salad and ice cream for pudding. Liz refused her coffee. Marisa said she'd have some, and this time DI Jones thought it might be a good idea to join her.

"I want to ring my parents," Liz said.

"Have you remembered any more?" Marisa asked.

"Not really, but I did have a recollection of being in a big house. Looking through the banisters down to the hall below and getting into trouble for it."

"I wonder why?"

"Perhaps because I could have fallen down the stairs." Liz shrugged. "I'm going to see if Mrs Robinson will let me use the telephone. Otherwise I'll have to go out into the storm and find a phone box."

She waited until Mrs Robinson brought the coffee, then asked permission.

"I'll have to charge you if it's a trunk call," Mrs Robinson said.

"That's fine. I need to call my parents in London," Liz said. "It's quite important."

"Of course. Go ahead, then." She motioned to the telephone sitting on a table in the front hall, next to an arrangement of dried flowers. Liz picked up the receiver, then dialled 01 for London, then their number. She waited, holding her breath while the number rang, and then heard her father's brisk voice: "324 0877."

"Hello, Daddy. It's Lizzie." She tried to sound cheerful.

"Hello, poppet. Coming to lunch on Sunday as usual? Want a word with your mother? She's been quite good for the last few days. No memory lapses at all."

"Actually, I want a word with you. I'm down in Dorset, on a story."

"Well, that's good. I thought you were stuck writing obituaries."

"This is tied to an obituary," she lied. "And I wondered . . . we've just visited a village called Tydeham. It was abandoned during the war. So I'm curious: Did we ever visit it? Did we know anybody there?"

"A village in Dorset?" He paused. "We went to Torquay on holiday once, when you were about seven. But that's Devon, isn't it?"

"But that was after the war ended," she replied. "I'm thinking about when I was a little girl, during the war. Is it possible we went there?"

"During the war? People didn't travel during the war. At least, not civilians. I moved around a lot before I was part of the invasion. But you and your mother, you were safely up in Shropshire. We didn't take any holidays until the war was over."

"I just wondered if we might have known people who lived in the village. They lived in a big house. Their name was something like Boddington?"

Mrs Robinson appeared beside her. "I've just remembered," she said. "It was Bennington."

"Bennington," Liz said into the receiver. "Their name was Bennington."

"In Dorset? Bennington? No, sorry, my dear. I don't recall ever having known a family in Dorset and certainly not visiting them during the war."

Liz took a deep breath. "I see. Oh well. Thank you, Daddy."

"You want to say hello to your mother?"

"Probably not. I'm using someone else's telephone. I just needed to make sure."

"Well, sorry I couldn't be more helpful," he said. "This village, is it part of your obituary story?"

"That's right," she said.

"Bennington." He paused. "Doesn't ring a bell. What did he do?"

He lost his home, Liz wanted to say. He was moved to a council house so that you army chaps could destroy his lovely manor house. "Nothing special. Give Mummy my love."

"We'll see you on Sunday as usual, then?" he asked.

"I expect so." She hung up.

Marisa had been hovering in the background. "Well?" she asked. "What did he say?"

"He said we'd never been anywhere near Dorset. We were up in Shropshire all the time during the war."

"That's strange, isn't it? You know what? Perhaps you saw a newsreel in the cinema of the village being evacuated. It was the sort of thing that might have made the news, don't you think?"

"I suppose so," Liz said hesitantly.

"You know how films make a big impression when you're a little kid. I had to be taken out of *The Wizard of Oz* because I was terrified of the flying monkeys."

"I don't ever remember going to the cinema until after the war," Liz said. "We lived quite a long way from the nearest town, and my mother didn't like cinemas. She's always been rather claustrophobic and scared of germs."

"It's a puzzle all right," Marisa said. "Sleep on it. Maybe you'll dream the answer."

"Maybe," Liz said.

CHAPTER 8

Marisa and DI Jones left the next morning. The inspector made a telephone call to the Met and came back to say that he was told this was clearly another red herring and that they should come back to London right away. "They said the Ministry of Defence isn't paying for you to lounge about in some seaside hotel. And what's more, don't you dare put your beer tab on expenses."

Clearly, whoever had been speaking knew DI Jones a little too well.

"Are you coming back, too?" Marisa asked Liz.

Liz considered this. "I think I want to stay down here a little longer," she said. "I'd like to speak to someone who lived in that village, just to make sure, you know."

"Of course. But how would you find them now?"

"There will be a record somewhere," Liz said. "Maybe in Dorchester?"

"Well, good luck, then," Marisa said. "I can't say I'm looking forward to going back. I expect I'll be taken off this case and put back on women who have been bashed around by their old man. I wish we'd found something." She sighed. "The longer it goes on, the less likely it is that the child is still alive."

After they'd gone Liz tried to make a plan. She asked about buses into Dorchester. Then she had a brilliant idea. Names would be on the gravestones in that village. If only she could take another look. But the army were not going to send someone else out. Maybe she could walk from the main road, if there was a bus going in that direction. It couldn't have been more than a mile or so. She went to enquire about buses and found there was one, going to Lulworth, but it only ran twice a day and had already left for the morning run.

Frustrated and wondering if she was wasting her time, she went for a walk along the esplanade. It was another bright, fresh morning. The breeze was tinged with salt and seaweed and felt delightful on her skin. She paused to examine a board on the seafront, marking the various tourist spots: Punch and Judy, donkeys, the aquarium—and then she paused, her heart rate quickening. At the far end of the beach, a path over the cliffs was shown. If that path continued, she could approach Tydeham from the harbour. It was a good distance, maybe three or four miles, but she had always been a keen walker, and she had all day. She stopped off at a bakery to buy a sausage roll and a bottle of lemonade, then she set off.

After the initial uphill slog, it was pleasant going with springy turf under her feet. At times a cultivated field came near to the cliffs, and she had to skirt around Brussels sprouts growing there. Then the land fell down to sea level, and she had to cross a small stream on to a beach before the path climbed again up the other side. It was certainly a good workout, she decided. But exhilarating. Doing something positive. She felt as if she was in a private world. Not another human for miles. The only sounds were the crashing of surf on to rocks below and the cry of an occasional seagull. Far out at sea, a fishing boat went past, heading for a distant harbour.

As she walked she had plenty of time to think. Her father had told her that she would never have visited Tydeham during the war, and yet the fleeting visions had been so real, as had that momentary feeling of dread. Could he have got it wrong? she wondered. He was, after all, away most of the time during the war. What if something had happened to her mother—maybe she'd had to go into hospital for a couple of days and had left her with friends? Perhaps those friends had come down here to visit a relative without telling Liz's mother.

It was a possibility, except Liz could remember no such friends. Not many friends at all, actually. Her mother was a very private person, shy amongst strangers, liking nothing better than to be at home with her husband and child. She had been involved in local activities, arranging the flowers at church, making jam with the Women's Institute—that sort of thing. But they rarely entertained in Shropshire and even less when they moved to London.

Liz was deep in thought when she came upon the fence. Barbed wire stretched out before her with a sign on it. "DANGER. UNEXPLODED ORDNANCE. KEEP OUT. MINISTRY OF DEFENCE."

Well, that made it clear enough. Liz hesitated. She had no wish to meet any unexploded shells or land mines. But the ground ahead of her was still smooth turf, and she would watch where she put her feet—if she could find a way past. Then she saw that one of the posts was rotting badly. She gave it a kick and it toppled obediently, so that she was able to balance on it to walk across the barbed wire. On the other side she had a feeling of triumph and continued on until she could spot the remains of the harbour below. There she sat on a rock and ate her lunch. Feeling fortified and ready for anything, she picked her way carefully down the hill until she clambered over seaweed-covered rocks and was at the steps leading up to the village.

The village street was eerily silent. Again no sound of birds, not even the sigh of the wind today. She walked past the old shop, past the pub, until she came to the churchyard. The gate creaked alarmingly as she pushed it open, the sound echoing back from the steep hillsides. She glanced around, but of course there was nobody to hear. Once inside in the graveyard, she put down her rucksack and took out the little notepad she had brought. Then she worked her way through the tombstones, struggling through dying weeds and tearing away rampant ivy. Many of them were badly corroded with lichen, but she could make out names. There were several Jenkinses and Thatchers, as well as Norton, Pierce and Lee. Then, off to one side, a very grand tomb like a little house: *Theodore Bennington, Esquire, of Tydeham Grange. 1797–1855.*

So at least that confirmed that the people at the big house had been Benningtons. Then, amid dying bracken she spotted another small grave. It, too, had been attacked by lichen, but she could see it was a newer addition. She read the words: *Dorothy Louise Bennington, aged two*. She couldn't make out the date. Suddenly she felt dizzy and had to rest against the mausoleum beside her. Dorothy Bennington, aged two. A swarm of ridiculous and improbable thoughts coursed through her head. After a fanciful childhood, Liz had learned the hard way to be a realistic adult, but now she found herself wondering the strangest things: Was it possible she had been channelling little Dorothy when she stood on the village street? If you'd asked her, she would certainly say she did not believe in reincarnation or ghosts. With all the current interest in gurus and Indian ashrams, the idea of reincarnation was now in vogue, so despite her lack of belief, she toyed with the idea that she was Dorothy Bennington, reincarnated.

Then a sudden breeze stirred through the churchyard, rustling dying leaves and sending them swirling. She shook her head. "Rubbish," she said and headed for the gate. At least she had names to check out now, even if they were all quite common apart from Bennington.

Liz was about to go back the way she had come, but she found herself focusing on the narrow path that led to the back of the big house. Would seeing it from this side trigger a memory? she wondered. Although she was hesitant about going through an overgrown area, she found herself moving forward, step by step, along what remained of the path, until she reached the stand of trees that must have marked the boundary of the Grange's property. Here the undergrowth was dense, and Liz hesitated, feeling foolhardy. If there was unexploded ordnance anywhere, it would be here. Then she saw something. Some woodland creature, a badger maybe, had created his own narrow walkway through the trees. She followed it, foot in front of foot, until she came out to gardens with the house beyond. This was clearly the back of the property with a kitchen garden and an orchard. Cox's Orange Pippin and Bramley apples hung from the branches of the trees, in spite of years of neglect. Brambles tumbled over walls. Lavender and rosemary had taken over the herb garden.

Liz found a former gravel path and followed it, her eyes on the house in front of her. Obviously facing the full force of the military invasion practice, this house had taken the brunt of the destruction. Only parts of the second story were still standing. There was a gaping hole at one side, and the Virginia creeper that had formerly been an adornment had swallowed up much of the walls in a riot of scarlet leaves, common at this time of year. It was actually rather picturesque if one didn't consider that it had once been a home where people had lived.

She found herself thinking again of two-year-old Dorothy. She had lived here, played in these gardens. Perhaps she had had a swing on a big oak tree. And now she lay in an overgrown churchyard where nobody could come to visit, and her house was no more. Liz found tears welling up in her eyes. She rarely cried any more, having shed too many tears after Edmond abandoned her. Recently all she had been able to feel was anger—anger at being treated unjustly by her newspaper and then new anger at the deceitful Mr Bob Green. She blinked back the tears in surprise at being so affected. Was it because so many people's lives had been ruined?

You don't know that, she told herself. *Maybe some of the people who lived in those cottages actually moved somewhere better, somewhere with modern plumbing or closer to a town where there were good jobs.*

But she wasn't really convinced. The kitchen gardens ended with a broad terrace. Off to one side she saw a grassy area surrounded by the remains of netting. A tennis court? It had been a nice place, Tydeham Grange. People had enjoyed living here. She went on to the terrace, moving carefully as the flagstones were cracked and at angles, and stared up at the house. Miraculously there was still glass in a couple of the windows on the ground floor. As she looked at this, she had another flash of a memory. She had peeked in that window, standing on tiptoe to see in. The window was maybe two and a half feet high, so she must have been really small. What had she seen inside? The thought provoked no negative feelings. She moved closer. Cobwebs stretched across most of the inside of the window. She peered in through a part of the glass not covered in cobwebs. As she tried to make out what was inside, something moved. Not something small like a rat or a cat. A big dark shape came into her line of vision, moving towards her.

Liz gave a scream, stepped back, tripped over an upended flagstone and went sprawling.

CHAPTER 9

For a second she lay there, unable to move. Her heart was still pounding, and she was conscious of a burning pain in her leg. A ghost. She had definitely seen a ghost. She attempted to sit up, wanting only now to get away.

"Are you all right?" asked a very human voice above her.

Liz looked up to see a youngish man staring down at her. He was wearing an old tweed jacket and dilapidated corduroy trousers. His dark hair flopped boyishly across his forehead, and he was wearing wire-rimmed glasses that gave him an owlish appearance. He was also looking rather scared.

"I think so," she stammered as she sat up and assessed the damage.

"What the hell were you doing?"

"I didn't expect to see anyone, and I tripped."

"You scared the daylights out of me," the man said. "I look up and there's a bloody white face staring at me through the window, then this unearthly scream and it vanishes . . ."

"I scared the daylights out of you?" she demanded, anger mixing with pain and fear. "How do you think I felt? I look into a house that hasn't been occupied since the war, and I see a figure moving towards me. It's no wonder I fell over and . . . oh bugger, I think my knee's bleeding. Look, it's ruining my trousers."

"Here, let me help you up." He reached out a hand and she took it, letting him pull her to her feet.

"Thank you. I'm sorry. I didn't expect to see anyone . . ."

"Obviously not since the place is off-limits," he said, still sounding annoyed. "Here, come and sit on this bench. I think it's still solid."

He led her over to a stone bench at the edge of the terrace. She sat and pulled up her trouser leg.

"It's only a graze," she said. "I'll live."

"I don't know where we could find water here." He was frowning. "There's been no plumbing since 1943. But I might have a clean handkerchief." He reached into a trouser pocket and produced one. "Fairly clean," he said. "Enough to mop up the blood."

"I don't want to ruin your handkerchief."

"I do have others. I may look like a tramp, but I'm usually quite civilized," he said with a slight smile. "But I have to ask, what on earth are you doing here? You can't say you came by mistake because it's almost impossible to get in."

"I was here yesterday, with two officers from Scotland Yard," she said. "An army man drove us here. We had a tip about the child that's missing."

"The child who was kidnapped in London? Why on earth would anyone think she was here? This would be the last place I'd take a child. You could get your foot blown off, for one thing."

"I agree, but a child resembling Lucy was seen in this area, and the officers felt they had to cover all bases."

"I see. And you're with the police, too?"

"No, I'm a newspaper reporter."

"Did they send you back to do some more snooping? I didn't see a car."

Liz shook her head.

"No, I came by myself, over the cliffs. I needed to see the place again."

"Why?"

"I had some questions I hadn't answered," she said. "But what about you? I should ask you the same questions. How did you get in? And what are you doing here?"

"Ah." He smiled wider, making him look even more boyish. "I have a good answer to that. This is my family's former home. I'm James Bennington. I'm doing a salvage operation."

"A bit late, wouldn't you say? There's not much left."

"Don't they say better late than never?"

"You're not thinking of trying to rebuild this place, are you?"

"Good God no. Even if we ever got clearance and the permits, I don't have that kind of money. But I thought I might salvage some choice items to take with me. For my father. It was his family's home for hundreds of years, you know. So I got permission, and I've been coming down at weekends, seeing what I could use. I've managed to get several of the marble tiles from the old front hall, and I thought I'd make Dad a patio. I've also taken a little fountain that was on a wall in the sunken garden. Oh, and one of the big oak doors. I'm hoping to use the timber from that to make him a table. It's lovely dark oak."

"You're good at that sort of thing, are you? With your hands?"

He shot her an embarrassed grin. "Not terribly. I'm an architect by profession so I know how to do all these things in theory, but give me a hammer and a saw and I'm liable to chop a finger off."

He laughed then. Liz laughed, too.

"I think it's very nice that you're doing this for your father. I'm Elizabeth Houghton, by the way. Liz."

"How do you do." He held out a hand for a formal shake. "Is it Mrs Houghton or Miss?"

"It's Miss." She wondered if there was a Mrs James but didn't like to ask.

"What paper do you work for?"

"*Daily Express.*"

"At least it's right-wing. My father would approve of that. I'm more left leaning myself."

"Me too," she agreed. "Not too far left, but I don't think a few people should have everything and the rest of us have nothing."

"You have nothing? You sound rather posh to me."

She laughed. "I'm the daughter of a brigadier, and I went to an expensive private school. But these days I don't like to ask my parents for anything. At my age, I should be self-sufficient. They'd love me to keep living at home. It's tempting except I should be able to make my own life. And I hate being stifled." She broke off, suddenly embarrassed about opening up to a man she had just met. "Sorry. I'm babbling on. It must be the shock of meeting a ghost."

James nodded as if he understood. "I'm curious. What exactly brought you back here for a second time? You must have established that the child is not hidden here. Surely there's no story in this place. It's all long over and forgotten."

Liz took a deep breath before answering. "I came back on a personal matter," she said. "Yesterday, when we were standing in the middle of the street, I had the strangest flash of memory that I'd been here before."

James shook his head. "I doubt that. It was evacuated in 1943, and you can't have been born . . ."

"I must look young. I was born in '41."

"But still . . . ," he said. "A tiny tot. What did you remember?"

"Just that I'd seen that pub. I knew it had a ship on the sign. And today, when I saw you, I had just remembered looking in that window. I'd had to stand on tiptoe to see inside."

"How strange." He was now looking at her intently.

"So I wondered if perhaps I had been brought down here for a weekend visit by someone who knew your family."

He studied her face. "I don't recall seeing you," he said. "Of course, I expect you did look a bit different in those days."

She laughed with him this time. "Were you alive then?"

"Oh yes. I was six when we had to leave," he said. "It wasn't actually bad for me. I liked being closer to a town and other boys to play with.

Here there had been two little girls, younger than me, and several much older boys, so I'd been pretty much left to myself."

"You were an only child?"

"My older brother was killed in the Battle of Britain. He was an RAF pilot. And I had an older sister I never met."

"Dorothy," she said.

"How did you . . . ?"

"I saw her grave in the churchyard."

"Smart of you. Yes. Her name was Dorothy. She caught meningitis when she was two and died in a couple of days. My mother was devastated. I never knew her, of course. I came along as an afterthought, but I don't think I ever made up for a daughter."

Liz examined her knee again. The bleeding had stopped. "Look, I shouldn't keep you any longer. I must be getting back the way I came. I don't fancy walking over those cliffs in the dark."

"If you'd like to hang on a little until I load up the van, I'll drive you back. Where are you staying?"

"Weymouth. Isn't that out of your way?"

"No problem. I'm not in any rush. And to be honest I could do with a bit of help in loading up the van if you're up to it with your wounded knee."

Liz smiled. "I've had worse. I'll be happy to help."

"The van's around the other side, at the front of the house." He stood up. "Are you sure you can walk all right?"

"Of course." Liz stood up, too. Her knee was still stinging, but she wasn't going to admit it. She followed him across the terrace, down two steps and around the side of the building. To their right there was an old rose garden. Miraculously some of the roses had endured, and a few last blossoms clung to old stems.

"This must have been so beautiful once," Liz said.

"I suppose it must. As a small boy, you don't appreciate beauty. I didn't like the rose garden because I once came off my tricycle and fell into a rose bed and got covered in thorns."

Liz tried to keep up the pleasant conversation, but the foreboding feeling she had experienced the day before was now palpable. She stared across the rose garden. Behind it was an arbor with a curved stone bench. A trellis sheltered it, now overwhelmed by a climbing white rose with flowers fading on long tendrils. White petals lay dying on the marble below.

"Oh." Liz stood stock-still, her heart pounding.

James looked back at her. "What is it? Are you all right?"

"There." Liz was pointing to the right of the arbor, with a look of horror in her eyes. "That's where they buried her."

CHAPTER 10

"What?" James spun to look at her.

Liz was still pointing. "Over there. See, behind the rose arbor. The ground dips down."

"Who? Who was buried there?"

Liz shook her head, almost as if coming out of a trance. "I don't know. I can't remember anything else. It just came to me that they'd buried someone."

"They?"

She shook her head again. "I don't know."

"This is all very strange," James said. "You don't look like the type of person who has wild fantasies."

"That's just it," Liz said. "I'm not. I'm usually a very sensible sort of person. That's why all this is so alarming."

"I wonder what you mean by someone being buried there? Was it someone from our house? Someone who had died? Then why wouldn't they have been buried in the cemetery?"

She paused, considering. "I'm wondering if it might have been one of the little girls."

"What little girls?" he asked sharply.

"From the war. The DI who was working the Lucy case in London told us he'd been assigned to several other missing children cases during the war. One was murdered. Two of them were never found. I just wondered whether I might be somehow channelling this." Then she broke off, giving an embarrassed laugh. "No, that sounds stupid. I've never shown any indication of being clairvoyant in my life. If I had been, I'd have known"—she was going to say about Bob Green being married—"several things."

"Someone who had been killed—deliberately?" He blinked as if trying to come to terms with this.

"I don't know. It just came to me in a sort of flash, and now it's gone again. But it can't have been good. I had this feeling of dread when we were here yesterday and again today as you and I approached this area."

"What do you think we should do? Go to the police?"

Liz put her hands up to her face, pulling the skin taut, then swept back her hair. "I don't know, James. It might all be in my head. I might have been remembering somewhere quite different that maybe looked like this. I mean, my father tells me I'd never have been here. I don't want to look like a fool. And yet . . ."

"If someone was buried here, and never found, then the police should know about it. Presumably a family would like to know about a missing daughter."

Liz nodded. She looked back at the arbor and the ground gently sloping down behind it. "I suppose we should tell someone."

"We could try digging ourselves, just to see if . . ."

"No. Don't let's do that." The words tumbled out and she grabbed at his jacket. She found she was shaking.

"I'm sorry," he said gently. "This is obviously quite distressing for you. Let's get out of here and decide how we proceed. It could have been something quite harmless, you know. Children don't always quite understand what's going on. It could have been someone's beloved dog."

"Maybe." Liz wasn't convinced.

He took her arm. "Come on. Let's get going. We'll go and have a drink somewhere. You look like you could do with a brandy. You're deathly white."

Liz allowed herself to be led away from the rose garden, around to the front of the house, where a white delivery van was waiting.

"I rented it from a company in Bournemouth," he said. "I don't own a car myself. It makes no sense, living in Central London. There's nowhere to park. My dad lets me borrow his car when I'm down visiting." He studied Liz's face. "Look, let's forget about loading up the van. The stuff can wait. It's not going anywhere. I think we should get you out of here as soon as possible. Come on." He opened the van door and helped her climb up on to the seat. Usually Liz was an ultra-feminist and would have insisted that she didn't need any help, thank you very much, but today she hardly noticed as he tucked her in, then closed her door. He went around and climbed in from the driver's side, started the engine and they were off.

As they turned on to the lane, Liz felt her anxiety abating. Had she been overreacting, imagining things? What if they dug there and there was no body? James would think her a fool. The police would think her a hysterical female. But that would be better than finding a body and having to figure out who it was. They didn't speak much on the ride back to Weymouth.

"Now to find a decent pub," James said. "There must be one somewhere in Weymouth."

"The Black Dog was quite nice. We went there yesterday."

"You'll have to give directions. I don't know this place well," he said. "In fact, I don't think I've been since I was a little boy. I remember coming right before the war. There was an ice cream shop and donkeys—both very important to a small kid." He smiled at the memory.

Liz managed to direct him to the esplanade and then to the pub. They parked and went in. The pub radiated a sense of warmth and well-being. At this early hour the room was almost deserted, apart from a couple of men standing at the bar. James sat her in a booth, then went to the bar and came back with a large brandy plus a pint for himself. Liz took a sip, feeling the warmth spreading inside her. She nodded. "Thank you. I'm sorry. I've completely messed up your day."

"Not at all," he said. "You've made it much more interesting. So let's try and make sense of this. Do you think your parents knew my family?"

"No. My father says they didn't."

"But did you live nearby?"

"Again no. We lived in Shropshire. That's why it's so baffling. My father says we would never have come down to the South Coast during the war. He was away in the army most of the time, and my mother was a nervous driver at best, and anyway there wasn't any petrol to be had."

"I guess it seems unlikely you were here." He took a long gulp of his beer.

"Most unlikely." She paused. "The only thing I could think of was that I might have stayed with family friends and they brought me to visit. But I don't know what friends they would be? My mother wasn't very social. We didn't have many relatives, much less relatives living anywhere near us. My father had cousins. My mother had an aunt, but I think they're all dead now."

James toyed with his glass. "What makes this so odd is that you would have been scarcely more than a baby. How much does one remember at that age? I don't think I can recall much before the war started."

"You remembered the ice cream shop and donkeys," Liz pointed out.

"Ah yes. But I think that might have been after war was declared. Life went on as usual until the bombings in 1940. So I'd have been three, nearly four." He looked up from staring down at the glass. "But the thing is that your father says definitively that you wouldn't have come here. What does your mother say?"

Liz sighed. "That might be a problem. She's having . . . memory issues, you know. The doctor says it might be the start of dementia. It's very worrying, actually. She always was . . . well, the nervous sort, but recently she's had episodes when she sounds quite confused." She stared past James to the log crackling in the fireplace.

"That must be hard for you," James said.

"Very hard. I feel guilty about not being at home for her, but then it's hard to take, to see a parent slipping away. She was all I had until we moved to London, and I had friends nearby."

"You can't be her caregiver, Liz. Your father's there, isn't he?"

"Yes. And a lady comes in to clean, so there's not a problem like that. Oh, and I don't want to sound as if she's gone quite bonkers. She's not wandering around in her nightdress, claiming she's Marie Antoinette or anything." She laughed, then fell silent.

"All the same, you expect a parent to be the strong one, don't you? Even when you're grown up, you sort of have that feeling that a parent is there if something goes wrong."

"Yes, I suppose you do."

He toyed with the glass again. "That's why it's odd that I'm suddenly the protector of my father. After we had to move out of Tydeham, he had a tough time . . . what with one thing and another. Leaving your family home is a huge shock, and then . . . my mother didn't take it well. Eventually he became a housemaster at a boys' school, largely, I think, to make sure he could keep an eye on me. Anyway, he enjoyed the job and stayed on until he retired a few years ago. The housemaster's job came with accommodation, and he has since moved into a small and practical bungalow in Bournemouth. We thought that would be a good idea so he was near theatre and concerts and would have an easy trip up to London, where I live."

He paused. She waited for him to go on. "But he's not very happy. He's not going gaga or anything, but he has slid into quite a deep depression. After being surrounded by noise and little boys, he's now in a place where he knows nobody and his life has no purpose."

"You didn't want him to move in with you?" Then she added swiftly, "I'm sorry. That was rude of me. I've no right to pry into your personal life."

James smiled. "My father is a very independent man, also a creature of habit. He wouldn't be good at sharing space with anyone, especially not me, who tends to be messy." He paused. "I suppose I should marry and give him grandchildren." He looked up, giving her a grin.

"Oh, so you're not married?" It must have been the brandy that had loosened her tongue. "I'm sorry. Prying again," she added.

"You're a newspaper reporter. You're used to prying," he said. "No, there is no Mrs James. I was in a long-term relationship that I assumed would lead to marriage when I was established in my profession, but she became very caught up in the protests that were going on—you know, ban the bomb, stop killing animals. You name it, she protested. And she fell in with a group of serial protesters, quit her job and the last I heard she was sharing a group squat in the East End. Making love not war. Isn't that what they say?" This time the laugh was bitter. "So how about you? You never found the right bloke, then?"

"I did," she said. "He was perfect, a mining engineer. He went off to Australia, and that was the last I ever heard from him. So either he found someone he liked better than me, or he's dead. Either way, I've learned to live without him."

The door opened, letting in a cold breeze for a moment, and a group of people came in, talking in an animated fashion before seating themselves at a table near the fire where Liz had sat the night before.

"What about your mother?" Liz asked.

"She died. When I was still a kid."

"I'm sorry."

"Me too. It would have been nice to have a mother taking care of me. Instead of that, it was boarding school at seven."

"My father wanted to send me off to boarding school," Liz said. "Everyone in his family had been. But my mother wouldn't let him. She was quite possessive about me and didn't want to let me go. I'd quite like to have gone—not at seven, but later, at thirteen. It might have been fun." She took another swig of brandy. "So what are we going to do?" she asked. "No, I don't mean that. This is not your problem. You've got to get back to your father, and presumably to work in London. I'll go to the local police here and report what I think I remember, and they can choose to dig there or not. I presume they'd have to get permission from the army first?"

"I'm sure they would. But look, I'm down with my father for a few days. I had a lot of leave owed to me. We worked non-stop on a big civic centre project in the summer, and I had to miss out on my holiday. I'm not due back until next weekend." He paused, turning his glass again. "You're staying here, are you?"

"Yes. Seaview Lodge. One of the hotels on the esplanade. Nothing grand."

"Why don't I come back in the morning and go with you to the police station? Then, if you like, we could drive over to see my father, and you could ask him about any connection to your family."

Liz shook her head. "I couldn't possibly impose, James. You've been kind enough, and I've already taken too much of your time."

"But I'd like to help," he said, "And to tell you the truth, I'm rather curious now. It's a mystery, all right, isn't it?"

"It is." Liz took another sip of brandy. The warmth had now come back to her fingers and toes, and she felt almost normal again. The whole episode at the house now seemed to have taken on an unreal quality, like watching a scene from a film. "If you really don't mind giving up your time, I'd really appreciate the support. As it is, they are going to think I'm a madwoman when I tell them."

"Tell me about your job at the *Daily Express*," he said, clearly wanting to take her mind off the shock of the afternoon. "What do you report on? Is it usually crimes?"

Liz sighed as she put down her glass. "Actually, at the moment I've been banished to obituaries. I was, I think, up-and-coming last year. I covered some political stuff. I liked to think that I'd soon be a lead reporter and get my own byline. And then, quite by accident, I hit on a story that could have been an utter scoop. I caught a well-known political figure visiting a high-class call girl who had a flat in Mayfair. It was all by accident. I saw him getting out of a car, I followed him and noted the building he went into, and the reporter in me checked on who lived there. And she was a model and escort, shall we say."

"Fascinating." James nodded.

"The more I dug into this, the juicier it became. Another of her visitors was a man attached to the Russian embassy. Suddenly I had my scoop, my first big story."

"So what happened?"

"I gave it to my editor. It turned out that the politician in question was a bosom friend of the owner of our newspaper, and the word came down to kill the story immediately."

"You could, presumably, have gone to someone else with it? Any other newspaper would have snapped it up."

"Ah." She smiled. "That did cross my mind, until I was given a veiled threat. I was told if I took it elsewhere, they couldn't vouch for my safety."

"Not such a veiled threat," he said. "How infuriating for you. The story that would have made your career."

She nodded. "At least I wasn't sacked on the spot. I think the editor likes me and felt badly for me. I was moved across to obituaries, where I couldn't do any damage. You can't do an exposé on someone who's already dead."

"Why did they send you down here on the trail of the missing girl?"

Liz stared past him, into the fire, where a log had now settled, sending up a trail of sparks. "I'm afraid they didn't. My flatmate is a detective with the Metropolitan Police. She was the one who was sent down here, following a tip that someone had seen a little girl who looked like Lucy in the vicinity. And I—I was feeling rather down and frustrated about my life, so I thought, what if I came, too? What if I was there when the missing child was found? I'd redeem myself with the newspaper and be doing something worthwhile."

"And they gave you permission to do this?"

Liz gave an embarrassed little grin. "Actually no. I telephoned in sick. I may lose my job."

"On the contrary—it seems to me you may now have a great story. What were you saying about the other little girls missing in the war?"

"It was the DI who told us. He was a new young policeman on the case. Three little girls who disappeared about the same time of year for three consecutive years."

"And were never found?"

Liz nodded. "One was. Found in a wood. Murdered. But the other two . . . no trace. He said it was pretty chaotic in the war. People moved around all the time. Kids were shipped off to the country for safety. You put your kid on the train with a label around her neck and hoped that someone would take care of her."

"I imagine it would have been hard to keep tabs on people. When a whole row of houses was bombed, people would scatter to relatives', to various sorts of temporary housing, wouldn't they? And presumably you'd only know where they were because they'd register their ration cards somewhere else."

"Ration cards. That's a good idea," Liz said. "Even little children had ration cards, didn't they?"

James smiled at her. "I can see you are already on the story."

"I don't know, James. It seems so ridiculously impossible that I have suddenly developed this ability to locate a little girl that Scotland Yard could never find. Surely you know when you are a child that you have psychic powers? I certainly never had any. I would have used them to see the questions on the Latin exam in advance."

This made him laugh. He glanced at his watch. "I should probably get going. My father will definitely start to worry if I'm not home by dark." He stood up. "I'll drop you at your hotel first."

"Not necessary, James," she said. "It's only along the esplanade, and I could do with a walk to process what's just happened and to decide what I'm going to say to the police."

"I'll see you in the morning, then," he said. "About nine thirty? We don't want to bother the police too early."

"It's really kind of you. I hate to . . ."

"Liz, I want to do this," he said. "No more arguing."

"All right. Thank you." She stood and followed him to the door.

～

It felt strange eating dinner alone at the hotel that evening. As she was the only one dining, Mrs Robinson clearly didn't feel she had to go to much trouble. It was another tinned soup followed by what Liz guessed was a Sainsbury's steak and kidney pie covered in a lot of gravy. Then tinned peaches and custard to follow. This didn't really matter to Liz, who was suddenly overcome with exhaustion. It wasn't just the physical exertion of walking several miles along a coastal path; it was the emotionally draining experience of the afternoon. She tried to put the whirring thoughts to one side. It was impossible to make sense of what had happened. But one thing did occur to her: she found James Bennington rather nice. She tried to squash this thought instantly. *Oh no, Liz. Not another man. You'll probably find out he is really married or a pervert or a secret serial killer or . . .* She broke off this thought, staring at her cup of coffee in horror. What if it was a member of his family she had seen burying a body?

CHAPTER 11

After dinner she asked to use the telephone again, worrying a little that the trunk call charges might add a whopping amount to her bill. The landlady nodded with enthusiasm, however.

"Your friends have gone back to London, eh? And they didn't find anything? But you, with your reporter's nose—you think there's still a story down here . . ."

"I still have one or two things I need to follow up on," Liz said. "I'm afraid it doesn't look as if the little girl was brought down here, but I think I might have an interesting piece to write on Tydeham. You know, a nostalgia article about what was lost in the war."

"Oh, I see." She looked clearly disappointed and not really interested in nostalgia, which was what Liz had hoped. She didn't want the woman listening in to her telephone call. She knew she could have gone out and rung from the telephone kiosk, but that involved putting in coins, and she wasn't sure how many she had left. She waited until she heard the kitchen door slam and then dialled the flat.

The phone rang several times, and Liz was concerned that Marisa had gone out. She was just about to put the receiver down when the phone was picked up and a bleary voice said, "Hello?"

"Marisa, it's me. Were you asleep?"

"Yeah. I was," said the voice. "I was knackered after this trip. I didn't sleep at all well at that awful hotel. The bed was full of lumps. The springs were so bad, every time I turned over, one of them gave a loud twang and I woke up again. To make matters worse, the train back was full of a party of school kids going up to London, and they didn't stop shouting at each other and running up and down the aisle all the way." She paused. "Where are you? Are you coming home tonight?"

"No, I'm still down here in Weymouth. I may stay a few more days. Something weird has happened, Marisa." She paused. "I went back to the village today. After yesterday I felt I just had to see it again, to make sure . . . to see if I could find out more, you know, the names of the people who lived there."

"How did you get back in? You didn't get Corporal Dave to drive you again?"

"No. I sneaked in the back way. I took the path over the cliffs and came down to the harbour."

"Wasn't it fenced off up there?"

"It was. I managed to climb past the barbed wire."

"You've become very daring recently, Liz. You were always such a goody-goody. This can't be the same Lizzie Houghton who didn't want to fly the nun's underwear from the flagpole at school." She chuckled, then asked, "So did you find out anything more?"

"I went back to the big house, and you won't believe this, Risa, I bumped into the son of the former family. James Bennington. He was retrieving items from the old house for his father's new property."

"That's good. What's he like, this James Bennington? He sounds posh."

"He is. Very. But nice. Kind."

"Attractive?"

"In a way. Sort of serious looking, but that may be the glasses. But listen, that isn't what I want to tell you. I had another flash of memory while we were going around the house. I remembered seeing somebody being buried in the garden."

"Buried? As in a dead body?"

"I think so."

"Crikey." Marisa sounded shaken. "Do you know who?"

"No idea. I don't remember who was doing the burying or who was buried. But it just came to me, Marisa. What if I was having some kind of vision about Little Lucy? Or what if I was seeing one of those little girls the DI talked about?"

"What are you going to do?"

"James is coming back, and we're going to the police in the morning. They may not take it seriously, of course. But it's up to them, isn't it?"

"Of course they should take it seriously. What if it is Little Lucy, and you somehow picked up the vibes . . . ? I'll tell DI Jones in the morning and see if we need to come back down. But guess what? It seems Jones and I have now been added officially to the task force, so I'll find out more tomorrow about what they now know. I'll keep you updated, okay? And I'll see if we should mention this to anyone."

"I suppose it depends who they dig up," Liz said. "If they decide to dig."

"You're right. Okay. I'm going back to sleep. Ring me tomorrow. I want to hear more about posh James Bennington."

"Marisa, I don't need a bloke, all right? My track record in that department has not been good. James will probably turn out to be queer or about to go into the priesthood or has just . . ." She stopped. She was about to continue with the joke and say just murdered his mother. Not funny. "I'll talk to you tomorrow."

And she hung up. As she went up the stairs, she wondered if Mrs Robinson had been listening in. Did they have an extension in the kitchen? Then she thought about the *Daily Express*. Could this be a story for them? Young reporter solves old murder? Village of secrets? She decided to call Ted Benson, the editor, in the morning. It was taking a risk, but it might be worth it.

Liz did not sleep well that night. Her bed was not as lumpy and bumpy as Marisa's had been, but a squall had come in from the sea and the windows rattled as they were peppered with rain. She stared at the ceiling, conscious of being alone and far from friends and family, half afraid to fall asleep in case her dream recreated the disturbing memory. She told herself that might be a good thing—if she could identify the body in her dream, it would help everyone. Eventually she fell asleep, awaking to find early sunshine painting streaks of light on the wall behind her bed.

On Saturday morning, breakfast was an overcooked scrambled egg. Clearly the food was going to deteriorate with each day. *But I won't be staying much longer,* she thought. *After today I can go home. Back to London. Away from all this.*

She finished breakfast, put on make-up and made sure she looked presentable before James arrived. He pulled up in a rather grand but ancient Bentley.

"Sorry about the car," he said, smiling as he got out to open the door for her. "My father's since before the war. He's rather proud of it. It reminds him of the days when he was somebody. It reminds me of driving a hearse. And it eats petrol at an alarming rate." He closed her door and came around to the driver's side.

"So I told my father all about meeting you," he said, "and he doesn't remember anybody called Houghton, especially not a brigadier's family. He said when he was in the army, he was a lowly lieutenant and would not have hobnobbed with a brigadier. But he would like to meet you." He glanced across at her. "Although he's very concerned about someone burying a body on our land. He immediately thought it would be something to do with the army, after they took over the place."

"Army?" Liz looked surprised.

"Yes, he said he'd bet it was some drunken soldier who picked up a local girl, brought her there to have his way with her, she fought back and he accidentally killed her. So he and his mates had to bury her rapidly. It does make sense, doesn't it?"

"Except that how could I have seen that? I couldn't have been in the village after the army took over. Nobody could." Liz hesitated. "I suppose they did all move out when they were supposed to? Nobody could have stayed behind?"

"They'd have been rather stupid if they did," James said. "There would have been shells landing on them. Come to think of it, the army came with lorries and simply shoved everyone's belongings in. Apparently they promised my father that the manor house would be left untouched—but look at it. They didn't care. I still remember my father's face when we came back after the war and were allowed to see the damage. He just stood there, and tears ran down his cheeks. I'd never seen him cry before, not even when . . ." He paused.

"When what?"

"When my mother died."

"I'm so sorry. How awful for you, and for your father."

James nodded. "She suffered badly from depression after my sister died and then my brother was killed. Having to lose her lovely house and move into a poky little farmworker's cottage was just too much for her, I suppose." He stared straight ahead as the car pulled out into traffic at a roundabout. "Ah well. It's all long ago now. I've got over any grief I had. So let's go and face the fuzz. I checked out where the police station is on the way here."

They drove along the esplanade, then turned on to the Dorchester Road, the way Liz had driven previously with DI Jones. Liz found her heart was beating very fast as they parked the car on a side street and then walked up to the red brick building. She had been dreading this moment, spending half the night telling herself that it didn't have to be done. She could go back to London, say nothing, and nobody would be any the wiser. But she couldn't, even though she was sure they'd take her for a crazy person.

There was a young, freckle-faced PC sitting at the desk. They asked if a detective was available. The constable's eyes grew large when Liz said it was about reporting a possible body.

"Oh right, then," he said in his broad West Country burr. "I'll go and tell him, right away, then."

Soon they were escorted through to a back room where a man resembling DI Jones was just making himself a cup of tea. "Come on

in. Sit down," he said. "I'm DI Fordham. I'll be with you in a minute."
He added several spoons of sugar to the cup, stirred it noisily, then sat
opposite them. "Now what's this about a body?"

Liz tried to explain. It was complicated. The visit to the village. The
flashback of memory.

DI Fordham was frowning. "Hold on a minute, young lady. You
say you saw a body actually being buried. When was this?"

Liz felt her face flushing bright red. "I'm not sure. That's just the
problem. It must have been when I was a little girl, because that village
has been off-limits since 1943."

"So you're telling me that you now remember seeing a body buried
before 1943?"

"I know it sounds absurd," Liz said. "But I visited the village with
a team from Scotland Yard who had a tip about Little Lucy."

"They were here, a couple of days ago," DI Fordham said.

"Yes. I was with them. We went to the village, and suddenly I knew
I'd been there before. I couldn't make it out. I called my parents, and
they said I would never have been there, so I was confused. I went back
again yesterday, to see if any more memories were triggered, and I met
Mr Bennington, whose family used to live in the manor house."

"Oh right." The name seemed to ring a bell with the inspector.
"Bennington. I knew your father. What were you doing out there? Isn't
it still off-limits?"

"I was given permission to salvage anything I could use from the
house," James said. "Frankly there isn't much. It is all in ruins. But I met
Miss Houghton there, and we were walking around the house when she
stopped and turned white and told me she remembered seeing a body
buried." He paused, glanced at Liz, then continued. "We wondered if
we should check it out ourselves, but then we thought it might be a
crime scene and we shouldn't disturb it."

DI Fordham nodded as if this was a sensible notion.

"Another thought that came to me," Liz said. "Again it sounds
absurd, but I was with the detectives from the Met, and we were looking

for the missing girl. I wondered if somehow I was picking up vibes and she was the one buried there?"

For the first time the DI looked interested. "You do this sort of thing often, do you? Psychic sort of thing?"

Liz gave an embarrassed chuckle. "No, never. I'm a newspaper reporter. I'm usually quite sensible, so I don't want you to think I'm deranged."

"Newspaper reporter, eh?" A suspicious look crossed his face. "I know you lot. Anything for a story. You'll have us out there, digging up what turned out to be a dead dog."

Liz stood up. "Look, I really didn't want to come here. I knew how you'd take it and that you'd think I was a complete fool. But I felt I had to do the right thing, just in case it was important, just in case you located a missing person. All right. I've told you. I've made my report. We can go, James."

"Keep your hair on, love," DI Fordham said. "You've made your report, and I suppose we are obliged to follow through, especially after what you said about Little Lucy. We'll soon be able to tell if it was a recent grave or not. But I'll have to get on to the army again to get clearance, and then you can come with us and show us the exact spot. That probably won't be for a day or so. The army doesn't exactly move at the speed of lightning. So where can we reach you?"

"I'm staying at the Seaview Lodge," Liz said. "But I'm not sure how much longer I can stay down here. My newspaper will want me back in London." This was a slight exaggeration, but he nodded.

"I'll try and light a fire under them and see if we can go out there tomorrow, then. All right? I'll leave a message at the Seaview. This may be wasting everyone's time, but who knows?"

James stood, too. "Thank you for your time, sir," he said.

"Don't mention it. A good man, your father. Give him my regards."

Liz glanced at James as they came out into the fresh air. It was amazing in England how knowing the right person changed everything.

CHAPTER 12

"Well, that went as well as can be hoped," Liz said. "I think having you along made a big difference. The lord of the manor's son. At least I wasn't some drug-riddled hippie hallucinating after LSD."

James smiled. "I think you did rather well. This must have been hard for you."

"I hate looking like a fool," Liz said. "I always have. But thank you for coming all this way to give me moral support. I was going to volunteer to come back to your house and help you load up, but you haven't got the van today."

"No, the bloke I rented it from needed it. Besides, I promised my father I'd take you to meet him. Maybe you'll learn some more when you talk to him."

"Oh, thank you. I'd like that," Liz said. "If you're sure you have the time."

"If it was a choice between having my father tell me exactly how he was growing his prize begonias and having him chat with you, I'd choose the latter." This time he looked directly at her as he smiled, and she felt the connection in his eyes. A little unsteady now, she replied, "I'm glad I beat out begonias at least."

They followed the Dorchester Road until it picked up the A road across the county, and it took just under an hour to reach Bournemouth. Liz could see immediately why James's father was depressed. The house was a new build, nice enough but on a cul-de-sac of identical homes, each with a small front garden and many with a suitable car—Rover or Volvo—parked in the driveway. After having been raised in Tydeham Grange, this must still feel like a comedown.

"At least he hasn't put gnomes in his front garden yet," Liz commented as she spotted some across the street.

"I did volunteer to get him some for Christmas." James shared an impish grin. "He told me where I could put them. A rather blunt man, my father."

They pulled into the driveway of a house on the end of the cul-de-sac, and Liz let James enter first.

"We're here, Dad," he called out as they stepped into a narrow front hall.

"In the sitting room," came the voice.

Liz followed James into the room at the back of the house. It was the classic English suburban home with French doors leading to a patio. Beyond this a lawn surrounded by flower beds and a view of more back gardens backing on to it. At this time of year, the roses had been cut back and the garden had a desolate appearance. The sitting room was over-furnished with chairs and a sofa that were rather too big for the size of the room. There were a couple of good oil paintings on the walls— one of a hunt and one of a house that must have been the Grange in its prime. James's father was sitting in an armchair, a rug over his knees.

"I've been watching rugby on the telly," he said. "A replay of last Saturday's Wasps versus Saracens. Good game." He got up to switch it off. "But let's see who we've got here." He put aside the rug and stood up.

"Dad, this is Liz Houghton," James said.

James's father was a tall man with a shock of iron-grey hair and a neatly trimmed moustache, rather like her father's. His eyes drooped at the corners, giving him a rather sad look, but the eyes sparkled as he held out his hand to her.

"It's a long time since a pretty girl has come to call," he said. "How are you, Miss Houghton?"

"I'm pleased to meet you, sir," she said. As she took his hand, she studied his face. Did it stir the least whiff of memory? She didn't think so.

"James, go and put the kettle on, there's a good chap," Mr Bennington said. "And take a seat, young lady." He waited until James had gone before saying, "So James tells me a strange story about you. That you have a memory of coming to our little village when you were a small child."

"That's right. I don't remember much. But standing in the street, I remembered the pub and the sign swinging in the wind with the sailing ship on it."

"Extraordinary. And you were born which year?"

"Nineteen forty-one."

"Then you'd only have been two at the most. And the war was on. Not a lot of travel."

"And I asked my parents, but they said I'd never have come here during the war. That's what's so odd. I wondered if a family friend might have brought me."

He peered at her, then shook his head. "I can't say your face rings a bell, although I suppose you might have changed a bit during the last twenty-something years." Then he chuckled at his own joke. "Houghton, you say your name is? And your mother's family?"

"O'Brien, although I never met any of them. She was originally of Irish ancestry. Her parents were out in India and died young."

Mr Bennington frowned. "I don't recall ever knowing a Houghton or an O'Brien. Of course my wife might have done, although I can't recall her having visitors during the war, apart from her sister." He broke off as the kettle shrieked in the kitchen, and there was a muttered curse as James either burned himself or dropped something. "I was home, you know," he went on. "I served in the Great War, but by the second I was a bit too old, and anyway because we had the home farm, I was in a protected occupation."

"I wonder," Liz said, "whether I might have been brought to visit someone else in the village."

"I very much doubt it," Mr Bennington said. "My tenants were all, shall we say, humble folk. Farm labourers, fishermen. Not our sort at all, although it's no longer fashionable to say that kind of thing." He gave an embarrassed little grin, then called out, "What's keeping the tea, boy?"

"It's brewing," came the shouted reply. "Where have you put the biscuits?"

"The barrel's staring you in the face!"

"Oh. Right."

Liz had to grin this time. Then she reverted to their conversation. "Can you give me a list of all your former tenants? I expect the police will want one, and I might want to check on them, too."

"Really, I don't see . . . ," Mr Bennington started to say, then corrected himself. "Jenkins at the shop. Tom Pierce at the pub. Lee in the end cottage, Purvis, Thatcher and then Norton."

"Would you have any idea where I'd find them now?"

Again Mr Bennington looked a little annoyed. "I haven't really kept up. And I expect some of them are no longer with us. The Nortons must have been in their late fifties. Reg and Mary. Tom Pierce wasn't young either, but then neither were the Jenkinses. Bert Thatcher was too old to be called up. Frank Lee was serving in the merchant marine, and so was William Purvis. But as to where they are now . . ."

"Presumably you had servants at the Grange?" The idea had just come to Liz. Was it possible they had visited a former servant? Highly unlikely from a different part of the country, but still.

"Just Joan Lee during the war. She did the cooking and cleaning. Did it bloody well, too. Real old countrywoman who would pull out a wardrobe to dust behind it." He smiled at the memory. "Her daughter, Maggie, had been a maid, too, but she went to join the Auxiliary Territorial Service. The women's army. Most of the families had one member serving somewhere. But as I said, I don't know where you'd find them now. They were moved just up the road to Osmington or

Preston initially, if they didn't have someone to go to. The Jenkinses went to her sister's in Dorchester. I remember that."

James came back bearing a tray with three cups and saucers and a small plate of chocolate digestives. Liz took a cup and helped herself to a biscuit. She realized that they had not mentioned the body. Was he waiting for her to bring it up? She took a bite of biscuit, appreciating the crumbly sweetness, then looked up. "James told you about my very strange experience."

"The body, you mean? He said you remember seeing someone bury a body."

"That's right."

"Well, I can tell you, absolutely definitively, that nobody buried a body in my garden while I was in the house. We had a perfectly good cemetery for that sort of thing, although we did bury the family dogs. But that was on the other side, at the edge of the woods by the tennis court. I suppose the gardener could have buried a dead rabbit." He said this in a jovial, almost joking manner, but Liz saw a brief, sharp glance pass between James and his father.

"You had a gardener, then?" she asked.

"During the war it was only Bert Thatcher who helped out. We had turned most of the lawns into vegetable production. He would have noticed if there had been anything funny going on—especially a burial." Again he seemed to be taking this lightly, but Liz sensed he was being a little too hearty.

"This whole experience has been very unnerving for me, Mr Bennington," Liz said. "I'm not the sort of person who believes in the supernatural, and yet you tell me I'd never have been to the village, and my father said the same thing. I find myself wondering if perhaps I was seeing someone else's experience—if that is at all possible. It did occur to me that we were looking for a missing girl, and perhaps she has been buried on your grounds."

"The little girl who is missing in London, you mean?"

Liz nodded. "Exactly. I was with the team from Scotland Yard, who had a tip she was seen down here. What if I somehow sensed her presence?"

"I'd say a load of hogwash," Mr Bennington said. "I don't believe in communication with the spirits myself, although my late wife tried hard enough to reach our son. You heard that Simon was shot down in the Battle of Britain? It devastated my poor wife. Me too, of course. Such a bright boy, only just nineteen."

"Did she ever manage to communicate with him?" James asked.

Mr Bennington shook his head. "Never did. Although she did claim that Dorothy came to her in a dream and said she was happy to be an angel. She found that comforting, poor woman." He stirred his teacup savagely, then added, "Anyway, we'll know in a day or so whether your body was just a figment of your imagination. Let's pray it is."

Mr Bennington did not invite her to lunch, although he did shake her hand and say he was delighted to meet her, and he hoped James would bring her again when all this business was cleared up. Liz was thoughtful as James drove her back to Weymouth. Strange and unnerving ideas floated around her head: James's mother, who was distraught, consulted spiritualists and had then died. Was it possible that she had killed someone? Even if Liz suspected that this thought had occurred to Mr Bennington and perhaps James, there was no way she could ask.

"I hope they can get to this quickly," James said. "If it drags on, I'll have to go back to work, and I don't suppose you want to stay down here indefinitely either."

"I don't," Liz said. "For one thing, it's costing me money to stay at the Seaview, and for another, my paper would expect me back at work. The obituaries are piling up, no doubt."

James chuckled. But then he turned to her. "If this really turned out to be Lucy, you'd have a scoop, wouldn't you?"

"I would. But I realize it's a far-fetched idea. It will probably turn out to be a dead cat, if anything, and I'll get scolded for wasting police time."

"But we have to know."

"Yes. We have to know."

~~~

James dropped Liz off outside the Seaview. It was too early for a drink this time, and he didn't suggest having a late lunch together. Liz suspected he found the whole situation uncomfortable. Having someone state that they'd seen a body buried on your property could be unnerving. And she didn't know if it was a long-held memory or a modern-day psychic vision of some kind. She wondered if he had come to believe she was off her rocker. Maybe he saw traces of his mother's depression and belief in the afterlife in her and it worried him. Instead she thanked him for the ride, they parted politely, and he agreed he'd meet her at the site whenever they were given permission to go there.

Mrs Robinson did not appear as Liz let herself in. She went up to her room and lay on the bed, listening to the rhythmic sound of the waves outside her window, trying to decide what to do. She knew she would have to call her boss at the paper, tell him the truth and probably get into trouble for being a loose cannon again. And she should report in to Marisa to see what they might have found. And she should start writing. She had been used to writing every day before the boredom and routine nature of obituaries had stifled her creative juices. But now her mind had already formed headlines. The village that time forgot. Does it hold a secret for the present? She was about to take out her typewriter when her stomach reminded her she hadn't eaten. She got up, splashed some water on her face and decided to call the newspaper from a phone box, not from where Mrs Robinson could overhear.

The day was bright, but the wind off the sea was bitter, and she wrapped her scarf more tightly around her neck as she walked along the esplanade, past the old stone pier, then around to the harbour, with its line of old pastel-coloured cottages fronting the water. Sailboats bobbed at their moorings. Fishing boats were tied against the far side, one still being unloaded while gulls screamed and circled overhead. It was an attractive setting, full of life, and she paused to admire it. Her stomach growled, and she was tempted to have lunch before making the phone call. But she had to get it over with. She went into a newsagent's, bought a paper, paid with a pound and was grudgingly given change. Thus equipped with sixpences and shillings, she found a phone box on the quay and dialled the number, only remembering as she did so that the weekend shift would be on duty.

"*Daily Express*," said the bright female voice. Daphne probably.

"Daphne, is that you?" Liz asked.

"That's right. Who's this?"

"It's Liz Houghton. Who is in charge of the newsroom today?"

"Mr Tomlins."

Tomlins. Not the easiest of men to get along with. Old-school. Gruff and to the point. He had been second in command when the affair with the MP blew up a year ago.

"Could you put me through to him?"

"What shall I say you want him for?"

"Possible news story."

"Okay. Hold on . . ."

Liz waited, finding it hard to breathe. Then the gruff voice. "Tomlins. Newsroom."

"Mr Tomlins. It's Liz Houghton. Remember me? I'm now in obits."

"What do you want, Miss Houghton?"

Liz cleared her throat before saying, "I'm down in Dorset, and I think I might have a story."

"Dorset? What are you doing down there?"

"I came down with a team from Scotland Yard, looking for Little Lucy."

"Who assigned you to this?" His voice was sharp. "I don't see any record . . ."

"Nobody, sir. I seized the opportunity. It was probably quite wrong of me, but I got the chance and I took it. I'd like to find her. We all would."

"And you didn't clear this with your boss?"

"No, sir."

"Houghton, I thought we'd been through this before with you. Didn't going off on your own almost cost you your job?"

"I know, sir. But what if she is down here? What if we find her before the police do?"

"What are you saying?"

"Just that I might have stumbled upon a grave . . ."

He swore. "And the local police? Have they been informed?"

"Yes. They are getting permission to go in and dig. I thought I might stay down here to report, if that's all right. They might not get what we need for a day or two. It's not as if obituaries can't survive without me."

He gave a heavy sigh. "Houghton, you'll drive me crazy one of these days. You are just not a team player. And you are too bright for your own good, you know that."

"Yes, sir. But I may stay down here? And report what the police find?"

"I suppose it can't hurt. They're not getting anywhere here, that's for sure. How did you come upon the grave?"

She was not going to say it was a vision. "A tip, sir. It's in one of those abandoned villages from the war. Off-limits to the public. We were allowed to search it."

"I see." Another long pause. "And the police have reason to think that this might be the missing child?"

"They have to follow through on all tips at the moment. It may just be someone's dog," Liz said. "But it's worth a try, isn't it, sir?"

"All right. A couple of days. I'll clear it for you." A pause. "And Houghton?"

"Yes, sir?"

"Anything you find, you report straight to us, understood? No going off on your own."

"I understand, sir."

The telephone beeped for another shilling, and Liz dropped it in only to find he had hung up on her. She felt quite shaky as she came out of the phone box. "Food," she said to herself and went into the nearest café, where she ordered fish and chips. The portion was huge and satisfying, washed down with a big mug of strong tea. Afterwards, she felt renewed and revived, ready to tackle whatever came her way. As she walked along the quayside, she let herself fantasize about finding the body, being interviewed by the BBC, gaining new respect at the newspaper . . . until she remembered that this was a little child, someone's daughter, and finding the body would bring heartache and grief.

CHAPTER 13

That evening she telephoned Marisa, giving her the news that she had permission to stay on and do a story. Marisa also had news to share about the missing child.

"We've attended a briefing and learned a bit more about the family. Not as straightforward as everyone thought. Anthony Fareham, the dad. Up-and-coming in the city. Some talk about running for Parliament. But it turns out it's not his child."

"She's not?"

"No, he met Susan, his wife, in the South of France. She was a young widow with a baby. She'd been married to a Frenchman who had been killed in a motoring accident. Word has it that Fareham might be queer and wanted the respectability of a family, you know."

"Oh, I see. That does complicate things, doesn't it?" Liz said. "Do we know for sure the real father is dead? Is anyone looking in France, in case one of the father's family wanted the child?"

"Exactly. I gather they've put Interpol on to it. And then there's the au pair, who was watching Lucy when she disappeared. She's Swedish, and was very attached to the little girl. So we have to ask if someone might have spirited her to Sweden. This is unlikely, but at this stage, who knows?"

"If Anthony Fareham is up-and-coming in the city, he must be doing well. Could it be a question of ransom?"

"They'd have heard by now. It's been a week."

"At least if she was taken to France by her real father, or someone in his family, she'd still be alive, which would be good news, wouldn't it?" Liz said. "They're going to be digging up where I think I saw a body, so we'll know soon. I'm hoping in a way it isn't Lucy, but in another way it would make my career." She paused. "That's a really callous thing to say, isn't it?"

"I understand," Marisa said. "If I were you, I'd want to restore my good name with the paper and make them take me back to the newsroom. So you're staying down there in Dorset until they dig?"

"I spoke to the editor, and he gave me a couple of days. We should know something as soon as they get permission to dig."

"That's convenient. Plenty of time to get to know James."

"Marisa," Liz snapped, "don't keep trying to hook me up with a man. I notice that you're the same age and you're not exactly settling down."

"I haven't found the right one yet, darling." Marisa laughed. "And I'm still enjoying sampling the menu. But this James seems rather right for you."

"I've only just met the chap. And I sense he's keeping his distance. Well, wouldn't you if a strange woman said she had a vision about a dead body? But he did take me to meet his father."

"That's a good sign."

"No, I asked to meet him. I wanted to know if he might possibly remember me or my family."

"And did he?"

"Not at all. I asked him for the names of all the other residents in the village. He didn't think it was likely I'd visited any of them. Not our sort, was what he said. He's a good old-fashioned snob like my father. They'd get along well."

"I'd better go," Marisa said. "Another date with the chap from the Met."

"Ooh, getting serious."

"Not at all. He's taking me to dinner, and I'm in need of a good meal."

"Before you go," Liz interrupted, "did you speak to DI Jones about my theory that this could possibly be one of his earlier missing girls?"

"I did. He seemed quite upset and didn't want to talk about it. He said he should never have let my irrational friend join us in the first place. I think it haunts him that after all these years, he didn't manage to find them."

"Then let's hope this might be one of them. At least then he'd know. He'd have closure, wouldn't he?"

"Knowing you failed and it was a bad outcome. That's the last thing a copper wants to hear. Look, Liz. I have to go. Let me know when you have news. Bye." And she was gone.

Liz went up the stairs and got undressed, still conflicted. What did she really hope they would find when they dug? If it was Little Lucy, then she'd have the story she dreamed of. Byline Liz Houghton, reporting from the scene in Dorset. But it would be a terrible tragedy. The nation would mourn. If it was a body from long ago, it would mean more questions and not a lot of answers. In a way she found herself hoping that there was no body there at all. She'd look like a deranged counterfeit reporter, but at least she wouldn't break any mothers' hearts.

~~

The next morning Liz was woken to the pealing of church bells. *Sunday,* she thought. She had quite forgotten what day it was. She sat up, sighed. It wasn't likely that the police would get anyone out on a Sunday, so she'd have a day with nothing to do. A glance out of the window did not look promising for walks on the beach. A grey morning with a blustery wind whipping whitecaps on a leaden sea. The sort of day to stay indoors and watch telly. She hadn't checked whether there was a telly in the lounge or whether she'd be allowed to watch it during the day.

She went down to breakfast, hoping for a Sunday full English but was disappointed to find it was cornflakes, followed by tomatoes on toast. She was just helping herself to marmalade when there was a ring at the front door. Liz heard Mrs Robinson saying, "Oh right. I'll give it to her. Thank you." She came into the breakfast room. "That was a policeman with a note for you," she said, her face alight with anticipation. "They must have found something."

She handed Liz the note and hovered in the doorway, clearly not going to leave until she knew the contents. Liz opened it, her hand shaking a little. It said, *Army is sending out someone this afternoon. Be at the station by one.*

"Well?" Mrs Robinson's voice sounded sharp.

"They want me to accompany them. Something I've seen may help them."

"What is it?"

"I'm afraid I can't tell you yet. It's an ongoing investigation," Liz said.

"But it's still Little Lucy you're after?"

"It may be," Liz said.

"Poor little kid. When they find out who did this, I hope they are hung, drawn and quartered." With that, she made a grand exit.

Liz finished breakfast, then wondered what to do until one. She presumed they would also be notifying James or his father, assuming James had not already gone back to London. He'd said he had to be back at work on Monday. She didn't have his telephone number, so there was nothing she could do about it. Outside the weather was still not encouraging: a heavy overcast with a buffeting wind and the promise of rain. Not the sort of day you'd want to be digging up a grave. But she was now aware she might be on to a story. She went upstairs, got out her portable typewriter and began: *Liz Houghton, reporting from the Dorset Coast. I came down here on a tip. Someone had spotted a little girl in the back of a dirty Morris Minor. Our search led us to the village of Tydeham, a strange, haunted place, abandoned since the war.*

She went on to describe the ruined cottages, the cracked pavement, the feeling of utter desolation. *What happened to all those lives suddenly disrupted? Did those people make new and better lives for themselves, or did they never really recover from what they had lost?*

This could be a nice feature story in itself, she thought, looking up from her typing, wondering how to title it. The village that time forgot. The lost souls of Tydeham. Memories of a forgotten village. Yes. She nodded with satisfaction. She'd stay down here and try to trace the rest of the villagers this week, and maybe she could turn in a good story, whatever happened today. She went down to the front hall, took the telephone directory and carried it through to the sitting room. It felt bleak and cold, with the gas fire not lit and a draft coming in through the bay window. She examined her notepad. There was a Purvis in Weymouth. She copied the address. Several Lees in the area. Several Pierces. No mention of a Jenkins, but she had been told they moved to Betty's sister in Dorchester. Not much chance of locating them, then. There were two Nortons, one in Poxwell and one in a place called Langton Herring, wherever that was. And a Thatcher in Osmington, which was the closest village to Tydeham. That looked promising.

Liz copied down addresses and telephone numbers, but she didn't feel like ringing any of them that morning. She really didn't feel like settling to anything until she knew the truth. Mrs Robinson coming up to make up her room spurred her into some sort of action. She would go and visit the Purvis who lived in Weymouth and maybe telephone some of the others if she could find a phone box in a quiet area. At least it wasn't raining today. The early clouds had dispersed, although a bank of grey fog hung across the horizon out to sea. Breakfast had been sadly lacking, and the first thing she did was to look for a café to get a coffee and a bun. But the town had fallen into a Sunday stupor. Every shop she passed was shuttered. The streets were empty, and only a distant church bell told her that some people were out and around on this day. On the harbour wall a couple of brave men in oilskins were line fishing. She finally found a café open opposite the station. The coffee wasn't memorable, and the bun was stale, but they fortified her, and she set off to find the address of Purvis.

It turned out to be a small dead-end street close to the station, definitely a less glamorous part of the town and not visited by tourists. The houses were a row of two-up two-down terraced houses, as seen in the backstreets of any city but less dirty than those in London or any industrial area. Some of them had been spruced up, with tubs of late chrysanthemums or ornamental bay trees outside newly painted front doors. Two little girls were playing outside their house, sitting on their doorstep, having a tea party with their dolls. They looked up as Liz passed.

"Do you have a cup for me?" she asked.

"You're too big," one said scornfully and handed the minute teacup to her teddy bear.

Liz knocked at Number 42. The door was opened by a round middle-aged woman wearing a pinny, her hair tied up in a scarf.

"Yes?" She looked at Liz suspiciously. "You're not canvassing for the election, are you? We're busy, and we know who we want to vote for."

"No, I'm not doing that," Liz said. "Are you Mrs Purvis?"

"Yes." Now the expression was really wary. "It's not bad news, is it? Not about William?"

"No. I just wondered if you were the same Purvis family who used to live in Tydeham?"

"That's right."

"I'm really glad to have found you," Liz said. "I'm a newspaper reporter, and I'm doing a story on the village." She had decided on the way there that she would keep the interview impersonal. "I wondered if you might have a minute or two for a couple of questions?"

"I don't see why they want to do a story on it now," the woman said, folding her arms across her bosom. "The time to do a story on it was when they wouldn't let us go back after the war. When we realized we weren't ever going back. They'd promised us, you know. But I gather there was nothing to go back to. They'd flattened the whole thing. Bert

Thatcher got to see it. He said you wouldn't believe your eyes. You'd hardly recognize the place. And the old Grange, what used to be such a lovely big house, all the windows blown out and the roof caved in. That wasn't right, was it?" She realized she had been talking a lot and stopped. "Have you seen it for yourself? Been out there?"

"I have," Liz said. "And it's very sad. You can hardly believe that anyone lived there once."

Mrs Purvis brushed down her apron. "Well, what can you do? It was wartime. Lots of folks had their homes flattened, didn't they? All those poor blighters in the East End. They never went back home either."

Liz gave a sympathetic nod.

"At least we're not too far from our roots here, and William's still working the fishing boats," Mrs Purvis went on. "Makes quite a decent living. And my girls aren't too far away—one's married and lives in Lyme Regis and one in Weymouth here, out on the new estate towards Chickerell, so I get to see them plenty, and my grandchildren, too." She paused again, then gave an embarrassed chuckle. "Look at me, keeping you here on the doorstep. Would you like to come in? It's a bit of a mess because I was doing the hoovering, but if you don't mind sitting in the kitchen."

"That's very kind," Liz said. "I won't keep you long." She followed Mrs Purvis in, down a dark and narrow hallway to a spotless little kitchen with just enough room for a red Formica table and two chairs. Mrs Purvis put the kettle on the tiny gas stove as Liz took a seat.

"Now, what was it you wanted to know about the village?"

"What it was like before you had to move, for one thing," Liz said.

"Life was quite hard, that's what I remember," Mrs Purvis said. "In many ways we're better off here. We were quite cut off, you know. We grew all our own veggies and kept chickens . . . If you wanted anything from the shops, you had to wait until someone with a van or a tractor could give you a lift. We never had a car in those days. Never had the money. William used to be a fisherman. They had two boats in that little port. William went out with Reg Norton and his son in one and Frank Lee with Bert Thatcher's son, Johnny, on the other. He was killed in the war, Johnny was. And one of the Lee boys, lost on D-Day and he'd only just joined up. His mum made him wait until he was eighteen, and off he went, proud as punch, and only lasted a month or so."

The kettle boiled and she made the tea. "That's how it was, wasn't it? I was lucky that my William came back safely. Merchant marine he was. On the North Atlantic convoys, but he said to me, 'I guess the devil didn't want me.' Frank Lee was also merchant marine, and he survived. So did his other son."

Liz duly made notes in shorthand and nodded as a steaming cup of tea was placed in front of her.

"So let me get this straight . . ." And she read off details about each of the names Mrs Purvis had mentioned. "Have I missed anybody?"

"There were the Jenkinses at the shop," Mrs Purvis said. "I heard they moved to Dorchester and he died quite young, and I believe she lives with her sister. Oh, and the Pierces—Tom used to run the pub. And he was lucky. He fell on his feet. He got another pub to run out towards Shaftesbury. I don't know if he's still there. He'd be quite old now. I reckon he was over fifty when we all left, so that would make him eighty, wouldn't it?" She chuckled. "I never was much good at maths. We didn't get much schooling in those days."

"Was there a school in the village?" Liz asked. "I don't remember seeing one?"

"Before the war there used to be a schoolteacher who'd come in, and there were classes in the village hall," Mrs Purvis said. "But during wartime Ed Jenkins used to drive the kids up to the school in Osmington, and the big boys took the bus to the secondary school in Weymouth—if they ever went, that is! The bus wasn't too reliable, and neither were the boys." She shook her head as she took a seat opposite Liz. "All they wanted to do was be old enough to join up and fight. And look where that got them."

"Were there many children in the village at the time you had to move?"

"Apart from our two little girls, there were only the Lee boys, and the Pierces' son. But he didn't go to school. He was a bit touched, you know. Something wrong with him. I expect they'd have a name for it these days. He used to have fits. I was always a bit scared of him, if you want to know the truth." She paused, spooned sugar into her tea, then added, "Of course there was the Benningtons' son, poor little chap. Living out there at the big house. Nobody to play with. They had some kind of nanny or governess for him, but then she went away. I think she joined up. So many people did." She took a big gulp of tea. "I'm not sure what more to tell you."

"That was everyone who lived there when the order to evacuate came?"

"It was. Oh, apart from the vicar, but he didn't really live there. He was in charge of two churches, and he only came out to us a couple of times a week. A very earnest young man, I remember. No sense of humour at all. You should have seen Bert Thatcher taking the mickey out of him. Oh, he loved to pull the vicar's leg."

"What was the vicar's name?" Liz asked.

"The Reverend Pomfrey—Cyril Pomfrey. Now there's a prissy name for you, isn't it?" And she gave a deep, throaty laugh. "He always was holier-than-thou. Loved to talk about sin and punishment."

"Where is he now?"

"Oh, he did quite well for himself. I believe he's now the assistant bishop over in Exeter, or is it dean of the cathedral? One of those important jobs. But he'd be retirement age now, if priests are allowed to retire."

As Mrs Purvis spoke, Liz was trying to think what other questions she wanted to ask. She tried the important one first. "Mrs Purvis, do you remember seeing a little girl who looked like me? Because I think I visited the village once."

Mrs Purvis stared at her, frowning. "I can't say I do. When would this have been?"

"Just before the village was evacuated. In 1943."

"I don't remember any visitors then, my love," Mrs Purvis said, slipping into the West Country affectionate mode. "I would have remembered if you'd come to see someone in the village. My girls would have been excited about someone to play with. How old were you?"

"Only two."

"And you remember it? My word, that's good memory, isn't it? My Sheila, who was three at the time, says she can't remember the village at all. Were you visiting the folk at the big house?"

"Mr Bennington says he doesn't think so."

"Oh, you've seen Mr Bennington, have you? How is he doing? I hear he retired and moved."

"Yes, he's in Bournemouth now. In a new housing estate. Not too happy about it."

"Well, he wouldn't be, would he? Having grown up in that lovely house and all the grounds and the trappings. Now he's just ordinary like everyone else. What's the boy doing, I wonder?"

"James? He's an architect in London."

"Oh, so you've seen James, have you?"

"I have."

Mrs Purvis paused, thinking. "So what's this all about, this article of yours?"

Liz felt herself turning red. "I wanted to remind people what it was like to lose a whole village, and how everybody has coped since. Are you still in touch with some of the other residents?"

Mrs Purvis shrugged. "Not really in touch. I heard that Reg and Mary Norton had both passed away. And Ed Jenkins. I get a Christmas card from the Thatchers, and I see Joan Lee sometimes. But we're not really close. We've all had to make our own way since the war."

"What about Mrs Bennington?" Liz asked.

Mrs Purvis looked shocked. "Oh, but she died years ago. Didn't they tell you? Took her own life, so we heard, poor soul."

"Oh," Liz said. "How tragic." She felt terrible that James hadn't mentioned how his mother had died.

"It would have been during the war, or right after it. I don't suppose she could cope with being put in a cottage after having been used to that big house and servants to wait on her." She leaned closer. "I did hear that she was always on the frail side, you know."

Poor little boy. Liz's heart went out to him. His mother taken from him when he needed her most, when there was a war on and things were scary enough as it was.

"So when she was alive, did you have much to do with her?"

Mrs Purvis smiled now. "We weren't matey or anything. She was polite enough. She'd ask about the children when we saw her. Gave everyone a little gift at Christmas. But we weren't ever invited to tea, if that's what you mean." She took a sip from her own cup of tea. "No, my dear, in those days the lines were clearly drawn. They were gentry, and they didn't mix with the likes of us." She put down the teacup, then looked up again sharply. "But I'll tell you one thing. She was never a happy woman."

Have I learned anything? Liz wondered as she came away. She knew where to find Bert Thatcher, the Lees and the vicar. And she also knew that Mrs Purvis did not remember seeing her. So it was unlikely that she had visited one of the former villagers. But she now had several intriguing thoughts that played around in her head: the holier-than-thou vicar who talked about sin and punishment. The Pierces' son who was "a bit touched" and Mrs Purvis had been afraid of him. And the fact that James Bennington had had a governess or nanny who had gone, maybe to join up. Intriguing thoughts of "what if" floated around her head. Could one of them have buried a body? But that still didn't answer the question of how she had been there to see.

CHAPTER 14

At one o'clock Liz reported to the police station. She had wondered if she should eat an early lunch, but her stomach was in knots, and she had only managed a few bites of a ham sandwich and a cup of tea at that same station café. DI Fordham was waiting in the reception area with a uniformed constable.

"Right, let's get this over with, shall we?" he asked impatiently, his look saying that she was annoying in the extreme for wasting his valuable time. "The army is sending a bloke to meet us at the village and unlock gates and things. Trust the army to be quick and efficient for once, when I was looking for an afternoon watching the football."

The back door of a police car was opened, and DI Fordham ushered Liz into the seat, then got into the front himself, beside the constable who was driving. He was an older man with flaming-red hair.

"Sorry you had to miss your Sunday dinner, Hanson," DI Fordham said.

"Me too. The missus got a leg of pork this week. She does the crackling a treat. And the sage stuffing. Still, I suppose she'll warm me up a plate when I get home." He stared straight ahead as he drove. "What's paining me more is missing Weymouth Town playing football. I've got a nephew on the team. He's pretty good. Hopes to make the professionals some day."

They drove in silence for a while as the last buildings of the town were left behind. Liz felt as if the trip was taking ten times as long as usual. She wanted to break the silence, but she also didn't want to initiate conversation.

"What about the young chap from the manor house?" the constable asked at last. "Is he meeting us there?"

"Supposed to be," DI Fordham replied. He turned back to Liz. "You two know each other, I gather?"

"We only met when I bumped into him at the village. He was trying to salvage some pieces from the house for his father's new home. We've chatted a couple of times, that's all."

"So exactly how is this Bennington chap allowed on to the property when he feels like it?" DI Fordham asked, again with judgement in his voice.

"I believe he applied for permission to salvage," Liz said. "It was his family home that the government destroyed, after all. They were never paid restitution."

"Had to live like the rest of us, Constable." Fordham turned to the bobby beside him and gave a deprecating little smirk. "Imagine that. No servants. No acres of ground. What a shame, eh?"

Liz bit back any comment she might have made.

"And you, Miss Houghton. Newspaper lady, eh? Hoping for a juicy story out of this? My clairvoyant brilliance found the missing girl?"

"I'm really hoping it's not the missing girl, Inspector," Liz said. "In fact I'm hoping it's not anybody, and you tell me I've wasted your time and we can all go home. Believe me, I'm not enjoying this at all."

"Well, we'll soon know the truth," he replied.

An army Land Rover, this time driven by a private, was waiting at the lane and led them until they came to the track leading to the manor house.

"Leave your vehicle here, sir," the private said. "You can ride with me from now on."

They piled into the open jeep. It was decidedly chilly.

"How come this way is open when the rest is surrounded by barbed wire?" DI Fordham asked as they bumped over the muddy track.

"This part's always been open, sir," the private said. "It's the only way to reach these fields, and they were needed during wartime. But there was barbed wire blocking off the manor house and the village. Mr Bennington got permission to have that removed so that he could get at the house and see if anything was worth salvaging."

"He wasn't worried about being blown to pieces?" DI Fordham sounded as if he was enjoying this thought.

"He had to sign a liability waiver. On his own head." He, too, chuckled.

They came through the stand of woodland, and there was the house ahead of them with the van already parked outside. James emerged from the house when he heard the jeep approaching. His eyes lit up when he saw Liz, which she found strangely satisfying.

"Right," DI Fordham said. "You've got your shovel, Constable, and another for the private. Let's get going. It's going to rain again before long, if I'm any judge of weather." He eyed Liz. "Right, Miss Houghton. Lead us to the spot."

Liz started to walk around the house. As she came to the rose garden, she felt the sense of dread returning. She didn't want to go any closer.

"It's over there," she said, pointing. "See to the right of the arbor, where the ground slopes down. It was there."

"Show us the exact spot."

"I don't want to come any closer," she said, her voice shaking.

"And I don't want to be here at all, but we're here now, and we have shovels, and we don't want to waste any time digging in the wrong spot."

"I can't tell you exactly," Liz said. "I think my view was partially blocked by the arbor. I just know it was right behind it. Not too far down the bank." She paused, looking at the inspector. "You have to realize I had one flash of memory and then it went again. I can't picture anyone digging or who was being buried. I just knew. That's all. So I can't really help you."

"Right, let's get to work," DI Fordham said. He crossed the rose garden on one of the gravel paths and went around the arbor.

"There's a stream here," he said. "Lots of lovely mud. Okay, boys, let's get digging."

Liz was standing like a statue, her face frozen as she stared across the rose garden. James moved closer to her and touched her arm gently. "Why don't you help me load up the van," he said. "I'm sure you don't want to watch this."

She gave him a grateful smile. "You're right," she said. "I've been dreading this moment."

He led her back around to the front of the house. Several slabs of white marble were stacked by the former front door. Together they carried these to the van. As they stood outside, she could hear the scrape of shovel on earth, and it set her teeth on edge. James noticed her discomfort.

"There's a lovely green stone fireplace," James said. "But I don't see how I can get it out without the whole wall coming down on me, and I don't know where I'd use it if I salvaged it."

"Let's take a look," she said.

"Watch your step," he warned. "Just follow in my footsteps. I've forged a path that is safe."

They stepped over the threshold until they were standing in the remains of what had been an expansive foyer. A dark oak staircase went up one wall to a balcony beyond. The carved wooden banister continued all the way around. Liz stared at it, then shook her head.

"This isn't the house," she said.

"What?" James stared at her.

"I had another flashback of standing on the balcony, looking down through the railings of the banister, and I got into trouble for it. Someone said, 'What are you doing out here?' and I was dragged away. But it couldn't have been here because you can't see down from the balcony."

"So this whole vision you had might have been from another house altogether?"

Liz chewed on her lip. "It might."

"Which might mean that the body was buried in quite another place?"

"I don't know." She snapped out the words, then said, "I'm sorry, James. This whole business has shaken me up more than you can imagine."

"I'm sure it has. Let me show you the fireplace," he said. He had cleared a narrow path of debris to various rooms and now led her to his right, into what had been an impressively large drawing room. Liz could make out several pieces of rather grand and ornate furniture under a layer of collapsed ceiling plaster. The fireplace, against the far wall, was indeed magnificent. "I think it's agate," James said. "Wouldn't it make a wonderful centrepiece in any room?"

"Not your father's house," Liz said. "That room is already over-cluttered."

"Yes. Isn't it? He insisted on taking all his old furniture from his housemaster's cottage, although I offered to buy him new and more efficient pieces suitable for the size of the rooms."

"He has to have something to cling on to," Liz said. "I do feel for him in that faceless estate."

"I do, too, but I'm not sure what to do about it," James said. "I live in a flat, and he can't afford the sort of house he'd like. Schoolmasters don't exactly make a lot of money, do they?"

Liz nodded. "The panelling in here is lovely, too. You should try to salvage some of that. In fact I bet you could sell a lot of this stuff to people who want to incorporate old elements into a new build."

"I could, if I had the time," James said. "Unfortunately I have to earn a living. I'm just taking what might cheer up my father and might possibly be useful for him."

Liz's sharp eyes had been scanning the room, trying to picture what it had been like before. Then she noticed something sticking out of the debris.

"What's this?" she asked, taking a step forward.

"Careful!" James grabbed at her. "You might step on something."

"You cleared this path and you survived," she said, a little shakily because he had scared her.

"Ah, but I live a charmed life." He grinned. "I can't tell you the number of times I fell out of trees, or did something stupid at school. Besides, I'm not exactly reckless. I moved really carefully with a long stick to probe ahead."

"But look over here. What is it?" Liz lifted a piece of collapsed ceiling, and beneath it she pulled out a lovely little marble statue. It was of a young shepherd boy with a dog beside him.

"Oh, I remember that," James exclaimed as she handed it to him. "My mother loved it because she said the face reminded her of Simon, my older brother."

"I wonder how many other family treasures are still hidden here?"

"Probably quite a few," James said. "We had to pack in such a hurry, and then we knew we were going to a small cottage, so a lot of stuff had to be left behind. As you can see, we couldn't take much of the furniture."

"What a shame. All those lovely pieces."

James shrugged. "I don't suppose they were that lovely. They would have been once, but most things were well worn by the time I remember them. I do remember that I had to leave my rocking horse. That was a huge blow to me. I loved old Prancer. He was one of those big rocking horses that cost a fortune in antique stores these days. I used to ride him all the time and pretend I was in a race, or riding with the cavalry . . . all sorts of things." A wistful smile came over his face. "Mummy said I was too old for it anyway when we had to leave it."

"I wonder if we could still find it if we looked?" Liz said.

James chuckled. "I don't think I'd fit on it any more. But at least you've found this. My father will be thrilled."

"Should we see if we can find any other treasures?" Liz asked.

"We probably shouldn't tempt fate," James said. "One small gift from the past." He stroked the marble statue lovingly. "And then it's time to move on."

As he said this, Liz heard a shout from outside the house. She gave James a startled look.

"We should probably go and see," he said. "Come on. Chin up."

As they came around to the side of the house, Liz heard a man's voice saying, "Gently now. Careful."

The men looked up as Liz and James came towards them.

DI Fordham straightened up. "You were right, Miss Houghton," he said. "We've found a body, or rather a skeleton. Just where you said."

"A skeleton?" Liz could hardly make herself utter the words. "Then it's not . . ."

"It's not a small child at all. It's an adult and most likely a woman."

CHAPTER 15

Liz stood, staring at the piled of upturned earth. She wanted to peer into that hole, and yet she was afraid to.

"A woman?" she said at last.

DI Fordham nodded. "Looks like it. Finer bones. A few strands of long blonde hair around the skull."

When she didn't answer, he went on, "Does this stir any other memories? Any idea who it might be?"

Liz shook her head. "None at all. I've no idea. You'd have to check if there were any women who were reported missing around here before October 1943. James's father suggested it might have been a soldier bringing a girl out here on a date, and she fought him off and he killed her by mistake. But then how would I ever have seen that?"

"How would you ever have seen any of it?" DI Fordham snapped the words. "We'll need to get forensics out here, and then maybe they can tell us more. But in the meantime we'll need details from you, and of course we'll need to interview your parents, if they are still living."

"Yes. Yes, of course." Liz stammered out the words. "They live in London. My mother . . . my mother will not be what you might call a reliable witness. She's in the early stages of dementia. Sometimes she's quite bright and lucid, and other times she's off with the fairies."

"Really?" DI Fordham stood looking at her. "Where did you live in wartime?"

"In Shropshire. Outside Shrewsbury."

"That's a long way from here."

"Exactly." Liz nodded. "None of it makes any sense. I'm sure we wouldn't have come down here. My mother didn't like to drive, and my father was off in the army."

"In the army, was he?" DI Fordham showed interest in this.

"Yes. He was a brigadier."

"A brigadier. Well, that's a bit different, isn't it?"

"What do you mean?"

"Top brass like that always have people around them. Drivers and clerks and batmen. They don't just go off on their own."

Liz gave an incredulous laugh. "You're not suggesting that my father might have brought a woman here and killed her? Inspector, you don't know my father. The most upright of men in the world. A career soldier. Discipline and duty were drummed into me. Besides, he'd hardly have brought me with him if he planned to murder a woman."

"No, of course not. Sorry, Miss Houghton. I didn't mean to suggest." He gave an embarrassed shrug. "But I will need to talk to them."

"Yes. I understand. I'll give you their address. And I do have friends at the Met, if you'd like to arrange for someone else to interview my parents, rather than making the trek up to London yourself."

"Thanks for the offer, but I'd like to hear things straight from the horse's mouth, if you don't mind. Just to get the feel of this case for myself. We'll go through old missing persons reports, naturally. And take it from there." He turned back to the two men, standing, shovels in their hands, and watching the interaction. "We'd better leave it for now, men. In case forensics say we've buggered up a crime scene. We'll need to get a tarp to cover this up before it rains. Hanson, can I leave that to you? We'll drive Miss Houghton back to the station, and you and Private Adams come back here with the tarp to secure the area."

"Very good, sir," the constable said.

"And you, Mr Bennington," the inspector said. "We'll need contact information from you, from your father and a list of the other residents at the time of the evacuation."

"Oh, right." James looked at the van. "Should I follow you, then?"

"You can leave the van here, if you like," the constable said. "I've got to come back with the tarp anyway. No sense in driving that big thing where you don't have to."

"Thank you," James said. "Much appreciated."

He fell into step beside Liz. "Are you all right?"

"I think so. A bit shaky, but now more confused than anything. I had convinced myself we'd find a small child's body. Now I have no idea."

"Let's hope they find a missing person from the time so that we know more," he said. "So that we can put this behind us."

She saw then that he looked rather shell-shocked, too. Was he thinking that his family might have had something to do with the body? His mother, who had been upset and unstable at the time? Liz wanted to ask him about the governess Mrs Purvis told her about, but she didn't want to put a thought into his head that might not have been there.

They piled into the Land Rover and bounced back to the waiting police car at the top of the lane.

"I wonder if we should be posting a guard at the site, sir?" Private Adams asked. "If word gets around there's a body been found."

"I think we're fairly safe on that," DI Fordham said. "Most people will not know there's a way to reach the house through the fields. They'll arrive at the front gate and see the barbed wire and the 'Keep Out' signs. But maybe we can ask the army to put back some barbed wire across the track until forensics have finished with the body."

They parted from the Land Rover and its driver. He did not look too upset about this and indicated he'd be waiting at the nearby Nag's Head pub. Liz and James got into the back seat of the police car. As they drove away, James patted her knee. "It's going to be all right, don't worry," he said.

She gave him a grateful smile. "God, I hope so. It's a bit nightmarish, isn't it? You think you are leading a normal, if boring, life, and suddenly you find yourself mixed up in a murder case, when you know you can't have been there."

"There must be a rational explanation," he said. "There is for most things."

At the police station she gave the DI her address in London, her parents' address and also the information she had gleaned on various people who had lived in Tydeham at the time of the evacuation.

"Most helpful, Miss Houghton," DI Fordham said. "I see you've done your homework. Still, I suppose you journalists are trained to do this sort of thing. Now if you could just get to the bottom of who this woman was and why you knew about it, I'd be grateful."

"So would I," Liz said.

"You'll let me know if you have any more visions, won't you?"

She couldn't tell if he was joking or not. "I'll be in touch if I find out anything more."

She waited while James gave his own details, noticing that he lived in a smart new development in the city, in an area that had been flattened in the war. She had been to visit a friend who lived there, and it was the sort of place she'd like to live herself. She deduced James made a good salary. The units were not cheap. She watched him as he dictated his father's address and telephone number. She must not read too much into his friendliness. He was a nice person, being kind to a damsel in distress. Nothing more. This whole business was strange enough without the complication of a man.

"Right." James stood up. "I'll ride back with your constable to pick up my car, shall I?" He turned to Liz. "Do you need us to drop you off at your hotel first?"

"Oh no. I can walk. It's not far. The walk will do me good," she said. "And I'm not sure whether I'm going to stay down here any longer. I should probably be getting back to London."

"Really?"

She nodded. "I thought I might have a story here, but obviously it's all gone pear-shaped. Now I don't know what to think, and I'm pretty sure I'll have to do some damage control with my parents."

"Damage control?"

"Yes, for involving them in something so unpleasant. I'll be accused of upsetting my mother. Daddy is very protective of her these days."

"But what if they know something?"

"They don't. My father already told me, most emphatically, that I would never have come here during the war." She gave him a smile. "Well, goodbye, James. Thank you for your support. I've really appreciated it."

"Glad to help," he said. "I'll let you know if there are any developments on this end. And Liz—might I call you when we're back in London?" Before she could answer, he went on, "I have to go back tonight anyway. But now you've got me interested in what other treasures we might be able to find at the house. Dad's going to be chuffed about the statue. Perhaps you and I could go down together one weekend, if you're not too busy?"

"Yes, I'd like that," Liz said. She felt herself flushing like a schoolgirl. So much for not allowing a man into the picture to complicate things further.

CHAPTER 16

Liz put off the telephone call she had been dreading until she had rung Marisa.

"Yeah? Who is it?" Marisa mumbled the words.

"Did I wake you up again?" Liz said. "Sorry, it's me."

"You bloody well did. I didn't get to bed until nearly three this morning."

"Hot date with the fellow cop?"

"You could say that. We went to a folk club after dinner, and then to some kind of all-night café with a group of people we met there. Really interesting types. Although not my scene at all. All those songs about saving the world and peace for all."

"And you'd have to grow your hair, too."

Marisa laughed. "So you're still down there? In the dead zone of Weymouth?"

"I am."

"What news?" Marisa asked. "Did they find a body?"

"They did."

"And was it . . . Lucy?"

"No, it wasn't a child at all. It was an adult woman."

"Blimey. That complicates things, doesn't it? Buried recently, do you think?"

"No, it's a skeleton. I've no idea how long it's been there."

"Could be ancient. Medieval. That would be useful for you, wouldn't it? At least you couldn't have been around to witness it."

"Yes, but I'd come across as a right nutter," Liz said.

"Better to be a nutter than to be involved in a murder scene."

"That's true." Liz sighed. "I think I'll be coming home. There doesn't seem any point in staying down here any longer. I've pretty much established that nobody remembered me as a child, and if this story has nothing to do with Lucy or the other three missing girls, then I don't have a reason to stay."

"Mysterious missing woman from the war and you being psychic? That's not a story?"

"I don't think it's one I want to tackle. It's too disturbing."

"You'd have a chance to see James if you stayed on."

"James has to be back in London. He's going back this evening."

"Ah. Now it all becomes clear."

"Shut up." Liz chuckled. "And for another thing, I don't think I can take Mrs Robinson's cooking any more. It's gone downhill every day. It will be gruel in a day or so. And I want to be back in a place that makes sense. I feel like I'm living in a twilight zone."

"Come on back, then. We had the day off, but I'm dying to get to work on Monday morning and see if they've learned anything more about Lucy."

Liz hung up and then waited. Light was now fading, and the wind, outside the telephone box, had picked up. Even as she stood there, the glass was peppered with a squall of rain.

"Do it," she said to herself. "Do it and get it over with."

She dropped the coins in, taking deep breaths before she dialled her parents' number.

"Is that you, Lizzie?" her father's rich voice barked down the phone line. "Where are you? Your mother was most disappointed that you didn't show up for lunch today. She made a lemon meringue pie, your favourite."

"I'm sorry, Daddy. I'm still down in Dorset." She was annoyed with herself at the sense of guilt she felt about this. Missing Sunday lunch. Letting her mother down. She realized how good they were at making her feel beholden to them.

"What on earth for?"

"Still researching a possible story. But I'll be coming home in the morning, and I did want to warn you that the Weymouth police may be contacting you."

"Contacting us? What the devil for?"

"I told you I had a memory of being in that village before, didn't I?"

"And I told you it was absolutely impossible. You must have imagined it."

"Yes, I know that. But I was back there, at the manor house, and I had a sort of vision of a body being buried."

"A body? You mean a dead body?" His voice had risen several tones.

"They usually are, Daddy. But yes. A dead body. Buried on the grounds of the manor house."

He paused. "How extraordinary."

"And the thing is, Daddy, that they started digging and they've found a skeleton."

"The missing girl's body?"

"No, an adult. Probably a woman."

"Well, I'll be damned. Do they have any idea who it might be?"

"They're going to be consulting old missing persons records. But they asked for your address and telephone number, I presumed to corroborate that I was up in Shropshire during the war and didn't come anywhere near Dorset."

"And why do they think it's a skeleton from that time, pray?"

"They don't. Except the village was fully occupied until 1943."

"You can bury a body in the dead of night, even when a place is occupied, I would have thought."

"Anyway, they must think they have the time right because my visions are of being a small child there. Before October 1943."

"This is ridiculous, Lizzie. You were a toddler, and there was no way you'd have been anywhere near the place." His voice was rising.

"I know, Daddy. I know." She fought back panic. Her father could be terrifying when he was riled.

"This will be most upsetting for your mother, you realize? Police on the doorstep."

"I did point out that she hasn't been very well."

"That's a fat lot of good if they show up and want to ask her a lot of stupid questions."

"I'm sorry. I'm really sorry. I'm really confused about all this. I don't know what to think. What to believe. I'm beginning to wonder if I'm going batty."

"You know, Lizzie," he said, his voice gentler, softer now. "Now that I think about it, you used to have awful nightmares when you were a small child. And those games of pretend. You lived in another world most of the time. And you had a lot of imaginary friends, didn't you?"

"I suppose I did. Mrs Gumboots, remember her? And the Troddle family with all those children?" She gave a little laugh. "They had to come shopping with us."

His voice took on a new tone. "I'm wondering whether those friends really were imaginary, or were you channelling someone else's life somehow. Yes, I know I'm the most sane and sensible man in the world, and I can hardly believe I'm saying this, but I can't think of any other explanation. There are things that just defy belief, you know. When I was in India as a young man, I saw things you just couldn't explain, but they were happening before your eyes. It's possible you do have a clairvoyant streak. Your mother's family is Irish, after all, and the Irish are known for their second sight."

"Gosh," Liz said. "That's a bit too much to take in. But it did cross my mind that maybe something like that was happening. I found a little girl's grave in the village. She'd died when she was two, and I did wonder whether she was somehow calling out to me."

"Who knows? Well, let's hope they discover who this woman was and put an end to the whole business, and life can go back to normal."

"I do hope so," Liz said. "And I'll come up to the house if you get word when the police are coming to visit."

"I can't think it would take long," her father said. "We give them our former address in Shropshire. We tell them your mother did not have a motor car at the time and you never left the area. That's simple enough, even for a policeman, isn't it?"

Liz hung up, promising to come to Sunday lunch, if not before. It had gone better than she had hoped. But it had left her with more unanswered questions. That her father, her quintessential soldier father, should suggest that she was maybe picking up vibes from someone else's life was highly disturbing. And if she really was channelling little Dorothy Bennington, who had died of meningitis at the age of two, then was it Dorothy who had witnessed a body being buried? Maybe that governess?

∿

Dinner at the Seaview was a surprise after the cornflakes and toast. It was a Sunday roast with all the trimmings. Mrs Robinson looked quite sad when Liz said she'd be leaving in the morning.

"I've been called back to work in London," Liz said.

"Really? Did you find anything important during your investigation down here?"

"Maybe," Liz said. "We located a body, but not the little girl. A skeleton from long ago. They're going to be searching through missing persons files."

"Fancy that. A skeleton, you say. From how long ago?"

"I've no idea," Liz said. "I don't know how you can date skeletons. It could be from the Middle Ages for all I know."

"Oh, the Middle Ages." This was clearly not interesting for Mrs Robinson. "Not much of a story in that, is there?"

"I'm afraid not."

The wind had turned into a gale by the time she went to bed, and she lay there, listening to the buffeting on the windows and the sound of the waves. "I want to go home," she said out loud. Even obits seemed safe and sane at the moment.

A LITTLE GIRL

The little girl sat on the floor, hugging her knees to her chest. She was cold and lonely and a little scared now. The fairy lady had promised she'd be back soon, but it had been a long time. There was only one window in the room. It was high up and dirty, with a cobweb in one corner, but the little girl could see that it was getting dark. She was afraid of the dark. At home she always had a nightlight in her bedroom with a pretty pink shade. She was also hungry. She realized that she'd missed lunch and now tea. An image of teatime came into her head: the fire in the fireplace, and sometimes Mummy would let her make toast or crumpets and they'd spread lots of butter and honey.

She realized by now that the fairy lady had probably tricked her. Mummy wasn't going to meet them, and there were not going to be any puppies. In fact she now suspected that the fairy lady was rather a bad witch in disguise, and she was now a prisoner in the witch's castle. It wasn't a very good castle, she had to admit. No moat around it. No dragon or magic mirrors. It looked like an ordinary building from the outside . . . not a very nice house at all.

She was very disappointed in the fairy lady. When she had first met her, the fairy lady had seemed so nice. That day she had first appeared in the bushes, she had whispered that she had to be a secret person or she would vanish again. They had played secret games together in the bushes, tea parties for gnomes and elves, and the fairy lady had told her about her magic castle and how she could make herself very tiny and how she could fly. She had promised the little girl that they'd fly to her lovely white castle on a hill as soon as it was safe. They had to stay here right now because there were bad people around and it wasn't safe to move. But soon it would be safe, and off they'd go to the white castle in the country where the little girl could play with the bunnies and kittens and have a pony to ride.

It had all sounded so wonderful and exciting.

She had been a bit surprised when the fairy lady appeared outside the bushes and beckoned her to come over. "Guess what?" she said. "Your mummy sent me to fetch you. She's waiting at the pet shop for you to choose that puppy you talked about."

"The one with the long ears?" the little girl had whispered back.

"That's the one. Can you come right now?"

And so she squeezed through to the fairy lady. The lady had wanted her to ride in a pram. The little girl was indignant about that. She was much too old. But the fairy lady said they had to hurry in case someone else bought the puppy first. Because of that, she had allowed herself to be put inside the pram and pushed. Only it wasn't to the pet shop.

"I want to go home," she said out loud, but nobody was there to hear.

CHAPTER 17

Liz caught the first train back to London in the morning. Here the weather was calm and bright, the sun warm on her face as she came out of the Parsons Green Underground Station. The humble streets of Victorian houses looked particularly attractive, and a fresh breeze came from the Thames, giving the day an almost spring-like feel. *Home*, Liz thought. It was good to be home. Now that she had distance between herself and the abandoned village, she felt that she could think clearly again. She had somehow been contacted by a spirit from the past—little Dorothy, she suspected. A spirit who had been unable to send out a message before because the village had been abandoned. Well, now the message had been delivered. The body had been discovered. They would identify it, and then the spirits of Tydeham could again rest in peace.

I can get on with my life, Liz thought. This jerked her back to reality. Did she really want to return to the newspaper, back to the boredom of obits? To see Miss Knight smirking? To tell Bob Green what she thought of him? And what about Lucy and those three little girls from long ago? Surely there could be some kind of story there, if she could find out what happened to at least one of them. DI Jones had been on the team that had tried to find them and had not succeeded. She had to accept the truth that someone had abducted those girls, maybe murdered them and buried them. The pressing question was: Had he resurfaced after all these years and taken Little Lucy? Which might mean a really juicy story—devastating for all concerned, but still juicy. In journalism they were trained to detach themselves from emotion. Just the facts.

She had sort of been given permission to investigate Lucy, and ergo any link between the two cases, hadn't she? She toyed with the idea, wondering how one would start to hunt for a child who went missing all those years ago. She'd talk to DI Jones, she decided.

Marisa was never the tidiest of people, and the flat looked as if a tornado had swept through it. Marisa's new white boots lay on the floor inside the door, her dress over the sofa, her bra dropped inside the bedroom door. If Liz hadn't known better, she might have thought that Marisa had brought back her date and the clothes had been ripped off in the heat of passion. Had this been the case? No wonder Marisa was lacking sleep! Mechanically Liz bent to pick up stray items of clothing and dumped them on Marisa's bed. Then she washed up the dishes that had been piled in the sink. When the place looked presentable again, she found she was pacing the room, anxious to do something. Now she wanted to get her hands on the case files for those three earlier missing girls. Was it the done thing to show up at Scotland Yard, asking to speak to Detective Constable Young? She didn't think Marisa would thank her for it.

But she should call her boss. And she wasn't looking forward to that! He was perfectly suited to being head of obituaries—meticulous, a stickler for details and completely without humour. He always wore a bow tie, of which he had a large selection. He also had a neat little moustache and hair parted in the middle. A throwback to a bygone age. Liz dialled the *Express* and was transferred. Mr Pettigrew's neatly clipped voice came on the line.

"Hello? Miss Houghton?"

"Yes, Mr Pettigrew. I wonder if Mr Tomlins has spoken to you or left you a message?"

"I have received several strange messages during the course of the last week, Miss Houghton," he said. "Frankly, I'm not sure what is going on. Firstly, I'm told that you are at death's door with a stomach upset and can't come in to work. Then I am told that you are somewhere on the South Coast, following a tip about a missing child. How that falls into line with the jurisdiction of your current position at the *Express*, I cannot fathom."

"I'm sorry, Mr Pettigrew, but my roommate is a detective with the Met and she was given this tip about Lucy, so I thought that maybe this might be a terrific scoop for our newspaper. I had to jump at the chance to go with her."

"And was it?"

"Was it what?"

"A terrific scoop for our newspaper?"

"The tip did not pan out, but some interesting new facts have come to light. A woman's dead body in an abandoned village. Three missing little girls from long ago. I still think there might be a story for us."

She heard the dramatic sigh on the other end of the line. "Miss Houghton, when will you learn that you are a very junior reporter at a major newspaper and your job is to be a team player, not to go shooting off on wild-goose chases of your own?"

"I do realize that, Mr Pettigrew. It's just that this seemed too good to miss. If they had found Little Lucy down there, and I'd been in on it, just think."

"But you were wrong. You've wasted company time, and I suggest you report back to work immediately if you value your position with us."

"Mr Tomlins did seem to say I could take a few more days until they have exhumed a dead body."

"Whose body?" His voice sounded sharp now.

"We don't know yet."

"Possibly the child?"

"No, an adult."

"Then I don't see what this has to do . . . Miss Houghton, it seems to me that you are getting yourself embroiled in something that is none of your business. I suggest you return to work immediately."

"I can't do that, sir. I have to know."

"Need I remind you that you are employed in the obituaries department? I expect you to be working on obituaries, not joyriding around the countryside digging up bodies."

"But I might have a really good story for the paper. And I do have an in with the Met investigation for Little Lucy."

"Return to work immediately or you risk getting the sack."

Liz took a deep breath. "So be it then." And she hung up.

Afterwards she was so shaken that she had to pour herself a splash of Marisa's vodka. *You wanted to leave anyway,* she told herself. *You planned to give notice. And if you get some sort of good story, you can go to a competitor with it as your entrée.* This seemed like a good idea. She found that the fridge was rather bare and went out to buy groceries. Marisa came home at five thirty.

"Welcome home," she said to Liz. "Oh, and you cleaned up. Sorry, I intended to do it, but I was knackered after last night."

"You didn't bring him back here, did you?"

"What do you take me for?" Marisa laughed. "I have more pride than to bring a man back to a rubbish tip like this place. Besides, I don't think he's the bloke for me. He was really into this folk-singing stuff. And they all seemed a bit hippieish for me. You know, all the blokes with beards, all the girls with hair over their faces. Not my scene at all." She flung herself down on to the sofa. "So, anything new to report?"

"No, I left early this morning. They'll be searching records for missing persons. But you know what, Marisa? I'm still intrigued by DI Jones's unsolved cases—the three little girls. What if there is a connection? I think someone should look into it. Correction—I'd like to look into it. Any chance you could find me the files in the archives?"

Marisa raised an eyebrow. "You want me to raid police archives for you?"

"How about we ask DI Jones and have it done officially? He'd like to find out the truth, wouldn't he? And he's busy doing other things.

What if I could prove some kind of link? A murderer who had never been caught?"

"If the police couldn't come up with anything at the time, what chance do you think you've got now?"

Liz shrugged. "Maybe not much. But I'd like to give it a try."

"What about your paper? Did your boss okay this?"

"Absolutely not. He told me I was likely to be sacked. I said fine. I was thinking of quitting anyway."

"Golly, that's brave."

"No, it's not. It's proactive. I'm worth more than obits. I'm a good journalist. And I'm going to prove it to those creeps."

"Good for you. That's more animation than I've seen in you for a long time." She sat up, smoothing down her skirt. "But Lizzie, one thing did occur to me. About your visions in that village."

"Yes." Liz looked up.

"This may seem completely off the wall, but I've been wondering how you could ever have been there when your family says you were miles away."

"My father even suggested I might be channelling another person, or a departed spirit. And if my father can say that . . . it gives one pause, doesn't it?"

"I've been thinking of something less fanciful. Listen to this: What if you were one of those little girls who went missing?"

"What?" Liz stared at her. "That's absurd. How could I be?"

"Well . . . you told me your parents had you late in life. You were a surprise miracle baby, right?"

Liz nodded.

"What if they couldn't have a child? But a child was found abandoned—one of those little girls, maybe—and your father got the chance to bring you home and adopt you."

Liz gave an incredulous laugh. "That's ridiculous."

"Is it? It was wartime. They probably didn't check records very well. And he was a brigadier—able to go all over the place."

Liz shook her head emphatically. "Good thought, but not true. I can remember my mother singing to me when I was a wee thing. She'd sing 'Golden Slumbers' to me and rock me on her lap. And I think we must have had a power cut because there was lamplight making the room all cosy. It's one of my first memories. In fact all of my early memories are of my parents and our house."

"It was worth a try," Marisa said.

"And I'm supposed to be the one with the overactive imagination." Liz laughed. "But you're right. It was a good hypothesis. It would have explained things nicely. Except the skeleton."

"Except the skeleton," Marisa echoed.

CHAPTER 18

Liz lay awake that night, listening to Marisa's rhythmic breathing, unable to shake disturbing thoughts from her mind. She knew in her heart that Marisa's idea couldn't be true, but it still haunted her thoughts. Right, she decided, she would go to Somerset House, where birth and death records were kept, and ask to see her birth certificate. That would prove conclusively who she was.

Marisa was up and spreading Marmite on toast when Liz surfaced the next morning.

"I've decided I'm going to find my birth certificate," Liz said. "That should show you that your notion is false."

"Good idea." Marisa took a bite of toast. "I'm sorry. I upset you. The idea sprang into my head. One explanation, wasn't it?"

"As good as any right now," Liz replied. She opened the kitchen cupboard, took out a bowl and then grabbed a box of muesli. "But I'd dearly love to see the notes on those missing girls. Any chance you could arrange a meeting with your DI and I could ask him?"

"You know what he felt about you interfering with police work, Liz."

"But this wouldn't be interfering. It would be resurrecting a cold case that the police are not prepared to do themselves. And it would help him, wouldn't it? Put some closure on things if I could find out what happened to at least one of the girls." She poured on the milk.

"And if it did turn out to be a serial killer of children and there was some hint he might still be operating . . . well, think about it."

Marisa nodded. "Worth a try. I'll meet you at noon and see if we can trap him in the cafeteria."

"Brilliant. Thank you."

"I can't promise he'll be there. If we're sent out, I'll leave a note with the bloke at the front desk."

Liz nodded. "Fair enough. I wonder what time Somerset House opens?"

"Not this early if they are civil servants. I wouldn't chance it before ten."

Liz sat at the counter and started to eat. Marisa had gulped down her toast in a few bites and was now examining her hair in the hall mirror. "Got to dash," she said. "Briefing at eight thirty. See ya." And she was gone.

Liz finished breakfast, cleaned up the kitchen, then walked up to catch a number eleven bus. It would take much longer than the Tube, but it went all the way to the Strand and Aldwych, and it was a pleasant way to travel. Besides, she wasn't in a rush. Westminster Cathedral went past. The Houses of Parliament, Trafalgar Square. A proper tourist-eye version of London, looking attractive on a bright and breezy autumn day. What's more, there was a bus stop almost opposite Somerset House. She crossed the road and paused at the entrance arch, admiring that large courtyard and the elegant Georgian palace built around it. All rather intimidating, but there was a man in a cubby at the entrance, and he directed her to the national registry rooms. Here she had to fill out a form with name, date of birth, name of parents and county of birth. She handed it to the woman at the counter. She was told to take a seat and wait.

She waited and waited. The clock on the wall ticked annoyingly every thirty seconds. Footsteps echoed on wooden floors. Muted conversation wafted in from open office doors. And the clock crept closer to noon, when she was supposed to meet Marisa.

She went back to the counter. "Excuse me, but I filled in the form over an hour ago, and I just wondered . . ."

"Sometimes it takes a while," the woman said shortly.

At last a young man with a worried expression called her up. "I'm sorry," he said. "We couldn't find anyone fitting your description having been born in Shropshire."

Liz's heart did a rapid flip. Could Marisa have been right?

"However," he went on, "we did more of a search on that date of birth, and there was an Elizabeth Marie Houghton with the same parents' names born in Somerset. Is it possible you got the wrong county?"

"I don't know . . ." Liz stammered the words. She had always assumed she had been born in Shropshire, but was it possible that she had been born elsewhere and then they had moved when she was too young to remember? "I suppose it must be right if you have the names of my parents."

"Then do you want a copy?"

"Yes, please."

He went off again, presumably to some kind of copying machine. This involved another long wait until he came and handed her an envelope. She waited until she was outside the building before she opened the envelope.

Elizabeth Marie Houghton. Born April 8, 1941. Parents Henry Hurst Houghton, 48—profession Brigadier, His Majesty's Armed Forces. Maureen Marie Houghton (née O'Brien), 44—profession Housewife. Address: Brackleberry Lodge, Clareborne St Mary, Nr. Wincanton, Somerset.

Somerset. Not Shropshire at all, but at least a hundred miles away. She stood looking at it for a long time. This was definitely her birth certificate. But why hadn't she known that she had been born in Somerset? She gave herself the answer immediately: because she had never asked. She had just taken it for granted that the little house in Shropshire had been her home until they moved to London. But of course it had been wartime. People moved around. It was possible their home had been requisitioned, or bombed even.

In the distance she heard Big Ben chiming the three quarters. She'd better hurry if she wanted to meet Marisa and her DI. She dropped down to the river and caught the first Circle line train from Charing Cross Station, hoping that St James's Park was the nearest stop to the new Met offices. *Why did they have to move the bloody police headquarters from the Embankment?* she thought as she waited impatiently, strap-hanging on the Tube. At least she knew where that was. She had never been to this new HQ, although Marisa said it was a much nicer place to work, lighter and with modern loos.

She sprinted up the steps at St James and was relieved to find herself on the corner of Broadway, only a few steps away from the new New Scotland Yard. And Marisa was waiting outside.

"Good. You made it," she said. "And I got DI Jones to hold us a seat at his table." She saw Liz's expression. "Or rather hold me a seat. He doesn't know you're coming yet. We'll spring that on him once he's got his food and he can't escape." She chuckled. "So, did you find your birth certificate?"

They entered the modern marble foyer, and Marisa led Liz to the back of the building.

"I did," Liz said. "And it's all in order, except for one thing. I didn't know I was born in Somerset."

"That's easily explained," Marisa said. "Your family could have been staying with friends, or taken a place temporarily while your dad was posted there."

"Yes, of course." Liz nodded. "Makes sense."

The cafeteria was noisy, with the clatter of pots and pans and voices echoing. Marisa spotted DI Jones, now in conversation with another older plainclothes officer. The man nodded to Marisa and went on his way, holding a tray.

"I've brought Liz," she said. "I thought you'd like to hear what she's found in that village."

DI Jones eyed her warily but didn't say anything. He went back to a plate of cauliflower cheese and a sausage.

"Sit down. I'll get you something," Marisa said. "I can't guarantee the flavour. What would you like?"

"Oh, just a sandwich, I think. And a cup of tea," Liz said.

"They do a decent ham salad. Will that do?"

Liz nodded. She slid on to the bench opposite the DI.

"So I gather you didn't find one of my little girls," he said, looking up from his food.

"I'm afraid not. But there was a body at the manor house. The skeleton was an adult woman."

"And could have been there for donkey's years," he said. "Except that you thought you saw her buried."

"That's right," Liz said. "They are going to go through missing persons files, so I just have to wait and see. But your case has now piqued my interest, Inspector. I'd really like to see if I could follow up on your missing girls. You never know, something may have come to light in the meantime. Is it possible that I could have access to the archives on them?"

"My little girls! Absolutely bloody not." He had raised his voice, and diners at other tables looked across at them. "I don't know why you've the nerve to think you can do what a trained police team could not."

"I was just thinking . . . ," Liz said hesitantly. "What if it really was a serial killer of children, Inspector? What if he's resurfaced and he's taken Little Lucy? Wouldn't you want to know?"

"I think that's bloody rubbish," he said. "There have been plenty of other children killed in the years between. I don't see why you think there could be any connection with something that happened twenty-something years ago."

"Didn't you say that the little girls looked similar?"

"All little girls look cute and adorable. Stop thinking about it. A complete waste of time. Leave police work to the police, young lady."

Liz gave him a hopeful smile. "I only want to help. Maybe I'll come up with nothing, but it's worth a try, isn't it? It's not going to cost you either time or money, and I can't do any harm after all this time."

She saw him hesitating, thinking this through. "I can't see how the hell they can be connected," he said, still glowering at her. "Or what an adult woman's body in an abandoned village has anything to do with any of these cases." Then he sighed. "But I suppose anything that brings us closer to finding Lucy . . ." He didn't finish the sentence.

"Have you found out any more?" Liz asked.

"I'll tell you one thing we haven't found," he said. "And that's her real father. The French police have identified the name the mother gave us. He was indeed killed in a car accident around the time the baby was born. But there was no marriage certificate, and they haven't located his family so far. It seems he might have come from Algeria. Perhaps they got married in England or another country. Perhaps they weren't legally married. Who knows? But anyway, there don't seem to be family members we can find who might have wanted to kidnap the child, so that's another dead end."

Marisa returned with a tray and put a plate of ham salad and a cup of tea in front of Liz. As she began to eat, DI Jones finished his own meal and pushed the plate away. "Well, I should be getting back to work," he said. "I'll leave you women to natter." And he left.

Marisa looked at Liz. "So how did that go?"

"Not sure," Liz said. "He did sort of hint that it couldn't do any harm. If you could nudge him, or maybe go through those channels yourself, that would be great."

"I can't promise anything," Marisa said. "We are rather busy right now, you know."

"But you could find time to ask?" Liz looked at her hopefully.

They finished eating, and Marisa rushed off to a meeting. Liz came out of the building, uncertain what to do next. Then she made a sudden decision to go and see her parents. She wanted to hear why she had never been told that she was born in Somerset. She hopped on the Tube, changed to the Bakerloo line and headed up to Finchley Road. From there it was a longish walk to her parents' house, close to Hampstead Heath. It wasn't a huge property but on a street of posh houses, with Jaguars and Rovers parked in driveways.

"Well, this is a surprise," her father said when he opened the front door. "Your mother will be thrilled. She was so disappointed when you didn't come to lunch on Sunday. We have some lemon meringue pie left over that she made for you specially. Your favourite."

"I'm sorry, but I told you I was on that assignment in Weymouth. I didn't get back until yesterday."

"Of course. Any more news on that yet?"

Liz shook her head. "And I take it you haven't had a visit from the police yet?"

Liz's father put a finger to his lips. "Let's not talk about it. I don't want your mother upset. But no. No visit yet."

She came into the front hall, savouring the familiar smells of home—the brand of furniture polish with lemon, a whiff of her mother's favourite perfume, L'Air du Temps.

"Look who I've found," her father said brightly as they came into the living room. Her mother was sitting in an armchair, a magazine in front of her.

"I thought I saw Alice coming up the front path," she said, looking up with delight on her face, "but it's you, Lizzie. My little girl come home. How lovely." She reached out her hands to her daughter, and Liz went over and took them. She noticed that her mother seemed to have shrunk again. She had been a big woman, tall, statuesque, imposing. But now she was a shadow of her former self, perpetually confused with a worried look on her face. "But why didn't you come for lunch, Lizzie? You didn't come on Sunday, did you? You should have come today. I'd have made a cottage pie with the leftover beef. Proper food. I know you don't eat well at that silly flat."

"I had to have lunch with some people, Mummy." She bent over to kiss her. "Who's Alice?"

Her father shot her a warning frown. "One of her school friends," he whispered. "She keeps having conversations with school friends. Mostly dead school friends, I fear. Still, if it keeps her happy." He shrugged.

Liz sat down beside her mother, holding her hand. "How are you, Mummy? You're looking well." Her mother was dressed as if she was going out to lunch. She was wearing make-up, pearls, a brooch in the shape of a peacock. The effect was to accentuate her present frailness.

"I'm very well, my darling. All the better for seeing you. You didn't come home this Sunday, and I made you a pie, too."

"I'm sorry. Dad said there might be some left?"

"I think there is if Mrs Croft hasn't eaten it. She steals a lot of our things, you know. And she eats our food."

"Now Maureen, you know that's not true," the brigadier said. "She's an invaluable help, and we're lucky to have her."

"So you say." Mrs Houghton's face was stony. "I could manage just fine without her."

She got up and swept from the room. The brigadier sighed. "She is getting more difficult. Accusing that poor woman of eating her cake when she's forgotten she had it for tea. And she couldn't manage without her. Several times recently she's turned the gas on the stove, then gone away and completely forgotten about it. Still, one does what one can."

"You may eventually need a nurse for her."

"Yes, I've thought of that. Luckily we are not without funds. We'll face that hurdle when we come to it."

"So Daddy, I've got a question," Liz asked, having rehearsed a plausible reason on the train. "I had to get a copy of my birth certificate, for some pension scheme at work, and I see I was born in Somerset. Why didn't you tell me?"

He shook his head, patting her on the cheek. "Did you ever ask? I don't think the subject ever came up. We were in Somerset only briefly, my dear. Our house in Kent, the family home I grew up in, was requisitioned by the army, and we had to get out in a hurry. Your mother was expecting you and was naturally upset. Luckily an army pal was being sent abroad and said we could use his house for the time being. So that's where we went, until he came back. You were born there. Then Bristol and Bath were being bombed. Your mother felt we were too close to them. She didn't feel safe, so we looked for a place far from any industry or dockyards, where no bombs were likely to fall. And we found the house in Shropshire. A nice enough little place, wasn't it?"

Liz was taking this all in. "But what about your ancestral home in Kent? I didn't know about that either. Was it lovely?"

"A very attractive place, actually. Broxley Manor. I was lucky to have grown up there."

"Why didn't we go back after the war?"

A pained look crossed his face. "Because the army had trashed it. The gardens were overgrown. The house would have needed so much work done to it. It would have cost more money than I had. We decided to sell it to a developer. It was pulled down and is now a housing estate."

"You got a decent amount of money, I suppose?"

"Not that much. Certainly not what it was worth. Or had been worth. Still, the war made things hard for a lot of people. At least we always had a roof over our heads. And we're happy enough here, aren't we? Lucky we're now in London within reach of good doctors for your mother, and where you can come to us when you need us."

"Can they actually do anything for her?"

"Probably not. I keep hoping, but . . ."

He looked up as Mrs Houghton came in. "I've searched everywhere for that lemon meringue pie. See, I was right. That woman ate it."

"I'm sure she didn't, my dear. And even if she did, we can't begrudge the woman a piece of pie, can we? She does work awfully hard for us."

"I don't see why we need her at all," Liz's mother said. "I could manage perfectly well. You always liked my cooking, didn't you?"

The brigadier put an arm around her shoulders. "My dear, you have worked all your life making a lovely home for us. Now you deserve to take it easy and let someone wait on you. It's your due."

She turned to look at him. "Yes, but how do I fill the hours of the day? That's the question. The days seem awfully long. For you, too. How do you fill your days?"

"You must both find a new hobby," Liz said brightly. "Take up ballroom dancing."

Her mother laughed at this. "Ballroom dancing? Didn't anybody tell you your father has two left feet?"

"Well, painting then, or table tennis. Something to challenge you, Mummy."

"I find my jigsaw puzzles challenging enough. And I can't seem to do the crossword any more."

"You used to do lovely embroidery and crochet," Liz said. "I remember those pretty little dresses you made for me."

"If I made you a pretty little dress now, you wouldn't wear it," her mother said. "But I do hope for grandchildren one day, then I'll get to work again. Isn't there anyone in the picture at the moment?"

"Not at the moment," Liz said.

"Don't let life pass you by, my dear. I'll never understand why you turned down that nice boy—what was his name?"

"Edmond, you mean? He went to Australia."

"No. Not him. I never liked him," she said angrily. "The other one. What was he called?"

"You mean Alistair?"

"Yes. What a dear boy. So right for you. And a good family, too. A family who lived nearby."

"Mummy, he was dull. And he had no sense of humour. And his mother was so possessive. It wouldn't have worked."

Mrs Houghton shook her head, making tut-tutting noises. "Well, I liked him," she said. "You are not getting any younger. I know, why don't you let Daddy find you a young officer? That's what my parents did. They introduced me to your father."

"I expect I'll find the right man some day, Mummy," Liz said. "I had better be getting back. I've some work to do. But I will try to come this Sunday if I can. You can make another lemon meringue."

"I will. I will." Her mother looked overjoyed. Liz kissed her.

"I'll see you out," her father said. He escorted Liz to the front door. "So good to see you, my dear child. And you've seen what a tonic you are for your mother. She brightens up immediately when she sees you. I don't suppose you'd think about coming home to live again? It would mean a lot to her."

"Daddy, I'm twenty-seven. I have to get on with my life," she said. "I do try to come home as often as I can." She put her hand on her father's arm. "I know this is hard for you. It's hard for me, too, to watch her slipping away." She reached up and kissed his bristly cheek. "Bye, Daddy. I'll see you soon. And let me know if you hear from the Weymouth police."

"I'll send them away with a flea in their ear, that's what I'll do," he said. "There's no point in coming to us. We'll just tell them exactly what you've already said. Waste of their time and money. If they talk to you, tell them they can telephone. I don't want your mother worried."

"All right. I'll do that. I did give them your number."

"Henry? What are you chatting about without me?" came her mother's voice.

"I should go," Liz said. "Bye, Dad."

"Goodbye, my dear child." He gave her a smile, but she saw him glance back towards the living room with worry in his eyes.

A LITTLE GIRL

The little girl was running. She was running as fast as she could, but her legs felt that they were weighted with lead. She glanced behind her. The thing was still there. She didn't know exactly what the thing was, but it was big and dark and it was coming for her. However fast she ran, it was still coming behind her. Up the flight of stairs. Along the long, dark hallway. She could see the door at the end. If only she could make it. She reached the door. The handle wouldn't turn. She looked back to see the thing right behind her, reaching out a bony hand . . .

She screamed and woke up to find herself lying in her own narrow bed. Another nightmare. There were so many these days. As if the bombing wasn't enough to worry about. She sat up, her bare feet reacting to the cold linoleum of the floor. Maybe Mum was still up. If she was in a good mood and had been to the pub, she'd sometimes make the girl a hot drink and let her sit by the kitchen stove for a while.

She tiptoed to the stairs and saw a light still shining from under the kitchen door. Mum was still awake! She had almost reached the kitchen when she heard a deep, masculine laugh. The girl froze. HE was there again. The girl did not like him. He was big and rough and he scared her. She peeked through the keyhole. Mum was sitting on his lap, and he had his hand up her skirt. Anger replaced fear. She barged into the kitchen.

"Stop touching my mum," she said, sounding braver than she felt. "My dad wouldn't like it."

The big man stood up, tossing Mum aside. "Are you talking to me, little girl?" He came towards her. She could smell the beer on his breath, and his eyes looked bloodshot.

"Yes." She stuck her chin out bravely. "My dad's far away in the army fighting, and he wouldn't like you coming here to see my mum."

"Go back to bed, now," Mum commanded, but the big man stood in her way.

"You should learn to keep your trap shut, kid," he said. "No one's asking for your opinion. Now get lost." He slapped her across the face so violently that she reeled backwards. But her fighting spirit was aroused. She ran at him, pummelling him with her fists.

"You're a bad man. I hate you. Leave us alone." She screamed out the words.

"Want to fight, do you?" He gave that nasty laugh again, grabbed her by the neck and brought his fist slamming into her face.

She heard Mum say, "Bill. No. She's only a little kid . . ."

But he went on hitting the little girl until she dropped to the floor. The last thing she saw was his boot, coming at her . . .

CHAPTER 19

When Liz got home, having negotiated the beginning of rush hour, despite being offered food at her parents' house, she realized she had hardly eaten all day. She had only picked at the ham salad—besides, it was not filling. Now she didn't feel like cooking. She went around the corner to the Indian takeaway and brought back tikka masala and a naan. *Mummy was right,* she thought. *I don't cook for myself.* When Marisa arrived home, she stopped in the doorway.

"I smell Indian food," she said.

Liz nodded. "I picked it up from that place on the Wandsworth Bridge Road," she said. "There's enough for two if you'd like some and aren't going out to dinner with handsome policemen."

Marisa beamed. "I'm starving and I'm not going anywhere. In fact I plan to go to bed early and catch up on sleep."

Marisa set the table while Liz dished up. "We made one tiny step of progress this afternoon," she said as Liz put the plates on the table. "Another policewoman and I were allowed to speak to the au pair who was with Lucy when she was taken. She's feeling really guilty because she says someone left a Swedish newspaper on a bench in the park, and she was reading it while Lucy played. She said she could see the park gate and it was closed, and they were the only people in there, so she didn't think Lucy could come to any harm while she played."

"So she wasn't watching all the time?"

"Apparently not."

Liz frowned, her brain ticking into action. "Could it be that some-one planted the Swedish newspaper, knowing that the au pair would pick it up and read it and not be watching?"

"That thought struck me, too," Marisa said.

"That would mean it was a carefully orchestrated kidnapping, not a random snatching of a child."

Marisa nodded. "But it doesn't get us any closer as to who might have wanted to take the girl. Was it a paedophile who had been watching her, a kidnapping for ransom, or was it some kind of revenge action against her parents?"

"The au pair might have been reading the newspaper, but if Lucy had cried out, she would have looked up. And if someone had carried Lucy out of the park, she would have seen."

"True."

"Was it possible she was small enough to have squeezed out between the railings?"

"That's a possibility. But then her kidnapper wouldn't have been able to slip out that way. And there really was only the one gate."

"What a puzzle." Liz sighed. "Well, we can't do anything right now, so let's eat this before it gets cold."

The tikka was hot and satisfying, and they mopped up the sauce with the naan.

"I went to see my parents," Liz said as she put down her knife and fork.

"You did? To ask them about the birth certificate?"

"Yeah. All a perfectly reasonable explanation. I didn't know, but they lived in my father's ancestral home until the war, a big fancy house, until it was requisitioned by the army. They had to find somewhere to go, and a pal in Somerset lent them his home. Then my mother was afraid of the bombing in Bristol and Bath, so they moved as far away as possible."

"Makes sense." Marisa popped the last of her naan into her mouth. "So how is your mum?"

"Going downhill, I'm afraid. Now she's saying the cleaning lady is stealing from her and eating her food. Oh, and she's having conversations with dead school friends."

Marisa gave her a sympathetic smile. "It can't be easy for your dad."

"Not for me either. All those years it was just my mother and me when Daddy was away. She was my rock. She looked after me so well." She got up, went over to the kettle and poured hot water on to a tea bag. "My father suggested that it would help her if I came back home to live. I'm sure he's right. Am I being selfish to want to stay here and live my own life?" She turned to look at Marisa. "I love my parents, but I feel smothered there, even at the best of times. You've seen them. They hover over me, trying to please me, making me feel guilty if I don't do what they want. And now, with my mum sinking like this . . . I don't think I could handle it."

"You shouldn't have to," Marisa said. "You're a good daughter. You visit often. But you have to make your own life. You want to find a bloke and settle down, don't you?"

"Of course."

"Speaking of which, what about James?" Marisa gave a cheeky smile.

Liz gave her an exasperated look. "We only met a couple of times, Marisa. He seemed very nice, but I'm not sure if . . ."

At that moment the telephone rang. Marisa went over to it, glanced at Liz and said, "Yes, she's here. Hold on." She held out the telephone to Liz. "Speak of the devil," she whispered, and she raised an eyebrow.

Liz took the phone from Marisa. "Hello?"

"Liz? It's James. So you made it back to London?"

"Yesterday," Liz said. "There didn't seem any point in staying any longer."

"Have you heard anything more about the dead body?"

"Not yet. Did the police speak to your father?"

"They did," James replied. "He was extremely annoyed about it. They wanted details about everyone who had stayed with us, lived with

165

us. He told them nobody during the war, and they said it need not have been from that time." He paused. "I'm afraid you are not his favourite person at the moment for having your vision. He called you a bloody woman. Why couldn't she keep her séances to herself?"

"I'm sorry. I seem to have caused a lot of upsets," Liz said. "They haven't spoken to my parents yet, but my father is worried they will frighten my mother. She doesn't always understand things properly these days. I did tell you that she has the beginnings of dementia, didn't I?"

"You did mention it."

"It's sad, James. Her grip on reality isn't always there. My dad is scared she'll panic if police come to the house."

"Understandable. But you couldn't help it. You didn't invent a dead body for attention, did you? I saw your face. You were terrified."

Liz sighed. "I'm just praying they identify the remains and I can forget about it. And that I don't have any more flashbacks."

"What I really rang to tell you, Liz, was that my dad was thrilled with the statue. So excited to see it. He talked about other pieces that must have been left behind. I thought I'd go down again this weekend, and I wondered if you'd like to come, too, since you were the one who found the statue? You obviously have a good eye for these things."

The desire to be with James wrestled with the fear of going back to the place where the body was buried. But by then the body would have been removed from the rose garden. She made a quick decision. "I'd love to. It would be amazing if we found some more precious objects."

"Great." He sounded pleased. "There's a train at eight thirty to Bournemouth on Saturday morning. Shall I meet you at Waterloo? That's not too early for you, is it?"

"No, of course not. I'll meet you there, then."

"Terrific. Bye."

Liz put down the phone.

"Well?" Marisa said.

"He wants me to go down to the house this weekend. I found a marble statue in the rubble, and his father is thrilled to have it again. James wants to see if we can retrieve more stuff."

"That sounds exciting," Marisa said. "You and James, alone in the spooky, ruined house . . . how romantic."

"Shut up." Liz made a playful swipe at her. "He probably only wants me along because I had sharp eyes and spotted the first one."

"Oh yes, definitely. Only because of that. He likes you, Liz. And he sounds very suitable. Architect. Son of a good family. And he lives in London. Nothing your parents could object to."

Liz put her hand up to her mouth. "Oh God, Marisa. I've just said I'll spend the weekend with James, and I promised my parents I'd be there for Sunday lunch. Now what am I going to do?"

"Go with James, of course. Are you crazy?" She got up and carried the plates to the sink. "Liz, you can't spend your whole life trying to please them. Tell them you've got an assignment this weekend, which is true. You are writing this story about the abandoned village. This is another piece of it. And you say your mother is losing her grip on reality. Tell her Monday is Sunday. She won't know the difference."

Liz laughed. "You are so devious."

Marisa laughed, too. "I've had to be to get around a mother with eyes like a hawk. How else do you think I ever got to go on dates? No boy would have ever come to our house. My mum would have given him the third degree." She turned on the taps and ran water to do the washing-up.

Liz picked up the tea towel to dry. Inside her she felt a tiny bubble of excitement.

CHAPTER 20

Liz wasn't sure what to do when she woke up on Wednesday morning. She was conscious of a sense of urgency, of unanswered questions, and fought off feelings of frustration. She hadn't been told if they had identified the body at the abandoned village. Everybody had told her it was impossible that she had ever been there, when those flashes of memory were so real. The police did not seem to have got any further with the disappearance of Little Lucy, and there was no way that she could be involved in the case. So many questions and no answers. She stomped around the flat, turning on the hot water jug and grabbing a mug from the hook on the dresser.

She was wasting her time. What was the point of staying away from work, apart from getting herself the sack? She had not been able to glean any more information that she could use in a story. She had picked up a couple of things from Marisa about Little Lucy's family, but she had definitely not been given permission to use those, either from her paper or the police. She also had no information on the lost girls of long ago, even if the paper might think they were worth a story. And no more information on her dead body at the Tydeham manor house. So what was she doing, staying home? She should just go back to work, she told herself. But the thought of sitting at her desk in that room, writing an obituary of a former bishop or MP, seemed so unbearably boring after the excitement of the last week. She missed being in news. She missed the rapid heartbeat when she realized she was on to a story.

Maybe she could persuade DI Jones to retrieve the archives for her, and she could hunt for his missing girls. Although now that she considered it in the cold light of day, she had to admit that she stood little chance of succeeding. If a team of trained police detectives could not locate the girls around the time they disappeared, what chance would she have? She went over to the bay window and looked out. A woman was pushing a pram on the other side while a toddler clung to her skirt. Such a charming cameo. It struck her that somewhere around London there were mothers who probably still wondered about their daughters every day, and tried to remember what it felt like when a little hand held them tightly. She realized that she wanted to go on and to do what she could. If the paper wouldn't give her permission, then she'd do it alone and find a new job if she had to.

I have to write, she thought. She opened the folder with the typewritten pages she had begun on the village. Then a thought struck her. *He wants a bloody obituary. I'll give him one.* She put a sheet of paper into the typewriter and began.

Obituary of a Murdered Village

On October 8, 1943, a village died. Until then, there had been families in each of the cottages, going about their daily lives, hanging washing on lines, planting their back gardens, going off in their fishing boats. At the manor house there had been grand dinner parties. Children had played in the street. Hymns had been sung in the church, and at nightfall the men had gathered in the pub. And in one fell swoop, they were transported away, never to return . . .

She had almost finished the article when the telephone rang. It was Miss Strong from personnel. "Oh, Miss Houghton. You are at home. I've been getting conflicting messages about you. First I hear that you are off sick, and then that you're on an assignment. But your supervisor tells me that he expected you back at work. So perhaps you'd like to clarify?"

"I was trying to follow up on a story lead, Miss Strong," Liz said.

"So you weren't sick?"

"No. I had a tip about a missing child and followed my roommate, who is a police detective. The tip did not lead to anything, but I now have other story leads."

"But your supervisor has not authorized these, I gather. Are you not still attached to obituaries?"

"Yes, I am, but—" She was about to say she was working on a story when Miss Strong cut her off.

"Well, then. I'm afraid you are most definitely expected back at work."

She realized that Mr Tomlins had only given her a couple of days' grace. Those must have expired by now. An idea struck her. "How many sick days do I have left this year, Miss Strong?"

"Let me see." There was a rustle of paper. "You have five remaining. You had not taken any time off until last week."

"I'm afraid that I may be feeling sick right now," Liz said. "Please inform my supervisor."

"Really?" The voice sounded sceptical. "You are feeling sick? You will need a doctor's certificate when you return to work. You do realize that?"

"I'm sure I can obtain one," Liz said.

"Then there is nothing more to be said. Good day to you, Miss Houghton." The telephone was replaced. The tone had been icy. Liz stared at the receiver in her hand for a while before she put it down. Now she had done it. But she had five working days before she had to go back, if that's what she decided to do.

She made herself a cup of instant coffee and had just taken a sip when the phone rang again. "Hello?" she asked.

"Liz, it's Bob," said the smooth, deep voice. "I just heard that you're off sick. I'm so sorry. Is there anything I can do?"

"Oh, Bob. Kind of you to ring me," she said. "But there's nothing you can do. Just a virus. I have to wait it out."

"I could come over after work," he said. "Bring you something. Isn't it always grapes that characters bring people in books? I'll bring you grapes. And a bottle of wine. A nice Bristol Cream sherry, eh? I think you need cheering up."

She was about to tell him that she was highly contagious, but she changed her mind. It was time to stop the charade with Bob Green. "Won't your wife be expecting you at home after work?" she asked sweetly.

"What?" He gave a nervous laugh. "Oh, I'm sure she'd understand that I was visiting a sick colleague."

"She might, but my boyfriend wouldn't," Liz said. "He does get rather jealous."

"But I thought . . ." He stammered a little. "You never mentioned a boyfriend when we . . ."

"When you were flirting with me? Inviting me to your cottage for a naughty weekend? Just as you never mentioned your wife. I suppose we've both been remarkably reticent with the truth, haven't we, Bob? But thank you for telephoning me. I think I feel a little faint, and I should go and lie down. Goodbye." And she hung up. She caught a glimpse of her face in the mirror, and she gave herself a big grin. She had done it. She had not let a man get the better of her.

She went back to her typewriter and read through the obituary. It wasn't bad, she thought. But there was a body buried in that village that she hadn't mentioned. Could she include that? It would definitely give the story a little spice and intrigue, but until they discovered the identity of the skeleton, she felt uneasy about going on. She remembered the look between James and his father.

But there were the other stories. She looked again at the sheets of paper she had already typed. One on visiting the abandoned village, tying in the missing children. But that was no longer relevant. She crumpled it up and tossed it into the wastebasket. The other was on the missing children themselves: *As the country hunts for Little Lucy, we are reminded of other children who vanished, other mothers who bear lifelong grief. At the height of the bombings in the war, three little girls went missing, three years in a row, about the same time of year. The police hunted for them, but only one was found, murdered in a wood. Was there a serial kidnapper or killer at work during the war, and is it at all possible that he has reawakened and taken Little Lucy?*

Liz stared at it now. Too far-fetched. Why would a man who kidnapped and killed on a regular basis suddenly stop doing so for many years? She came up immediately with a good explanation: he had been in prison. He had served his time and just been released. She felt rising excitement. She had to tell Marisa right away. Picking up the phone, she dialled Scotland Yard and was told that DC Marisa Young was out on assignment. Liz asked for a message to be given to her as soon as she returned. Then she went back to her typewriter, and her fingers flew. *Has someone just been released from a prison or mental hospital? Why aren't the police looking into this? Has a serial killer struck again?*

Just before lunch, Marisa rang. "What is it, Liz? I got word that it was urgent."

"I had a fantastic thought," Liz said. "You know how we talked about the three little girls from long ago being linked to Lucy's disappearance? And it seemed too far-fetched to be true."

"Yes," Marisa said dubiously. "It does seem too far-fetched to be true."

"What if the person who took the first three girls was apprehended for something else—another child molestation charge, maybe—and has been in prison all this time? Or in a mental hospital, like the man your DI told us about? And now he's released and he's started kidnapping again?"

"Blimey," Marisa said. "That never occurred to me. That's brilliant, Liz. So I should check out anyone who was convicted of something resembling kidnapping or interfering with a child in some way . . ."

"And has just been released."

"Right. Of course he could also have been abroad all this time and just returned to England. I could get in touch with Australia, New Zealand, Canada and see if they had any serial child kidnappers who were never apprehended, or had been in prison there." She gave a sigh. "God, Liz, you've given me a huge headache here."

"But it may be important."

"Of course it may. You're too bloody clever."

"That's what Mr Tomlins in news said to me the other day. Anything more come to light on Lucy's kidnapping?"

"It's what we don't have that's interesting. Very few details on Lucy's mother's life in France or her husband. She did register the birth of a daughter there, stating father deceased. But not much more. Still, I don't suppose it's relevant if we don't suspect that the child was kidnapped by her late husband's family."

"I suppose this has nothing to do with the parents?"

"Meaning what?"

"Getting rid of an unwanted child?"

"Quite the opposite. Both of them seem gutted. And I don't get the feeling they are acting."

"Then I think we should at least take a peek at my theory. Share it with your governor." She took a deep breath. "And I'd like to help, Marisa. If you could get me notes on the missing girls, I could do some research of my own."

"You know what DI Jones is like. He's not going to hand over police archives to you, however useful you might be."

"There's no way you could get your hands on them?"

"Steal police archives for you? It's probably more than my job's worth, Liz."

"Pity," Liz said. "Anyway, keep me up to date, will you? About my released convict theory."

"I will, you bloody woman. You've given me a lot of extra work." Marisa chuckled as she hung up.

Liz made herself some grilled cheese for lunch, ate it quickly, then grabbed an apple and walked around the living room, biting into it. She was anxious to do something, but there was nothing she could do. So frustrating. But she realized this experience did tell her something: she needed to be back in a newsroom, doing something exciting and useful. Whatever happened, she'd look for another job with a newspaper. She made an instant decision. She took the obituary she had written on the village, put it into an envelope and addressed it to Mr Pettigrew. Then she was about to drop it in the postbox when the telephone rang again.

"Can you come over here right now?" Marisa asked. "I've got a few minutes before I have to be at a meeting, and I have something for you."

"What is it?"

"You'll see when you get here. Hurry." The call ended.

Liz grabbed her jacket and ran all the way to the Tube station, pausing only to drop off the obituary in the postbox for Mr Pettigrew. Ten minutes later she came out just down the street from New Scotland Yard. Before she could get there, Marisa stepped out of the doorway to a dry cleaners. "You made good time," she said. "Here, take this and go back the way you came."

She handed Liz a large envelope.

"What is it?"

"Notes on the missing girls. We have a photocopier now. I copied them for you. No one will ever know. But don't do anything silly, will you? Don't get me into trouble."

"Of course I won't. You're brilliant, Marisa. Did you run the released convict idea past DI Jones?"

"I did, and he pooh-poohed it. He told me not to waste our valuable time on cold cases when we had a hot one needing to be solved."

"But you're not going to listen to him?"

Marisa grunted. "I'm going to have a word with the superintendent who is head of the team, just to see what he thinks. And I may do a bit of digging on my own, now I know my way around the archives—just to see who might have been convicted around that time, and released recently."

"Good for you," Liz said. "We may be getting somewhere."

CHAPTER 21

Liz resisted the temptation to open the envelope on the Tube going home. She waited until she was sitting at the kitchen table and spread the papers out in front of her. The first thing she saw was a copy of a photograph clipped to a sheaf of notes. A faded black-and-white photograph of a sweet little blonde girl, holding a toy dog and looking up at the camera shyly. *Rosemary Binks, aged five* was written beside it.

Liz read the notes.

> *October 15, 1941. Whitechapel police received a visit from Mrs Ada Binks of 5 Tapp Street, Whitechapel. She stated that her daughter, Rosie, had been evacuated on September 18. She was told the parents would be contacted when the children were placed with a family in the country. But so far she had heard nothing.*
>
> *She had taken her daughter to the station and put her on the train, so she knew the journey started off well. The train was going as far as Yeovil in Somerset, with lots of stops along the way. She hadn't wanted to send her kid away, but she thought it was for the best, since they were being bombed incessantly. She said she couldn't leave London herself—never been out of the city in her life and wouldn't want to. Besides,*

her husband worked at the meat market, and she had to be there to take care of him.

It was only when she hadn't heard after a month that she got worried. Every child had a postcard with them to send home with their new address.

Liz read on. Police had travelled the train route, questioned other children. Children had been taken off the train at every rural stop and handed over to local volunteers who placed them with families. Other children had seen Rosemary on the train, but nobody had seen her on a platform. No local volunteer recalled seeing her.

Liz noted the address in London, and the route: Waterloo to Yeovil. But now that she studied it, she couldn't see what she could possibly do that had not been done. How could she interview people twenty-seven years later and expect them to remember?

She moved on to the next child. Gloria Kane. Also from Whitechapel. Romford Street. Again a copy of a faded snapshot, this time showing a skinny little girl not wanting to look at the camera. Mrs Kane told a similar story. *Child delivered to Waterloo Station and not heard from again. When asked which train route, she seemed unsure. Gloria's mother stated she wasn't too worried when she didn't hear. Child has her head in the clouds and can't write anyway. She only thought something might be wrong when she met Rosemary Binks's mother and heard about what had happened to Rosemary the year before. Those two girls had been friends in school.*

The police report stated that Mrs Kane seemed nervous, constantly twitching at the lace curtain and looking out of the window. *Checked the child's room and noticed the teddy bear on her bed. When asked if Gloria didn't want to take her teddy with her, Mrs Kane replied she was too old for teddies.*

Cut short the interview as she had to "run." Meeting a friend and going to the pictures. She did not seem particularly upset at missing daughter.

Scribbled note said, *Only one without bomb shelter in backyard. When asked, she said "Fate, ain't it? If a bomb's got your name on it, a shelter won't do no good."*

Liz copied down the address but wondered how to proceed.

There was no record of the girl who had been found, Valerie Hammond, who had lain surrounded with flowers like a fairy princess. Liz presumed it was because it was not considered a cold case. It had officially been solved with the arrest of the mentally challenged man. Still, she had enough to start with Rosemary and Gloria.

She checked out the A-to-Z street directory and found Tapp Street in Whitechapel, following up with the Tube map on how to get there. Then she headed out again. The journey was not as complicated as she had feared. The District line to Earl's Court, then change to the District line going east to Whitechapel. She came out on to a wide high street, bustling with various kinds of commerce. Buses and delivery vans moved past while the pavements were crowded with pedestrians. Old brick buildings stood next to new steel and glass, showing where the bomb damage had been.

She followed the A-to-Z through grimy backstreets of identical Victorian terraces until she came to Tapp Street. Then she stopped. Instead of the house she was expecting to find, there were several new blocks of concrete flats. Of course, she should have realized that the area had been badly bombed. But there was still a pub on the corner. The White Hart.

"We're about to close, love," the man behind the bar said as Liz stepped into the gloom of the interior. The place smelled of smoke and beer. Not too appetizing. The place was empty except for two old men nursing the last of their beers at a corner table.

"I don't want a drink," she said. "I just wanted to ask a question. I'm trying to find someone who used to live around here. I thought maybe you might know."

"When was that, love?"

"During the war. In 1941."

He had to chuckle then. "I was only a nipper at the time. And then I got evacuated. I had a smashing time down in Kent. Lots of good food. I didn't want to come home, I can tell you."

Liz approached the bar. "I'm writing a story about little Rosie Binks. Did you ever know her?"

"Rosie Binks? The one who went missing? Yeah. We went to the same primary school, but I never really knew her. She wasn't in my class. And she disappeared a good while before I was evacuated. Poor little kid."

"You don't happen to know where I'd find her parents now, do you? I can see that their house was bombed. Are they in one of the new flats?"

He frowned. "I don't know, love. I don't recall a Binks coming in here for a drink since I've been working here. My old dad might know, but he's moved in with my sister now, out in Gravesend." He pointed at the table of old men. "Ask old Will here, he's been in every day since God knows when. Hey, Will. Got a young lady here, looking for Binks. Any ideas?"

The old man lifted his head slowly and focused on Liz. "Binks?" he said. "You mean Albert Binks? Him what used to work down the meat market? The one who lost the kid?"

"That's right." Liz went over to him. "Do you know where I'd find them these days?"

"They moved away, didn't they, Charlie?" He turned to his neighbour. "Years ago. He was called up and went out to Africa, didn't he? That whole street was bombed, and I believe she went to live with her sister or someone. And I did hear that after the war they moved out to one of them new tower blocks. Lewisham, was it?"

"Could be," Charlie said unhelpfully.

"Yeah, I think it might have been Lewisham." He shook his head. "I couldn't tell you more than that. He ain't been back in these parts, that's for sure."

Liz thanked them.

"Aren't you going to buy us a drink for our trouble?" Will asked.

"It's closing time and you bloody well know it," the barman said. "Go on. Drink up and go home. Give your missus the thrill of your company."

"That will be the day!" The old man gave a wheezing laugh, but he drained his glass and got up. "Come on, Charlie. The mean bastard is kicking us out."

Liz went back over to the bar. "The other person I'm checking on is Kane? Mrs Kane, had a daughter Gloria."

His face changed instantly. "Gloria Kane? Oh, I remember her, all right. She was in my class and was supposed to be evacuated with us. The police asked us questions, but I don't think any of us recalled seeing her on the train. She was a funny little kid. Afraid of her own shadow. Now I think about it, I don't think she was well cared for, you know. She always looked a bit scruffy. And she fell down a lot. She always seemed to have bruises."

"Do you remember her mum?"

"Oh yeah." He grinned. "Dottie Kane. Who could forget her? Always dolled up like a dog's dinner. She comes in here sometimes, although I think the Blind Beggar pub down the street is her local. Mutton dressed as lamb, if you know what I mean." He gave her a knowing grin. "And I'll tell you something—when she comes in here, it's not usually on her own. And not with the same bloke either."

"What about Mr Kane?"

He chuckled. "I think she kicked him out years ago."

"So she'd likely still be living in the same house?"

"Probably. People around here don't move unless they have to."

Liz left the pub and stood breathing in the outside air, as smoky as the atmosphere had been inside the bar. Although officially coal fires were now banned, the law hadn't really taken effect and a pall hung over the East End. Why would someone choose to live here when they didn't have to? she wondered. Because it was what they were used to. Most people were scared of change. She remembered her mother not wanting to move to London when her father left the army, only doing

181

it because her daughter's schooling came first. But she had never really settled in or made friends in Hampstead. Her husband and daughter had become her whole life.

Liz sighed and set off for Romford Street, where she hoped to find Mrs Kane. There were no new buildings on this street, just the same grimy row of houses, all identical, all opening straight on to the pavement. The first attempts at gentrification had been made to some of the houses: brightly painted front doors, new bay windows, and a new Ford Consul parked outside. But not at Number 31. Dottie Kane's address. Grey lace curtains hung in the windows, and the front step had not been scrubbed like its neighbour's. Liz rang the doorbell, thinking it probable that Mrs Kane worked during the day and she was wasting her time.

But then, miraculously, the door opened and the woman stood there. Liz saw immediately what the publican had meant by mutton dressed as lamb. She had plucked eyebrows and thin red lips. Her hair had been dyed a brassy blonde, and she was wearing curlers. She had a cigarette stuck in one corner of her mouth.

"What do you want?" she asked, removing the cigarette.

"Mrs Kane?"

The woman frowned. "Used to be Kane once. Now it's Martinelli. Kane's been out of the picture for donkey's years now."

"I'm a writer," Liz said, "and I'm doing a piece on three missing girls back in the war. Do you have a minute to talk about your Gloria?"

Liz thought she saw a wariness come over the woman's face. "What sort of piece? Who do you work for?"

"A newspaper," Liz said. "I'm looking into the girls who vanished years ago, because the public is interested in a newly missing girl, Little Lucy. Might I come in?"

"I suppose so," she said. "Can't do any harm. But you didn't bring a photographer, did you? I look like shit today. Don't want me picture took."

"No photographer," Liz said. She followed the woman into the hall. The house smelled strongly of cigarette smoke. They passed two closed doors until they came to a kitchen.

"Right, let's get on with it," Mrs Martinelli said. "I have to be out of here in a little while, and I need to do my hair first."

Liz sat at the table. The kitchen reeked of frying and looked out on to a dismal little backyard. Whereas someone had made an effort with the houses on either side to spruce up their tiny back gardens with lawns, trellises and vegetable patches, this one was concreted over apart from a rockery at the back, decorated with several garden gnomes painted in garish colours.

"They look cheerful," Liz said.

"Oh yes. I love my gnomes." Mrs Martinelli perched on a stool across from Liz. "Always had my gnomes. Mr Martinelli wanted to get rid of them when he first moved in here. He wanted a veggie patch like the neighbours. I told him over my dead body."

"Do they remind you of Gloria?" Liz asked gently. "I bet she liked them?"

"My Gloria?" Mrs Martinelli shook her head. "She was half afraid of them. Someone told her once that they come alive at night, and after that she wouldn't go near them. She was such a timid little thing." She put a hand up to her mouth. "Poor little kid. Now you've brought it all back. What did you have to come here for?" She dabbed at her eyes, although Liz didn't notice tears.

"I'm sorry," Liz said. "Anything you can tell me about what happened to her?"

"She disappeared. That's what happened," the woman said bluntly. "I took her to the station, and then I had to be off to work, so I left her with the other kids, and then nothing. I didn't think much about it to start with because I thought she was probably having a smashing time in the country and she'd forgot to write home. But then I met that Mrs Binks at a working men's club dance, and she told me about her Rosie. So I started to wonder. She said I should go to the police, and I did, but they didn't do nothing, did they? They never found her." She gave a rattling cough, then leaned closer to Liz. "You know what I think? I think it was some soldier what took her. It was wartime, wasn't it? Everyone was moving around, all the men were in uniform, coming and going. No one would think twice about some man taking a little kid. And she was such a trusting little thing, she'd go with anyone if he promised her a sweetie or an ice cream. The poor little sod is probably buried now in some wood or field."

Liz noted the detached manner in which she said this. Almost as if she was describing something she'd seen in a film.

"What about Mr Kane?" Liz asked. "How did he take his child's disappearance?"

"He was off somewhere with the army. North Africa, I think. He didn't know about it until much later. Then he was upset all right. He said, 'If I find the bloke what did this to my girl, I'll kill him.'" She paused, thinking. "That was the one time I ever saw him display any kind of passion. Normally the most boring of men you'd ever have met. I should never have married him, but I was in the family way, so I didn't have much choice in those days."

"And Mr Martinelli? When did you meet him?"

"Him? Oh, he's only been around for a couple of years, ducks. Before him it was Mr Oakley. And before him Mr Dunbar. He was nice, but he had a weak heart. Dropped down dead one day. And Mr Oakley, he took to drink. But I reckon this one will be all right. He's got Italian ancestors so at least he's got a bit of passion in him. I like that."

"Let's get back to Gloria," Liz said. "Which train did she go on?"

"Train? How would I know?" She sounded impatient now. "I took her to the station. I left her with the other kids, and that's the last I saw or heard of her. I gather the cops asked other kids if they'd seen her, but none of them remembered her. Well, they probably wouldn't. She was such a shy, scared little thing, she probably tucked herself away in some corner on the train."

"And nobody remembers her getting off? None of the local volunteers remember her?"

"They didn't seem to." She shrugged. "Beats me. I don't suppose we'll ever know now." She glanced up at the clock on the mantelpiece. "I've got to run, love. I need to get these curlers out of my hair before I meet a friend."

From the way she said it, Liz suspected the friend was male.

She got up. "Well, thank you for your time, Mrs Martinelli. I'm really sorry about your daughter. It must be terrible, not knowing."

"Yeah. Terrible, that it is," she said. "All these years. Having nightmares about it. Poor little kid."

"You aren't still friends with Mrs Binks, are you?" The thought occurred to her as she walked down the hall towards the front door. "Rosie Binks's mum?"

"Haven't seen her in years," Mrs Martinelli said. "And we were never real friends, like. Bumped into each other occasionally. But that street got flattened in the Blitz. I heard they'd gone to one of them big new council blocks, out in New Cross, was it? Or Lewisham? Somewhere out there. All right for some. I said to my hubby, 'Too bad we didn't get bombed. The council would have given us a nice new flat.'" She glanced out of the window. "But then I wouldn't have wanted to leave my gnomes."

Liz came away with a sick feeling in her stomach. She suspected that Mrs Martinelli had not shed one tear over Gloria. She seemed more attached to her garden gnomes. They were the reason she didn't want to move away from a sooty little house . . . Liz stopped at the street corner, waiting as a bus went by, considering a dark thought that had come into her head. What if Dottie never took Gloria to the station at all? A child would certainly be an impediment to her very active love life. And the bruises on the little girl . . .

CHAPTER 22

It was the beginning of rush hour as she approached the Tube station, but she wanted to find Mrs Binks if possible, conscious of time slipping away before she had to make the decision to go back to work or to hand in her notice and find a new job. She studied the Tube map. No Underground service to Lewisham, so she caught the District line back to Charing Cross. Soon she was on a proper train heading to the southern suburbs. The train was already crowded, and more people got on at Waterloo and London Bridge, but it was only a few stations to Lewisham. Liz was directed to the town hall, where they were not pleased to see her. "We close at five," the girl said, glancing up at the clock that said 4:40.

"This shouldn't take too long. I'm looking for an address on a council estate here. It's my mum's cousin, and she's anxious to reconnect with her." She tried not to sound posh. "A Mrs Binks. Ada Binks. Or it could be Mrs and Mr Binks."

The girl shrugged. "I suppose I can see what I can do. I can't promise anything."

"My mum would be ever so grateful. She hasn't been well," Liz said, giving a hopeful smile.

The woman went away. Liz waited, watching comings and goings. A clock somewhere outside was actually chiming five when the girl returned. "I did find this," she said. "Binks. Albert. Would that be him?"

"I think it was Cousin Albert, yes."

"Here's the address, then. Bankside Avenue."

Liz took the piece of paper, thanked the girl profusely and hurried out. Crowds were streaming from office buildings and lining up at bus stops. Liz stopped to ask a policeman for directions and walked against the stream of people until she came to the address she had been given. It was a starkly modern concrete building with balconies running along the front. Liz didn't think it represented a much better way of life than the area she had just left. The lift was out of order, and she climbed four flights of stairs in a concrete stairwell that stank of urine and smoke. She was glad to come out on to the balcony. A couple of front doors were open. Radio music blared from one and from the other the smell of fish frying.

At last she came to the door she hoped belonged to the Binkses. The sound of TV news was coming from within. This was abruptly turned off and the door was opened.

"Yes?" The woman looked older than her years, with grey hair and a lined face with sharp cockney features. She eyed Liz suspiciously. "We're not buying nothing."

"I'm not selling anything," Liz said. "Are you Mrs Binks?"

"What of it?" Again the cockney suspicion of the outsider was evident.

"I'm Liz Houghton. I'm with a newspaper," Liz said "And we're doing a story about three little girls who vanished during World War II—you know, before Little Lucy. And I was told about your Rosie."

"Oh really?" The expression softened. "You'd better come in, then. You're lucky you caught me home. I only just got back from my daughter's. I babysit her nipper."

"Your daughter? Then your Rosie was found again?"

"Oh no, love. We had another kid when my hubby came home from the war. This is our Brenda's little boy I look after while she works. Kevin." She pointed to a photograph on the mantelpiece. "He's a lovely little chap. All smiles. It makes life worthwhile to be with him." And her face looked younger again as she smiled at the thought. "Well, take a load off your feet," she went on, indicating a chintz-covered armchair. "Now, what was it you wanted to know?"

"Everything you remember about Rosie and how she went missing."

Mrs Binks shrugged. "I remember like it was yesterday. We got the letter from the school saying the kids had the chance to be evacuated. I didn't want her to go, but then I thought I'd never forgive myself if she got killed by a bomb. So, I packed her little case. She insisted on carrying her stuffed dog, Bow-Wow. She loved him. Took him everywhere. We put the label around her neck with her name and all that. And her gas mask. She had to carry that gas mask at all times. That was the rule in them days. She was right loaded up, poor little kid. But she seemed cheerful enough when we got to the station and saw other kids she knew. Then they got on the train. They didn't let us parents past the barrier. But I waved and off she went." She stopped abruptly and stared out past Liz. "And that was the last I saw of her."

"The police looked for her, didn't they?"

Mrs Binks nodded. "They said they did. It was wartime, you know. The police force had better things to do than look for a little kiddie. But they checked along the line, and it seemed funny to me that nobody had seen her. You know they took kids off the train at every stop—and those were the days when every little place had its own railway station. People came and took kids home with them."

"Just like that?" Liz asked. "No sort of official list at each place?"

"Well," Mrs Binks said slowly, "there was always some volunteer ladies, and they kept tabs on who went where. The police said they questioned them all. But there was no mention of my Rosie on any of the lists. It was like she just vanished into thin air."

"You knew which train she had taken," Liz said. "Did you think of going to look for yourself when the police didn't find anything?"

A look of absolute horror came over her face. "What, me? Go down to the country, like?" She shook her head. "Oh no, dear. In those days I'd never been out of the Smoke, or at least only twice on a work outing to Southend in a coach. I wouldn't have known where to start." She sighed. "And it was wartime, wasn't it? You didn't travel around." She gave a sad smile. "These days it's different, isn't it? I thought coming out to Lewisham was going to the ends of the earth when we moved here, but then recently my daughter and her hubby have taken us on holiday to Devon. Lovely down there, isn't it? Have you been?"

"I have," Liz said. "It is lovely."

"So green, and the people are nice and friendly. I said to the hubby, 'I wouldn't mind moving down here when I don't have to look after little Kevin any more.'" She chuckled. "He thought that was daft."

"So no trace was ever found of Rosie?" Liz brought her back to the subject. "The other kids don't remember seeing her get off the train? Might it have been possible that she fell asleep on the train and didn't wake up until it arrived at the train yard and . . . someone found her?"

The hurt returned to Mrs Binks's face. "That's my thought. Some railway worker or tramp found her and took her. I console myself that she's now a bright little angel, looking down on me." She squeezed her eyes shut, as if this could shut out the pain.

The front door was not properly closed, and the sounds of the blaring radio down the hall wafted into the room. Suddenly Mrs Binks stiffened. "Listen," she said. A sweet expression came over her face. Liz recognized the song as Vera Lynn singing "There'll Be Bluebirds over the White Cliffs of Dover." A song that had been so popular in the war and was still often requested on the radio for nostalgia reasons.

"My little Rosie loved that song," she said. "And you know what she said to me?" She started to laugh. "She asked if we could have a bluebird sofa like the one in the song. She didn't understand the words properly, you see. Bluebird sofa. Bless her." She wiped a tear from her cheek. "She had the greatest imagination, Rosie did. So creative. Always dancing, making up songs, dressing up, drawing, painting. Oh, she loved pretending. 'I'm a fairy, Mum,' she'd say. 'I'm going to wave my magic wand and make the war stop.'" Her whole body shook with a big sigh. "Not at all like my other girl. Brenda is all no-nonsense and let's get on with it. She's doing really well in her career. Only twenty-two and she's already been promoted at her bank."

"I'm really glad you have her and your grandson, Mrs Binks," Liz said. "Is there anything else you can tell me?"

The woman thought. "Not really, love. She was a lovely little kid, my Rosie. You'll make sure your article says that, won't you?"

"Oh, I will," Liz said. "I promise. And I'll try to find out more for you if there's any way to do so. You need closure, don't you?"

The woman nodded. "I need to know what happened. Even if it's the very worst thing, I'd rather know. Then I can be at peace."

The song ended. Mrs Binks sat staring out of the window with a gentle smile still on her face. "A bluebird sofa. Bless her."

CHAPTER 23

Liz arrived home feeling tired and dishevelled. The Underground had been packed, and it had started to rain when she came out of the Parsons Green Station. There was no evidence that Marisa had been home—no kicked-off shoes or half-drunk cup of tea. The flat seemed cold and empty, and she turned on the gas fire before putting on the kettle. Wondering what there might be for supper, she opened the fridge and then the pantry. Nothing much there, but she was loath to go out again and spend money on takeaway, so she settled on her old staple, tomato soup and grilled cheese. She'd have liked a glass of wine, but she knew they'd drunk the last bottle the week before.

She turned on the telly, for the last of the six o'clock news. A police spokesman was giving updates on Little Lucy. "We are doing everything within our power to find this child and bring her safely home," he said. "We have mobilized every unit at our disposal. We have even sent a team over to France, as the child was born there. And we thank the public for continuing to send in tips. We are continuing to display her picture outside every police station, so if you see a child who resembles her, don't hesitate to telephone us."

"You have reason to believe the child is still alive, then?" a reporter's voice asked.

"We must always hope for the best until proven wrong," the police spokesman said. The camera cut away, and Liz spotted Marisa standing in the background. She felt a strange sense of pride that this was her friend and she was doing something positive. "If only . . . ," she muttered to herself, not sure what that meant. If only she could help to find Lucy? Or find out what happened to Rosie? Gloria? She still couldn't work out what had happened to herself in Tydeham. She paused, wondering if it might help if she saw a psychiatrist. Or maybe a psychic. She wanted someone to tell her that it was possible, that the dead had communicated with her, that she had channelled someone else's life. Because she had a nagging fear that she might be going mad.

She went over to her typewriter and back to her story. Three little girls, at exactly the same time of year, only one of them found . . . and went on to describe Rosie Binks, Gloria Kane and what she knew of Valerie Hammond. Was it possible that a serial killer had reawakened? Been released from prison or a mental hospital, or returned from Australia? Why weren't the police looking into this pattern? She finished the article and nodded with satisfaction. It was good. She'd take it to the paper in the morning.

~

Marisa arrived home close to ten o'clock.

"What a day," she said, flinging herself down on the sofa and kicking off her shoes. For once she was not wearing the new boots, but almost looked as if she could be in uniform again. Pleated skirt. Plain black tights and black lace-ups.

"You must be starving," Liz said. "There's not much in the fridge, but I could make you some grilled cheese."

"Oh, no thanks. The super took us to the pub, so I've had a meat pie and a pint. Not my favourites, but it was good. It sort of energized us all and reminded us to keep on going, even though it's now almost two weeks." She sat up again. "Hey, guess what? We interviewed the grandparents today. Susan Fareham's parents, I mean. They are quite posh, like you. They live in a big house in Chislehurst in Kent. Lovely place. Right on the common. I was sent with a female DI."

"Why her parents? Do they suspect she might have something to do with the disappearance of her own child?"

"No, not that. They want insights into background, including anyone who might possibly have a grudge. The latest theory is that she must have gone willingly with someone she knew. Otherwise, she would have cried out, or at least there would have been some kind of scuffle."

"But how could anyone have got her out of the park without the au pair seeing?"

"It has been suggested that she was small enough to have squeezed between the bars if someone had lured her from outside. But it would have been that she had wanted to go with the person."

"So family or friend, right?"

"Right." She paused, thinking. "One thing that's a bit weird is that Susan Fareham doesn't seem to have any friends. Not close friends in London, anyway. All the friends she mentioned to us are friends of them as a couple. More his friends. Influential people."

"It's not that strange," Liz said. "You can lose touch with single friends when you're home with a little child."

"But she has a nanny, for Pete's sake. She can come and go as she wants. And plenty of money." She wagged a finger at Liz. "And you know what else was strange? The parents seemed ill at ease with us. The wife was quite jumpy, I'd have said. She kept saying what a lovely mum her daughter was and how she adored little Lucy, but all the time her fingers were fiddling with her skirt and she kept glancing at her husband to see if she was saying the right thing."

"Gosh," Liz said. "Do you think they could possibly have something to do with it? That they know something?"

"I think they might know something," Marisa said.

"So where do you go from here?"

"I go where I'm told," Marisa said. "But I think we should dig into Susan's background some more. Former boyfriends. We don't know much except she went to study in France and met her husband there.

We have a team out there, lucky ducks, so maybe we'll learn more. But what about before she went to France?"

"How old was she?"

"They said she was nineteen."

"Pretty soon after she left school. Did she stay on to do A levels?"

"I think so."

"Where did she go to school again?"

"Farringtons. A boarding school near her home. She was a day girl there."

Liz came over and perched on the arm of the chair. "So why don't you go down there and find out who her friends were? She must have had friends in those days."

"I'd like to, but I don't think it's in the plan. Oh, and by the way, I expounded my theory to the super, about tying this case to the missing girls all those years ago. I don't think he was very impressed, so if I can find the time, I'm going to do some more digging myself, to see if there's an obvious case where a convict has just been released. Did you go through those pages I copied for you? At great personal risk, I might add."

"I did. And what's more, I've interviewed the two mothers of the missing girls. Very interesting. Complete opposites. Rosemary Binks's mother still grieves for her and spoke about what a wonderful child she was. But Gloria Kane's displayed no emotion whatsoever. I got the feeling she couldn't have cared less. I was told by a neighbour that there may have been a history of child abuse." She paused, collecting her thoughts before continuing. "The strangest thought came to me after I was there. I read in the notes that Gloria Kane was the only girl who didn't have a shelter erected in her backyard. It's all concreted over except a rockery with gnomes sitting on it. I began to wonder whether the child never even went to the station. Whether she was buried there, under those rocks. The mother refuses to move. Perhaps she's scared of getting found out."

"Blimey. I wonder how we'd proceed with that one," Marisa said. "There's nothing I could do right now. All our efforts are focused on finding Lucy. But once we've concluded this, and if by any chance we've found any connection . . . well then, we'll have that rockery dug up."

Liz nodded. "There were no notes on the other girl—Valerie. The one they found in the woods and the bloke was put in a mental hospital. So I couldn't tell what similarities there might have been."

"That's right. Her folder was with the ones I gave you, but when I opened it, it was empty. Maybe those notes have been moved somewhere else for a subsequent investigation. I'll have to ask DI Jones, but probably not right now. He's all caught up in this case and he's snapped at me when I've tried to tie it to his lost girls."

"But I thought he was the one who brought up the connection to start with?"

"I know. He was. But now he tells me to focus on the matter at hand and not throw out any wild theories." She reached up to pull the clip off her ponytail, letting that luxuriant black hair cascade over her shoulders. "That's better," she said. "It's been too tight all day. No, Liz, if you want to know, I think this case is really getting to him. He should never have requested to be part of the team. He's upset that we haven't found the child yet, and he's fearing the worst."

"He may not be wrong," Liz said.

"So what do you plan to do now?" Marisa asked.

"Obviously I'd like to trace that train journey to see if anyone had noticed Rosie Binks or had any idea what happened to her. I know the police would have already done that thoroughly, but what if there was someone who was reluctant to speak to the police—someone in the black market, for example? Or some child who was just too shy? I know it's a long shot, but I'd like to give it a try. I promised Mrs Binks I would. She needs closure, Marisa."

"You're taking a train to Somerset?"

"I thought that maybe James could drive me to some of the places when I'm with him at the weekend. Most of the stations are now closed, so I'd have no way of getting to those villages."

"With James, huh?" Marisa gave her a dig. "Getting serious."

"Risa, I hardly know him. He's nice. Friendly. Easy to talk to." Liz felt herself blushing.

"That's what they always say. We're just good friends."

"Well in this case it's true. He hasn't shown any romantic interest in me that I've noticed. And for heaven's sake, we've only seen each other a couple of times. But he'll have his dad's car, so it wouldn't be too far to drive to some of those villages." She shrugged. "He might not want to. His dad might not want to lend him the car. We'll just have to see. If not, I will go on my own." Suddenly she tapped Marisa on the arm. "I've just had a thought. I could go to Chislehurst for you and have a chat with that school. I could say it was a background story for my newspaper. Find out who her friends were and maybe talk to them? If that would help you at all."

Marisa met her friend's gaze, hesitating. "I'm not sure about that, Liz. You know what my governor would think of it. Interfering in a police investigation."

"I wouldn't be interfering if you are not planning to go there yourself. And besides, newspaper reporters are allowed to dig into background stories, aren't they? That's what I'll be doing."

Marisa nodded slowly. "I suppose so. And it might really help. As long as I don't officially know about it, nobody can complain, can they?"

"And it would be filling in a piece of the puzzle."

"It really would." Liz could see Marisa warming to the idea. "And I can't see how you'd be treading on our toes. Okay. I say go for it."

"I will. Tomorrow." Liz beamed. It felt good to be doing something positive.

CHAPTER 24

On Thursday morning Liz set off for Chislehurst and Farringtons School. It was a community on the edge of Greater London, but as soon as she came out of the station, it felt as if it was far removed from city life. From the station she learned she had to take a bus to the other side of the community. She sat on the single-decker, admiring the impressive houses set in their own grounds, and the leafy common, now with a carpet of yellow underfoot from the birch leaves. Two young girls on horseback cantered along the bridle path. The place had a country feel to it, with a pub beside the common and some thatched cottages. It was hard to believe it was only half an hour from Central London. It was stockbroker country, where rich men who worked in the city lived. Alighting from the bus, Liz walked up the driveway to the school. It was an impressive vista of yellow brick buildings surrounded by playing fields. A group of girls in their PE uniforms walked past carrying hockey sticks, chattering noisily.

Inside the main building it was warm and smelled of chalk. She located the office and was shown to the headmistress's study. The woman looked severe and middle-aged, with grey cropped hair. "Oh dear." She seemed flustered. "We have read about it in the papers, of course, but I'm not sure how we could be of any help at all. We have had no contact with Susan since she left us, was it six years ago now? I don't think she was particularly happy at school. Not the best scholar and did not intend to go on to higher education. She was persuaded to take a couple of A levels, but I believe she only passed one of them. So she left and we lost touch. She hasn't ever been back to open days. We did hear that she'd gone to France."

Liz duly made notes in shorthand, then looked up. "Would you happen to know who her friends were? And where we might find any of them?"

The headmistress paused, considering. "She was a day girl, wasn't she? I believe her friends would have been amongst other day girls. The boarders are always very thick together in their own little clique. That's probably why the day girls sometimes feel excluded, although we do our best to make them feel part of our society." She fidgeted with some papers on her desk, straightening them into a neat pile. "Our secretary would have a list of girls in her year, but Miss Jeffries might know better. She's the history mistress, and Susan took A-level history—though not with much success, I fear."

"And where would I find Miss Jeffries?" Liz asked.

"We have mid-morning break at ten thirty. If you go up to the teacher's common room then, you'll be able to catch her."

Liz thanked the headmistress and found her way up the stairs to the common room. She waited outside. Suddenly a bell echoed down the corridors, doors were opened and there was the sound of feet hurrying out of the building. Teachers began to appear, most of them older women with tired and grumpy faces. Liz stopped a more approachable-looking one and asked for Miss Jeffries.

"She should be along in a minute," the woman said. "You can't miss her. She's a big woman, and she wears her hair in a bun. Quite old-fashioned."

Liz waited until the woman who fit that description came along the corridor, in conversation with a small, wiry woman, a complete contrast in every way. Whereas Miss Jeffries was smiling, the other woman looked as if she had a bad smell under her nose. "I wouldn't have put up with it," she was saying as she approached. "What were they thinking?"

Liz stepped out. "Miss Jeffries?" she asked.

"Yes." The woman sized her up.

"I'm from the *Daily Express*, and we're doing a feature story on Susan Fareham's childhood. I'm told you would have known her quite well, and who her friends might have been."

The woman looked startled, then collected herself. "I wouldn't say that I knew her well. She wasn't the type that threw herself into school activities with great fervour. She did not play on any of our sports teams, but she did take part in the plays, now I come to think of it. Not the leads, you know, but small parts."

"Anything you could remember would be helpful." Liz gave her an encouraging smile.

"Would you like to sit somewhere? I can't take you into the common room as outsiders are not welcome there, but there will be an empty classroom along the hall." She set off and Liz followed, and they found themselves in a small classroom. Miss Jeffries pulled out the chair from the teacher's desk and sat, leaving Liz to place herself in one of the student desks.

"Now, what is it you wanted to know about Susan? And why does your newspaper think anything she did at school might be relevant in the disappearance of her daughter?" Her tone was not particularly friendly.

"I suppose we want the public to see her as a person and to feel sympathy," Liz said. It was the first thing that came into her mind. "We'd also like to know if she has made any enemies along the way."

"Goodness!" Miss Jeffries sounded shocked. "You mean to imply that somebody could have taken the child out of spite? In revenge?"

"I know they are looking at all possibilities," Liz said. "My assignment is more background. The mother's story, you know."

"All right. Fire away," Miss Jeffries said.

"I'm told she didn't particularly like school, is that correct?"

"I wouldn't say that." Miss Jeffries frowned. "She was in my advanced-level history course. I'm afraid she wasn't very interested and didn't apply herself well to her studies. She was an only child and, I suspect, rather doted on by her parents. Rather sheltered, too. I don't believe she knew what she wanted from life. Other girls knew they were going to be nurses or teachers or some such, but Susan expected to get married, I think."

"Was she interested in boys, then?"

Miss Jeffries had to smile at this. "My dear, there is not much opportunity to meet boys when you attend a school like this."

"So you don't know what she did when she left school?"

"She went her own way, that's all I can say. She never returned for Founder's Day as some of the girls do."

"What about her friends? Did she have particular friends, do you remember?"

Miss Jeffries frowned. "The day girls kept to themselves. So it would have been Molly Hartley, and what was the other girl? Trisha Brown. That's it. I remember seeing those three going around together. They all lived locally, so I imagine they did things together out of school hours."

Liz shifted on her hard chair, banging her knee against the desk. Why did schools make chairs and desks that were so uncomfortable? "You wouldn't happen to know where I could find any of these young women now?"

Miss Jeffries thought about this. "Well, their families probably still live in the area, so they will know how to contact their daughters."

"Yes, of course. Good idea." Liz gave an encouraging smile. "The school secretary will probably have their addresses on file, won't she?"

"Bound to. We never let alumnae slip through our fingers. They will be hounded all their lives for fundraising purposes." And she, too, smiled.

"I should let you get to your coffee before the break is over." Liz stood up.

"I don't mind about the coffee, but I'm dying for a cigarette," Miss Jeffries said. "I wish you good luck with your article. I wonder if anything you find will have relevance to Lucy's disappearance? I can't see how. I'm afraid it was a deranged individual, and the poor mite is long dead."

Back in the office, the secretary was dealing with a little girl who had lost her bus pass to go home. She handled this with great patience, then when the child went off, she turned to Liz. "Was the headmistress able to help you?"

"She was. But now I'd like to know about Susan's friends when she was here. You have the list of alumnae, don't you? I'm looking for a Molly Hartley and Trisha Brown."

"Oh, I remember Trisha," the woman said, nodding with approval. "Such a nice girl. A born leader. She went on to university, you know. Exeter. I believe the woman you are writing about was a devoted follower at school." She opened a filing cabinet and extracted a file of names and addresses. "Her parents live not far from the station. I'll write down the address. And the other girl? Molly Hartley? I believe I heard she got married. But I also have her parents' address." She printed it neatly on an index card, then handed it to Liz.

"Do you remember Susan yourself?" she asked, thanking the woman.

"Vaguely. She wasn't the type of girl who stood out, you know. She was polite, went around in that group with Trisha and then vanished."

Liz came away not feeling too hopeful about finding any useful information. Susan seemed to have been one of those girls who go to school because they have to and only want to get out as quickly as possible. There had been several like that at Liz's own school, most of them with one aim in life: to snag a rich husband. Susan had certainly done this now. But being an uninspired student somehow didn't translate to a girl who went off to France a year later. As someone who was coddled by her parents, that would have taken bravery and imagination. Had Susan hidden her true personality while she was at school? Liz hoped one of Susan's friends might know.

She caught the bus back to the station and then found Trisha Brown's parents' house. It was clearly a moneyed family, and the front door was opened by a maid. Mr and Mrs Brown were not home. They were visiting their daughter, who was now attached to the British embassy to Cairo. Did she wish to leave a message? Liz came away feeling not too hopeful about finding the second friend. She located the house easily enough. Chislehurst was not a big place. It was in a street of older detached homes. Not as prosperous as Trisha Brown's parents', but certainly of good quality. The gardens were immaculate, and there was a Jaguar parked in the driveway. This was a hopeful sign that the house was inhabited. She rang the doorbell. It was opened by a young woman in the process of wiping her front with a tea towel.

"Oh my goodness. Do I have baby food down my front?" she asked, giving Liz a grin. "Trying to feed a one-year-old solid food is no joke, I can tell you." She lowered the tea towel. "Now what can I do for you? I'm afraid my mother is not at home."

"Are you Molly Hartley?" Liz asked.

"Used to be. Now I'm Molly Jacobs. Married with two kids for my sins." She laughed.

"I know you're super busy, but I wondered if I could have a quick word about Susan Fareham. I'm from the *Daily Express*, and I'm writing a background piece on the family."

"Gosh. I know all about it, of course. That poor girl. I can't imagine what it would be like. I look at my two precious darlings, and I simply can't think what I'd do if that happened to me. I'd go to pieces." She must have realized that she was babbling on because she said, "Do you want to come in? It will have to be in the kitchen, and you may get hit by a flying food dish, but if you dare risk it . . ."

"All right." Liz laughed and followed Molly through the house to a spacious kitchen at the back. A sturdy baby sat in a high chair with bits of mashed carrot on his nose and in his hair.

"You see what it's like," Molly said. "Do you have children?"

"No, I'm not married."

"It's not exactly easy," Molly said. "The older one is taking his nap, and if I could just get this one to eat some carrots, I could put him down, too, and have five minutes of bliss." She wiped off the child as she spoke. "We're staying with my parents. Our boiler broke at the flat, so we had to come here. Now what would you like to know about Susan?"

"You two were school friends, I gather?"

"Oh yes. We were great friends at school. And with Trisha Brown, too. She's done awfully well for herself, you know. She's on the way to becoming an ambassador. We always knew she was bright. Sometimes I think I should have gone to university and done something special. But here I am, and I do like it most of the time."

She now addressed the baby. "See this lady? She's from a newspaper. So if you don't eat your food properly, your picture will be in the paper and everyone in the country will know that you've been a bad boy."

The baby stared at Liz, wide eyed. When the spoon came towards his mouth, he opened it like a baby bird, never taking his eyes off Liz for a second.

"That worked," Molly said, looking pleased. "Now about Susan."

"Did you stay friends with her when you left school?"

"To start with, yes. But I was at secretarial college, working jolly hard, and she . . . she didn't quite know what she wanted to do with her life. She thought she might be an actress. She is pretty, after all. But she sent for the admissions test for RADA, and when it came she showed it to me. 'Look at this,' she said. 'I have to memorize all these Shakespeare scenes. I can never do that. I never had a clue what anyone was saying.'" She fed the child another spoonful. "Of course her parents were only too happy to have her at home. They made such a fuss of her."

She broke off to wipe carrot from the baby's chin. "Then she got into singing at folk clubs. I think she loved performing, and this was an easy way. It made me laugh the way she sang all these protest songs as if she meant them, all about suffering and drugs and war, when she was actually living this life at a big house with Mummy and Daddy to spoon-feed her. But she met this bloke who got her interested in the protest marches, Ban the Bomb, you know. She started going to them, and suddenly it was full-fledged sit-ins, and love-ins and ban this and students rule. She started dressing like them, and next thing you know, she had moved into a squat with them in an abandoned building in Notting Hill. Her parents were beside themselves, but she wouldn't listen to reason."

"You're done." She picked up the child and held him on her hip. "They sent me to talk reason to her," she went on. "It was the most ghastly place you can imagine. Damp, mould on the ceiling. No furniture apart from mattresses on the floor, everyone was smoking pot, half of them were high on drugs, or apparently taking a trip on LSD. And it was clearly free love, if you know what I mean. Share and share alike, I got the feeling. I was most uncomfortable, and when the chap Susan liked suggested I join them for a threesome, I fled. I begged her to come with me. I told her she was making a mistake, but she told me to mind my own business and get out of her life. So I did."

The baby squirmed and whined. Molly picked up a pacifier and shoved it into his mouth. "I never saw her again, but I heard through the grapevine that she'd gone off to France, married and had a baby. All quite a shock. I wondered if the father was the bloke she had been keen on in Notting Hill. It didn't seem like her. So imagine my surprise when I saw her on the telly and she's married to some bigwig in the city, with her daughter missing. I felt I should go and see if there was anything I could do to help, but then I couldn't do it. I wouldn't have known what to say." The baby was making loud sucking noises. "Do you have any updated information that we don't have on Lucy?"

"Not really," Liz said.

"It's all rather hopeless now, isn't it?" Molly said, shifting the baby on her hip as he squirmed. "What I can't understand is why nobody saw anything. A square in the middle of London, for God's sake. There must always be deliveries, taxies driving past, or someone just glancing out of a window. Someone must have noticed a little girl being carried off."

Liz nodded. "I suppose the kidnapper seized the one lucky moment."

"Do you know Ladbroke Square? Is it always quiet? No bus route?"

"I don't know it," Liz said. "But I think I'll go and check on it myself tomorrow." She corrected herself. "I'm not involved in the actual crime investigation. I'm just a background person. But you never know. Sometimes background can be helpful. Thank you for your time."

"Glad to help," Molly said. "And I'm afraid my time is now up. Patrick here will start a full-blown tantrum if I don't clean him up and put him to bed."

She escorted Liz to the front door and waved as Liz walked down the front path. *Such a nice woman,* Liz thought. *If I had been Susan, I'd have wanted her as a friend.* And then she thought, *She's younger than me. Already settled with a family. And my life is just passing me by.*

CHAPTER 25

Liz arrived back in London in time to grab a late sandwich at the deli counter in Waitrose and bring it back to her digs. As she ate it, she consulted the A-to-Z and found that Ladbroke Square was not in Mayfair or Belgravia, as she had suspected, but was on the border of Kensington and Notting Hill. *Interesting,* she thought. Not too far from Susan's old haunts. But Notting Hill? That surprised her. She knew it as an iffy area of racial tensions with the West Indian immigrant community, and slum landlords—not the sort of place where a prospective member of Parliament's daughter was kidnapped from a garden. She set out again, taking the Circle line to Notting Hill Gate Station. She walked up Kensington Park Road, again surprised at what she saw. It was an area of prosperous white-fronted Victorian houses, each with its covered front porch. More like Kensington or even Belgravia than her impression of Notting Hill.

Ladbroke Square was composed of similar homes, fronting an expansive garden full of trees and shrubs. It wasn't hard to work out which house the Farehams lived in. There were two uniformed bobbies standing at the front door. There was a police car across the street by the gardens. Liz crossed the road and walked along the edge of the gardens. She noticed that the one gate still had police tape across it. The gardens were still out of bounds. They would have been anyway, she realized. There was a discreet sign reading "PRIVATE GARDEN. RESIDENTS ONLY." And there was a lock on the gate.

That made everything more complicated. Unless the au pair had left the gate open, a stranger could not have entered. No wonder she was at ease enough to have read her Swedish newspaper while the little girl played. Liz stood there, staring up at the house and then back to the gardens. *If only I could have a flash of clairvoyance right now,* she thought.

It was indeed a quiet area. There was a bus route at the far end on busy Ladbroke Grove, but on the square itself there was nobody in sight, although she could hear the hum of traffic on the nearby main roads. In the central gardens some of the bushes grew right up to the railing, poking through it in places. If someone had managed to grab Little Lucy, could they have pulled her through the railing? She stared at it, picturing a small child. It would have been a squeeze. Lucy would have objected, struggled, called out for her nanny. Someone would have heard her. Liz shook her head and walked on. She completed a tour of the park, examining the similar houses on the far side. And was none the wiser. It was as if the child had vanished into thin air.

Suddenly overcome with weariness, she returned to Notting Hill Gate Station and took the train home. *Why am I doing this?* she asked herself. *What do I hope to achieve? The police have experts working on it, and all I've found is that Susan once joined the counter-culture and lived with a group, squatting in an abandoned building not too far from her current address. That could hardly be significant since her husband would have made the decision where to live and might well have been occupying the home before he married her.* At least she could bring it up to Marisa. But the husband would definitely not want that part of his wife's life made public. No wonder her parents were jumpy.

Marisa was late again that evening. Liz stopped to buy a couple of frozen chicken dinners in case Marisa hadn't eaten. She ate her own watching television. The meal was unsatisfying, and she resolved to start cooking again properly, making the sort of comforting and nutritious meals her mother had always made for her. Even an omelette would be preferable to this. Thinking of her mother made her feel nostalgic. Their home had always been warm and welcoming, the meals always delicious, her clothes always washed and ironed for her. So why didn't she want to live there? She knew the answer right away. It wasn't just watching her mother slipping into dementia. She was twenty-seven years old. She enjoyed sharing the flat with Marisa, and she hoped to meet the right man, sooner than later. Besides, home had always felt a little like living in a lovely cage, or rather living in cotton wool, protected and safely tucked away from the big bad world.

Marisa arrived home about eight thirty. "Another pub get-together after work," she said. "I'll get fat if I have to have all this beer and chips." She took a seat beside Liz on the sofa. "So how did your day go? Did you visit her school and her friends?"

"I did." Liz recounted everything in detail.

Marisa listened intently. "Well, that's a turn-up for the books, isn't it?" she said. "All the time we've been portraying her as this upper-class girl who lived a perfect life, married in the South of France and now married to a golden boy. No wonder she wanted to keep the part about squatting in Notting Hill a secret. Very bad for his image if he's running for Parliament."

"I also went to Ladbroke Square," Liz said. "One thing that's interesting is that it's a private garden. You can only get in if you have the key."

"I noticed that," Marisa said. "That makes it hard to understand, doesn't it? Someone else had a key, noticed the au pair engrossed in her paper, took the child and walked out again. But I believe all the other residents of the square have been questioned with no red flags."

"Could a former resident have kept a key?"

Marisa shrugged. "Possible, I suppose. Or had a duplicate made on the quiet. But some of the houses have been turned into flats. So think how many people come and go." She sighed. "It's hopeless, Liz. I rather feel we're wasting our time, and we won't know anything until someone digs up her body, poor little kid."

"You have people looking into her past life in France," Liz said. "I suppose there is no point in looking into her hippie friends?"

"I don't think hippies are the sort who go around kidnapping children," Marisa said with a touch of scorn in her voice. "They are all for love and peace, aren't they? And I'm sure they make enough babies of their own without needing to kidnap one." She kicked off her shoes. "This new schedule is ruining my love life. I saw my new chap briefly in the hallway this morning, and he asked me out, and I had to tell him that I've no idea when I'll get off work these days. I hope he understood and doesn't think that I'm not interested."

"He works for the Met, doesn't he? He knows you're on a big assignment?" Liz said.

Marisa nodded. "I'm still planning to look into the released convict theory, although DI Jones said it's rubbish. But then anything a woman did would be rubbish to him. If I caught the kidnapper and brought Little Lucy back safely, he'd probably say that the bloke turned himself in and handed me the child. What a pillock. He's a pretty sorry excuse for a human being, isn't he? Nearing retirement, no wife, doesn't seem to have friends." She lay back on the sofa, stretching out her legs. "So, when do you have to go back to work? Or have you decided to leave?"

"I told the woman from personnel that I was taking sick days. She said I'd need a doctor's certificate when I come back. So . . . either I find one or I'll find myself out on my ear."

Marisa studied her for a moment. "Is it worth it, Liz? I mean, what are you actually achieving?"

"I'm asking myself the same thing," Liz said. "I could have found out that one of those missing girls from long ago was killed by her own mother, or by the mother's boyfriend, more likely, and buried in their back garden. I can't prove that. Just a hunch. I still haven't heard if the Weymouth police have identified the body, nor do I have any explanation about how I could have seen the burial. But I am going down there with James this weekend. Maybe I'll have another unexplained vision and all will be clear."

"That would be good," Marisa said. "At least I hope it would be good."

"It would stop me from worrying that I'm going bonkers. Do you know, Risa—I'm thinking of going to a shrink, just to make sure I'm not cracking up."

"Don't be silly. There's nothing wrong with you except you've been through a stressful time recently. And you're seeing James this weekend . . . that should cheer you up. Bring him back here. I'm dying to meet him."

Liz twisted a stray lock of hair. "I don't think we're at that level yet. Although we are staying at his father's house, so I suppose . . ."

"If you like him, let him know," Marisa said forcefully. "Don't let him get away like you did Edmond."

Liz frowned. "I didn't mean to let Edmond get away. He was excited about his dream job, and I wanted that for him. I assumed he'd ask me to come out to Australia when he was settled. He pretty much said that. But I suppose he might have met someone on the ship going over there. Who knows?"

"So what are you doing tomorrow?" Marisa asked. "Or are you spending the day deciding what to wear for James?"

"As to that, it will be jeans and an old sweater if we are rummaging through the rubble of his house." She paused. "But I might take a nice dress, just in case we go out in the evening." And she smiled. "And tomorrow. I'm not sure. I want to finish an article I'm writing."

"An article. On Tydeham? I thought you already turned in something like that."

"No, this is more exciting."

"Did your abandoned village article mention the body?" Marisa looked interested.

"No. I couldn't bring myself to mention it. Not until we know who it was. Just in case."

"In case what?"

"James's mother killed herself, Risa. She was a bit unstable, I think. And there was a governess who was there but left suddenly with no explanation. I'm trying not to put two and two together, although I suspect James and his father have had the same sort of thoughts."

"Again your vivid imagination is probably reading too much into things," Marisa said. "But you're right. I should probably steer clear until we know more."

"Good idea. I'm sure we'll check in with the police when we're at the house this weekend," Liz said. "Just to see if there have been any developments. I thought I might ask James to drive me to some of the former stops on the train down to Somerset on Sunday if we have time. On the off chance that I can come up with anything on Rosie Binks. I'm going to look for an old timetable. Do you think they have them at the station, or might a library be a better idea?"

"No clue." Marisa shook her head. "A reference librarian should know."

"Right. And where is the nearest library?" Liz grinned. "It's shocking. I haven't been to a library since I moved in here. So much for continuing to educate myself."

"I wonder if they'd have things like that stashed away at your newspaper," Marisa suggested.

"Possibly, but I'm not sure I can go in and then claim I've been ill all week, can I?"

"You said you have to get a doctor's certificate when you go back. How do you plan to do that?"

Liz gave her a knowing grin. "My parents have a private doctor. If I go and tell him I've been off with a sore throat and cough but now it's better, I don't think he'd have any problem writing me a note."

"How the rich live." Marisa got up. "I'm going to change into my pyjamas and watch some telly. There better be something funny on. I need cheering up."

"I think I'll just lie down and read," Liz said. "I haven't touched a book since this whole business started."

"That must be a record for you." Marisa grinned as she leaned forward to turn on the television.

∾

That night Liz had a disturbing dream. She was in a vast house with her father. "There are so many rooms," she said. "I don't know where to look next."

"I'm sure you'll find something hidden in one of them if you keep looking," her father said, "only you might not like what you find."

She woke up, lying in the still-dark room, trying to analyze this dream. The big house could be her father's ancestral home, but it could also be James's house and what she might find there when they went back. But again that dream had been tinged with the sense of dread. She tried to shake it off as she made coffee. Marisa had gone early, leaving the remains of cornflakes in the sink. As Liz cleared up she came to a decision: she would take her story on the missing girls in to the newspaper. Mr Tomlins had given her a few days' grace. She had obviously used these up, but she'd see him, show him the story and see what he thought. Then she'd decide how she felt about coming back to work.

She felt physically sick as she walked up Fleet Street and into the *Express* building. She was heading for the newsroom when she encountered one of the people she least wanted to see: Mr Pettigrew.

"Oh, Miss Houghton. You've returned, I see. Hopefully quite recovered and eager to get back to work. I've an obituary waiting for you—one of the ladies from the Women's Institute who organized making jam from turnips during the war. It was quite a successful enterprise, you'll find. You'll need to go down to Surrey to interview her children and fellow Institute members."

"I don't think I can do that today," Liz said. "I still have an assignment to complete concerning missing girls, and if this newspaper doesn't want it, I'm sure another one will." She started to walk away. "By the way, did you get the obituary I sent in?"

"That silly little piece about some houses that have fallen down?" he asked. "I don't know where you think that belongs in an obituary column."

"I see." Liz turned and walked away, her heels tapping on the linoleum floor.

"Never," she muttered to herself. "Never going back to obits. Never in a million years."

She found she was shaking as she pushed open the door to the newsroom, reacting as she heard the familiar clatter of typewriters and took in the heavy smell of smoke.

"Hey, Liz. I hear you were off sick?" one of the men called to her as she walked past. "Are you okay now?"

"I will be," she said. "Is Mr Tomlins in?"

"Last time I noticed," the man said. "In his cubby."

Liz continued across the room, trying to ignore the interested glances. What's she doing back here? She could read their thoughts. She saw Mr Tomlins on the phone through his glass door and waited until he had put it down before she tapped and entered.

"I've brought you a piece I've written," she said. "On the lost girls from the war. Possible tie-in to Lucy."

"You've managed to establish that, have you?" He was frowning. Not looking too encouraging.

"Maybe," she said. "No real connection, but I think it makes a good story, and it may keep up the interest in trying to find the little girl."

"Very well. Leave it here," he said. "I'll take a look at it. And then you'll be headed back to obits, I presume. Mr Pettigrew was annoyed that you were out."

"I'll be back on Monday," she said. "At the moment I'm on sick leave."

"You don't look very sick to me." There was the ghost of a smile as he said this.

She hurried out of the building before there could be any additional unpleasant encounters. From there she went straight to the Kensington Central Library. It was a big red brick building, not far from Hyde Park, and Liz sought out the reference desk. The severe-looking woman at the desk turned out to be not so haughty, and warmed as soon as Liz said she was doing an article on evacuated children.

"Let's see what we can find, shall we?" she said and scurried off. Not too long after, she returned with a copy of a timetable. "This is from 1944," she said, "but I think we can assume that the routes and times had not changed that much."

Liz carried it away to a nearby table and copied down every possible stop on the slow train to the West Country. There were a lot of them in those days. Every little village had its station. How easy to get around it must have been. Except that there were not many trains. Only that one at two o'clock in the afternoon going to Yeovil and Taunton. Fuel was too precious to waste on civilians, and troops would take the express train routes. As she handed back the book, with many thanks, to the librarian, she had another thought. "My father grew up in a big house in Kent," she said. "His family's ancestral home. It's been demolished now, but how could I find out where it was?"

"Did your father have a title?" the librarian asked.

"Oh, gosh, no." Liz gave an embarrassed smile.

"If the house was important enough, he'd be listed in *Burke's Landed Gentry*," the librarian said. "I'll find you a copy. Hold on."

She came back with an impressively bound tome. "Name?" she said.

"My father was Henry Hurst Houghton."

"And his father's name?"

Liz frowned. "I never met my grandfather. I believe his name was Gerald. Yes, I think that's right."

The woman skimmed through pages. "Ah, here we are," she said at last. "Houghton, Gerald Hurst. Broxley Manor, Farningham, Kent. Having issue: Henry Hurst Houghton, born November 21, 1892. That's him, correct?"

"It is. How clever of you." Liz beamed. "I hadn't heard about this place until recently. There is little point in going to see it, because it's now a housing estate."

The librarian sighed. "So many of the great houses have gone, I'm afraid. Too expensive to keep up, and of course it was impossible to find servants after the war."

Liz came away feeling a sense of purpose. She had all too many stations to visit, but at least she could go to a few with James, if he'd agree. And one day she would go to Farningham in Kent and see where her family's ancestral home used to be. She was impressed that her father had taken it so well, to be turned out of his family home and then to find it so damaged that he had no alternative but to sell it to developers. Yet she had never heard him complain, or even mention it. It was as if that part of his life had been sealed off.

A LITTLE GIRL

The little girl looked out of the carriage window as the train began to slow down. It was almost dark now, and it seemed as if they had been travelling forever. At first it had been fun to look out and see cows and horses in fields, but then it dawned on her that they were being taken far, far away from Mum and the whole world she knew. That's when she had first needed to pee. She always did when she was nervous. She had wet her knickers on the first day at Whitechapel Road Infant School. She thought the teacher was going to give her a good hiding, same as Mum would have done. But the teacher put her arm around her and said there was nothing to be scared of. Teacher was nice. She wished Teacher was with her now.

The strap on her gas mask dug into her neck. She wished she could take it off, but she had promised Mum she wouldn't. She wasn't quite sure what it was for, but she knew it was important. They had to practice putting on their masks when they had air raid drills at school. The masks had Mickey Mouse ears to make them look friendly, but when she put it on, she was scared that she couldn't breathe. It was just another thing that didn't make sense any more, like the loud, shouting voices on the radio or her dad going away dressed as a soldier, and now this train . . .

She held Bow-Wow, her stuffed dog, close to her, smelling his comforting smell and feeling his soft head against her cheek. He was so old that he hardly looked like a dog any more, but she couldn't sleep without him.

The train was definitely stopping. It was no use looking to see where they were. All the station signs had been taken down, and there were no lights from a nearby town. Just grey fields, grey trees, same as all the other places they had stopped. Ladies had come on to the platform and opened other carriage doors at each of the stops. Other children got out and had been led away. Now she wondered if they were the only ones left on the train.

"What if they've forgotten about us?" one of the big boys in the compartment with her said, grinning. "What if they shunt this carriage off to a siding and they find our whitened bones years later?"

"Shut yer gob, Billy, you're scaring the littl'un," another boy said.

That made her want to pee even more. She knew he was teasing. Boys were horrible teases. But what if nobody knew they were in this carriage? It wasn't a corridor train, so there was no toilet. She clutched Bow-Wow tightly and prayed, "Please God, please don't let me pee in my knickers."

Footsteps marched along the platform. The boys stood up, crowding the whole window.

"Who's left?" a brisk woman's voice called.

"Oi, we're still here." The biggest boy let down the window and opened the door from the outside.

"Right. Come along, then. Look sharp. And make sure you don't leave your gas masks behind." The boys jumped down, leaving the girl to wrestle her suitcase from the rack and then lower herself from the carriage. The boys were already talking to some ladies. She looked around, but there was no loo on this platform. Some of the people were already moving off, and anyway she felt too embarrassed to ask strangers. She looked at the other end of the platform and saw that a line of trees and bushes bordered a field. It came to her that she could pee quickly in the bushes and nobody would know.

She darted down the bank, squeezed through the bushes and into the field. The long grass tickled as she squatted to pee, but she didn't care. She was just pulling up her knickers again when a big dark shape came charging towards her. She noticed the huge head. The horns. From its mouth came a threatening snort. She had heard about bulls, but he was standing exactly where she had squeezed through the hedge. She gave a little scream and started to run. The bull came after her.

It was like a bad dream, looking for a place where she could escape from the field, but the hedge grew thicker and thornier as she ran. She could feel the bull's breath behind her. Gasping and sobbing, she managed to squeeze herself through and out into a lane. She looked back at the platform. It was empty. Everyone had gone.

She was too scared to cry. Maybe they'd notice she was missing and come back for her. She patted her suitcase with her things in it. That's when she realized she didn't have Bow-Wow. She couldn't leave without him, but she couldn't go back into that field. She started walking back, looking for the spot where she had squeezed through the hedge. Then she heard the sound of an engine. Headlights coming towards her. The motor car was coming fast. She flattened herself against the hedge, scared that the driver wouldn't notice her. But the car slowed. A window was wound down.

"Hello, what are you doing out here all alone?" The voice sounded friendly enough.

"The others went without me. I had to pee and I left Bow-Wow."

There was a pause.

"Why don't you come with me? We'll see if we can find the others."

"But I've got to get Bow-Wow first. I can't sleep without him."

"It's too dark now. We'll look in the morning."

The door opened. Inside the car, she could see only darkness.

She climbed into the car. The face beside her smiled as they drove away.

CHAPTER 26

On Saturday morning Liz was up extra early, plugging in the hot rollers for her hair and unable to decide what to wear. Marisa had been right. It did matter to her. She crept around while Marisa slept in, made herself a cup of tea and a slice of toast and Marmite, then set off for Waterloo. James was waiting by the departures board looking remarkably handsome in a big navy fisherman's sweater and corduroy trousers. His hair was still wet, as if it had just been washed. He looked not at all like a serious architect from London, and when he spotted Liz his face lit up.

"Oh, you made it. Great. I've already got our tickets."

Liz flushed. "You must let me pay you back for mine."

"Don't be silly. I'm employing you as my helper." He laughed. "Come on. Let's find a quiet coach."

They found one with only an older couple across from them and a man reading a newspaper in the far corner. The train pulled out of the station, gliding past grimy backstreets before it came to leafy suburbs. Slanted autumn sunlight made colours glow. It promised to be a beautiful day, and Liz felt a rush of happiness. Here she was sitting next to a charming man, on her way to a fun weekend's excursion. It seemed an eternity since that had happened. At least she hoped it would be fun: she was going to stay with James's father, who was angry with her, who had called her a bloody woman. And she was returning to a house where she had experienced the disturbing vision of a body being buried. So maybe not fun . . . but she was with James.

As the journey progressed, she recounted some of the things she had done during the week. She had heard no more about the body they had unearthed. As she said this, she watched the wife opposite look up inquisitively and decided to be careful in what else she disclosed.

"We'll stop at the police station just in case they've made some progress," James said. "But you haven't come up with any more recollections, have you? No more startling revelations? No more bodies buried on our grounds?"

Liz could see the woman now leaning forward as if she didn't want to miss anything. She gave James a warning glance, then shook her head. "No, nothing at all. But I'm going ahead with the investigation into the three little girls who vanished during the war. I think I mentioned it to you."

James nodded. "You did. And what have you found?"

"I visited two of the families, and I have the timetable for the route one of them took to Somerset." She hesitated. "I wondered if you can borrow your father's car and if we could possibly go to a couple of those villages. I know it's a long shot after so many years, but you never know—someone might have seen something that didn't seem significant then, but it might have struck them later. Or there may have been someone who didn't want to talk to the police."

James nodded. "All right. We'll have to see if my father is happy to let us have the car for the whole weekend. I hope we find something else for him at the house. He was so excited about that statue. He kept going on about how much my mother had loved it." He turned to Liz. "I think he's never stopped grieving for her. Never able to move on, you know."

"It must have been an awful shock," Liz said. "For both of you."

James's eyes held hers. She noticed they were an interesting green flecked with brown. "It was. I was at school. The headmaster called me and simply said, 'I'm afraid I've got bad news. Your mother has died. You father is coming to collect you. I expect you to be a brave chap and not make a fuss.' So I didn't. I don't think I cried once. I just felt as if I'd been turned to stone, you know."

Instinctively Liz reached out and put her hand over James's. "I'm so sorry. How ghastly for you. You were just a little boy, too. No one to hug you or tell you stories."

He blinked as if he was shutting out a tear. "The worst thing was that I don't think she ever cared for me very much. I was the replacement for my brother, whom she worshipped. A poor replacement, I'm afraid. She wasn't an easy woman, my mother. And yet my father adored her."

Liz decided to broach the idea that had been worrying her. "You had a governess, didn't you? Was she kind to you?"

"Tottie?" He laughed. "She was more nanny than governess, and she was a lot of fun, I remember. We played wonderful games together in the grounds and down at the harbour."

"What happened to her?" Liz could hardly bring out the words.

"She went away sometime during the war. I can't exactly remember when. But I know she went to join up. She said her brother had been killed and she wanted to do her part, not be stuck with us doing nothing useful. And I was just about to go off to school, so she wouldn't have been needed anyway. So off she went. I presume she would have come back to visit if we hadn't been forced out of our house."

Liz had her plausible answer. Tottie had left the family to join up. She wasn't the skeleton lying in that shallow grave. Or maybe that was just what a small boy had been told.

"What was she like, this Tottie?" Liz asked. "Was she a local girl?"

"No, I think she was some kind of family connection. An educated girl at any rate. Very tall and thin, I remember. She said they called her Beanpole at school." He smiled at the memory.

"But you've never been in contact since?"

James shook his head. "I think she was connected to my mother's family. Maybe she came to Mummy's funeral. I can't remember."

They sat for a while in silence. Suburbs had now been replaced by fields, some with cows in them, some with the remaining stubble of harvested wheat or barley. They rattled past small stations without stopping. Liz tried to read names, but they were travelling too quickly. To think that at such a station Rosie Binks would have got off the train, been taken away by somebody . . . She switched off her thoughts.

"Any updates on the missing girl?" James asked.

She saw the woman across from them prick up her ears again.

"Nothing that I've been told," she said. "My flatmate and her bosses have been very busy all week, but they haven't told me if they've made any progress." She decided not to mention her discoveries into Susan's past where they could be overheard. They chatted about innocuous subjects, the plays they had seen in London, a house James was helping to design for a rock star, complete with a guitar-shaped swimming pool. "It's a nightmare," James said. "The man has no concept of what is feasible. He says he doesn't want a wall here, and we have to tell him the house won't stand up without one. He's the type who believes money can get you anything you want."

"I suppose we all have our crosses to bear," Liz said. "I'm thinking of changing jobs."

"From the *Daily Express*? But surely that's a plum, isn't it?"

"It would be if I was appreciated and allowed to do the sort of real journalism I like. But not stuck in obituaries. Do you realize my boss has been there for thirty-seven years? Thirty-seven, doing the same job. I'd go mad."

"So where would you go?"

Liz shrugged. "I'm not sure. I thought if I had this story on the missing girls completed, I'd be able to take it to another paper."

"Or move to radio or television news?"

"That's a thought," she said. "I never considered it."

"You should. You're very pretty. You'd look good on camera."

Liz blushed bright red this time. "I don't know if I could picture myself talking to millions of viewers. But I'd love to be the person who put the story together."

Across from her, she heard the woman whisper to her husband. "She's a reporter. I bet she's on to that little girl, somehow. And they've found a body. Did you hear that?"

This is how misinformation is spread, Liz thought.

~~

At 11:40 they glided into Bournemouth Station. James said he usually took a bus to his father's house, but this time he insisted on a taxi. Mr Bennington opened the front door and greeted his son with obvious joy. Liz sensed he was more reticent about her. *Just as my parents have always been when I've brought a boyfriend home,* she thought. They had never taken to Edmond, although he always behaved like a perfect gentleman with impeccable manners. The only one they'd really approved of was Alistair, and the trouble was that Liz had not really taken to him!

"Well, here you are, and in good time," Mr Bennington said, holding out a hand to shake his son's, then hers. "Welcome, young lady, although I don't know if I should be glad to see you again after all the fuss you have caused."

"I'm sorry, Mr Bennington," she said. "I realize it must have been really unsettling for you. It certainly was for me."

"Have you now remembered who the bloody woman was?"

Liz shook her head. "Not at all. I have no other recollections, nor any explanation as to how I could have been there. In fact my parents state that I could not have been. My father, who is the most practical of men, even suggested I might be one of these people who gets messages from the dead. But I can't think that is true. At least I've never got one before."

"Well, don't just stand there. Come in. Coffee's just perked. James, show the young lady her room while I pour."

James led her down the hall and opened the door to a small guest room. It looked out on to the back garden. "It's not exactly the Ritz," he said. "The rooms in this house are all horribly small but functional, I'm afraid."

"Thank you. It's really kind of your father to let me stay."

"Oh, he loves company. He's always been quite a social man, so the school was good for him. There were always boys and other masters dropping in on him. Now he hasn't really found his niche here." He glanced back down the hall to see if they were overheard. "I feel rather badly about him. That I should be doing something. But I don't think he'd be happy in London, at least not in the sort of place I can afford. And he does enjoy walking along the seafront." He gave her an encouraging smile. "I'll go and help with the coffee. The bathroom is across the passage if you want to use the facilities."

Liz put her overnight bag on the bed, went across to the bathroom, checked her make-up (deliberately understated for the occasion) and smoothed down her hair in the mirror. Then she went to join James and his father. A tray with coffee and hot milk was already on the low table.

"Will you be staying for lunch, or do you want to set off straight away?" Mr Bennington asked.

"I don't know about Liz, but I'm starving," James said. "I didn't have time for breakfast."

"Well then, I've a treat for you," Mr Bennington said. "I picked up some local crab at the fishmonger's. And we've fresh bread, delivered this morning."

"Splendid." James rubbed his hands together. "I hope you like crab, Liz?"

"I love it. It's not something I ever eat. Too expensive in London."

They sat for a while drinking coffee, making small talk. The subject of the body did not come up. Then they went through to the dining room, where the table had already been laid with a white cloth and silverware, and enjoyed a delicious meal. It was only when they had finished that Mr Bennington asked, "So, does one gather there is no more information on this dead person on my land?"

"Not that we've heard so far," Liz said.

"We thought we'd stop by the police station on our way to the house," James said. "Just to see if they've found out anything more."

"Let's hope it turns out to be a skeleton from long ago. Or at least nothing to do with us."

He glanced at his son, but James was looking down at his plate.

After they had washed up, James and Liz set off in the Bentley.

"It's gorgeous down here, isn't it?" Liz exclaimed, catching a glimpse of blue sea. "It makes one wonder why we live in London."

"Because we have to make a living, I presume," James said. "I got hired by this firm of architects straight out of University College London. It was considered a plum assignment, and I suppose it is. I have a chance to work on big projects that I wouldn't have if I was in the provinces." He paused. "But I do miss the countryside."

"At least we can escape on weekends like this," Liz said.

They passed through small towns until they drew close to Weymouth.

"We should check with the police station first," James said. "Get that over with, don't you think?"

Liz nodded. "Good idea."

The town was busy, as shoppers were out in force on a fine Saturday afternoon, and they had to park the car down at the harbour before walking to the police station. Inspector Fordham was not in, but the constable who had been with him before was.

"No luck yet," he said. "We've come up with a list of several missing women from the time, but it's not that easy to locate next of kin for them. A couple were land girls and not from this area. Others have parents who have now passed away. But we'll get there in the end, I expect."

"But you do definitely think that this body dates from the war years, or could it have been much older?"

The constable frowned. "Not much older, from what we've been told. There was a shoe and a watch. The blokes at forensics seemed to take it for granted that it was buried after the village was evacuated."

"After?" James asked. "Why did they come up with that?"

"I've no idea. Maybe I misunderstood. At least it was from the war years. I know that much."

"Well, that was not very promising," James said as they came out again. "Still none the wiser."

"But I'm afraid it's not a fourteenth-century nun like you hoped," Liz said. "They should be able to identify her in the end."

"Yes, I suppose so." He said it quietly, as if he was thinking. Liz was dying to ask him whether he suspected who it could be, but it would have been too intrusive.

"Right. Now on to the fun stuff," James said as they returned to the car. They drove out of town, and finally down the narrow lane towards the old house. A flock of rooks scattered, cawing, as they approached. The house stood there, forlorn and rather magical now with its coat of ivy, its stonework glowing in autumn sunlight. It no longer looked menacing but more like one of the enchanted castles full of sleeping princesses she had imagined in her early years. There was no sign of the police cordon to the left of the house. It was, presumably, no longer a crime scene. Liz glanced across at it warily.

"Do you think I should go and stand there and see if any more memories surface?" she asked, anxiety returning.

"Do you want to?"

She shook her head. "Not really, but if it could help solve the mystery, then maybe I should."

"I'll come with you," he said.

They walked together in silence around the house until they came to the rose garden. Liz started down the path towards the arbor.

"It's gone," she said suddenly, looking at James in surprise.

"The body. Yes, I'm sure they took it away."

"No, I meant the feeling of dread. It's gone."

CHAPTER 27

"Tread carefully and let me go first," James said as they entered the house. "I've sort of learned how to clear a path, just in case we're about to step on a live shell."

"That's comforting to know," she replied, and he laughed.

They started in the sitting room where she had found the statue. There were portions of collapsed ceiling lying across much of the floor, impossible to move. They searched but found nothing else of note. Then they moved on. The former dining room had a giant beam lying across a vast dining table. It had once been highly polished oak but thanks to years of weather was now discoloured and peeling.

Liz gasped. "Oh, how awful to have to leave that table behind."

James was staring at it, too. "I know," he said, "but we moved into a small cottage. Most of our furniture wouldn't fit, and I don't think my father could find anyone to give it to. Most people don't have dining rooms this size." He gave a little sigh. "We only had two weeks to move out. We could only take what fit into a small van. But they did promise my parents that the house would be left untouched. We all assumed we'd move back in after the war."

"How unfair," Liz said.

"It was war, I suppose. Everything for the greater good, right?"

"What a horrible waste," Liz said, running her hand over a patch of the dining table that still retained a semblance of its polish. "I don't suppose we could take this and restore it?"

"And put it where?"

"I don't know. But it seems such a shame. A furniture restorer might like it." Then she peered over the beam. "Oh look. There's a brass bed."

It was sitting on the far end of the table, resting on a large chunk of ceiling. Beside it sat a water jug from the washstand in a bedroom, perfectly intact. James ducked under the beam and retrieved the jug.

"I don't know who would want this, but I'll take it anyway," James said.

"You could put flowers in it," Liz suggested.

He laughed. "I'm not the sort that puts flowers in things, but perhaps it has antique value and my father can sell it. Still, after surviving all this time, it does deserve to be rescued."

They carried it carefully to the front door.

"We could have taken the brass bed if you'd brought the van," Liz said. "It looks like it's all there."

"What would we want with a brass bed?"

"I gather they are quite fashionable these days."

"All right. We'll take it next time I bring a van."

They moved on to the kitchen, squeezing past the beam that lay across the dining room. James removed dust and debris most cautiously until they found an old kitchen scale, complete with iron weights.

"I'm not sure who could use this," he said, "but it seems to be all there."

"Again it's of historical value," Liz said, "And you could clobber someone with one of those weights."

"I didn't realize you were a violent person," he said, laughing. Then he stopped. "Oh, how about this?" An enormous iron stock pot stood on a wooden shelf. It was now rusted and in sorry state. "I don't know who'd want it," he said. "Unless you really are a witch and you need a cauldron."

"I don't make that much soup," Liz said. "But there are some other things of interest on that shelf. That china, I think—" She stopped abruptly as James grabbed her, nearly wrenching her over backwards.

"Don't move," he said.

Liz stared at him, confused. He pointed at the ground in front of her. A grenade lay at her feet.

"Don't touch it," Liz said. "Let's get out of here."

"No, it's all right, I think," he said. "The pin is still in. All the same . . ." He bent to pick it up, backed out with it and carried it to the front door. Then he hurled it far into the bushes. They waited for an explosion, but none came. James gave her a nervous grin.

"That was brave," she said.

"Brave? I'm shaking like a leaf." He glanced around. "I think we'll leave the kitchen for now. Let's go in the other direction." They passed through the sitting room and came to a former library. The lovely dark wood bookshelves that had once reached to the ceiling were now hurled across the room. Pages of books lay amongst debris.

"Oh," Liz said, her hand going up to her mouth. "How sad."

"I know." James stood beside her. "All those lovely books. I know my father took the best ones with him, but there were so many here. I remember this room as a child. Books everywhere you looked, and that old musty smell. I was allowed to look at some of them—a giant atlas of the world. I remember my mother showing me which parts of the world belonged to Britain."

"We must see if there are any books that can be saved," Liz said. Having grown up with a love of books, it was almost physically painful to see so many volumes scattered and destroyed. She started rummaging amongst the detritus.

"Careful," James said. "There is broken glass from the windows. And there might be more shells or grenades."

In her enthusiasm she had forgotten that point and hastily pulled back her hand. She cleared an area, then squatted to lift one book after another. The roof had collapsed completely here, and blue sky was above them, so every book she picked up was the victim of twenty-five years of rain and wind. Almost reverently she placed them aside, one after the other, until she came to a small leather-bound volume. *The*

Poems of Keats was still legible, embossed on the cover. She opened it, marvelling that the pages were still intact. Then, on the frontispiece, she read *Charlotte Mellinger*. And underneath, *To darling Tottie, with all my love, Ben.*

"Oh look, James." She held out the book to him. "This belonged to your Tottie."

James took it from her, turning pages carefully. "It's still perfect," he said. "How amazing." Then he frowned. "That's strange, though. What was one of her books doing in our library?"

"And who was Ben?" Liz asked.

He shook his head. "No idea. Obviously, her beau at the time. I wonder why she didn't want to take this with her when she left?" He handed the book to Liz. "You take care of it."

They searched some more but only found books that were mildly damaged and of little interest, until Liz gave a cry and bent to retrieve a small object. "Oh look, James."

She held out a well-worn toy soldier.

"Well, I'm damned." James took it, holding it in the palm of his hand. "One of mine. How did it . . . Oh, I suppose my nursery was above this. I thought I took them all with me, but I was always having battles all over the place, so this poor chap got left behind." He stuffed the toy into his pocket.

They searched but didn't find any more.

"But that would explain Tottie's book," James said. "Her room was next to my nursery. It must have fallen down, too."

Liz studied the book in her hand. But that still didn't explain why Tottie had left such a precious object behind.

Beyond the library was what James thought had been the morning room. It must have been pleasant once, with tall, dual-aspect windows looking out on to lawns and wide window seats, some still with faded cushions on them.

"I bet you used to sit here on sunny days," Liz said.

James frowned. "Not really. Most of my life was spent in the nursery upstairs. My mother was rather old-school—children should be kept in their own domain until needed." He gave a half smile, half grimace. "I came down on occasion and had to behave well. So I don't have fond memories of downstairs. But I loved my nursery. I told you about my rocking horse I had to leave behind, didn't I? Mummy said I was too big for such things. I wonder where that is now."

Liz looked around. "Part of the upstairs hasn't collapsed. Perhaps it's still sitting there."

"I don't think I'd want to try to get up those stairs," James said. "The whole floor is probably ready to cave in."

"You know what I'm thinking?" Liz said. "You're an architect. You could have this place rebuilt, as lovely as before."

"You've forgotten two things: one, that it would take a ton of money, which I don't have, and two, the slight problem that the army still has control of it."

"Then petition to get it back," Liz said, "and while you're at it, demand compensation for destroying a house they promised they wouldn't destroy."

James looked at her warily. "I didn't realize I was dealing with such a firebrand," he said. "Of course, you are right. We should have it back by now. There is no reason for them to hang on to it, apart from the danger of unexploded stuff. And we should get compensation. My father just sort of gave up after my mother's death. Losing his home, then his wife—nothing seemed worth it any longer. But I wouldn't have any idea how to start such an appeal."

"I could help," Liz said. "I work at a newspaper. People know how to find out almost anything." Then she stopped, realizing. "I'm sorry. I have no right to interfere in your life. It was kind of you to bring me here and I've enjoyed it, but I should mind my own business, keep my mouth shut and not upset you or your father."

James was gazing at her. "But you are right, Liz. Maybe we have given up without a fight. I mean, I was too young to understand properly or to do anything, but perhaps my father does need a kick in the behind to make him want to start living again." He reached out and put a hand on her shoulder. "And I think I quite like you interfering in my life."

Her eyes held his for a long minute. She got the feeling, with a shiver of excitement, that he was going to kiss her, but then he moved away. "Nothing more here, is there?" They picked their way out into the main foyer. "Now that you've got me started, there is so much good salvage work to be done here. The wood from that staircase, and the beams that have fallen. That panelling in the sitting room and that lovely fireplace. It's all usable. We'd need to bring in equipment and a team, and have somewhere to store them." As he talked, he walked ahead of her, looking around him and pointing excitedly.

"James, watch out!" This time she grabbed him.

A section of inner wall had fallen, and it had been pierced by some kind of large shell. It stuck up, metal and menacing, just where James was about to walk.

"Crikey," he said, stepping back hastily.

"We might have been blown to kingdom come."

"You're trembling." He put his hands on her shoulders. "It's okay."

"You're trembling, too." She attempted a laugh.

"I suppose it could have been a dud, but . . ."

Without warning he pulled her towards him and kissed her. She was surprised at the intensity of the kiss, half drew away, but then found herself responding.

"Was that all right?" he asked as they broke apart.

"You want me to judge a kiss?" She laughed uneasily. "On a scale of one to ten?"

"No, I meant was it all right to kiss you? I mean I don't know whether you are just being helpful or you just want to find facts for your story or . . ."

"Shut up." She put a finger on his lips. "James, I like you. I'm glad you kissed me."

"You don't have a boyfriend who will show up and knock my block off?"

"No boyfriend," she said. "There hasn't been anyone I care about for quite a while. I had my heart broken, but I'm definitely ready to move on."

"That makes two of us," he said. "Two wounded warriors, ready to tackle the world."

"Yes." She beamed at him.

His arm was around her shoulder as they made their way back to the front door. As they came out, she paused, looking back, taking in the foyer and the rooms opening from it.

I'm sure of it, she thought. *I was never in this house before.*

As they came out of the house, she had to glance to where she could just spot the remains of the police cordon and the trellis around the arbor. She peered at it, willing more memory to surface, but nothing did. She turned back to James, finding his arm around her comforting.

~~

"Is this all you found?" James's father examined the items they had placed on the kitchen table. "What were you doing all that time?"

James glanced at Liz. She spoke before he could. "Everything else that we could see was either too large to move or beyond repair," she said. "That lovely dining table could probably be refinished, but there's no way of getting it out with a giant beam across it. And all those lovely books in the library are so water damaged that they can't be saved."

He studied her. "You like books?"

"Love them. My flatmate will tell you that my books take up too much room. I have a proper library in my bedroom at home." She paused. "I was a lonely child. Books were my escape."

James's father nodded as if he understood.

"We did have a couple of adventures," James said. "First we found a grenade and then a whopping great shell, stuck through a wall."

"Bastards," Mr Bennington muttered. "Well, I suppose there wasn't that much of worth left behind in the first place. Except for the library. I took the valuable books, but we only had the use of a van for a couple of days and nowhere to store anything."

"I told Liz that," James said.

"And it was all so sudden. These army chappies appearing one morning, saying we had to get out in two weeks. Amelia was beside herself."

Liz reached into her handbag. "We did find this." She handed him the book. "It belonged to James's governess, apparently."

Mr Bennington turned the pages carefully. "So it did. Look at that. Charlotte Mellinger."

"Had she already left when you had to move?"

"Yes, she'd already gone a while before we had to get out. She said she wanted to join up and make a difference, not be stuck with us. Amelia was furious when she left, because she'd have to look after her own child. She didn't have a clue. She'd been waited on all her life, you see. But luckily Jamie was old enough to take care of himself by that time, weren't you, son?"

"I was six, Dad. I wasn't an infant. And you were planning to send me off to school soon."

Mr Bennington picked up a small china bowl they had rescued from the kitchen. "I do remember this. It held the sugar for breakfast. Do you think it's worth going back there again?"

"Dad, we've been thinking: maybe we could try to get the property back now. The army doesn't need it."

"For what?" Mr Bennington asked with bitterness in his voice. "I certainly don't have the money to raze and rebuild, and I don't think architects get paid that sort of money either."

"There might be compensation if we pushed for it."

"Ha. Fat chance of that. I don't think they ever gave compensation to all those poor sods who were bombed out of their homes, did they?"

"We still own land there, don't we?" James asked.

"We do. But it's leased to the farmer, and by law I'm not allowed to turn him out. I get a small rent from him, that's all." He paused, then added, "I'd give up crazy notions if I were you, son. I lost the home my family had lived in for six hundred years. I have to accept that. It's a different world now. No place for old buffers like me."

"Don't talk like that, Dad," James said. "You've got good years left in you yet. Anyway, we're starving. We've been working hard, shifting great bits of rubble. Had you planned something for dinner?"

"You know I'm not much of a cook, don't you? It's either a Sainsbury's meat pie or we go to the pub."

"I vote for the latter," James said. "Come on. I'll treat. All right, Liz?"

"Perfect." She smiled at him.

CHAPTER 28

"So, what time do you need to go back to London?" James asked Liz the next morning.

They had enjoyed a large breakfast, cooked by his father. In spite of telling them he was a terrible cook, he had managed a full English, complete with fried bread.

"I don't have to be back at any time at all," she said. "You're the one who has to go to work in the morning. I'm still hoping we might be able to follow up on my research today."

"One of the missing girls who took the train?" he asked.

"If that's possible. Do you think your father would let us have the car again?"

"Let you have what?" Mr Bennington came into the room, bringing a fresh pot of tea.

"Liz is writing a story about some little girls who vanished during the war," he said. "Maybe tying it in with Little Lucy. She wants to follow the train route one of the girls took down to Somerset."

"Rather a long shot after all these years, isn't it?" Mr Bennington asked.

"I know," Liz replied. "And maybe a complete waste of time, but just in case there is any connection . . . perhaps the person who abducted those girls has recently been released from prison? I'd like to follow up on anything like that."

"Oh, I see." He stared at her thoughtfully. "Well, I suppose there is no harm in it."

"I wondered if I could impose on you and borrow your car for another day? I'll be happy to pay for petrol."

"Don't be silly," he said. "The car is yours, or rather my son's, since I presume he'll drive. And you know what? I might come along. It's been a while since I've had a good outing."

"That's great, Dad," James said.

"That is if you don't think an old fogey tagging along will cramp your style?"

"Not at all," James said. "Liz and I will have plenty of time to see each other in London." Their eyes connected for a moment, which Mr Bennington noticed.

"Oh, so it's like that, is it? Jolly good." He nodded. "About time you had a sensible girlfriend after that ghastly what was her name?"

"Felicity, Dad. And don't pretend you've forgotten her name. You liked her. You were most encouraging, until . . ."

"Until she went off her rocker and started wafting around with her boobs hanging out, talking about saving the whales and butterflies."

Liz noticed that James had to smile. But a thought sparked in her head. James's ex-girlfriend had also become a protester and a hippie. Was there any chance she had bumped into Little Lucy's mother, Susan? And knew anything about her that might shed a light on the disappearance?

James offered to make a picnic lunch while Mr Bennington sat down with the morning papers. Liz assisted by buttering bread until they were interrupted by a loud shout. They rushed through to the sitting room.

"What is it, Dad?" James asked.

Mr Bennington was sitting, pointing at the newspaper. "I didn't realize I'd been hosting a celebrity," he said. Liz went to look over his shoulder. *HAVE PAST CRIMES COME BACK TO HAUNT US?* was the headline. *During the chaos of war, three little girls were evacuated to the country from London. They never arrived. Only one of them was ever found, murdered . . .*

"Oh gosh." Liz turned to James with an amazed smile. "He ran my story! How about that?"

"Good old you." James gave her a pretend fist pump. "See, Dad. I told you that you were entertaining a crack reporter!"

"Now if we can just find out what happened to at least one of those girls, then I can do the follow-up," she said.

Liz was still beaming as they set off, armed with maps and Liz's list of stations. They had printed her article. She had escaped from obituaries, at least for the moment. James drove with Liz sitting beside him. Mr Bennington insisted on taking the back seat. "Your expedition. I'm just coming along for the ride," he said.

"The first stop after London would not have been a large town. I don't think they'd have offloaded children in Salisbury," Mr Bennington said when Liz showed him her train route. "Tisbury is also quite large. I know the plan was to get the children out into the countryside, far away from the Home Counties, so that would mean all these following villages: Gillingham, Henstridge, Milborne Port, Ashdown Halt, Bradford Abbas . . ." He paused, looking up. "Where do they get these ridiculous names, I wonder?"

Gillingham turned out to be a sizeable town with an estate of new houses. It basked in Sunday morning slumber, its high street shuttered with nobody around. They asked at the police station and intercepted some old ladies coming out of church. Yes, they remembered the poor little kiddies coming out of the city. They remembered some of them going out to farms, and they certainly remembered the police enquiry, but nobody seemed to have any idea of where records of evacuated children might be found or who might have handled the placement of the children.

"I don't think we're going to have much luck with this," Mr Bennington said as they returned to the car. "Too many people moved around after the war, went to cities or immigrated to the colonies."

"Dad, it's the Commonwealth now," James said with a laugh. "I don't think Australia would like being called a colony."

"Same thing," he replied with a grunt. "All bloody colonials."

James gave Liz an amused glance. She was thinking that her father would probably have said the same sort of thing.

The next village they stopped at was Henstridge.

"I don't think they'd have billeted children here," Mr Bennington said. "There was an RAF station right next to it during the war. A perfect bombing target."

"Dad, you're being negative about everything," James said.

"I'm being realistic. Would you want your kid put at a farmhouse beside an airfield?"

"No, you're right," Liz agreed. "So probably not."

They continued along the A30 until they came to Milborne Port. Going was slow with Sunday drivers out to enjoy a fine autumn day. It was another large village where they found another cluster of elderly women loitering to chatter after church. The women were willing enough to talk, but they didn't learn much that was new. One of the ladies had been a volunteer when evacuated children arrived. Yes, they'd kept a list in those days, and of course the police had asked them about the little girl, but there had been no such child while she was working. They took good care of the children and made sure they went to good homes, she finished indignantly.

They were silent as they got back into the car.

"I don't know what I hoped to find, but it's been too long, hasn't it?" Liz said. "I'm sorry, I'm wasting your day."

"Not at all," Mr Bennington said. "When have I last spent a day with a pretty girl—oh, and with my son, of course."

"Let's stop for a picnic in the next village," James said. "I'm feeling peckish."

"After that enormous breakfast you ate?" his father declared.

"That was hours ago, Dad."

Liz observed them, enjoying the friendly banter. They left the main road and came to Ashdown Halt Station. It stood amongst fields with cows in them. It had the feel of being long deserted, its one short platform now with weeds sticking up through cracks in the concrete and the trim hanging from the station roof. It was also a good half mile out of the village of Ashdown.

"I bet that wasn't popular, having to walk at the end of a journey," Mr Bennington said as they saw nobody and drove on towards the houses. "Especially if you had a suitcase to carry."

Ashdown was smaller than the other villages they had encountered, and Liz could see why the railway no longer stopped at Ashdown Halt. It would have been almost as easy to drive into Sherborne and take the train from there. Nobody was coming out of church. The village shop was open, and a family emerged, the children licking ice lollies. They decided to picnic on a bench beside a playing field where a game of football was taking place. It ended amicably, and the players came over to retrieve their equipment.

"I think I'll go and talk to them." Liz got up and strolled across.

"You're the Ashdown team, are you?" she asked.

"No, we're bloody Chelsea, opting to play down here," one of the men said, getting a laugh from his friends.

"I'm from a newspaper," Liz said, "and I'm doing a story on missing girls."

"You mean the one in London?" one of the men asked, frowning now. "They haven't found her yet, have they? There are more who have gone missing?"

"No, I'm researching little girls who went missing years ago. One girl called Rosie Binks was evacuated during the war, came by train to somewhere along this route and was never seen again."

"I remember her," the man who had made the joke said.

"You saw her? You remember her?" Liz asked hopefully.

"No, I never saw her, but I remember the fuss about it. The police asked us lots of questions. I was a nipper myself at the time. None of us had seen her, but the police said she had her stuffed dog with her. They showed us a snapshot, and my brother found a toy dog like that a few weeks after."

"He did?" Liz's heart rate quickened. "Where did he find it?"

"It was in the field where Mr Johnson kept his bull. We told my dad, and we thought the worst, you know. That old bull had a nasty temper. We searched around, but we never found a body."

"Would you happen to remember who was in charge of the evacuees at that time? Who placed them with families?"

"I don't know, but my mum would," he said. "She's sitting over there, looking after the grandkids." He pointed at a bench closer to the playground where several small children were swarming over a climbing frame. "Our neighbour took in two of the evacuated boys. We didn't take anyone in because there were five of us and no room, but we helped out with food."

"What's your mum's name?" Liz asked.

"Adcock," he replied. Liz wondered if he was being silly again, making up a rude name, but he went on, "Daisy Adcock. I'm Brian."

"Liz," she said and held out her hand to him.

"You're not hoping to find the girl after all these years, are you?" one of the other men asked.

"No, but I'd like to find what happened to her. She still has a mother and father grieving, you know."

He nodded. "I don't know what I'd do if my little kid went missing."

Liz thanked them and went around the pitch to the playground. Brian's mother was sitting, knitting, glancing up occasionally at the children, who seemed to have no fear as they hurled themselves into space.

"Mrs Adcock?" Liz slid on to the bench beside her. "Your son sent me over to you." And she gave her the details.

"Oh, I remember right enough," the woman said. "Terrible business, that was. We all felt so badly about it. And when my son came home with her stuffed dog . . . well, we knew something bad had happened to her."

"Was there anyone nearby who was known as a child molester?" Liz asked.

"There was Old Ned," she said, saying the words cautiously. "He'd been known to ask a little girl to show him her knickers, but after the local policeman gave him a stern warning, he seemed to behave himself. The police from London did question him a lot, but they never got anything out of him. I think he was too scared that they'd finally come for him. He wasn't quite right in the head, you know. And he's long since passed away."

The children on the climbing frame squealed, making their grandmother glance up again. "You be careful, or you'll split your heads open and have to go to hospital," she said, then went back to her knitting.

"Do you remember who was in charge of the evacuees in those days?" Liz said. "Not that it will help much, but I was wondering whether anyone saw this child on the platform or anyone kept a list. We've had no luck so far in other villages."

"I can tell you that," Mrs Adcock said. "I was helping out that day. I'd made sandwiches for the kiddies. I knew they'd be hungry when they arrived. And I can tell you there was no little girl like the one in the photograph. There weren't many children left by the time the train got to us. It was all boys, I think. Older boys. Rough-looking types. They went out to a couple of farms, and I know those farmers got good unpaid helpers out of those boys."

"Thank you." Liz got ready to stand up.

The woman paused, staring out across the football pitch. "You asked who was in charge, and I've been thinking. It must still have been that Miss Gresham-Goodge. She was the lady from Ashdown Hall, and she ran everything. You know the type: Girl Guides, Cub Scouts, the lot. She was the one who put herself in charge, but I'm trying to remember if she was still there on that actual day the child disappeared. I don't remember her bossing us around the way she always did, but I don't think she'd moved away yet. Maybe she was just late that day. She wasn't the best time keeper."

"She moved away?"

"That's right, dearie. One day we got the news that she'd gone. Quite a surprise, I'm telling you, because she was the last of an old family who had lived here for generations. I'm not sure if it was because the army wanted to take over Ashdown Hall or because she had to go take care of her sick sister in Devon. We heard the sister was very ill."

"Whereabouts in Devon, do you remember?"

She thought for a while. "I believe it was near Tiverton, I think she said. And do you know what? She never returned. We never saw her again. Ashdown Hall was used by the army during the war, then sold after the war, what had been in her family for generations, and it's now a girls' school. Ashdown House, it's called. You can just see the chimney pots of the building sticking up over the trees."

She put down her knitting and started to stand up. "I'd better rescue those rascals. One of them is going to fall at any second, and I'll never hear the last of it from my son."

Liz stood up, too. "Thank you very much. You've been most helpful."

"Not at all, dear, although I don't know why they are raking up the past again after so long. No good can come of it, can it?"

Liz crossed the pitch to where James and his father had already opened the picnic basket and were eating ham sandwiches.

"Learn anything?" Mr Bennington asked. "You had a good long chinwag, I could see."

"I did, actually. She was here."

"The girl who vanished?"

Liz nodded. "At least her stuffed toy dog was found in a field near the station. A field occupied by a bull."

"Gosh," James said. "Do you think the bull killed her?"

"That's what these people thought, but they searched and never found a body."

"Maybe she ran away from the bull and someone found her," Mr Bennington said. "I presume they questioned everyone in the area. But it could have been someone driving past . . ."

Liz sighed. "Hopeless," she said. "I don't know why I ever thought this story was a good idea. We could drive around and question all the farmers with fields near the station, but they are hardly likely to tell us if they kidnapped and killed a little girl, are they?" Then she stopped. "There was one mention of a man who wasn't all there. Old Ned. He'd ask little girls to show him their underwear, but Mrs Adcock said he was harmless. Perhaps he wasn't."

"Where is he now?" James asked.

"Long dead, I'm afraid."

"So we'll never know," James said.

Liz nodded. "But the strange thing was that Mrs Adcock was helping out that day, and she said there was no little girl on the platform. It was all boys."

"But they found her dog?"

"Or a dog that looked like hers," Mr Bennington reminded them. "I presume there was more than one dog made in that pattern. Maybe it was a popular toy model that year. It could just have been coincidence."

"It could have been." Liz stared thoughtfully. "Although toys were precious in the war, weren't they? A child wouldn't be so likely to mislay a beloved toy . . ." She thought for a moment, her train of thought interrupted by the squeals from the playground of children having fun. "Perhaps it wouldn't hurt to go and talk to the farmer who owns that field. Just in case."

"Not until I've finished my lunch," Mr Bennington said. "Sit down. Make the most of the sun. Have a ham sandwich, or there's a pork pie."

Liz sat, hiding her impatience. For the first time she had an important clue. The child had dropped her dog in a field. Her precious toy dog she took everywhere with her. That in itself was significant. Also interesting was that nobody had seen her on the platform.

"I suggest we go into Sherborne for a beer after this," Mr Bennington said. "But we'd better hunt down Liz's farmer first."

They loaded the picnic basket and got back into the car, driving back towards the train station. Liz noted that there were no houses along that lane until you reached the actual village. It wasn't a place where a stranger would be likely to have been hanging around without being noticed. They stopped the car and Liz got out. The gate to the station was now locked, but Liz climbed over the fence easily enough. She went up the ramp to the platform. On one side there was a tiny station building. A window was broken, and Liz peered in. There was nothing but a small waiting area with a bench and a ticket booth beside it. She walked out on to the platform, stepping carefully over cracked paving stones. From this vantage point there was a good view over the surrounding countryside. At one end of the platform, there was a small car park beside the lane. But at the other end, a line of bushes grew beside a field. It now had cows in it, grazing peacefully. Liz scanned the area beyond and noticed smoke coming from a chimney two fields further away. That had to be the farmhouse.

She clambered back over the fence and got into the car. "I've spotted what looks like the farmhouse," she said.

"I must say you are remarkably agile," Mr Bennington commented. "Leaping that fence like a young gazelle."

"Hardly a gazelle," she said, laughing, "but I was a tomboy when I was young. We had an orchard, and I was always up in the trees."

"In Shropshire, you said?"

"That's right. Not far from Shrewsbury. It was a nice place to grow up, but quite remote. There weren't any other children to play with nearby."

"So you played pretend games in your garden and retreated to your books?" James said.

"That's right. My own little world."

"Just you and your mother?"

"Most of the time. Daddy was off in the army. We had a local woman who came in to help with the housework a couple of times a week, but that was it."

"Ah, here's what we're looking for," James said and turned into a muddy track leading to a farm. As they pulled up in front of the house, they saw that a man and woman were unloading groceries from an estate car. They looked up, puzzled, as James brought the car to a halt.

"Can I help you?" The man came towards them.

Liz got out. "I'm sorry to disturb you, but I wondered if I could ask you a few questions about this farm during the war years."

"You're lucky to have caught us. We've just been doing the weekly shop. There's a grocery shop in Sherborne that's now open on Sundays. The locals are scandalized." He laughed. "What did you want to know?"

"I'm doing an article about a missing child in this area from 1941, Rosie Binks. I don't suppose you were the farmer in those days."

He threw back his head and laughed. "Hardly. I was five at the time. That would have been my dad. He's more or less retired now, and I've taken over the running of the farm."

"Where would I find him?"

"Sitting watching the telly and keeping an eye on the kids, I expect," the man said. "I'm Colin Johnson, and my dad's Jim Johnson."

"I'm Liz Houghton," she said. "I work for the *Daily Express*."

"National newspaper. Fancy that." He looked impressed. "I suppose there's interest in Rosie Binks because of the current missing child case. They haven't found her yet, have they?"

"I'm afraid not."

"Well, I suppose you should come in, but I'd better help my wife with these groceries, or I'll never hear the last of it."

She followed him into a typical country kitchen. There was a cast iron stove on one wall, pots hanging up and the delicious smell of roasting meat. He put down the bags he had been carrying on the table then called, "Dad, are you decent? We've a visitor."

He indicated that Liz should follow him through to a small sitting room. It contained chintz-covered armchairs and sofa with a big brick fireplace in which a log was burning, and a television on a stand. An old man was sitting in one of the armchairs, and a baby lay asleep in a carrycot on the coffee table. He saw Liz and attempted to get up.

"Who's this, then? Not the visiting nurse on a Sunday."

"She wants to ask you about the farm during the war," Colin said loudly. He turned to Liz. "He's a bit deaf, you know."

"I am not. I hear perfectly if you don't mumble," the old man said.

Liz perched on an arm facing him. "Mr Johnson, I'm writing a story about missing children from the war. They tell me in the village that Rosie Binks's toy dog was found in your field, a couple of weeks after she disappeared."

"That's right. That field by the station where I used to keep the bull. He was a mean old bugger, so we thought he might have had a go at her, but we searched, with my dog who had a good nose, and we never found nothing. It was like she'd vanished into thin air."

"Do you happen to know who else was on the train and might have gone to local people?"

"A few boys. That's what we heard. In fact the wife went down there, and we took two of them in. Scrawny little runts they were when we got them, but you should have seen how they filled out with good food. They turned into good little workers, both of them."

"How old were they?"

Mr Johnson glanced up at his son, who had come back into the room. "How old would you say, Colin? About seven and nine at the time. They stayed with us two years, and they enjoyed helping out on the farm."

Seven and nine. Liz had half formed an idea that a bigger boy might have taken Rosie down to those bushes when no one was looking. But not seven and nine.

"And there were other boys?" she asked.

"I think there were three more. They took them in at Parson's Farm, and I heard that he worked 'em hard. Too hard, as I heard. They didn't stay long but went back to London."

"Did you have farmworkers in those days?"

He shook his head. "All the men were called up, my dear. I had some land girls, but they were about as useless as a bull in a milking parlour. We tried to teach them to milk, but they never got the hang of it. Kept getting the bucket kicked over. That meant the wife and me were up at five every day with no break. It was hard times, I can tell you."

Liz stood up. "Thank you for your time, sir. How do I find Parson's Farm if I wanted to visit it? I'd like to find out about the other boys."

"I can tell you where it is, but Fred Parsons don't live there no more. They upped and went to Australia after the war," he said. "Now it's a new young bloke fresh out of agricultural college with lots of barmy ideas." He gave a wheezy chuckle that turned into a cough.

Liz came out to find James playing with the family dog while he chatted with Mrs Johnson.

"Ready to go?" he asked Liz.

She nodded, apologized for interrupting their Sunday and got back into the car.

"Did you learn anything there?" he asked.

"Not much. He helped look for the girl with his dog but found no trace. There were some bigger boys who stayed at Parson's Farm, but the Parsons have gone to Australia. I thought maybe a bigger boy might have had bad intentions, lured a little girl down to the bushes . . ."

"Then her body would have been found," James said. "Or at least some trace of her would have been found. The dog would have sensed something."

"Yes. It's all a bit hopeless, isn't it?" She sighed. "I'm sorry. I shouldn't have brought you out here on a fool's errand."

"Not at all. I've had a delightful picnic," Mr Bennington said. "Now let's drive into Sherborne and have that beer, shall we?"

CHAPTER 29

They were retracing their route to the main road when Liz noticed a signpost going off to their right. "Wincanton 13," it said. And beneath it "Clareborne St Mary 8."

"Oh," she exclaimed, making James brake hurriedly.

"What is it?"

"I've just seen the place where I was born. Clareborne St Mary. It's only eight miles away. Do you think we could possibly . . . ? Only I've never seen it. I didn't realize until very recently that I was born in Somerset. I thought I'd spent my whole life in Shropshire."

She heard the words coming out in a rush and stopped, embarrassed. "Sorry. It's just I had no idea it was anywhere near here and . . ."

"Of course, why not. I'm sure we'll pass a pub along the way to keep the old man happy," James said. He backed up and swung the car to the right. It was a narrow lane, bordered by high hedgerows. They passed only an occasional cottage as they continued north. Liz found it hard to breathe. She didn't know why it was so important to see where she was born, but she knew she had to. At last they saw the sign "CLAREBORNE ST MARY." It was hardly big enough to be called a village. There were a few cottages made of yellow Somerset stone and a pub called the Green Man, and off to the right was St Mary's church with a fine square tower.

"Do you know the exact address?" James asked.

"All it said was Brackleberry Lodge, Clareborne St Mary, Somerset. We could ask at the pub."

"Best idea you've had all day," James's father said. He got out with enthusiasm, and he went ahead of them into the pub. The interior was dark with wood-panelled walls, and the air was heavy with smoke as several old men stood at the bar, pipes in hand. Mr Bennington ordered beers for himself and James and a cider for Liz, and they exchanged pleasantries about the weather with the barman until Liz dared to ask if they knew where Brackleberry Lodge was. She had half feared that it had been torn down like so much after the war, but the barman nodded. "About half a mile out of the village going towards Wincanton. You know the Petersons, do you? Nice young couple recently moved down here to be closer to his mother in Wincanton."

"I wanted to see the house because I was born there," Liz said.

The barman frowned as if trying to remember her. "How long ago was this?"

"Nineteen forty-one."

He laughed. "I was a teenager then, but I've lived around here all my life. What was the name?"

"Houghton. My father was Brigadier Houghton."

"Oh, right. I do remember some army family coming in for a while. Wasn't the house owned in those days by another army bloke, and your family came and stayed there for a while?"

"That's right," Liz said. "I was born there, apparently."

"Really? Then old Doc Storey would most likely have brought you into the world."

"Is he still alive?"

"Not only alive but he should be in here later. Eighty-three and still walks a couple of miles a day."

"So how do I get to the house?" Liz asked.

The barman gave directions. Liz turned to James and his father. "Maybe your dad might like to stay here while we drive out to take a look?"

Mr Bennington thought it was a splendid idea, and by the time they left he was already chatting with the old men at the bar. They drove for about a mile out of the village until they came to an impressive brick gateway. Beyond it was a curved drive and, set far back from the lane, a large white-painted house with what was probably a wisteria vine climbing around the front door. Liz stared at it, trying to take it in. No memory stirred.

"Do you want to see if anyone is home?" James asked.

"I think I should, if you don't mind."

James drove up to the house. Liz got out and rang the bell. It was opened by a young woman.

"I'm afraid this is awful cheek," Liz said, "but I was born in this house, and I've never seen it again, but we were in the area so I wondered . . ."

"You want a look inside?" the woman said. "I can't vouch for it being tidy. We've three boys, so you know what that's like, but you're welcome to come in for a moment."

"You're very kind," Liz said. "Have you lived here long?"

"No, only a year. We moved south to be near Ian's mum."

She stepped back to allow Liz inside. Liz came into the front hall, stopped, looking around. A wooden staircase ran up the right side, and above was a balcony with a railing.

"Yes," she said out loud. "This was it. This was the house."

"Ah, so you remember it from your childhood," the woman said fondly.

Liz continued to stare at that railing. She had looked through it, watching people come in through the front door, and someone had said, "What are you doing out of bed, you naughty girl? You can't let people see you in your nightgown." A woman's voice. Not her mother's. Softer. Gentler.

"I can show you the rooms, if you like, but we've had them completely redecorated. It was pretty run-down when we moved in." Obediently Liz went into a sitting room, now littered with toy trucks, where three small boys and a man were watching rugby on television, then a dining room, and a big, friendly kitchen. They were all decorated with white walls and modern Scandinavian furniture, and no spark of memory stirred for Liz. She thanked the woman, and they left again.

"Well?" James asked.

"This was the house I remembered," she said. "The one where I looked through the balcony railings and saw people below and I was taken back to my bedroom."

"You must have been very young," James said.

"I must. My father said we were only here for a year, but a one-year-old wouldn't remember things, would she?"

"Obviously you did."

They drove back to the village, where Mr Bennington was engaged in lively conversation over the state of the world and the stupidity of a war in Vietnam. Dr Storey had arrived at the pub, and Liz told him that he probably delivered her. He frowned, staring at her. "I don't remember doing so," he said. "You were living at Brackleberry Lodge? No, it must have been the midwife. Although I do vaguely remember your family coming in during the war. It was just your mum and dad and a nursemaid for you, wasn't it? No other servants, although I believe your parents had Mrs Gurney come in and clean. Now it's coming back that you must have had chickenpox when you were about two. I can picture you with spots all over you. Not a pretty sight." And he laughed.

"Are we ready to move on?" Mr Bennington said, "because if not I'll need another pint."

They got back into the car. "You're awfully quiet," James said as they drove away. "Did seeing that house upset you?"

"No, but I'm trying to make sense of things," Liz said. "You see, I remember the house, and I remember having chickenpox. Not much about it, but I can remember they made cotton mittens for me so that I didn't scratch myself. I can picture big blue-and-white gingham hands. And the doctor said it was when I was about two. But my father said we only stayed there for a year."

"He had a lot on his mind during a war," James said. "And he was away most of the time. He probably didn't remember places you lived that accurately."

"Yes, probably," Liz replied, but as they drove away, she was thinking that she had lived close enough to Weymouth to have gone to that abandoned village.

CHAPTER 30

They drove home, James's father in a good mood after his beer and chat. *He needs company,* Liz thought. *He's lonely.* They got back to the house in time for tea and cake, then James glanced across at Liz. "I need to be getting back to London," he said. "There are some things I have to go over before work tomorrow."

Liz nodded. "I'll go and pack up my things."

"There's a train at five thirty," James said. "We can make that if we hurry."

"I'll drive you to the station," Mr Bennington said.

"That's not necessary, Dad. We can call a taxi."

"No problem. The car's out there and ready."

James insisted that Liz have the front seat beside his father.

"This has been most refreshing," Mr Bennington said, giving her a smile. "You must come down more often, young lady. It's been good for me. And good for my son, too. He looks better than he has done for months."

"I can't tell you how much I've enjoyed myself," Liz said. "Thank you so much. I just wish we could have come up with more treasures in your house."

"A lot of things are in demand as building materials these days, Dad," James said. "That panelling and those beams . . . if we could get a salvage crew in there, you could probably make a pretty penny."

"There's a big difference in the army letting us nose around for bits and pieces and bringing in a demolition crew," Mr Bennington said. "It's still army property, remember."

"Then we should see about having it turned over to you again," Liz said. "They don't need it now. It's just a question of safety and a thorough check for explosives. I bet they could do that really easily if we made a fuss. I'll find out who the local MP is and get his help. It's a potential tourist site, after all."

They came to the station and bade farewell to Mr Bennington. Then James and Liz walked together on to the platform. The train was already in the station and, miraculously, they found a compartment to themselves.

"That was quite a weekend, wasn't it?" James said, coming to sit beside her when he had put the bags on the rack. "I have to tell you it was the best time I've had in ages."

"Me too." Liz looked up at him. He took her chin in his hands and kissed her. "Finally," he said. "I have you to myself. It was impossible to get rid of my father."

"He had such a good time with us, James," she said. "He really came to life, didn't he?"

"Wouldn't it be great if we could get the house back?" James said. "I've no idea where the money would come from to rebuild, but it would certainly give my father something to live for."

"I told him I'd check with the local MP. I'll do that as soon as I can," Liz said. "When I've got some of this other stuff sorted out."

"That would be super." He slipped an arm around Liz. She snuggled against him, her head in the crook of his neck, and gave a small sigh of contentment.

The train pulled out of the station as daylight was fading.

"We accomplished a lot in one weekend, didn't we?" he said.

"We found your tin soldier." She sat up, giving him a playful nudge.

"We found the house where you were born. And you remembered it."

She nodded, serious now. "And the doctor remembered I had chickenpox."

"But he didn't think he'd delivered you."

"No. Knowing my mother and how nervous she was at having a baby late in life, I think it's quite possible that she went to a nursing home in a big town for the actual birth. Into Taunton, perhaps. Or even up to Bath."

"And we did find another clue into the disappearance of your evacuated child."

"I think we can safely say that she got off the train at Ashdown Halt. Then someone took her. But I don't know how we'd ever find out who. Old Ned who looked at girls' knickers? I suppose I could return and find out where he lived and if it was possible he could have buried a child. Or those bigger boys from London who went to work on a farm." She hesitated, considering this. "I don't think anyone else in the village would have been a suspect, or someone we spoke to would have mentioned it." She stared out of the window where lights were coming on across a pretty rural landscape. "It's a pity that the woman who organized the whole thing moved away. She'd have had names and addresses, and she might even be able to give an opinion about what happened to the girl. I wonder if I could track her down in Devon?"

"If she's still alive," James said. "How old was she?"

"They didn't say, but if she was the type of spinster who ran things, she was probably in her forties or fifties."

"So she could still be going strong, organizing Girl Guides in Devon." James chuckled. "But Devon is a big county. How would you know where to start?"

"Brian's mother thought it was near Tiverton," Liz said. "That would be a start. She had such an unusual name it wouldn't be hard to look her up if she owned property, or her sister did."

"What was it?"

Liz frowned, trying to remember. "Gresham-Goodge."

"Yes, there can't be too many of them around," James said.

"She was the last. The family seat in Ashdown is now a girls' school."

"The last of the Gresham-Goodges," James said, smiling at her. "That's pretty dramatic. But having had to give up our own family seat, I feel for her."

"Apparently we had to do that as well," Liz said. "I hadn't realized until recently that my father's ancestral home was in Kent. The army took it over, just like your house, and after the war it was so damaged that Daddy didn't have the money to repair it. It was sold, and now there's a housing estate on it. It must be so painful for so many people in the same situation, like your dad."

"Life moves on," James said. "It's a different world. You need servants to run those big houses, and after the war nobody went back into domestic service. And you need money to maintain those houses and heat them, too."

"That's true," Liz said. "Maybe that's why we moved to a much smaller place after the house in Somerset." She paused. "But the doctor said I had a nursemaid. She didn't come with us when we moved. I'm trying to remember . . . I know we had a lady come in and clean in Shropshire, but I suppose I was old enough that I didn't need a nanny any more." She glanced up. "Probably as soon as I didn't need my nappies changed. My mother would have been squeamish about such things."

The lights came on in the carriage. They settled into companionable silence, Liz's head still on James's shoulder. She felt perfectly content until worrying thoughts nagged at the fringes of her consciousness. The house in Somerset, close enough to have made the journey to Tydeham. A little girl's stuffed dog dropped in a field. And now Little Lucy, still not found.

She sat up suddenly. "James, I've been thinking. Your ex-girlfriend . . ."

"All over and forgotten," he said.

"No, I don't mean that. You said she became a hippie and lived in a commune. I wonder if it's possible she knew Little Lucy's mother? How many people live in communes or squats? They all seem to be involved in protests and love-ins. Do they all know each other?"

"Possibly," he said. "But what good would that do?"

Liz shrugged. "I don't know, but it's another avenue to explore, isn't it? Lucy's mother, now married to a prospective member of Parliament was part of a counter-culture not too long ago. She failed to mention this during the investigation. Why? Because it would damage her husband's reputation? Or could it be because of something else?"

"Such as what?"

"I don't know, but I thought if we spoke to your Felicity, maybe she could shed more light on Susan's past."

"You think this child was kidnapped because of her mother's past?" James asked, his voice suddenly sharp. "Why?"

"I've no idea. But in journalism we fill in pieces of the puzzle. Either this child was taken by a random person and she's long dead, or she was taken for a reason—not for ransom, or that would have been demanded and paid by now, but to punish her parents? Revenge?"

"I suppose we could go and talk to Felicity," James said. "I don't know where she's living now, but her parents will. I could telephone them tomorrow and take you to visit her if you like."

"That would be brilliant." Liz gave him a spontaneous kiss on the cheek.

He chuckled. "I think this must be the only time my new girlfriend actually begs to visit my former one."

His new girlfriend. Liz savoured the phrase. It felt good.

CHAPTER 31

Liz opened the door of the flat and was met with the appetizing aroma of garlic and herbs. Marisa was sprawled in front of the TV, an empty plate on a tray in front of her.

"Hi there. That smells good," Liz said. "You must have been home. You can't cook like that."

Marisa leaned forward and switched the TV off. "You've got a bloody nerve," she said.

"What do you mean?" Liz stopped, surprised.

"You might have told me you were writing that article for your newspaper and that they were going to print it," Marisa said.

"I didn't know. It was a complete surprise when we saw it this morning."

"Well, you might have run it by me first," Marisa said. "I had DI Jones on the phone absolutely blasting me to high heaven. He blamed me for giving you details and letting you write it."

"But it can't have done any harm," Liz said. "In some ways it might have helped."

"Of course it could have done some harm." Marisa's voice rose. She was always so easy-going that this alone was shocking. "Don't you realize that if our hunch is true and a former kidnapper or killer has started working again, we've now alerted him that we're on to him? DI Jones is really regretting that he told you about the missing girls in the first place. I think he's already got into trouble for attempting to resurrect a cold case."

"I'm sorry. I really am. It never crossed my mind that I should clear this with anyone. Frankly I just wanted to get back to writing more than obits, and this seemed like an interesting take on current news." She came over and sat beside Marisa. "And I've got more to share, although I promise I'll share it with DI Jones first. I've found out a bit about what happened to Rosie Binks, although it's not good news. We know where she got off the train." And she filled Marisa in on the details.

"Wow. You think somebody took her from that field," Marisa said. "I don't know how we'd ever find out who. You can't ask people twenty-something years later if they remembered seeing someone with a little girl."

"The station is about half a mile from the village," Liz said, "but there were a lot of people at the platform to welcome the children and to place them. Surely someone would have seen or heard if Rosie had screamed, and the only road goes past the platform and into the village."

"So we have to think about someone grabbing her, dragging her into the bushes, killing her there and then . . ." Marisa shuddered.

"Only they searched with dogs and her body was never found."

"Well, I came up with something interesting, too," Marisa said. "I went back over the archives on Saturday when the place was quiet, and I found out a man called Alfie Hutchins was arrested in 1943 for sexually assaulting a string of children. He was given a lengthy prison sentence and was released last year."

"Oh." Liz stared at her. "Was he ever in Somerset or Dorset?"

"He was at an army base on Salisbury Plain during the war," Marisa said.

"Close enough."

"And where is he now?"

"They are not quite sure. He's finished his sentence, so no probation. I'm going to see tomorrow whether my guv will want to track him down. Oh, and there's something else, too. We had another chat with the au pair because she's asking to return home to Sweden, claiming she was traumatized by this whole thing."

"That's suspicious."

Marisa shook her head. "I don't think so. I don't get the feeling that she had anything to do with the kidnapping. But there was one thing. I asked her to tell us about Lucy. She was saying what an imagination she had, always playing these amazing games. She said Lucy had a pretend friend whom she played with in the gardens. A fairy who could do magic." She paused, staring at Liz. "I just wondered what if it wasn't a pretend friend at all. What if it was somehow a real person?"

"Hiding in the bushes in the gardens?"

"That's what I wondered."

"But how would he or she get in?"

"Good question. But the au pair might not have noticed on other occasions that there were other people in the park. She might always have used the time to read or write letters home and not bothered too much if the child was happy."

"But aren't we sure there was nobody else in the park that day? And they couldn't have got out without the au pair seeing them."

"That's the problem. Although . . ." Marisa paused again. "Two things. A pram was stolen from outside a house on a nearby street a few days before Lucy disappeared."

"A pram? A proper baby's pram?"

Marisa nodded. "And it just happens that a crossing guard at a primary school remembers someone pushing a pram that morning, walking really fast, he said."

"What sort of person? Male or female?"

"He thinks it was a woman, but he couldn't be sure. Wearing a black sweatshirt with a hood, black trousers."

"Not much to go on. Have they ever recovered the pram?"

"Not that I know of."

"I do have one suggestion," Liz said. "We know that Susan Fareham was briefly with a hippie community before she went to France. Well, it turns out that James's ex-girlfriend also went off to become a hippie, living in some kind of communal setting. I just wondered how much these people interact with other hippies or squatters or protesters or whatever. Is it possible that James's girlfriend met Susan?"

"And if she did?"

"I've been thinking," Liz said slowly. "What if Susan didn't go to France to get married there? What if she went to France because she was pregnant? Her upright and respectable parents whisked her off to France and fabricated the whole widow thing."

"Go on." Marisa was staring intently now.

"What if this might have something to do with the real father of the child?"

"Possible, I suppose. I'd still rather bet my money on the newly released child molester, if we can track him down."

"But it can't hurt to question Felicity, can it? James is going to find where she's living now."

"It certainly can't hurt. So, James and you? Any progress there? Do you like him?"

"I do. I really do. And there is progress. I can't believe I'm saying this, but it seems that he likes me, too."

"Well, hooray for that," Marisa said. "Have you eaten? Mum sent me home with a ton of food, including her fish stew. Sorry if it's stinking up the place a bit. But there's plenty left if you haven't had dinner."

"I haven't. We just got back to London, and I'd love some food." She went over to the kitchen and shovelled some of the stew on to a plate. It was an interesting mixture of vegetables and fish in a rich red sauce. Liz tasted a mouthful before she carried it over to the table and sat down.

"So the weekend with James was good?" Marisa asked, stressing the last word.

"It was very nice, thank you." Liz started to eat.

"That's all I'm going to get? It was very nice, thank you? What sort of answer is that?"

Liz put down her spoon. "We got a lot accomplished. There, does that satisfy you now?"

"You know bloody well it doesn't."

"All right. We did some more salvage work at the house. Didn't find much more, but we talked about reclaiming the property. I've promised to see if I can stir up a local MP to request it back from the army."

"We? Reclaiming the property?" Marisa raised an eyebrow.

"James's father reclaiming his property," Liz said. "He needs a purpose in life right now."

"And you're just helping out of the goodness of your heart, I take it?"

Liz looked up from her stew. "Things are progressing quite nicely, if you must know," she said. "We have kissed, on several occasions, and he referred to me as his new girlfriend."

"At least something is going right, somewhere in the world," Marisa said. "But no news on your buried body?"

"Nothing at all. Maybe we'll never find out. If it was wartime, people moved around a lot, didn't they?"

"But you saw it," Marisa said.

Liz paused, considering this. "Yes," she said. "I saw it."

When Liz went to bed that night, she lay there, listening to Marisa's steady breathing, trying to handle conflicting thoughts and emotions. She was thrilled that she and James had made such a wonderful connection, but she couldn't keep all the troubling thoughts at bay. Not just the concern about what they might learn that would help find the missing child now, but worry about what had happened to the children in the past and how she could ever find out why Rosie Binks had left her dog in a field. Why Tottie's precious book of poems was left behind in the library, and whether she could possibly be the woman whose body had now been exhumed. Which would mean it had something to do with James's family, his unstable mother who had killed herself. And if that was not enough, the underlying realization that she had once lived within fairly easy reach of the abandoned village. She could have gone there.

CHAPTER 32

James telephoned early the next morning. "I'm dashing off to work, but I just spoke to Felicity's parents. They gave me her last address but said she may not still be there. These people squat in an abandoned building until they are turfed out, then they find another one. But we can go after work today if you like."

"That's brilliant, James."

He gave an embarrassed little clearing of the throat. "It was rather awkward, actually. They got the wrong end of the stick. They thought I was trying to get her back. Her father said, 'If anyone can do it, you can, James. You'll make her see sense and come back to us.'" He hesitated. "I didn't have the heart to tell him that I didn't want her back, that I'd moved on." When she didn't reply, he said, "I had such a good time this weekend. I hope you did, too, although it was obviously distressing as well. It seems so hopeless, doesn't it?"

"I'm afraid so. I'm inclined to believe that the character they called Old Ned wasn't quite as harmless as they thought. Or perhaps it was an accident. We know he liked to look at little girls' underwear. What if he grabbed her and she started to scream, and he killed her to keep her quiet?"

"Quite possible. A big man who doesn't realize his strength. If he put his hand over Rosie's face to stop her from screaming, he could easily have suffocated her."

"But they never found the body."

"Unless it was buried in his back garden."

"That's a thought. We can follow up on that. But right now I'm anxious to meet up with Felicity."

"Do you want to go this evening?" he asked.

"Where is it?"

"It's one of the old warehouses over the Thames in Whitechapel. Not the most savoury of neighbourhoods. I could meet you somewhere?"

"Where do you work?"

"Mayfair. Curzon Street."

"How posh."

He laughed. "It is. A frightfully upscale clientele. How about we meet at Charing Cross? That's easy for us both to get to."

"All right. What time?"

"Shall we say six? I usually get off at five, but sometimes we have to work later."

"Six is fine with me. Outside the station?"

"Great."

Liz was smiling to herself as she hung up. For the first time in ages, she felt excited, energized. It was clearly a long shot, but what if the groups who squatted around London did know each other, and did cooperate in finding places to move to each time they were thrown out?

She glanced at the clock, thinking that she should go in to work. But she needed that doctor's certificate before she returned, and that would mean going to her parents and having her father telephone and explain things. And frankly she couldn't handle seeing them right now. Her mother would be distressed that she had missed Sunday lunch yet again. Liz would feel guilty. Instead she decided to stay home and write a follow-up to the missing girls.

She embarked on a description of how they traced the movements of Rosie Binks, but when she had finished, she realized that it was still an incomplete story. In a way she hoped that Marisa would track down the newly released child molester and he would confess to the murder—not just of Rosie Banks, but of Lucy. Then she stopped. Of course she didn't hope any such thing. She hoped that Lucy was still alive somewhere.

~~~

At six o'clock she came up from the Underground to see James already standing outside the station, looking for her. He gave her a kiss, as if this was now the most natural thing in the world.

"Right," he said. "Ready to venture to the seediest part of the city?"

"Let's go." He took her hand, and they headed back down to the Tube station. It was still the height of rush hour, and they stood, pressed against each other, which she found a little disconcerting. The crowd had thinned when they finally got off at Whitechapel.

"I looked at the map," James said. "We have to go this way to the river."

They crossed the high street, now teeming with both motor and pedestrian traffic, then the noise and bustle died away as they entered an area of warehouses. Fog had drifted in off the river, and the dark shapes of tall brick buildings loomed out of the mist. An occasional streetlamp glowed eerily in the fog. The hoots of tugs on the river echoed forlornly. From somewhere nearby came the sounds of shouts and then running feet. Liz shrank closer to James, and he slipped his hand into hers.

"Down this alley, I think." His voice sounded shaky, as if he, too, didn't feel quite safe here.

Who would ever want to live here? she wondered.

James peered at a street sign, nodded and led her forward. "This must be the building."

A double door gaped open. Inside was pitch dark.

"We should have brought a torch," Liz said. "Is this the right place?"

"I think so."

"Surely nobody can live here?" But as she said the words, they heard the sound of a guitar being played somewhere over their heads. And they picked up the smell of onions frying. As their eyes got used to the dark, they saw a flight of stone stairs going up in one corner.

"Careful." James's grip tightened on her hand as he led her past old packing crates and pallets. Up they went and came out on to a broad landing. Still there was no sign of light, but the guitar was still strumming, and they picked up the sound of voices off to their right. They followed it. Faint light glowed from under a door. James gave Liz a look before he went forward and tapped on it. The guitar and conversation stopped. The door was opened and a face peered out.

"What do you want?" said a man's voice.

"We're looking for Felicity Pearson. Does she live here?"

A woman pushed in front of the shadowy male figure standing at the door. "James? Is that you?"

"Hello, Felicity," he said. "Can we talk for a minute?"

"If you've been sent by my parents to lure me back home, the answer is no," she said. "They've tried everything else. I suppose they thought you'd be their trump card."

"That's not why I've come," James said. "Can we find somewhere to talk? It's awfully dark and cold out here."

"I suppose you can come in." Felicity opened the door wider, and they stepped into a room. As well as the scent of frying onions, the smell of marijuana was heavy in the air. On the floor were several mattresses. There was no electric light, but there were candles on a window ledge and on a table in the far corner, beside what looked like a gas ring and sink. A girl was standing there, stirring some kind of large pot. In the half darkness, the impression of a witch at her cauldron came to Liz. Several figures were sitting or lying on the mattresses. One nearby was smoking a joint. The guitar player was propped up against a wall and had started strumming again.

"You can sit here." Felicity plopped down on to a mattress and patted it beside her. Liz could now get a better view of her. The first thing she noticed was that Felicity was quite beautiful: long, dark hair now hid one side of her face. She was wearing some kind of long, flowing dress but had a knitted shawl over her shoulders. The whole impression was of somebody from the Georgian era. Elizabeth Bennet transported to seedy surroundings.

James glanced at Liz again before sitting beside Felicity, then Liz followed suit.

"So to what do I owe the honour of this visit?" Felicity asked. Her voice was distinctly upper-class but tinged with London accents, no doubt to make her fit in with her fellow inhabitants. "Are you missing me dreadfully?" She tossed the strands of hair back, revealing her whole face, and gave him a challenging smile.

"That's not why we've come," James said.

"We?"

He turned to Liz. "This is my friend Liz Houghton. She's a newspaper reporter. She's following up leads on the missing child."

"Which child is this?"

James stared at her. "Little Lucy. Surely you've been seeing the news?"

"We don't bother with the outside world here," Felicity said. "No television, radio or newspapers. We are our own private kingdom, you know. We don't recognize the government of Britain. We obey our own laws. We're frightfully democratic."

"Anyway." James gave a little cough. "This child was kidnapped two weeks ago now, and they are trying to work out who might have had a motive to take her."

"Some deranged sicko, I should think," Felicity said, now lifting that heavy, dark hair and letting it fall back across her shoulders. *She's trying to seduce James,* Liz realized and felt a pang of jealousy.

"If not, then it might have something to do with her family. That's why we came to see you."

"Does your friend not have a voice?" Felicity asked.

"I do. I was being polite and letting James speak first," Liz said. "But what we've discovered is that the child's mother, Susan Fareham, was once living in a squat like this, and we wondered if it was possible that anybody here might have known her."

"Susan Fareham?" Felicity frowned. "Never heard of her."

"Her maiden name was Upton," Liz said. "Her parents lived in Chislehurst. This would have been three or four years ago. I understand she joined a group of people who were squatting in Notting Hill."

"Does she mean Sky?" a man lying on the next mattress asked.

"Sky?" Liz turned to him.

"That's what she called herself, but I believe someone said that her given name was Susan. If so, she was one of the Wilds."

"The Wilds?"

The man made an effort to sit up. "They adopted a communal surname. Wild. Changed it by deed poll. So they were one family. Sky and Lark. Lark was the other girl. Skylark. Get it? They were very close. I'm not sure if they were lovers, but probably. And then there was Traveller. I kind of got the impression they were a threesome."

The girl who had been standing at the stove picked her way over to them. "I remember them," she said. "Traveller. He was at that folk club. He was groovy." She looked absurdly young.

"Do you have any idea where they might be now?" Liz asked.

The girl shook her head. "Someone told me that they were starting a commune out in Kent. They had taken over an old farm and were going to grow their own produce and be self-sufficient."

"Great idea," the man who had been talking to them said. "We should do that."

"You can't be stoned all day if you have to work the fields, Graham," one of the other shadowy figures commented, and there was general laughter.

"Do you know where in Kent?" James asked.

"Not sure." The girl shook her head again. "But I think out past Gravesend."

"And what happened to Lark? Did she go with him?"

"I don't know what happened to her," the girl said. "I never really knew any of them."

"Wasn't one of the girls pregnant?" the man asked. "I have this vision of a girl with lots of curly hair and a big belly."

But nobody answered.

No more information was forthcoming. James got to his feet and held out a hand to Liz. "We should be going. Sorry to have disturbed you."

"So is this the new girlfriend?" Felicity asked.

"That's right."

"Take good care of him," Felicity said. "He's a good bloke."

"Don't worry. I intend to," Liz replied.

~~

The fog had thickened while they were inside, and the alleyway now lay indistinct ahead of them. A fog horn sounded close by, echoing back from the tall buildings.

"Well, that was unsettling," James said. "How can people want to live like that? What do they do all day?"

"I suppose some of them might work to support the others," Liz said, "or they collect unemployment and stay there and get stoned."

"I can't understand it." James's voice was clearly upset. "She was such a fun-loving person. So bright and ambitious. She studied fashion design, and she worked for a magazine. And now look at her. Is that what drugs do to people, do you think?"

"I'm sorry you had to see that, James." Liz touched his sleeve gently. "It can't have been easy."

"At least it told me one thing," he said. "And that is I'm well and truly over her."

"It told us something else," Liz said. "Susan was pregnant when she left those people. There was no French husband, just as I suspected."

"And her current husband couldn't possibly let this information leak out. Do you think somebody knows? Somebody is actually black-mailing them right now, and there might be negotiations going on that we know nothing about?"

"I should get home and tell Marisa," Liz said.

"You're deserting me, out here in the fog?" He slipped an arm around her. "The first time we're actually alone together?"

"I would love to spend more time with you," Liz said, "but this is important, James. I just feel I can't relax and enjoy anything until this is all settled. I don't know where this all leads from here, but the police might. But at least we can put them on to the right track." She gripped James's hand more tightly as car headlights loomed out of the fog ahead of them. "And it may mean that Little Lucy is still alive."

"At least I'm going to take advantage of this bloody fog," James said. He put his arms around her, pulled her close and kissed her. The kiss was warm but not passionate, more of belonging than desire, and Liz found it just right for the moment. *He understands what I need,* she thought and found this satisfying. They walked on to the Tube station, their arms wrapped around each other.

CHAPTER 33

"You're suddenly the one who is gadding around," Marisa greeted Liz as she returned home, "and I'm the boring homebody. Were you out with James?"

"I was, as it happens," Liz said, "but it wasn't a date. James found the address of his ex-girlfriend. We went to see her. It was an awful place, Marisa. An old warehouse by the Thames in Whitechapel. There were a whole lot of hippies just lounging around on mattresses, smoking pot. It smelled really bad. My eyes are still watering. I could tell James was quite shaken up by it."

"So you found the ex-girlfriend?"

"We did. And it turned out that some people in the room knew Susan Fareham or at least knew of her. She called herself Sky in those days. And she was part of a family who called themselves the Wilds. She was involved with a man called Traveller, and also very thick with another woman called Lark."

Marisa shook her head, laughing. "The names they invent!"

"But the important thing is that one of the people we saw suggested that she was pregnant. So that proves what we've suspected—she was already pregnant when her parents whisked her to France and there was no French husband who died."

"Interesting." Marisa nodded.

"James and I wondered if there was something in this story that Susan and her husband are paying to keep quiet. Someone may be blackmailing them, using the child as a bargaining chip."

Marisa looked worried. "Don't you try and go anywhere with this information, Liz. It's now a police case, remember. No stories for your bloody newspaper. If you interfered in any way, the kidnapper could decide it was safer to kill the child. We are trained in these things."

"I understand. I'll stay well away," Liz said. "Although I'd dearly like to be there if Lucy is found. That would be the biggest scoop of any career, wouldn't it?"

Marisa frowned. "It would be more likely that she was handed over somewhere secret at dead of night. Left beside the motorway, perhaps." Then she paused. "But well done for what you've found out. You may have helped a lot. It's quite possible the background is the key." She got up, carrying an empty wine glass and dirty plate towards the kitchen. "There's still more food, by the way. We won't have to cook for weeks. Help yourself if you haven't eaten."

"I haven't. James wanted to stop and get some dinner, but I thought I should tell you as soon as possible."

"You turned down dinner with James to rush home to me?" Marisa looked back, grinning. "I am touched. I hope he wasn't jealous."

"Shut up!" Liz chuckled.

"The old girlfriend, what was she like?"

"Beautiful," Liz said. "Or at least I'm sure she was when James knew her. Now she was half hidden under hair and voluminous clothing. Why do people want to make themselves look like that? The other girl in the room looked like a witch. In fact the whole atmosphere was spooky, like stepping into some kind of magic den."

"It's the drugs," Marisa said. "They are like bats, avoiding the light."

"Thank God you and I are 'normal,'" Liz said.

"Speak for yourself. I don't ever want to be normal. I want to be exceptional." Marisa did a fake strut across the room. "So shouldn't you have gone back to work?"

"Probably," Liz said. "But I'm not going to. I still have things I want to know. I'd like to chase down the woman who was in charge when Rosie Binks went missing. I was told she moved away to Devon to take care of her sick sister around that time. I thought I might go there, maybe early tomorrow morning."

"That's a long shot, isn't it?"

"It is except . . ." She chewed on her lip, realizing that it was an expensive long shot. "Except if she was the sort of efficient woman who ran everything, how did she let one little girl get off a train and vanish?"

"It can't hurt to follow up, I suppose," Marisa said. "Although if she was the type you suggest, I bet she's been racked with guilt all these years that she let the child be taken. You'll be reopening old wounds."

Liz considered this. "But I'd still like to know. I feel that now I've started down this path, I shouldn't stop until I've tried everything. I still think the other missing child, Gloria Kane, was buried in that backyard by her mother, but I don't know how we'd ever get permission to dig and find out. One would have to have quite conclusive evidence, right?"

Marisa nodded.

"And there's the third little girl. Little Valerie Hammond. The one they found. You said her file was empty, which makes me wonder whether they've taken the contents because there was something in it that does link her to the current kidnapping. Or . . ." She paused, letting the idea form in her head. "There was something in that file that someone doesn't want anyone to know about."

"Like what?" Marisa sat up sharply.

"Like they tracked down someone they suspected of her murder, but he was in some way connected to the police, or had a lot of influence, the way they stifled my MP case."

Marisa put a hand to her mouth. "Oh my God, Liz. You don't think that DI Jones was somehow involved and that's why he's so paranoid now? He fits the profile, doesn't he? Never married, socially awkward and gets himself on the case . . ."

"Let's hope not," Liz said. "That would be awful."

"I'll try and find out more about why that file is empty," Marisa said. "And if I don't see you in the morning, enjoy your outing to Devon. You must be funding that South West Train route singlehand-edly at this time of year."

"Not funny," Liz said. "I'm burning through money I don't have and may not even have a job. But James suggested I try and move to television or radio journalism. I've no idea how, so don't ask me."

"You have devoted parents who would be willing to cough up money if you asked them, I'm sure," Marisa commented.

"I know, but I'm not going to ask them. Nor am I going to move back home." Liz went through to the bedroom and started to undress.

〰

Liz had set her alarm for six, knowing that she wanted to take a day trip to Devon and not have to spend the night. She wasn't sure how much she could accomplish in one day, but she still had this strong feeling that she should be doing something, that she was on the verge of getting somewhere, although she wasn't sure what that "somewhere" was.

She woke to darkness, fumbled and muttered as she tried to dress without waking Marisa, then headed straight for the Tube and Paddington Station. There was an early train going to Exeter and stop-ping in Tiverton. Liz grabbed a cup of tea and a bacon butty, enjoying the latter as the train pulled out of the station. It was a bright autumn day with clouds racing across a light-blue sky. She felt excited and ener-gized, as if she was doing something meaningful for a change. She'd provided a vital clue in the disappearance of Lucy, and maybe she'd come one step closer to learning what happened to Rosie Binks.

〰

She let herself daydream a little, breezing into the newsroom and hand-ing in the story in which she had solved not one but two cases of abducted children. No more obituaries for me, she'd say. Either you give me back my job in the newsroom, or I'm off. It felt wild and heady and a little scary, but she decided that now was the time to make a stand.

The train pulled into Tiverton at 9:45. She went first to the town hall. If Miss Gresham-Goodge or her sister owned property nearby, they paid rates to the council, and she'd be able to find their address. The young man she spoke to was suspicious when she asked her question.

"They are my mum's cousins," Liz said, noting how easily lying was coming these days. "We lost touch, but my mum is anxious to see them again."

"Right." He disappeared, leaving Liz standing in a cold entry hall, where a chilly wind accompanied everyone who came or went. He seemed to be gone for a long while, then returned shaking his head. "Nobody of that name, I'm afraid. At least not within our jurisdiction. If she lived out of the town, she'd be paying her rates to the county, wouldn't she?"

Fighting back frustration, Liz came out into the cold air. The weather had worsened, and dark clouds now promised rain. The county records were presumably kept in Exeter. That meant another train ride. If Miss Gresham-Goodge had moved far enough away from a town, how would Liz ever track her down without a car? She wandered through the centre of the old town, trying to think. From what she had been told about Miss Gresham-Goodge wanting to run everything, she'd have been involved with a local church. Liz headed towards the tall square tower and found herself at St Peter's church, on the banks of a river she presumed must be the Exe. It was a gloriously ornate building, maybe a little ostentatious for a small market town, and Liz thought immediately that it would be the sort of place that someone like Miss Gresham-Goodge would be attracted to. She went to the rectory and enquired. The current vicar was a younger man, who shook his head. "No, the name doesn't ring a bell, I'm afraid. We have plenty of well-meaning ladies in the altar society, but the lady you seek is not one of them." He paused. "There are several other churches in the town, and of course in the surrounding villages, too, if you happen to know where she lives."

"That's the point," Liz said. "I only know that she moved somewhere near Tiverton to be with her sick sister. And I don't know if the sister was married or not."

"That's a problem, isn't it?" He gave her a pitying look. "I'm sorry, but I have to go. We've our autumn craft fair in the church starting today. It's always a big thing around here. Artists come from all over the county. You should take a look."

Liz was about to say that she had things she should be doing, but at that moment the first spots of rain fell on them.

"Looks like it's going to pour," he said. "Better hurry."

Liz didn't dispute this but hurried with him across the churchyard and in through the ornately carved doorway. Inside there were rows of booths with everything ranging from paintings to crocheted dolls. Liz allowed herself a brisk walk up and down the aisles, admiring fine woodwork and pausing to examine jewellery. She came to a booth and stopped to look at the needlework. Her mother would like this, she thought. Mummy had always done embroidery and all kinds of needle crafts. *Perhaps I'll take her a piece from here,* she thought.

"Can I help you?" The owner was a woman about her age, with long, fair hair that framed her face with wispy curls. She was dressed in a long skirt and waistcoat that were probably hand woven. She gave Liz an encouraging smile.

"You have some lovely things," Liz said. "I thought I'd take a piece for my mother. She used to do this sort of thing, but now, with the dementia, she can't follow patterns any more."

"Oh, how sad," the woman said. "I do this as a hobby. My real job is textile design."

Liz noticed some cushions and hangings, decorating the back of the booth, then she froze. One of the sofa cushions was a striking fabric design of bluebirds on a yellow background. She felt the hair on the back of her neck standing up. She remembered the photograph of the small girl with long, fair hair, the girl who was so imaginative, so creative. Surely it was too much of a coincidence . . .

"Is this a fabric you designed?" she asked, trying to keep her voice casual while working on what to say next.

"It is. One of my favourite patterns, as it happens."

"May I know your name?" she asked.

"Jenny. Jenny Worth." The woman was still smiling.

"Oh. Thank you." Liz reached to take the cushion.

"You like that one? Good choice. Would you like me to wrap it up for you?"

"I thought it would look good on my sofa," Liz said. "What do you think of a bluebird sofa?"

There was no doubting the woman's reaction. Her face registered incredulity, her mouth open, eyes staring.

"What?" She recovered quickly. "Oh yes. Absolutely. It would make a lovely sofa. I do have a bolt of it . . ."

"I think I know who you are," Liz blurted out. "You're Rosemary Binks."

"That's right. That was my original name." The woman nodded, still relaxed, still smiling. "How on earth did you know?"

"Your mum told me about the bluebird sofa."

She was frowning now. "My mum? She was killed in the bombing when I was a little kid. I was brought up by a relative."

"So Worth is not your maiden name?"

"No. It's my married name. My maiden name was Gresham. Jenny Gresham."

"Then your relative is Miss Gresham-Goodge?"

She gave an uneasy chuckle. "No Goodge. Emily Gresham. That's my aunt's name."

"Does she still live around here?"

Jenny was looking at her oddly now. "No. She's gone into a retirement home near the coast. She got bad arthritis, and she's pretty much bedridden. I go to visit once a week."

"And her sister? Is she still alive?"

Jenny frowned. "I don't know of any sister. I didn't think we had any relatives. I certainly never met one. Aunt Emily never mentioned one. She used to say, 'You and me against the world.'" She stopped. "Look, what is this about? You tell me you remember my mother, but you're no older than me."

"My name's Liz Houghton. Could we go and talk somewhere?" Liz said. "I see there's a café at the far end." Then she added, "I have some important news for you, and I think you should be sitting down."

"All right." Jenny nodded, then turned to the man at the next booth. "Adrian, would you keep an eye on the stall for a few minutes? I'll be back."

"Of course, love." He smiled at her.

Liz led her to where chairs and tables had been set up to form a small café. It was quite busy, but they found seats in the corner and ordered two coffees. Liz took a sip of hers before she looked up to find Jenny staring at her.

"It's not bad news about Aunt Emily, is it?" she said. "You're not her solicitor?"

"No. It's good news for you, I think. But maybe bad news for your aunt."

"What do you mean?"

Liz had been thinking how to phrase this. "You left your parents when you were evacuated, right?"

"That's right. My mum put me on that train, and I never saw her again."

"You got off the train at Ashdown Halt."

"Is that what it was called? How do you know that?"

"Because I've been there. I asked about you. But nobody remembers seeing you on the platform. What happened?"

Jenny toyed with her spoon, stirring the cup. "I wanted to go to the bathroom. I desperately needed to pee. There was no loo on the train as far as I knew. And I didn't want to wet my knickers in front of everyone when the train stopped. There were women waiting for us. The big boys pushed in front of me. I ran behind the building down the bank and into the bushes. I had to get through the hedge first. I had just found a good place to pee, with no stinging nettles, when I looked up and there was this bull coming towards me. I was a city kid. I didn't know about bulls, but he looked terrifying. He was snorting and charging right at me. I dashed back into the bushes, where he couldn't reach me, and tried to find a way back through the fence."

She looked up at Liz, willing her to understand.

"By the time I came out and went back on to the platform, everyone had gone. There was nobody around. I didn't know what to do, so I started walking. Then this big car pulled up beside me, and the lady asked me who I was and told me to hop in. She took me back to her lovely big house. It was like a palace to me. She told me I'd be safe with her, and I was. We stayed there for a while, just the two of us in this big, big house, and then she said she'd had some bad news. She said my parents had been killed in a bombing, and she was now going to take care of me and be my new mummy. And we were going to move away to a place where I could go to a good school and be happy." She paused, still toying with her coffee cup. "And that's what we did. We drove away and we moved here. And I've had a wonderful life. She took great care of me, I had a good education, then I met and married a lovely chap, and we've two little girls now. Aunty Emily loves to see them—and spoil them, of course." She stopped, staring at Liz intently now. "Why are you here? What did you want to tell me?"

"I'm afraid your whole life has been a lie," Liz said. "Your aunt Emily may have taken good care of you, but she stole you. Your parents are still alive."

"No. That can't be true." Jenny's voice rose. "No. It's not true. After the war, we did a school trip up to London, and I went to find the street where I was born, and all the houses were flattened. Gone."

"That's right. But your parents moved out to a new flat in Lewisham. I've been there. I met your mother. She told me about the bluebird sofa and how artistic you were."

"No." Jenny shook her head violently. "It can't be true. Can it? My mother's alive?"

"And your father. And all these years they've grieved for you. They had the police searching for you, you know. No trace of you was ever found, except your toy dog in a field two weeks later, so everyone expected the worst. That you'd been abducted and killed."

"Oh, how terrible." Jenny put her hand to her mouth. "My poor mother. All these years. Why did Aunt Emily do it, do you think? What made her lie to me?"

"To start with, she was probably just doing the right thing," Liz suggested, not sure at all that this was true. "Taking you in because you were lost. Doing her job to find a placement for you nearby, but then she fell in love with you, and she couldn't let you go. And she realized what a perfect chance she had. Nobody knew you were there. Nobody had seen you except her."

"So she moved away with me. To a place where nobody knew us." Jenny spoke the words slowly, as if digesting them as she said them.

Liz nodded. "It was wartime. Everyone moving around. Nothing was permanent. Not easy to check on who was bombed and killed. Easy to register her as your guardian."

"Yes."

There was a long silence. In the hall a voice was announcing tickets for a raffle. The tea urn hissed. Coffee cups clinked. There was light chatter. But Jenny sat, frozen like a statue.

"What am I going to do?" she asked. "If I tell people the truth, Aunt Emily will go to prison, won't she?"

"I don't know. I suppose she might."

"I don't want that to happen. She was always so kind to me. She's an old lady and not well. I want her to live out her days in peace. And yet . . . and yet she robbed my parents of their daughter. They didn't see me grow up or go to my first dance or win prizes at school."

"Your parents can meet your daughters now," Liz said. "And you've got a younger sister. Born after the war. She's got a little boy."

"I've a sister?" Jenny's face lit up. "I can't believe it. It's too much to take in. I have to talk to my husband, Jeremy. Decide what to do next. Of course I want to see them, but I have to think."

"I understand," Liz said. "It's overwhelming right now. Look, I'll give you their address, and what you do is up to you."

"I have to see Aunt Emily first," Jenny said. "I have to hear the story from her own mouth. I have to see if she shows any remorse for what she did."

Liz took out her notebook, writing down the Binkses' address and phone number, also her own.

"Telephone me when you come to London," she said. "I could come with you when you first go to your parents if you want me to. Give me your address, too. Would you like me to break the news to them, or would you rather do that?"

"I'd like you to," Jenny said. "I don't want one of them dying of a heart attack when I turn up on their doorstep." She stared across the hall. "All these years," she said. "All these years of picturing my mum blown to pieces and my dad killed in the army. How can I ever make it up to them?"

"By being alive and well. That's it, isn't it?" Liz stood up. "I should go. You've a lot of thinking to do. You need time to process this."

Jenny stood up, too. Their coffees remained undrunk. "I must get back to the stall, I suppose. I can hardly leave it now, just when the place is filling up." She started to walk back, then she turned abruptly to Liz. "What is your role in all of this?"

"I'm a newspaper reporter, doing a piece on lost children, and your name came up. I traced your parents, and I was told that Miss Gresham-Goodge moved near Tiverton. It was pure chance that I came in here today. If it hadn't been raining, I probably would never have come in."

"So you're going to include me in your story." Jenny was frowning now. "Then everyone will know about my aunt Emily. The police will find out. They'll come after her, won't they?"

"It's a tricky one," Liz said. "Give me time to think."

"I can't let her go to prison, Miss Houghton," Jenny said. "It would kill her."

"I understand."

"You've done the good thing. You've reconnected me with my family. Do you have to include us in the story?"

"I'll see if I can find a way around it, but once you meet your family, other people will know. It will be general knowledge."

"I suppose it will. Gosh, it's complicated, isn't it?" Jenny stared at her, and Liz saw the worry in her eyes.

"Talk to your aunt first," Liz said. "Maybe there are ways to protect her. She could always say that she genuinely believed your parents were dead. Or even that you looked like an undernourished child, and she realized she could give you a better life."

"She's not the type who lies easily," Jenny replied. "She was always very hot about doing the right thing . . ." She paused. "Except when it really mattered."

They walked back together. It was only then that Liz noticed the sign above the booth. It was painted with plants and flowers, and it said, "ROSEMARY AND THYME."

A LITTLE GIRL

The little girl was finding her suitcase too heavy, and the gas mask bumped up and down across her front as she walked. It was warmer than usual, and she felt hot and clammy in her good coat. But Mum had insisted she wear it. "You'll be cold once it's winter," she said. "And then you'll thank me that I made you wear it."

The little girl dumped the suitcase and opened the buttons of the coat. That was better. She stood on the corner, gulping in big breaths of air that blew in from the river. She was quite excited about going to the country. She had only been out of London once, on a school outing to the seaside for the day. That had been exciting. She wondered if they'd be taken anywhere near the seaside now. Her mum didn't know. "You'll find out when you get there," she had said. The little girl could see that her mum was upset she was going. That was why she didn't want to come to the school with the other mums. She claimed she had to be at work in the factory on time, but the little girl suspected it was because she knew she was going to make a fuss and cry.

The girl lifted her suitcase again. It weighed a ton. She reckoned her mum had packed every single thing she owned into it. On she staggered, waiting for the traffic light to turn before she crossed the busy street. Then she turned into a quiet back road. Here it was peaceful after the traffic noise. Nobody else in sight. Only the sound of a radio voice giving the morning news from an upstairs window. It wasn't far to the station now. She could see its roof, sticking up behind the rows of houses. The suitcase handle was making her hand burn. She put it down and spat on her palm. She wasn't aware to begin with of the big black car that drew up beside her.

"Do you need a lift somewhere?" The man inside the car had wound down his window.

"It's all right. I'm only going to the station," she said.

"The station? By yourself? Are you running away from home?" He asked it almost as a joke.

"No!" She could tell the man was teasing in that annoying way grown-ups had. "I've got to meet my class, and we're getting on a train out to the country," she said. "We're being evacuated."

"Well, I'm driving past Victoria Station, as it happens. How about I take you that far? That will save you lugging that heavy suitcase, won't it?"

The little girl hesitated. She had been warned about strangers. But the man looked like someone's uncle. What's more, he had a posh voice and he was wearing a uniform, so he must be all right. And the suitcase was jolly heavy.

"Thank you, sir," she said. "It's very kind of you."

"Not at all. We all have to help each other when there's a war on, don't we?" He came around and opened the back door. "Put your case in there." And then the passenger door. "Hop in. That's right. Off we go, eh?"

And off they went.

CHAPTER 34

On the journey home, Liz felt as emotional as Jenny Worth must be feeling. On one hand it was a sense of triumph. She had followed the clues and found the truth. She was a good investigative reporter. And when she wrote the story . . . then she stopped. She could never write the story now, because if she did, an old woman would go to prison. She mulled over everything she had learned. No bathroom on a train, leading to a little girl having to retreat to the bushes, being chased by a bull, finding everyone had gone. And at that very day, the organizer was late . . . *What small things can change our fate?* she thought.

Then she sat up suddenly, staring at her reflection in the train window. A flash of inspiration had come to her about Lucy. The man in the squat had said, "Wasn't she pregnant?" And she had assumed it was Sky. What if it wasn't Sky at all? What if it was Lark? And what if Sky . . . Susan . . . had taken another woman's child? Sky had been in love with the man, Traveller, hadn't she? But another girl was having his baby . . . a girl she had also loved. And she felt betrayed, maybe? Jealous?

She sat impatiently, waiting for the train to pull into Paddington Station. Once there, she sprinted for the Underground and rode the Circle line around to St James's Park. At New Scotland Yard she was disappointed to find that DC Marisa Young was not available. Out on a case, she was told. No idea when she'd be back. Liz could leave a message.

With no other option she scribbled out on the piece of paper offered her, *Have to talk to you right away. We may have got something wrong about Susan. Important. I'll be at the flat. Call me.*

She was so temped to go to Ladbroke Square herself, to speak to Susan and find out the truth, but Marisa had made it very clear that she should not interfere in a police investigation. Anyway, she doubted that Susan or her husband would want to speak to her—the press. She also wanted to see Rosie's parents and give them the good news, but she needed to be close to the telephone for when Marisa called her. Reluctantly she got back on the Tube, then walked to the flat. The smell of garlic still lingered, and she realized she hadn't eaten all day. She warmed up the last of the stew but found that she was too excited to eat. Her new theory thundered through her brain. Where was bloody Marisa? Why didn't she telephone?

The call didn't come until five thirty.

"You're home?" Marisa said. "I thought you were going to Devon."

"I was. I did and I'm back," Liz replied. "Look, can we talk right now? It's important. I may have a vital clue about Lucy."

"We have just come back from Kent," Marisa said. "You know, the commune you told us about? We talked to the man who knew Susan. The one who calls himself Traveller."

"And?"

"I'm afraid you got it wrong. It wasn't Susan who was pregnant. It was the other girl. Lark, she called herself. Her real name was Joan. He said that Sky, or Susan, was sort of in love with her. And with him, he thinks."

"That's exactly what I figured out, Risa. Listen, what if Lark had the baby and Sky took it and passed it off as her own? And Lark wanted her daughter back."

"There's only one thing wrong with that," Marisa said. "Traveller said that things went wrong with the pregnancy towards the end. Lark was really into drugs by that time. She was taken into some kind of clinic. Sky went with her to give her support. And . . ." She gave a dramatic pause. "And he never saw either of them again. But he heard that Sky had gone back to her family and that Lark had killed herself. Jumped off a bridge, apparently."

"And the baby?"

"He assumed the baby had died, too. He thought she'd had complications with the delivery and that was why she killed herself."

"But what if he'd got it wrong? What if the baby lived? What if Lark didn't kill herself? And now she has come to reclaim her child?"

"It sounds like a good theory," Marisa said. "It would be easy enough to go through death records if Lark still lived in the city. If she'd gone home to somewhere in the country . . . well, that would take time, wouldn't it?"

"We have to speak to Susan right away," Liz said. "Can we go over there right now?"

"We?"

"I'm the one who came up with the theory. You can take me along as a friend who knew Susan's family. I promise I'll let you do the talking."

"I'd have to clear it with my DI first," Marisa said. "At the Met we don't just go shooting off on our own. That would get me back on foot patrol in an instant."

"Talk to your DI."

"Okay. I can't promise anything. See you then." Marisa hung up.

Liz changed into her most conservative suit, brushed her hair and put on a hint of make-up. It was important to make the right professional impression with Susan, and with anyone she had to meet at the Met. The Tube was packed, and she tried not to get squashed and creased as she rode to St James's Park Station, emerging into the last streaks of daylight and the glow of the city beyond. Marisa was waiting for her, as was DI Jones.

"So Marisa says you might have more for us on this case?" he asked. "She told you we checked into her background with the information you provided? Nothing that gets us anywhere, I'm sorry to say. Susan had a brief fling with the counter-culture. Her friend Lark got pregnant,

Susan was miffed because the bloke liked Lark better, and Susan went home to Mummy. Lark was into drugs, the pregnancy had a bad outcome, and she topped herself."

"But what if that wasn't how it happened?" Liz said. "Marisa told me that Sky was close to Lark and went with her to the clinic. What if she took the baby, and that made Lark try to kill herself? Only she didn't succeed . . . she found out where Sky was living, not too far away in Notting Hill from their old squat, and she plotted to steal the child back."

DI Jones was eyeing her warily. After a long pause, he sucked in through his teeth and said, "I suppose it could be possible."

"It's the only logical solution we've come up with so far," Marisa said. "Perhaps there is a police report on Lark's attempted suicide. It depends if she used her real name or went by Lark Wild."

"Lark Wild." He shook his head, giving a deprecating snort. "It's about time those people cleaned themselves up and got a job."

"Anyway." Marisa stopped him before he could go on. "It's worth a visit, isn't it, guv? Just to see Susan's face when she finds out what we know. I think we could take a good guess about whether Liz's idea could be true."

"I'd have to clear it with the super," he said after a pause.

"Can you do that now?" Marisa asked. "I saw him a little while ago. And if we're wrong, it can't do any harm, can it? We haven't spoiled the investigation."

"I suppose not." He stared from one woman to the other. "You two go alone. Better coming from another girl her age. I know how you women like to natter and gossip together."

Liz ignored the sexist remark. "Thank you, sir," Liz said. "We won't let you down."

He gave her a hard stare. "I should have refused to let you join us when we met in Weymouth. You've been nothing but a headache for us ever since. Who did the dead body in Tydeham turn out to be?"

"They haven't identified it yet." She wondered whether to tell him about Rosie/Jenny but decided it could wait. First she had to tell Rosie's parents. Before that, she had to see if her hypothesis led to finding a missing girl today, in London.

"Do you want me to ask the super for you, guv?" Marisa said.

"No, I bloody don't," he said. "You stay right here until I get back."

They watched him walk away. "He's having a hard time with not wanting to believe that we may be right, or that we've come up with a lead he hadn't thought of," Marisa said when the inspector had vanished into the lift. "Any time a woman shows initiative, he feels threatened. Thank God he never married."

"It's hard to imagine any woman wanting to be his wife," Liz said. "I wonder if he was always like this? People change over the years, don't they?" She paused. "You didn't ask him about the empty file, did you?"

"I did," Marisa said. "He said he'd no idea. It was wartime. Things got lost. Or it might have been lost when they moved from the old building. But he didn't look too worried."

They waited, watching a stream of employees, police and civilian staff leave for the day, buttoning up coats against the cold. The stream had slowed to a trickle by the time DI Jones came back. They couldn't tell from his face what the news would be, as he looked grim.

"He said why not," DI Jones said. "He said we're not getting anywhere, so he's willing to try anything right now. However kooky it is."

Liz nudged Marisa. "Ready to go, then?"

"I'll get my coat."

As the DI started to walk away, Liz couldn't resist saying, "I may have some news for you soon about one of your missing girls, Inspector."

"My girls? From the war?" She saw the spark of interest in his face battling with disbelief.

"That's right. Some good news."

"I'll believe it when I see it," he said.

"I have a couple of people I need to check with first."

Marisa reappeared, slightly out of breath, and Liz headed for the Tube station when Marisa grabbed her sleeve. "We'll take a taxi," she said. "The Underground is crazy at this hour." She managed to hail one, and soon they were heading past Buckingham Palace and around Hyde Park. "The super will be telephoning to let them know that we're on our way," she said. "It's better if we are seen to arrive in a taxi. More official looking."

Liz was chewing on her lip, unable to calm her excitement as the taxi came to a halt in stopped traffic on Kensington High Street. What if they were on to something important? What if her hunch was correct, and they found the child alive and well? It was almost too much to hope for. It was as if Marisa was thinking the same sort of thing, as neither of them spoke as they drove up Church Street and past Notting Hill Tube Station.

CHAPTER 35

When they finally came to a halt in Ladbroke Square Gardens, the cabby leaned back. "I have to drop you here, love," he said. "On account of the police cars still being outside that house where Little Lucy was taken."

"That's fine," Marisa said and paid him, not mentioning what their mission was.

There was a police constable standing guard at the front door. Marisa showed him her warrant card, and they were admitted to the house. Susan Fareham came down the stairs to meet them. She looked elegant in a long blue gown that set off her porcelain skin and blonde hair. She was quite lovely, Liz thought. No wonder Anthony Fareham was smitten with her when he met her in the South of France. *She looks like a perfect politician's wife.* She paused on the bottom step, eyeing the two young women with suspicion.

"I was told that . . . ," she began.

"Mrs Fareham, I'm DC Young from the Met." Marisa stepped forward. "And this is a reporter friend who has been helping us with our enquiries into the disappearance of your daughter."

"Your superior said you might have news for me? Or at least a new lead?" Her voice sounded posh and polished, and it was hard to imagine her lying on a mattress in that warehouse amid so much squalor. Perhaps her heart had never been in it, Liz thought. Perhaps she had met those people and fallen for either Traveller or Lark or both. Or it had been an experiment or act of defiance.

"We have what may be a new lead," Marisa said. "If we may come in and talk to you?"

"Of course. In here." She led them into a sitting room that was furnished with a tasteful light-blue three-piece suite and low white tables. There were several large houseplants, a couple of pieces of modern art on the walls, and an ormolu clock on the mantelpiece. Radiators gave a pleasing warmth, even though there was no fire in the fireplace. It was the sort of room that shouts money and breeding.

"Please take a seat." She motioned to the sofa, and they sat.

"Mrs Fareham," Marisa said. "This may be painful for you, but we hope you can be completely honest with us. We promise whatever we say in this room will be confidential."

"You've received a ransom note?" Her voice quivered.

"No. We've had no communication with the person who took your child, but we hope you might help us to locate her," Marisa said.

"I don't see . . . ," Susan Fareham began.

"Mrs Fareham," Marisa said, "we have been looking into your past history. We have now been able to put most of it together."

"Meaning what?"

Liz saw a shiver of alarm cross her face.

"Sky?" Marisa said. "Tell us about when you were called Sky."

Susan's fair skin flushed bright red. "Oh," she said. "You know about Sky."

"And Lark and Traveller," Marisa said. "We have spoken with several people who knew you in those days."

"All right. I suppose having a rebellious period, experimenting with a different way of life, is something most young people try." She now sounded defiant.

Liz decided she had been silent long enough. She thought that her own cultured accent might establish more of a bridge than Marisa's pronounced London vowels.

"Mrs Fareham," she said, "perhaps you can explain why you took Lark's baby."

There was a stunned intake of breath. Susan opened her mouth to say something. "But I . . . Whoever told you . . ." Then it was as if something deflated. "How did you ever find out? Nobody knew. Nobody, I swear."

"So you don't deny it?" Marisa said.

"My husband must never know." Susan reached across and grabbed Liz's hand, squeezing it tightly. "It would be the end of everything if he knew."

"We do understand," Liz said.

"But how can any of this help me get Lucy back?"

On the mantelpiece the ormolu clock chimed six thirty.

"It may be vital," Liz said. "Can you tell us what happened and why you ended up with your friend's baby?"

"Because I knew she'd let her die," Susan said. "We all experimented with drugs, but some more than others. I stuck to pot after one bad trip with LSD. But Lark, she got more and more into it. And then she found heroin. Before the baby was born, there were complications. She wasn't eating well. She wasn't taking care of herself. She'd become a real addict. When she went for a check-up at a clinic, they admitted her for the sake of the child. I went along for support. I was . . . close to her, you know. We talked of it as our baby. Finally the poor little thing was born, and I saw right away that she wasn't going to take care of the baby. She ignored her when she cried. She forgot to feed it. Breastfeeding didn't work, and she wasn't washing the bottles properly. And the drugs had changed the way she felt about me. She said some cruel things, like she didn't want me in her life any more. So I made the decision. I'd save the baby. I took her and ran. And showed up at my parents' house, claiming I'd just had the child."

She looked from one face to the next, wanting to see approval. Liz gave her an understanding nod.

"They were wonderful. They whisked us away to their place in the South of France. Managed to smuggle the baby across the Channel in their car. No problem. And once there, we invented a good story for me. One that was acceptable to the sort of people my parents mixed with. And then I met Anthony, and the rest is history. I didn't worry about meeting my old set again because we would never cross paths and I looked so different. I heard through the grapevine that Lark had killed herself. I thought I was completely safe." She stopped abruptly, as if the thought had just come to her. "Are you saying that the kidnapping had something to do with one of them? But why?"

"What we're wondering," Liz said, "is whether Lark didn't die. Whether she wanted her child back."

"But that's absurd," Susan said. "I was told she jumped off a bridge. Then she survived?"

"We are not sure yet, but our people are looking into it. And the place where you were once squatters was not far from here, was it?"

"Not far at all. Only a few streets away. On Freston Road just off Bramley Road." She shuddered. "Awful place, actually. We drove past a few weeks ago. I thought that so ironic when Anthony first took me to our house. Of course, I couldn't tell him that this part of London was not unfamiliar to me." She sat there, staring past Liz and Marisa at the wall, where there was a painting of the Scottish Highlands. "Are you trying to tell me that Lark took my daughter? How could she? Kristina swears that nobody came into the gardens and she could see the gate all the time."

"Is it possible that your daughter was small enough to squeeze through the railings?"

She considered this. "I suppose, but why? She wouldn't go with a stranger. She knows better than that."

"What if the person wasn't a stranger?" Liz said. "You told the officers that your child was very imaginative. She had a pretend friend she played with in the bushes. A fairy, I believe. What if that fairy was actually a real person?"

"Lark, you mean?"

Liz nodded. "And she groomed your daughter. Won her trust. And at the right moment she lured her away."

"Oh God." Susan Fareham sunk her head into her hands. "Lark used to be so . . . appealing. Such fun. The way her eyes sparkled when she smiled. And she had a soft, gentle voice. She'd know the right things to say. Any little girl would be entranced . . ." She looked up, her eyes pleading. "If she's taken Lucy and she's still on drugs, she won't know how to care for her any more than when she was born. How do we get her back?"

"Did she have connections outside of the city?" Marisa asked. "Family somewhere she might go to?"

Susan shook her head. "She was estranged from her family. Her mum kicked her out when she was sixteen, after the mum's boyfriend started getting interested in her. She came from up north. Bolton. But she wouldn't go back there. She said she hated it. She loved the feel of the city."

"But might she have gone down to one of the new communes?" Liz asked. "DC Young was at the one in Kent today where Traveller now lives."

"Traveller? You saw him?" Liz saw the flicker of interest in Susan's face.

Marisa nodded.

"How is he?"

"Doing well, I suppose," Marisa said. "They are growing veggies and plan to be self-sufficient."

"Oh, how wonderful." A wistful look flashed across her face for a second. "We talked about that. Finding some land. Making our own little community. Sharing everything."

"Was Traveller the father of Lark's baby?" Marisa asked.

Susan shrugged. "Hard to tell. As I said, we shared everything. She liked to think he was. She was in love with him. But he liked me better,

I think." She sat up, alert again, "What is the next step to finding my daughter?"

"Tracking down where Lark might have gone with the child. We don't know if she's still involved with one of the hippie groups or if she's on her own. She'd need money to support a child. Does she have a job? But as we've said before, this is all supposition until we find out whether she really did jump off a bridge and whether she was killed."

There was a silence, punctuated only by the ticking of a clock.

"You don't happen to have any photos of Lark, do you?" Marisa asked. "It would be helpful to let our people know who they are looking for."

Susan stood up. "I might have one. Wait here."

She left them alone. Marisa made eye contact with Liz. "I hope to God we're right after raising her hopes like this. I wouldn't want to be the one now to tell her we've discovered the child's body."

"It makes so much sense," Liz said. "It's the only reasonable explanation. It has to be right."

They looked up as they heard Susan's feet tapping down the tiled hallway. She came in, holding a small snapshot. "This is all I have," she said. "We were not really into modern things like cameras. But we were at a street fair once." She handed Marisa the photograph. It showed two young women, their long hair windblown, arms around each other, laughing for the camera. Sky's hair was medium brown, but Lark's was dark, and a mass of tight curls stood out from her head. She was wearing a dark-red kaftan that exposed a good deal of her breasts, and she looked exotic, with sparkling eyes and a beaming smile.

"May we borrow this?" Marisa held out her hand. "We'll take good care of it, I promise. I'll have copies made, then return it to you."

"All right." Susan was clearly ill at ease. "But what if Anthony somehow gets wind of it? What if he finds out why we're looking for her? What if we find her and she spills the beans? What am I going to do?"

She grabbed Liz's hand again. "If we find her, will I go to prison for kidnapping? I only did it because the baby was going to die. Oh God."

Now she put her head into her hands. "This is so complicated. I don't know what to do next."

"I presume it's up to you whether you leave Lucy with her birth mother," Marisa said. "Your decision entirely. We can go away and pretend this conversation never happened."

Susan shook her head wildly. "No. I must have my daughter back. She's all . . ."

She was going to say, "She's all that I have," Liz thought with interest. Was the rumour true that Anthony Fareham was gay and just wanted a wife and child for respectability? Liz felt deep compassion for the woman and what she was going through.

"We have to hope that, if this turns out to be true and we find Lark and your daughter, Lark can see how much better off she will be with you, and what a good life you can offer her," Liz said.

"You do realize she could prove the child was hers if she had to," Marisa said. "There would have been a birth certificate and a record at that clinic."

Susan gave an almost imperceptible nod. "But then my parents had a second birth certificate issued in France. Lark would have to prove that my Lucy was the same child as her missing baby." She appeared to think this over. "That would take money for a court case, wouldn't it? I'd have to ask Anthony. Tell him the truth."

"My suggestion would be to come to some kind of agreement—let her visit and you raise the child," Marisa said.

"Yes. I'd be prepared to do that, only . . . only what would Anthony say?"

"If he wants his family with him when he runs for Parliament, I suspect he'd keep quiet," Marisa said. "Do you want us to look for your daughter and return her to you, then?"

"Of course I do. More than anything."

Marisa stood up. "We'll have every available officer on it, you can be sure, Mrs Fareham. Let's hope for the best, shall we?"

CHAPTER 36

"How about that!" Marisa looked at Liz as they stood in the darkness of Ladbroke Gardens. City sounds were muted and sounded far-off, and Liz could hear tree branches creaking and tapping against the railings in the stiff breeze. "Your hunch was right. Lark has to be alive, doesn't she? And she must have taken back her daughter. I need to get back to the Met and put out an all-points bulletin for Lark. Let's see what info they've dug up on her."

"Wait." Liz grabbed at her coat. "I've been thinking. If Lark lured the girl away and had her squeeze through the railings, how did she get her out of the square without being seen? From that photo she's a rather striking woman. People would have noticed. And what then? Surely she doesn't have a car. They get on a bus? The Tube?"

Marisa grabbed her arm. "Remember a pram was reported stolen, and the one statement we got that someone walked past a crossing guard, pushing a pram and walking really fast? Someone wearing a hood and dark clothing?"

"So she didn't go far!" Liz grabbed her arm now. "What if she's gone back to that squat they used? Freston Road? Where it joins Bramley Road? That's close by, isn't it?"

"I think so. There will be a map at the bus stop, I expect. Come on, let's go and see."

Together they hurried from the square. There was no map at the nearest bus stop, but two men standing outside a pub pointed them in the right direction. It was further than they thought.

"We should have taken a cab," Marisa said, pausing and breathing hard. "My feet are killing me."

"It can't be far now," Liz encouraged.

They set off again, through a maze of small backstreets, some seeming to be genteel and well maintained and others horribly run-down, with broken glass on the pavement and loud music blaring from open front doors. At last they came to Freston Road. They passed a row of ordinary terraced houses. Cooking smells came from one of them, onions and spices. It all looked like any other street in London until they came to a shop with its window boarded up. Several young West Indian men were standing outside the pub on the corner.

"Hello, ladies, want to meet a real man?" one of them called out. "One who can show you a good time?" He had a strong Caribbean accent.

"Too busy," Marisa said. "I'm a police officer, and we're on a case."

"No kidding? You're joking, right?"

"No joke," Marisa said. "I can show you my warrant card if you don't believe me. Now perhaps you can help. I'm looking for this woman. Come into the light. The one with all the hair. Have you seen her around here?"

"A white woman, is she?" One of them squinted at the photograph.

"Could be." Another leaned closer, too. "No. I don't think I've seen her."

"Wait a minute." The first man pushed them aside. "I think I've seen her. But she had her hair under a woolly hat."

"Any idea where she might be living? On this street?"

"Ain't no white people living here no more," one of the men said.

"What about an empty building where some hippies used to squat?" Marisa asked.

"Oh, the old factory. They got turned out some time ago now."

"Where is it?"

"See that big red brick building there? That's it. They took it over for a while. My mum tells me they left a hell of a mess. Used all the cupboards as lavatories. She was so glad when they went. She said they must have brought in every rat for miles."

"Thank you," Marisa said. "You've been really helpful."

"Are you sure we can't buy you young ladies a drink?" the first one asked.

"Tempting, but I have to report back to the Met, or they'll send a car out looking for me," Marisa said.

"So what's this woman done?" one of them asked.

"She might have kidnapped a little girl." She hesitated. "You haven't seen a little girl on this street? Long blonde hair, about three years old."

"If she kidnapped her, she wouldn't let her go wandering around now, would she?" the first man said. "She'll have her hidden away somewhere or taken out into the country."

"Right," Marisa said. "We'll go and check out that old factory, just to make sure. Thanks for your help."

"No problem, darlin'," one of them said. "Always willing to help the police, aren't we, boys?"

There was laughter behind them as they walked away.

Another street down they came to the big brick building. It definitely had a derelict feel to it. The windows at ground level were boarded up, and no lights shone out from the upper levels.

"Doesn't look promising, does it?" Marisa turned to Liz. Liz was still in awe at the calm way Marisa had handled the encounter with the young West Indians. The door was also nailed shut. Liz went around to the side of the building. There was a narrow side alley with dustbins.

"Look, there's another door round here," she said. She pushed it, and it swung open. Marisa came to join her. "I wish I smoked," she said, "then I'd have matches or a lighter on me. It's too dark to see anything, isn't it?"

Liz stepped inside, cautiously, one step at a time. Once inside, her eyes accustomed themselves to the darkness, and she could just make out a wooden staircase going up against one wall. The banister had fallen away, and it did not look inviting.

"Surely nobody can be living here," Marisa said.

"There are dustbins outside," Liz said. "See if any of them have been used lately."

They both went back into the alley. Marisa took the lid off the first dustbin, then stepped back, reeling. "Phew. It don't half pong."

They both peered in. Inside they could make out food wrappers, orange peels.

"Look at this." Liz reached in and pulled out an empty milk bottle. She put her nose to it and sniffed. "It's gone off, but it's not that old," she said. "Look, it's almost liquid at the bottom. If she had a child with her, she'd want to give it milk, wouldn't she?"

"You really think she's up there with Lucy?" Marisa asked.

"Somebody was here recently," Liz said. "The alley only goes to the back of the building. Nobody else would be using the dustbins."

"Unless someone living nearby knew there were empty bins here and took advantage of them." Marisa stared up at the tall blank facade.

"But an empty milk bottle," Liz said. "Other people put their bottles out for the milkman, don't they? They don't dispose of them."

Marisa was still staring at the blank wall of the building, hesitating.

"Should we try and go up?" Liz said. "We could go to that shop on the corner that's still open and buy a couple of lighters so we can see where we're going."

But Marisa shook her head. "I don't have authority to do that. If she's really there and we're going to make an arrest, it will need the proper team. We can't risk anything happening to the child. I'll find a phone box and try and catch the super before he goes home. You wait here, but don't go up."

"All right." Liz sat on the bottom steps while Marisa disappeared into the night. Inside was completely still. Then Liz thought she heard a floorboard creak. Ears now finely tuned, she went cautiously up that first flight of stairs to where it opened to a landing. Total darkness met her. There was a faint smell of rot and decay. She paused, listening. Then she froze. From above she heard a tiny voice singing softly, "Twinkle, twinkle, little star."

A LITTLE GIRL

The little girl sat on the mattress on the floor, hugging her knees to herself. "Twinkle, twinkle, little star," she sang. Mummy had said that singing makes you feel better, but it didn't make her feel that much better right now. She felt sad. She couldn't see any stars from the dirty window. The one candle on the shelf did not light the whole room, making scary shadows, and the smoky stick that the lady had lit again made it smelly and strange. She hated the dark, hated everything about this room. She was cold and hungry. The fairy lady didn't seem to care. She was lying on the mattress now, her eyes closed. The little girl didn't know if she was asleep or just thinking. She did a lot of thinking.

"Are you awake?" the little girl dared to ask at last. "I'm hungry."

"You had a hamburger just this afternoon. From Wimpy's, remember?"

"That was yesterday," the little girl said.

"Oh yeah. Right." The fairy lady sat up, then stood up. "Oh, it's dark already. I suppose I can go out and get us something to eat."

"How long do we have to stay here?" the little girl asked. "When can we go to your magic place in the country?"

"Soon," the fairy lady said. "Very soon. You have to be good and quiet just a little bit longer so the bad people don't find us first. Okay?"

"Okay," the little girl said, but it wasn't really okay. She had started to wonder if there really was the magic place in the country the fairy lady had told her about. After all, she had told fibs before.

The fairy lady picked up her shawl and wrapped it around her shoulders. Then she went to the window and looked out. "Oh no," she said. "No. They're here. They've found us. Quick. Up you get."

"Where are we going?" The little girl picked up the fear in the lady's voice.

"On an adventure," the lady said. "Give me your hand."

The little girl obeyed. The lady led her on to the landing and pushed open a door. Stairs went up.

"Where are we going?" the little girl asked again. "Are we going to see my mummy now? Can I go home?"

"I'm your mummy," the fairy lady said. "I'm your real mummy. The other mummy was just pretending. Come on."

The little girl went with her, unwilling, but the hand held hers firmly. Up the rickety steps until they came out on to a flat roof. Around them lights of the city sparkled and twinkled. Noises of cars and voices floated up to them.

"What are we doing up here?" the little girl asked. "Are we hiding?"

"No, we're going to fly away," the lady said. "We're going to fly to that magic place I told you about. The white castle on the hill with the green grass all around it and the lake with the swans, remember? We're going to fly there."

"I can't fly," the little girl said.

"But I've brought fairy dust with me," the lady said. "I'll sprinkle some on you, and then you can fly very well."

"Will I get wings?" the little girl asked.

"Invisible wings," the lady said. "But they work really well. Come on. Climb up here. Are you ready?" She looked down at the little girl. She was giving an encouraging smile. "Here is the fairy dust now. Sprinkle, sprinkle. Now you're magic like me. And when I say go, we fly off the roof. Ready?"

The little girl didn't feel any different. She glanced behind her to see if any wings might have appeared. Then she gasped. A big dark shape had appeared in the doorway.

"Now!" the fairy lady shouted.

"No, I don't want to fly. I want to go home to my mummy." The little girl tried to wrench her hand free from the fairy lady's grasp.

The big dark shape became a tall man in a dark-blue uniform. He hurtled across the roof, grabbed the little girl and snatched her away. The fairy lady looked back to see more dark shapes emerging. She turned to face outward and flew away.

CHAPTER 37

Marisa had followed the officer, while Liz stood at the bottom of the steps. For a long moment, there was silence, then she heard a scream from the street. She looked out in time to see a person come hurtling down, hair and clothes streaming out behind her, almost as if she was flying, before she hit the pavement with a sickening thud. Another policeman stepped forward.

"Everyone stand back. Go on. Go home. There's nothing you can do."

For a terrifying moment, Liz tried to see whether she had the child with her amongst all that clothing. She made herself take a step forward, even though her heart was pounding so loudly that she could hardly breathe and felt as if she might vomit any minute. Other people rushed to the scene as a police constable appeared. "Stand back, everyone," he said. An ambulance bell rang in the distance. Then Marisa appeared, the little girl in her arms.

"The lady flew away," the girl said.

"That's right, dear. She flew away," Marisa said, steering the child away from where the body lay on the street. "And guess where we're going to go now? We're going to take you home to your mummy and daddy."

"Really?" The child's face lit up. "I'm going home?" And she hugged Marisa fiercely around the neck.

Afterwards there was a lot of explaining to do, a lot of meetings and interviews with police, with newspapers and TV. Marisa was the one in the spotlight. WOMAN POLICE CONSTABLE CRACKS THE CASE said the billboards at the newsstands. LITTLE LUCY SAFE. Liz was content to remain in the background, but Marisa's super was impressed and appreciative.

"What on earth made you two ladies come to that conclusion?" he asked. He was a big, jolly-looking man with a moustache and a head of curly grey hair.

Liz explained. Susan's past history. The meeting with the hippies. One of them pregnant. What if . . . She did not add the final piece of the puzzle. Meeting with Jenny in Devonshire and learning about a woman who took another woman's child, passing it off as her own. She hadn't yet come to terms with how she was going to handle that.

He nodded. "Good work. We could use more brains like yours, young lady. Would you like to come and join us?"

"You mean join the police?" she asked.

He nodded.

Liz had to smile. "I'm afraid I'm not very good at obeying rules," she said. "I'm in trouble with my newspaper at this moment."

"Not for long, I'd have thought," he said. "You've got the scoop, after all."

∿

The evening wound up late, at the Old Star pub. Liz sat quietly, enjoying the noise level and camaraderie of the Met officers. Marisa seemed quite at home and held her own in the banter. Everyone seemed to be reacting as if it was their own daughter safe and back home with her family. Liz allowed herself a small bubble of pride that she was part of this.

DI Jones came over to stand beside her, putting down his pint on the nearby table. "You said you might have news on the other cases?" he asked. "The ones from long ago?"

"I might," she said.

"You've solved one of them?"

"I might." She grinned. "I need to check with a couple of people about how much information I can share, but I think you'll be happy."

"You've found the girls?" he asked. She watched his face, now part hopeful, part wary.

"At least one of them," she said.

"And was there a link to this current investigation?"

"Luckily it turned out to be simpler than that, didn't it?" Liz said.

DI Jones frowned. "What do you mean?"

"I mean who was the rightful mother," she said.

~~~

That night Liz sat up late, writing away. She phrased the story carefully, not mentioning that Lark had been Lucy's real mother and that Sky/Susan had stolen her. She implied that Susan's brief brush with counter-culture as an impressionable teenager had led her to meet Lark, a troubled girl who had envied Susan and later succumbed to drugs and illusions. She knew she was not telling the whole story, but it was a case of making life bearable for the living and especially for Little Lucy. Nothing could be gained by her adopted mother now going to prison or having Lucy taken into foster care.

In the morning, she breezed into the *Express* offices and went straight to the news chief. "I have a story for you," she said. "How I found Little Lucy. Would you like it, or should I take it to another paper?"

Of course they wanted it. Liz handed it in, told her story and requested that she be reinstated in the newsroom. That request was granted. Then she went to Lewisham and broke the news to Jenny's parents, treading carefully on the subject of Aunt Emily, hinting that the woman really thought Rosie's parents had been killed in the bombing. That seemed the kindest thing to say at this moment. If Jenny wanted to tell them otherwise, it was up to her. There were tears from both of them. And hugs.

∾

"So you've done it," James said. They were meeting for a drink that evening at the Kings Arms on Whitehall Street, near his office in Mayfair. He had seen Liz on the television news the evening before and telephoned, excited for her. "How marvellous. Everything turned out well."

"Apart from that poor woman who threw herself off the roof to her death," Liz said.

"She must have had mental problems all along, don't you think?" James asked.

"You're right. It turned out she'd been a troubled soul for some time. She tried to kill herself once before. She was in a mental hospital and then in a drug treatment centre. She might have made a full recovery, but she went to see the place she had once squatted and saw Susan with Lucy in the neighbourhood nearby." She looked up at James. "Isn't it funny how small coincidences can alter a whole life?"

"Like you deciding to visit our house in the village when I happened to be there," he said. "I'd only been once before. A different day, and we'd have missed each other."

Liz returned his smile, but then said, "It still doesn't explain how I had such vivid memories of the place or who the person buried there was. Nobody can tell me. Except. I do now know that I lived in Somerset when I was very small. Someone could have taken me to Tydeham. But who?"

"Without telling your parents?" he asked.

Liz shrugged. "That does seem strange. It could all have been quite harmless. A local person where we lived could have had a relative there, taken me for a day out. Maybe my mother was sick, or had to go up to London."

"None of which explains the body," James said.

"No. It doesn't explain the body." She toyed with her wine glass. "I really hope they make a positive identification soon, and it's nobody I could have known. Nothing to do with me. And perhaps I have psychic powers."

"I'm not sure I want to be with a girl with psychic powers." James was half joking. "You'd know what I was thinking."

Liz laughed at that. "And what are you thinking right now?"

"That I'd like to be somewhere more private where I can kiss you properly."

"I might rather that you kissed me improperly," she said, her gaze teasing.

"I'm sure that can be arranged, too." They sat for a long moment, their eyes locked.

She took a swig of wine. "Are you going down to your father again this weekend?"

"I can't, I'm afraid. I promised a friend I'd help him move. I'm known for my brawn in architecture circles, you'll note." He demonstrated a muscle flex.

Liz laughed. Then she said, "I'll probably have to go to my parents' anyway. I'm usually there for Sunday lunch, and the last two weekends you've lured me away."

"You make me sound like an evil seducer."

"Now that would be fun." Her eyes held his for a long minute, and she felt a twinge of desire in her belly.

"I can see there's a side to you I know nothing about," he said.

"Not really. The only exciting life I've led so far is through books."

"I'd say finding two missing children and a buried body are pretty exciting."

"And finding you."

He reached across the small glass table and took her hand. "Ditto." He gave her hand a squeeze. "So are you going back to work? The paper gave you a hero's welcome?"

"I'm going to start on Monday, back in the newsroom. But tomorrow I thought I might go to Kent, to see the place that was my father's ancestral home. The house itself is no longer there, but I still think I'd like to visit the area."

"Of course you would," James said. "We have this need to know where we came from."

"My birth certificate says I was born in Somerset," Liz said, "but I could have been conceived at that house in Kent. My parents had to leave when the army took it over."

"It seems to me the army has a lot to answer for."

"It was a war, James. At least we weren't invaded. We did win."

"That's right. But you and I are collateral damage. We both lost the homes we should have had."

"We're not doing so badly, are we?" she said.

He reached out and took her hand, squeezing it. "Not badly at all."

CHAPTER 38

The train ride through sprawling outer suburbs was not a long one, and Liz disembarked at Swanley. It was one of those simple and functional villages that had sprung up because of the railway, and Liz walked down a modest row of shops until she came to the A20, the main road to Dover, where traffic roared past. From here there was a bus to Farningham, this time a pretty and ancient village feeling quite removed from the nearby London sprawl.

"The new estate, love?" a milkman finishing his rounds answered her. "On the other side of the main road."

"Is that where Broxley Manor used to be?"

"The old manor house? Yeah. That's right. Pity they tore it down. It was a good-looking place. But I heard the family moved away and didn't want it back after the war."

"It was my family," Liz said. "My father said he didn't have the money to fix it up after the army left it."

"Bastards, pardon my language," he said. "Well, there's not much you can do about it now, love. It's all streets of nice new houses."

"Were you born before the war?" she asked. "I wonder if you remember my family."

"Not me, love. I was ten when the war started, and anyway we were living over in Hextable." He paused, considering this. "I hoped it would go on long enough so I could join up. Shows how bloody silly boys are, doesn't it?" He placed an empty crate on his milk float, climbed into the driver's seat and drove off.

Liz found a place to cross the main road and made her way to the new estate. "Broxley Manor" was the name at the entrance, but she could not see one trace of the old house. Not one old tree was still standing, just rows of nearly new homes, each with its television aerial and washing flapping in the back garden. *I'm glad Daddy didn't come with me to see this,* she thought. She returned to the main part of the village, set well away from the bustle of the main road. It had a pretty main street with a few shops, a couple of pubs and a grey stone church, standing amongst the weathered gravestones of its churchyard. Liz went to visit this first, thinking that there would be her father's baptismal records and the family tombstone, and found the vicar at home in the next-door vicarage. He was an elderly man whose face lit up when she told him who she was.

"I remember your father quite well," he said. "I came here as a young man, and he was around my age. We were all proud when he was accepted at Sandhurst. Then off he went to India, met and married your mother out there. Of course they wouldn't have been married in our little church anyway, since she was a Roman Catholic with family from Ireland."

"But you remember when they lived here?"

"I do. They came back for a short while before the second war. Broxley Manor was a splendid house in those days. They ran it as if there had never been a Great War. They still had servants and house parties. Employed half the village, I should think."

"But then the war came, the army took over the house and they had to move away," she said.

"Oh no, my dear," he said, shaking his head. "It wasn't exactly like that. I heard he offered his house to the army. Did the noble thing, of course. And it was used as a training facility for spies." He gave a dry chuckle. "Of course they never told us that, but we guessed something was going on there. Something very hush-hush."

"So there weren't ever soldiers billeted there? They wouldn't have trashed the place?"

"I don't think so. I'm sure there were a few military men stationed there. I know they didn't employ any of the local people, which made us guess that it was a secret sort of operation. And a barbed wire fence around the grounds and guards at the gate." He gave her a knowing nod.

"I wasn't even born," Liz said. "I was born when they lived briefly in Somerset."

"Of course you were," he said.

"I suppose my mother could have been expecting me before they left."

"She could have. She never mentioned it, and I know they were hoping for a child, so perhaps she didn't want to jinx anything until there was a successful birth."

"I expect so," Liz said. She tried to think of other questions to ask but couldn't. She wondered why she had bothered to come. She had learned some things that didn't agree with what her father had told her, and that was disquieting. It seemed that he had twisted facts more than once, but she had no idea why.

"Perhaps you'd like to see the family grave now that you're here," he said. "We have to make it quite quick. I've a parish council meeting at eleven thirty."

"Thank you." She followed him to the door.

"Matthew, if you are going out, make sure you put your coat and scarf on," came a voice from the sitting room. "Remember your chest. It's cold out today."

The vicar grinned. "She fusses a lot. I had bad bronchitis last winter." But he stopped at the hall stand and did as she had told him.

They came out into a blustery wind. Brown leaves swirled up, and the path was sodden underfoot. They went through the low gate into the churchyard, and the vicar came to a halt by an impressive marble mausoleum. On the sides were inscribed the names of various Houghtons: *William Houghton, 1751–1824, Mary Houghton, 1629–1631 . . .*

"Some of them didn't live very long," Liz said.

"Life was hard in those days," the vicar replied. "You caught a disease, and off you went. I'd have been gone last winter if it hadn't been for penicillin."

Liz walked around all four sides of the mausoleum and found herself wishing she had brought flowers to place in the empty flower holder in front of it. Nobody was mourning the Houghtons now.

"I don't suppose anyone really remembers us any longer," she said.

"Oh, you'd be surprised. There are several older people who used to work for your family who still live around here. Fanny Boswell was your cook in those days, and her husband, Dan, worked in the garden. And Edie Jones was one of the maids. She married Luke Jones, and they still live here over by the mill. They've grandchildren now."

"It sounds as if there were a lot of servants."

"There certainly were. I don't think your mum ever lifted a finger, you know." He grinned at her. "Proper lady of the manor she was in those days. When you moved away, people were having bets with each other that she'd never be able to cope without people to wait on her."

"So she didn't take any of them with her?"

"Most people wouldn't have wanted to leave their homes here. When you have roots in a place, you tend to stay put. But hold on a minute. I do believe I heard she took Alice with her."

"Alice?" Liz was suddenly alert.

"Yes. Young girl she acquired from the orphanage. She wasn't from around here. Nice, cheerful type. Pretty girl, but a bit of a flirt, I think. Popular with the young men when she grew up. Some said she'd gone off to be married, but I believe your mother took her when they moved. She'd grown quite fond of the girl."

"You don't know where she'd be now?"

"I've no idea, my dear. Your parents might have kept in touch. I'd ask them." He started away from the tombstones. "I take it they are in good health?"

"My father is. My mother is sadly slipping into dementia. Some of the time she's lucid, and others she's in her own world."

"Oh, I am sorry. She was such a lively, fun-loving lady. I can well see why your father married her. Lots of parties when they were here."

The church clock tolled the half hour.

"I must leave you now, I'm afraid. My parish council meeting. Miss Pargeter will give me an awful scolding if I'm late again."

"Of course. Thank you very much," she said. "By the way, do you happen to remember what Alice's last name was?"

The vicar paused. Frowned. "I do," he said after a while. "It was Alice Thatcher."

CHAPTER 39

Liz found her hands were shaking as she sat on the train on the way back to London. As green fields and orchards gave way to sprawl, she tried to process what she had just learned. Alice Thatcher. The one person her parents had taken with them. Fun loving. Flirty. Could it be coincidence that she had heard that name before? One of the former residents of the abandoned village in Dorset was Bert Thatcher. A common enough name, but . . . She was an orphan, the vicar said. She wasn't from there.

And the name. Alice. Her mother had thought she saw Alice on the garden path when Lizzie arrived for a visit, and her father had made light of it. She keeps having conversations with school friends. *Only it wasn't a school friend. It was me.* Alice was the one maid they had taken with them when they left. Why? Why was this important? Why was her mother so attached to Alice that she had to come to Somerset with them, and then what happened to Alice that she didn't accompany them to Shropshire?

Liz stared out of the window as fields gave way to suburban back gardens. What she was thinking was so preposterous, so unbelievable that she didn't even want to put words to her thoughts. The couple who had longed for a child but were never lucky enough to conceive. And Alice was flirty. The men were attracted to her.

What if I am Alice's child? she asked herself. She tried to picture Alice, but no image came. Then the thoughts became even darker and more confusing. *What if Alice had me with my father? Because my mother couldn't. But what then? Alice stayed on as nursemaid until . . . until she found herself a bloke? Left to join up? Or?* She framed the next sentences with difficulty. Lark had been Little Lucy's real mother and had come to reclaim her child and paid with her life. *Did Alice try to take me?* she asked herself. *And the body I saw being buried . . . somebody killed her. Her boyfriend? A random soldier? Or somebody closer to home?*

I can't bear this, she thought. The burden of finding out about Jenny's true parents was bad enough. Old Aunt Emily could face prison for kidnapping if the news became public. But if someone had killed Alice . . .

I have to see Bert Thatcher first, she decided. I can't go to my parents until I'm completely and utterly sure.

When the train reached Victoria Station, she sprinted for the Underground and got off at Waterloo, waiting impatiently for the next train to Weymouth. It was after four by the time she arrived. Once there she could not bear to find out about buses, but took a taxi from the station.

"Osmington. That's a fair way out," the taxi driver said.

"It doesn't matter. It's important." Liz blurted out the words. "I'm in a hurry."

After she said that, the driver drove like a man possessed, swinging around hedgerows, clipping corners so that she gave a silent prayer of thanks when they arrived in the village. It wasn't hard to find out where the Thatchers lived. Everyone in the village knew Bert. Bert Thatcher, eh? They said with a smile. What's he done now?

Liz walked up a track through a small field to their cottage, and the door was opened by a big man with grizzled hair whom she assumed was Bert himself. Breathlessly she explained why she had come.

"Alice?" He gazed at her with interest.

She realized she probably looked sweaty and unkempt the way she had rushed.

"I did have a niece called Alice. My brother's child."

"Really? Can you tell me about her?"

"Not much," he said. "I never really knew Alice. My brother and I weren't that close. He was a lot older than me, you know. He went off to sea while I was a nipper. Fought in the Great War, and then he went and married a German refugee girl. You can imagine how well that went down! Anyway, he was killed somewhere abroad, and we heard that his wife had met a bloke and gone back to Germany with him, leaving their child in an orphanage in England." He paused, realizing that they were standing on the doorstep.

"You'd better come inside. We're letting the heat out." He opened the door for her to step into a tiny front parlour. A log burner was giving off good warmth, and it was snug and cosy. He patted a well-worn armchair, and Liz sat.

"That child was Alice?" she asked.

"That's right. We'd only met her once when she was a baby. My wife was horrified when she heard what they'd done to her. Really angry. 'That's what you get for marrying a bloody Kraut,' she said. We felt bad about it, but we couldn't do anything. We had three of our own and a fourth on the way, and our cottage was bursting at the seams."

"So did you ever meet her afterwards?"

"Oh yes. We kept in touch. We sent her food parcels and the like, and before the war she came to visit us. She'd become a very pretty girl. A bit like you. And she said she'd got herself a good position in a big house, and she was well treated and liked it there."

"Did she mention a young man?"

He chuckled then. "Too many, so I believe. She said she wasn't ready to settle down yet, and besides she was holding out for something better than a farm boy."

"And what about later, after the war? Did you see her again then? Did you get letters from her?"

"Never heard from her again after the war. And when we didn't hear anything after the war, my wife said, 'I bet she's met one of them Yanks and gone off to America with him.' So that's what we thought."

He gave a nod of satisfaction, then tilted his head on one side, like a bird. "Why the interest in our Alice?"

"Because it was my parents she worked for. I must have known her when I was a small girl, but I don't have memories of her, so I wanted to fill in the missing pieces. Maybe get in touch with her again."

"I'm afraid I can't help you there, miss," he said. "Like I told you, not a peep out of her after the war ended. I'd check the records for war brides."

"You're sure she didn't come to visit you during the war? When I was a little girl? She didn't bring me with her?"

"How would she have known where to find us?" he asked. "We got turned out of our village, as you've probably heard. Only had two weeks to pack up everything and get out. I was lucky enough to get a cottage here, on account that I worked on the farm and was needed. The wife wrote to Alice at the address she'd been given, but it was returned, saying the building was now occupied by His Majesty's Government. I reckon they grabbed all the good properties, don't you? And made a mess of them."

"That's right," Liz said. "My father didn't have the money to fix up his house after the war. And your village is only a ruin now, isn't it?"

"Ruined beyond repair," Bert said. "A right sad sight, it is. Our little community scattered and gone. A sad day for us all. I don't think the wife ever got over it. She's not been the same woman since. And the grand lady at the big house, Mrs Bennington—well, she never got over it either. She killed herself. I felt for her poor little boy. I wonder how he's doing now?"

"James? He's doing well," Liz said. "I see him quite often. He works in London."

"Does he now? The wife will be glad to hear that. She was worried, you know. 'I hope he doesn't take after that mother of his,' she said. The wife reckoned Mrs Bennington had always been a bit funny in the head." He stopped and put a hand to his mouth. "Here, listen to me going on when I shouldn't. If you know the young gentleman, then you won't take kindly to me saying bad things about his mum." He gave an embarrassed grin. "My wife says I never know when to keep my trap shut."

"Oh, that's all right, Mr Thatcher," Liz said. "I won't take any more of your time. I have to get back to London tonight. But thank you for your help. I don't suppose you have a photograph of Alice, do you?"

He frowned. "We may do somewhere, but it's the wife who knows that kind of thing, and she's off with her sister today. But she was a pretty girl. A lot like you. Blondish hair, a nice smile."

~~

It was dark by the time Liz returned to Weymouth. She had found no way of summoning a taxi, and buses were few and far between, so in the end she had begged a lift from a delivery van that had stopped at the pub. When she reached Weymouth, she was tempted to go to the police station to see if they had found out any more about the skeleton. It was a female, they had said. They'd found some blonde hairs. She looked a bit like you, Bert Thatcher had said. *My uncle Bert.* She toyed with the words, trying to make sense of them. And the next thought that came to her: *How can I ever talk to my parents about this? But I have to know the truth. I've a right to know who I am.*

She fidgeted impatiently on the train back to London, not getting in until after ten.

"Well, there you are at last," Marisa said. She had already changed into her pyjamas and was lying on her bed reading. "I began to wonder if you were spending the night with the elusive James."

"The relationship hasn't progressed that far," Liz said. "I wish it had been something as nice as that. But I've had a rather overwhelming day, Risa." She plopped down on to her own bed, kicking off her shoes. "You'll never imagine where I've been."

"I thought you said Kent."

"That was the first place. I found the site where my father's old home had been. It's all neat little houses now. But then I met the vicar, and I think I may have unlocked the mystery."

"Go on." Marisa sat up.

Liz explained, step by step. When she had finished, Marisa looked at her, long and hard. "Do you think that maybe you are jumping to too many conclusions, Liz? You're still feeling high from finding a missing girl who was taken by her real mother. And you located one of the missing girls in Devon. That girl was also kidnapped and taken from her real family. So you may be trying to fit yourself into this pattern." She swung her feet over the side of the bed, facing Liz. "Couldn't it simply be that Alice was a helpful girl with no family ties so the logical one to take along when your mum was pregnant and needed help? And she stayed until something better came along. She met a man and married him. Or she joined up and went into the forces."

"But what about my mother thinking she saw Alice coming up the front path when I came into the house?"

"Maybe she had grown fond of her. Thought of her as a younger sister or daughter? Maybe it's her dementia? All you need to do is to ask your parents about her. Then you'll know."

"I suppose so. I'm afraid to find out, actually. I keep thinking that Alice is the body I remembered seeing buried."

Marisa lay back again. "Too much drama. You read too many crime novels. Get undressed and go to sleep. I have to get up early. Meeting at eight."

Liz undressed and lay down, but she was too wound up to sleep. She glanced at the clock. Ten fifteen. Perhaps it wasn't too late to telephone her father. He had always been something of a night owl. Her mother would have gone to bed hours ago, but she'd be asleep and the phone should not disturb her.

"I have to know," she said. "I can't go to bed not knowing."

She tiptoed out of the bedroom, closing the door quietly behind her, and picked up the phone. It only rang once before it was answered.

"Sorry to phone you this late, Daddy," Liz said, in answer to her father's clipped "Houghton."

"Well, if it isn't the celebrity," her father said. "We saw you being interviewed on television when you helped to find the missing child. Your mother was so excited she almost fell off her chair. She had been upset that you'd missed another Sunday lunch, but when she saw what you'd been doing she was so proud. She kept saying, 'That's our daughter, Henry. On television. A hero.'"

"Not a hero, Daddy. We were lucky we got there in time. Just a hunch that paid off, thank goodness. But it was all rather horrible."

"Yes, I imagine it would be. Woman threw herself off the roof, didn't she?"

"That's right. I saw it."

"We all see things we wish we could unsee," the brigadier said. "Especially during war. I've had a few nightmares in my time. So what's up? Did you suddenly realize you'd been neglecting your poor old parents?"

"Daddy, I want to come round and see you in the morning. I want to see you both."

"Splendid. Let's see if your mother's up to making something good for lunch. It has to be something she still remembers how to cook. We've had some rather funny combinations lately. She put Bisto in the custard. What do you fancy?"

Liz took a deep breath before she said, "Daddy, I want to talk to you about Alice."

"Alice? You mean your mother's imaginary school friend?"

"No. I mean Alice. The real Alice. The one who was your maid in Kent. The one you took with you to Somerset."

"What about her? A very pleasant girl. Your mother was fond of her."

"Daddy, I've been to Farningham. I talked to the vicar there. And I talked to people in Somerset, too, at the house where we used to live. I've met Alice's uncle."

"Her uncle?" Now he did sound surprised.

"Bert Thatcher. The one who lived in Tydeham."

"Good God."

"I've been putting the pieces together, and now I want you to tell me the whole truth."

"Meaning what?" His voice was sharp.

"The truth about who I am."

"What nonsense is this, Elizabeth? Who has been feeding you lies?"

"Daddy—I need you to tell me. Am I Alice's daughter?"

"Of course not. Utter rubbish."

"I'm coming over in the morning, and I'm going to ask Mummy."

"That would be most unwise. You'd only upset her. You know how fragile she is these days. I'm shocked, Elizabeth. Why would you want to hurt your mother?"

"I don't want to hurt her. I just need to know. I'll see you tomorrow, all right?" And she hung up. She found she was breathing hard. Was she going mad to believe what she did? And did she really want to know?

CHAPTER 40

After the telephone call Liz felt physically sick. *It's my parents,* she told herself. *If what I believe is true, I'll have destroyed their life. Wrecked our relationship forever. And I'm all they've got.* She corrected this. *They are all I have got.* But she couldn't let it drop. Not now. It was like a gnawing wound inside her. She had to know.

Would her father share any of this with her mother? Would she even remember? But she had remembered Alice, all right. She had seen Liz coming up the front path and thought it was Alice.

Liz made herself a slice of bread and jam with a cup of Horlicks and finally forced herself to go to bed. Marisa was already sleeping peacefully.

Lucky you, Liz thought, looking at her. *You know where you came from, who you are. It hasn't always been easy for you to be an outsider, but at least you know.*

She got into bed and finally fell asleep from sheer exhaustion.

In the morning she was woken by Marisa bustling around, muttering swear words to herself as she looked for her hairbrush, a shoe and various other objects she had lost.

"I can't be late for the bloody meeting," she said. "Why didn't the bloody alarm go off?"

Liz obviously couldn't slow her down by telling her what she planned to do. When she had gone, Liz got up and paced the room, still in an agony of indecision. *Go over there right now. Get it over with*, she told herself. In the cold light of morning, she asked herself whether Marisa had been right. She had been reading too much drama into something that could be easily explained. Alice was a nice young woman with no ties. She had come with them to Somerset to help out during the pregnancy and birth, then gone off when she was no longer needed. End of story. Except a body had been buried in an abandoned village. And her family had moved from Kent to Somerset and then from Somerset to Shropshire. And her mother had been described as formerly being a fun-loving woman who gave parties. Something had happened. Something had changed their lives.

She was putting on lipstick when the phone rang. She stared at it for a long minute before she picked it up.

"Miss Houghton?" The voice on the other end sounded cheerful. "It's Jenny. Jenny Worth. I just wanted to tell you that I've talked to my mother. My real mother. I'm coming up to meet my parents this weekend. I wondered if you'd like to join us, since you were the one who made this happen?"

"Oh, no," Liz said. "I think it should be private between you and them. Unless you feel you need support from an outsider."

"You know, I did feel that. It might be awkward. I'm still not sure what to tell them about Aunt Emily. I can't lie and say she's dead. I can't even lie and say she didn't know what she was doing. But I don't want her punished either. What do you think I should do?"

"If it were me, I'd say she is now in a care home near the end of her life and no good can come of recriminations at this point. You can say she did what she thought was best—that she was giving a child a better life. Your parents live in a council flat in a not very nice part of London. You've had every advantage."

"That's true. I have. And I'm happily married and I'm doing what I love. I've no complaints at all. But that's the problem, isn't it? I feel so guilty."

"None of this was your fault, Jenny. Just look at the plus side. Your parents thought you were dead. Now they have a chance for a relationship with you, and new granddaughters. They'll be thrilled. And you have a sister. You'll be happy, too."

"I hope so," she said. "I really hope so. And I do want to thank you for what you have done. You were awfully clever."

"Sometimes I think I'm too clever for my own good," Liz said, attempting to laugh it off.

She had only just put the phone down when it rang again. This time it was Marisa.

"Oh good. You're home. Look, DI Jones has been bugging me to know what you've found out about his missing girls. Can we meet him for lunch?"

"I have to go over to my parents'," Liz said.

"You've talked to your dad, then? What did he say?"

"Blustered. Denied everything I said."

"See. I told you that you were imagining things and there was a perfectly normal explanation."

"Maybe. I just felt he blustered a bit too much. And he told me I wasn't to upset my mother. I'm going over there now. I want to hear it from him in person. I want to see his face."

"Good idea. Let's hope we can settle it forever. But can't you swing by here for a coffee later? He's so worked up about it."

"Not before I've seen my parents, Marisa."

Marisa gave a little sigh. "I'll tell the DI you'll meet him as soon as possible but you have a family crisis on your hands."

"Thanks," Liz said. She hung up.

Liz finished doing her hair and was putting on her suede jacket when the phone rang again. This time it was her father.

"Oh, you're still there. I wanted to warn you—the doctor is with your mother. I'm afraid it doesn't look good."

"Oh no. What happened?"

"I'd rather not talk about it over the phone. I'm rather upset, as you can hear, but you need to come as quickly as possible."

"Of course, Daddy."

She snatched her handbag and ran to the nearest Tube station. Guilt threatened to overwhelm her. *I did this,* she told herself. *I telephoned late at night. Mummy overheard, and now something terrible has happened. She had a heart attack or a stroke, and it's my fault.*

The Tube seemed to take forever, doors opening and closing at a snail's pace, people taking their time to get on and off. She wanted to scream. Move. Hurry.

At Finchley Road Tube Station, she spotted a taxi and hailed it.

Her father must have been watching for her because the door was opened before she could knock.

"Oh, you've come. Thank God," he said.

She saw his face—stricken, ashen.

"How is Mummy?"

"She's . . . not with us any more."

"She's gone? You let her go?"

"She's passed away. Dead."

"She's dead?" Liz blurted out the word.

Her father gave what sounded like a cross between a cough and a sob. "When I came in with her morning tea, I couldn't wake her. I called the doctor. I thought she must have had a heart attack, but the doctor said she must have taken too many sleeping pills. And sure enough, we found the empty bottle."

"Where is she?"

"Still on her bed. She looks so peaceful." He swallowed back a sob, turning it into a cough again. "I can't believe it."

"Did you tell her, Daddy? That I was coming and I wanted to hear the truth?"

"She overheard our phone call. She wanted to know."

"Let me see her."

"Of course. You'll want to say goodbye." He gave a sigh, led her upstairs and opened the bedroom door. Her mother, that statuesque woman she remembered, now lay like a small shrunken doll against a white pillow.

Liz tried to form the words. "She killed herself because I was coming and she couldn't bear to tell me, is that right?"

"No. Not at all. I'm sure that wasn't it. It may have just been an accident. That's what I said to the doctor." He stared at her with a distraught face. "I always put out the right pills in a dish beside her bed. And I did that last night, I'm sure. But she had taken the bottle from the bathroom. I suppose we have to admit that it was a deliberate act." He paused again, staring down at his wife's body now. "But I didn't want the doctor to know that. I didn't want her death to go down as suicide. The doctor understood. He's been treating her. He knows what she was like."

"So there won't be an inquest or anything?"

"He doesn't think so. Unsound mind, you know. Much better all around, don't you think? You can't be buried on consecrated ground if you kill yourself, can you? Maureen would want a proper burial."

"But you think she killed herself deliberately?" Liz asked, still not taking her eyes from her mother's body. How peaceful she looked.

"I'm sure she killed herself because she couldn't face the future that awaited her—not knowing who she was and who we are. She was always such a proud person. She would have hated having to be fed and bathed . . ."

Anger and guilt raged inside Liz. "And this just coincidentally happened to be when I was about to come to hear the truth about my birth? Come on, Daddy. You know that's why she did it. You two have been keeping a secret from me all my life, and Mummy couldn't bear to face up to it."

"I suppose so." He gave a long sigh. "Poor, dear woman. I'm so very sorry . . ."

Liz could not take her eyes from her mother. Another thought was forming in her head. Her mother who was now so confused, so removed from reality. Had she really managed to work out how many pills to take? And ignore her religion that thought suicide was the ultimate sin? She tried to wrestle with the nagging idea that was forming—too horrible to be true, and yet . . . She looked up, staring at her father. "She didn't kill herself, did she, Daddy?" she said, hardly daring to say the words. "You killed her! You killed her because she wanted to tell me the truth and you didn't! There was no way she could have worked out how many pills to take, the way she was right now." She took this one step further, staring at her father as the horrifying truth dawned on her. "Oh my God. It was you." She blurted out the words before she could weigh whether it was wise to do so. "And you killed Alice, didn't you? That's why Mummy was always so uneasy all her life. The vicar in Farningham said she was so fun loving. She gave parties, and then she turned herself into a recluse because—"

"Stop!" He barked out the word, a soldier used to giving commands. Liz took a step back, alarmed at the look on his face. "That's not how it was at all." Then the bluster left him, and he said in a low voice, "All right. You are correct. I did kill your mother. I put her out of her misery. But I did it for her, because I loved her."

"I don't understand. What misery?"

He took a deep breath. "She wanted to go and confess everything. When she knew you were coming, she wanted to turn herself in. She said it was time she took her punishment and paid for her sin. I had to stop her."

"Turn herself in?"

He gave a shuddering sigh. "I didn't kill Alice, my dear. Your mother did. And she wanted to confess. She was going to go to the police in the morning and I couldn't stop her, that's what she said. If she did that, they'd have locked her up or put her in a mental institution for the rest of her life. I couldn't let that happen to her, could I?" He put a hand on Liz's shoulder. "Let's go and sit down. And I think we both need a stiff whisky."

Liz followed him downstairs, moving mechanically, and numb, not able to take in everything she'd heard. Her father poured two glasses of whisky, handed her one. She sat. Sipped. Stared at him.

"So answer me this one thing," Liz said. "Are you my real father? Did you have me with Alice?"

His face flushed red. "Absolutely not. I was completely and utterly faithful to your mother. She was the love of my life. I adored her. You've got it all wrong."

"You'd better start at the beginning," she said.

"That's right. From the beginning." He took a gulp of the whisky, then held the glass in his hands, staring down at the amber liquid. "Alice came to us from an orphanage. She was a nice, cheerful girl. Willing. Helpful. Your mother took to her right away. But she was always keen on the young men. Too keen, I'm afraid. She came to us one day and told us she was in the family way. The young man had been shipped abroad, and she had no way of contacting him. She was desperate and didn't know what to do. We talked it over, and it seemed like a miracle. We had wanted a child, but it never happened. And here was one, being handed to us on a plate, so to speak. We arranged for her to go to one of those places unmarried mothers go to. A nice one. In the country, where she was well looked after. You were born. We picked you both up, and we all went to a house we rented in Somerset. Far away from anyone who knew us. A new life. It was perfect. Ideal. Your mother was so happy. Alice stayed on as your nursemaid. And then . . ."

He paused.

"Then?" Liz asked.

"You started to grow up. Such an adorable little girl. But you liked Alice better. When you fell down, you ran to Alice for comfort. You wanted Alice to tuck you in. Your mother got jealous, I'm afraid. Things came to a head when you told your mother to go away one night because you only wanted Alice. That really upset her. So she gave Alice the sack. I was away at the army camp, or I might have intervened and smoothed things over. That night Alice took you and ran off. Your mother contacted me at the camp in a panic, but when I arrived home, she was gone. She had followed you and Alice." He had been staring down at his tumbler. Now he looked up at Liz. "Your mother followed her to Tydeham. Presumably Alice had gone there, hoping to find her uncle, Bert Thatcher, but the village was empty. I suspect Alice had gone to the manor house in the hope of finding it still occupied, but it was locked up. Your mother found her in the rose garden and tried to take you. Alice resisted. They got into a horrible shouting match. Alice said she'd go to court and tell the truth and they'd give the child to her. Your mother said the only birth certificate listed her as the parent."

He paused again. "It turned physical. She gave Alice a shove. Alice fell and hit her head on the corner of a marble bench in the rose arbor, and it killed her. Your mother was in a panic. At that moment I arrived. Luckily I met the man who had given them a lift. I calmed her down, and we talked it through. Nobody around for miles. Nobody could have seen. The village was now off-limits. And as far as we knew, Alice was an orphan with nobody in the world. So we buried Alice. We had told you to wait in the car on the other side of the house, but you must have got out and seen us."

"We moved to Shropshire right after that," Liz said. "Far away from anyone who knew us."

"It haunted your mother for the rest of her life," Brigadier Houghton said. "She was never the same woman again. As the dementia took over, she became more and more riddled with guilt. She wanted to tell you the truth and then to go and confess."

"Poor Mummy," Liz said. "Poor Alice."

CHAPTER 41

Liz stayed with her father while a policeman came and took particulars. He was young and kind and sympathetic, nodding when the brigadier explained that she had severe dementia and must have mixed up her medications. "I watched her when she took her pills," he said. "I watched her last night. But she must have forgotten and got up after I left her and taken more. She mixed everything up recently. I was just telling my daughter that she put Bisto in the custard."

"Would you say she was in a depressed state of mind, sir?"

"Not really. She got angry on occasion when she realized what she was becoming and that normal life was slipping away."

"Do you think she could have done this deliberately, then? Ended it all while she still could?"

"It's possible, I suppose, but I don't think she was that type of person. And frankly I'm not sure she was coherent enough to work out what kind of pills to take."

"You said you put out pills for her?"

"That's right. Every morning and night. She took blood pressure medication and iron tablets and at night a fairly strong sleeping pill the doctor had prescribed. With her dementia, she got anxious when it became dark."

"And these strong pills were kept where?"

"In the bathroom cabinet. I didn't realize she even knew where the pills were kept. But I found the bottle beside her bed. I presume she took several of them."

"You realize there will have to be a post-mortem exam, sir?"

"Of course. But I really hope this was a horrible accident. She was a religious woman. She'd want to be buried on consecrated ground."

"You have my deepest sympathy, sir," the young policeman said. "Arrangements will be made to come for the body shortly. But you can go ahead and plan for the funeral."

The brigadier accompanied the policeman to the front door. They shook hands. Liz had watched the whole scene unfold as if it was a drama at the pictures. She was too numb to feel anything, too confused, too shocked. She tried to understand her father's motivation if everything he told her had been true. Of course they would have put her mother in a women's prison if she confessed to killing Alice. Then Lizzie would have had no mother.

∿

"Well, that's that." Her father came to sit beside her and finished his whisky with one swig. "Went as well as could be hoped, I suppose."

Liz examined his face. "You don't seem very cut up about it," Liz said.

He stared at her, frowning. "My dear child, I've been through two wars. I've watched friends be blown to pieces. I learned to shut off emotions long ago. But believe me, I will never stop grieving. She was the love of my life. I don't know how I'm going to carry on without her."

The brigadier reached across and took her hand. She didn't pull it away but instead sat there as if turned to stone, joined with him in his misery.

"I hope you might stay on here for a little while, Lizzie," he said at last. "Just until I know what I'm going to do and how I'm going to cope. I've never been much good with the housekeeping side of things. Mrs Croft will come in and clean, I expect, but still . . ."

Liz stood up. "I have to go out and think, Dad," she said. "This has all been too much. I just can't process it." And she ran for the door without waiting to grab her jacket. She walked fast, not noticing the cold wind with the promise of rain. She kept walking until she reached Hampstead Heath. Here the wind blew strongly enough to take her breath away. London lay spread out below her. She pressed on, as if walking fast enough might stop her from thinking and feeling and realizing what had happened.

At last, out of breath, she sat on a bench, staring out at the clouds heavy with rain racing in from the west. *I lost my mother,* she thought. *The only mother I've known, who loved me and protected me. Only she wasn't my real mother, who also loved me. I don't know what to think. And my father, who has just killed my mother, talks calmly about my moving in with him to take care of the housekeeping, as if nothing bad has happened at all.* It was just too much to take in.

She found herself wishing that James was there. She could telephone him. He'd come. He'd lost a mother. He'd know the right thing to say. But she couldn't tell him the truth, could she? It was a burden she'd have to bear alone.

She could not bring herself to go back and act as if life was going on as normal. How could she give her father the love and reassurance he wanted when she was fighting back anger and disgust and betrayal?

"What do I bloody well do?" she shouted aloud, into the wind. "Do I forgive him because he thought he was doing the right thing? Do I forgive both of them? Do I have to believe that killing Alice was a horrible accident?" The wind sighed and moaned through the trees. *What about Alice? Should I tell the police I know the identity of the body? But then they'd arrest my father. He's all I've got.* She toyed with this last phrase. *All I've got.* She tried to see what he might be going through, making the decision to kill the woman he loved to protect her from a future trial. *It had been an accident, Mummy had said.* That might have been true, but she had given Alice the fateful shove. And borne the guilt for the rest of her life, living as a recluse, clinging on to the daughter for whom she'd risked everything.

As Liz tried to understand, she let compassion overtake the anger. Two people who had longed for a child, thought they'd been blessed with a miracle, fought to hang on to her, and then had done everything for the rest of their lives to keep her true identity secret. Her father would be devastated without her mother, she thought. *I have to stay with him for a while, and try to understand, however hard it's going to be.*

The first drops of rain splashed on to her. She stood up and started walking home.

∽

Later that day Liz telephoned Marisa to let her know that her mother had passed away and that she was going to stay with her father at least until after the funeral. "Tell DI Jones I'm sorry I can't meet him right now. He'll understand," she said.

"Do you want me to come over to be with you?" Marisa asked. "It must be awful for you. Did you find out the truth about your birth? Did she kill herself rather than tell you?"

A thousand different answers went through Liz's head. "I did find out, and it's complicated. I can't talk about it now. Maybe one day when this is behind me." Liz couldn't imagine telling her friend what her father had done. She was with the police, after all.

"I can understand that," Marisa said. "The dementia. It must be awful to know what you are becoming and not be able to do anything to stop it. I'm so sorry, Liz. My mum drives me bonkers, but I'd be gutted if I lost her. Let me know if I can do anything for you, all right?"

"Thank you. There's nothing anyone can do right now," Liz said.

∽

After thinking carefully what she was going to say, Liz telephoned James.

"Do you want me to come over right away?" he asked.

When she hesitated, he said, "Look, I can leave early. I'll come. You shouldn't be alone. What's the address?"

"Don't come to the house," Liz said. "This isn't the right time to explain and meet my father. I'll meet you at the Finchley Road Tube Station."

She didn't have to wait long. When he put his arms around her, she gave a big sob and the tears started to flow. Until that moment, she had been unable to shed a tear. Now she sobbed on to James's shoulder, not caring they were on a busy street.

"I'm sorry," she murmured. "I'm wetting your jacket."

"It's okay. Go ahead. It's good to cry." He held her close, stroking her hair. "I never cried for my mother. You should cry all you want to."

They went into a nearby coffee bar, and he sat her down in a booth at the back, bringing two coffees. She told him what had happened to her mother, not able to bring herself to tell the whole truth at that moment. He listened, his eyes holding hers.

"You'll get through this, Liz," he said. "I want you to know that I'll be there for you. I'll always be there for you."

She saw love in his eyes.

"You will come to the funeral, won't you?"

"I'll come over any time you want me to," he said. "Maybe now is not the best time to meet your father, but I'm here whenever you want to talk."

"Thank you." She reached out and took his hand. "I'm lucky I found you."

"The luck is mutual," he said. "And if you want something to cheer you up, you'll be pleased to know that I've put in an official request for our property to be returned to us or for suitable compensation to be given. It will be interesting to see what happens, and in the meantime, I'm drawing up plans to rebuild the house. A pipe dream, I know, but . . ."

"Oh, James. I'm happy for you. Your dad would be thrilled."

His eyes held hers. "When you're feeling better, I'd like your input, too. A house needs a woman's touch. That's what too many male architects don't understand."

"Yes. I'd be happy to . . ." She gave him a watery smile, and a tiny sliver of hope crept into the darkness.

How funny, she thought. *I'm related to Bert Thatcher, who lived next door to James when he was growing up. It's as if we've both come full circle.* She wondered if she could ever tell James the whole truth of it.

∾

The funeral was a quiet and sombre occasion, with only James and Marisa as well as the faithful cleaning lady present, apart from six young army privates as pallbearers. The whole ceremony felt unreal, and as Liz stood at the gravesite and watched the coffin lowered in, she had a strange feeling of déjà vu—that small child coming around the big house and seeing Alice's body being buried in the earth.

∾

Liz returned to work at the newspaper during the day, but despite her conflicted feelings, she came home to her father in the evenings to make sure he was eating properly and had company. Her father suggested she go through her mother's possessions, keep anything she liked and donate the rest. She was loath to do this, but she saw how hard it would be for him, so she agreed, putting piles of clothing on to the bed in the spare room—nothing that would have fit her. She lamented that the fur coat was too large, considered having it refitted for herself, then decided she wasn't a fur type of person.

There were a few good pieces of jewellery that she was happy to keep.

"Are you sure you don't want to sell them, Daddy? They'd probably fetch quite a bit of money," she said.

"Oh no. You have them. She'd have wanted you to," he said, "And don't worry about me. I have plenty of money for my needs and enough to pass along to you. I'm thinking that I should sell the house and move into one of the armed services clubs. That will be good for me. Lots of old codgers to natter with."

"Is that what you want?" She looked at him. "I could always . . ."

"No, darling. You have your own life, and it's about time you got on with it. That nice new fellow. He'll take good care of you."

Liz went back to the jewellery. Apart from the few good pieces, there was a large wooden box of costume jewellery—not at all to Liz's taste. But she admired the box, clearly from India, where her mother had grown up. She tipped out the various brooches and necklaces and was surprised to find the bottom also fell out, and beneath it a thick envelope. Curious now, she opened it. It contained a stack of letters. She recognized the handwriting at once as Edmond's. Reinforced by the Australian postmark.

"Oh," she said. "Oh no."

One by one she read them. *My darling Lizzie. You'll love it over here. I can't wait to show it to you.*

Why haven't you written? Didn't you get my last letter? I'm so worried. I can't understand, Lizzie. I thought you loved me.

And then the final one.

Since you've made it quite clear that we will never have a future together and you want nothing more to do with me, I have found a nice girl. She's a nurse at the flying doctor station out near the mine. She'll never replace you, but I can't be lonely and sad for the rest of my life.

"Oh, Edmond," she said, her eyes brimming with tears. "All that time thinking I'd forgotten about you." Was it too late to write, to make things right? Then she thought about James. She would write to Edmond one day and let him know that she hadn't forgotten him, but now they had both moved on. She thought about her mother, so desperate to cling to her adopted daughter that she would act in this way. And she decided not to tell her father about the letters. She went down to the sitting room where a fire was burning in the hearth, and after saving one envelope for his address, she burned the lot.

Having done that, having dealt with all the lies and this, the ultimate betrayal, she felt the bonds of guilt and responsibility to her parents slipping away and knew she was free to move on.

∿

Liz called Marisa and arranged a meeting with DI Jones. "Why don't you come to the house here," she said. "It would do my father good to have some company, and I'm getting to be a passable cook."

They both came, the DI wearing a suit.

"Good of you to invite us, Miss Houghton," he said, looking a trifle uneasy in these surroundings.

Liz brought them into the sitting room and poured a beer for the DI, wine for the rest of them. After he'd had a good swig, the DI turned to her. "I didn't realize when I first met you that you are a top-notch reporter. I don't know how you managed to find out anything when we couldn't. So which little girl have you found?"

"Rosie Binks," she said. "And possibly Gloria Kane. As for the third girl, Valerie, we knew her fate, but I couldn't look into anything more because her file was empty. I don't know if you were still investigating who killed her or you know who did it."

"No. We don't know," he said. "We did look into that file and go to see the old bloke, the barmy one who we thought had killed her. He's now living with his sister and couldn't remember much, except to say he'd never have harmed such a beautiful little angel. We're fairly sure he didn't do it, and we know now that he had nothing to do with Little Lucy. But what about Rosie Binks? You found her? Alive?"

Liz related the story to him. And the pieces of luck. The finding of the toy dog in the field, going to a craft fair in Tiverton because it had started to rain and seeing the fabric with the bluebirds on it. Such tiny things that had swung a whole story.

"So why didn't we hear about the toy dog?"

"Because it was found by a child. I don't suppose they put two and two together at the time. They did look for her body, but of course they didn't find it."

"Well, I never." DI Jones shook his head, smiling at the same time. "The bluebird sofa. I'd never have remembered that. And the woman that kidnapped her? She's still alive?"

"She's dying. In a nursing home. Rosie would rather that you let her die in peace."

"She put us through a lot of grief," he said. "She put those parents though hell."

"She thought she was doing the child a favour, Inspector. Ragged little girl from the East End. Undernourished. Parents not likely to survive the bombing. And she had money and position. She could give the child a good life. You can understand that, can't you?"

"I suppose so. And what about Gloria Kane? Have you figured out what happened to her?"

Liz expounded her theory. He nodded as she was speaking. "That's what went through my head at the time. The mother didn't seem to be too concerned that her daughter was lost. And the mother clearly had a man living in the house, although she denied it. So you think the kid's buried under that rockery, eh?" He toyed with crumbs of bun on his plate. "I don't suppose the bigwigs will think it's worth getting a search warrant to have it dug up at this stage, although I would like to know. I'll try to press them to do it. I could do with some closure."

"So what about the third girl—Valerie Hammond?" Marisa asked. "The one whose body you found? What were your suspicions at the time?"

"Not much to go on," he said. "Mother had to go to work, so she left the kid to walk to the station, where she was supposed to meet the others. But nobody remembers seeing her at the station. It was all rather chaotic, though. Several schools all milling about. Easy for kids to get lost. We did check at each of the stops on the train journey, but there was no record of her being placed with a family. So we have to assume that someone grabbed her when no one was looking. Of course, at the time we took it for granted it was that man, Dan Harkness. When he was found, placing flowers around the girl's body, his first words were 'I didn't mean to . . .' We took that for a confession, even though he never admitted he'd killed her."

"So why did you then decide he wasn't the one?" Liz's father asked.

"When the other two girls were reported missing, he was already in custody, wasn't he?" He took another big gulp of beer. "Dan Harkness had an alibi for both. We decided it might be a serial killer. But it turns out it wasn't a serial killer, after all. So now I'm thinking that maybe Dan did kill Valerie. Or perhaps it was one of the soldiers from the army camp nearby. We'll never really know."

There was silence in the room. The log on the fire shifted, sending up a shower of sparks. Then the DI drained his glass and put it down on the table. "But at least we can surmise now, and we know about Lucy and two of the girls from the war. Always better to know, isn't it? Better than not knowing."

Was it? Liz wondered. Would it have been better if she'd gone through life thinking she was the brigadier and Maureen's daughter? Better if she'd never found the forgotten village? *But then I'd never have met James,* she thought. *I'd never have written the stories that got me back into doing what I love. Everything in life happens for a reason.* She caught Marisa staring at her, and she smiled.

EPILOGUE

A few weeks later Liz stood outside the shell of Tydeham Grange, looking around her as the wind swept through bare branches and the first drops of icy rain spattered on to frozen ground. It was the first time she had returned to the village since she learned the truth, since so many things had happened that had shaken the very foundation of her life. She took a deep breath and walked around the side of the house until she came to the rose garden, now, in the winter, just a collection of bare stalks rising from bare earth. The leaves had fallen from the climbing rose over the arbor, and she could now clearly see the elegant curve of the marble bench with its sharp corner that had killed her mother.

The past weeks had been a time of processing, of coming to terms with the deaths of two mothers. Trying to understand that the woman she had thought of as her mother all her life had killed the woman who had given birth to her. An accident, so she was told, but she'd never really know. Now she realized that both her mother and her father could be devious and unscrupulous. She wasn't sure about anything any more. Those letters from Edmond had shaken her almost more than finding out the truth of her birth and of Alice's death.

She had tried to recall more of Alice—how she looked, how she felt. Liz only had that one memory of her voice, chiding her at the top of the stairs, but it was a sweet and gentle voice, even when Liz had been naughty. Alice had loved her, of that Liz was sure. But the outcome could never have been good. When Liz was too old for a nanny, what then? Would she have stayed on as a faithful family retainer? Would she have been too tempted to tell Liz the truth? Would she have found a man and married him, and wanted her daughter? Liz sighed. Nothing was straightforward, was it? Right and wrong, good and evil. Lucy and Rosie and her own life, all complicated by people who rationalized they were doing the best for the child.

She'd never know who her real father was either. She wondered if she was the result of an imprudent one-night affair or a loving relationship. She liked to think of a handsome, witty and kind young man who had gone off to fight, who had perhaps written letters home to a sweetheart who no longer lived at Broxley Manor and had returned from the war to look for her. She hoped that was the case.

She had also had to come to terms with a father who had helped cover up the death of her birth mother and killed the only mother she'd ever known—out of love. She had to believe that. She had always known that he worshipped his wife, so it had to be out of love. Her life would only have been a gradual descent into fear, anxiety and helplessness. But there would always be that nagging sliver of doubt. Had everything happened the way he told her? She would never really know.

So much she would always wonder about now. She felt a great bond with Jenny. They had both been given the very best upbringing, adored in every way, and yet it was not the upbringing they should have had. Would they have been happier with their real mothers? The fact was that their real mothers would have been happier with them and were deprived of it. At least she had done the right thing for Lucy Fareham. She was undoubtedly far better off with Susan than she would have been with Lark.

Liz took a few steps forward. She could see the place where the body had lain, although the earth had been replaced and tamped down again. Now it no longer filled her with dread, just sadness for poor Alice. She looked up as she heard footsteps behind her.

"There you are," James said. He came up to her and put an arm around her shoulder. "You should have asked me to come with you if you'd wanted to visit the gravesite. I know how hard it must be for you."

She looked up at him, glad she had told him everything, the tears in her eyes more for his understanding than for her loss. "I'm still trying to come to terms with it all," she said.

"It's too much, all at once. Take your time," he said. "You know I'm here any time you need to talk. You'll get through this, my darling. You're strong."

"I'll try to be. Any you've been so wonderful." She managed a smile. "Now we've just got two fathers to feel responsible for. Maybe we should move my father into the next-door house in Bournemouth, then they could entertain each other."

"We can move them both in here when it's rebuilt," James said. "I'll modify my plans so that there is a wing each for them."

"A wing each? What are you designing, Buckingham Palace?"

James laughed. "Well, maybe a little bungalow each for them on the grounds."

"You haven't even got the planning permission yet."

He shrugged. "One has to be hopeful and look ahead." He paused, looking at her with great tenderness. "And dream."

"Yes," she agreed. "Be hopeful and dream."

His grip around her shoulder tightened. "Come on," he said. "Let's get back to work. I want to see if we can make the stairs safe enough to find my rocking horse."

Their arms wrapped around each other, they walked back towards Tydeham Grange.

Sunday Express, November 24, 1968

Obituary of a Murdered Village

Elizabeth Houghton

When war broke out across Britain, Tydeham was a village like any other: families lived there, were born, died and were buried in the churchyard. There were farmers, fishermen and the lord of the manor in his big house. Quiet little lives, cut off from the turmoil of the outer world. Not that the war had passed them by: fathers and sons were off serving in the armed forces. Some had already been lost—in a torpedoed ship, or a plane going down in flames. The village of Tydeham had known its share of joy and sorrow and had lamented its dead.

But everything changed in the autumn of 1943. Tydeham was selected, picked from amongst every village in Britain, for a special mission. Because Tydeham lay on the South Coast, with a small harbour, in a narrow valley. And an invasion was being planned across the Channel, an invasion that would finally put an end to the war. But an invasion could not be left to chance.

There needed to be practices, drills so that nothing went wrong. A place that resembled the coast of Normandy was needed. And Tydeham fit the bill. White cliffs around it, like those of Normandy. What's more, it possessed nothing of historic value apart from the square-towered church, and Tydeham Grange, the manor house whose residents actually owned the land on which the houses of the village were built.

And so it was chosen. The inhabitants received a letter, giving them two weeks to pack up their belongings and leave. Temporary housing was found. Lorries came and carted away lives, or as much of lives as would fit. Stuff was left behind—clotheslines and boxes of Ovaltine, onions in the ground and, at the manor house, a beloved rocking horse. Of course the manor house was different. The lord of the manor had been promised that his house would be safe, untouched, ready for him to return to after the war ended, should the invasion succeed.

They left, with much grumbling and a few tears, expecting to come back one day. But they hadn't been told that the invasion practice was with live ammunition. Houses were blown to smithereens, and only crumbling walls were left, looking like the remains of a lost civilization. There was nothing to come back to. Even the manor house that should have been left untouched got its share of the shelling. The roof caved in, and beams landed across the dining table that had seated twenty.

And now the village lies, off-limits still, with barbed wire around it and unexploded shells, its crumbling walls buried under ivy and creepers. Nobody tends the graves in that churchyard. They lie hidden under weeds and bracken. The former inhabitants have made new lives, some more successfully than others. But they all carry with them the ache for a lost time and place, when they had lived their peaceable lives away from the world in a small hamlet called Tydeham.

HISTORICAL NOTE

This story is based on a real place. The village is called Tyneham. It lies on that stretch of the South Coast of England: a small, unimposing place, one main street, only a few residents—which was why it was chosen for invasion practice.

Tyneham sits abandoned today, just as I have described my village—the shells of houses overgrown with creepers, the whole area returning to nature. It is now open to the public on certain days. You can stand on that lonely street, hearing the wind whistling through broken buildings, and think that you hear the laughter of long-ago children at play. Certainly the sort of atmosphere to inspire a creepy story!

While British nomenclature has been used throughout the novel, the use of arbor versus arbour is intentional.

ACKNOWLEDGMENTS

As always, I'd like to thank Danielle Marshall and the whole team at Lake Union, as well as my wonderful agents Meg Ruley and Christina Hogrebe. You all make working with you such a joy.

AUTHOR BIO

Photo © Douglas Sonders

Rhys Bowen is the *New York Times* bestselling author of more than sixty novels, including *The Paris Assignment, Where the Sky Begins, The Venice Sketchbook, Above the Bay of Angels, The Victory Garden, The Tuscan Child,* and *In Farleigh Field,* the winner of the Left Coast Crime Award for Best Historical Mystery Novel and the Agatha Award for Best Historical Novel. Bowen's work has won sixteen honors to date, including multiple Agatha, Anthony, and Macavity Awards. Her books have been translated into many languages, and she has fans around the world, including more than seventy thousand Facebook followers. A transplanted Brit, Bowen divides her time between California and Arizona. For more information, visit rhysbowen.com.